The Ripper Secret

Jack Steel

**SIMON &
SCHUSTER**

London · New York · Sydney · Toronto · New Delhi

A CBS COMPANY

First published in Great Britain by Simon & Schuster UK Ltd, 2012
A CBS COMPANY

1 3 5 7 9 10 8 6 4 2

Simon & Schuster UK Ltd
1st Floor,
222 Gray's Inn Road
London WC1X 8HB

www.simonandschuster.co.uk

Simon & Schuster Australia,
Sydney

Simon & Schuster India,
New Delhi

A CIP catalogue record for this book
is available from the British Library

Paperback ISBN 978-1-84983-753-8
Trade Paperback ISBN 978-1-84983-752-1
Ebook ISBN 978-1-84983-754-5

Typeset by M Rules
Printed and bound by CPI Group (UK) Ltd, Croydon, CR0 4YY

Prologue

1870
Under the Haram es-Sharif (Temple Mount), Jerusalem

'I need more light,' Warren said, the whites of his eyes the only feature visible in his blackened face. 'Pass me that lantern.'

A few feet behind him, a second figure, his face equally filthy and his clothes just as invisible below layers of dirt, stepped closer and passed him the Davy lamp, the dim light casting giant wavering shadows on the rocks around them.

'What is it?'

'The entrance to another chamber,' Charles Warren replied, his voice echoing from the rock walls that tightly enclosed that part of the labyrinth, 'or at least I think that's what it is.'

Sergeant Henry Birtles shook his head. He'd virtually lost count of the number of chambers and passageways and shafts, rock walls and ancient stones that he'd seen in the three years that he and Warren had been working on the site. At first, it had been quite exciting, wondering what the next day's or week's excavation would reveal, but as time passed and all they found were yet more chambers filled with rubble and debris, his enthusiasm for the job had waned markedly.

And it was hard, draining work, because of the heat, the

humidity, the cramped and confined underground spaces they were forced to work in, the sheer physical labour needed to tunnel their way into the hidden places they'd found, and of course the circumstances, which were, at best, somewhat peculiar. Because, although their presence in the old city of Jerusalem, where they'd lived for the previous three years, had been authorized and approved, Birtles had no doubt that what he and Warren were doing was actually illegal. He also had no doubt of the likely consequences if they were caught.

'So is it a chamber, sir?' he asked.

'Yes,' Warren replied. 'It looks as if it's open on the other side, but the entrance is low and very tight. I'll take this lamp and try and slide through. You stay here, just in case I meet any problems.'

On several occasions, when they'd entered chambers that were comparatively clear, they'd found evidence of rock falls, and the possibility of one of the men being trapped by a boulder dropping from the roof was always uppermost in their minds. Whenever they entered a new space, their normal practice was for one of them to carry out an initial inspection, while the other waited in a safe – or least a safer – location. Fate or chance had decreed that this time it was Warren's turn to go first.

He stretched his hand out in front of him, pushing the Davy lamp through the restricted entrance he'd found, then crawled forward, steadily easing himself through the narrow gap and into the open space which lay beyond. The entrance itself was clearly man-made, not a natural fissure in the rock, and appeared to be the top of a very low arch formed from the massive stones they were used to finding underneath the Temple Mount.

In fact, it was only by chance that Warren had spotted the square corner of one of the stones and realized there was an entrance there at all – the earth had been piled up so high against the wall that most of the masonry had been invisible. It had taken them the better part of half an hour to shift enough of it to reveal the entrance, which was extremely small: they guessed only about three feet high and the same wide. They hadn't cleared it all, just opened it enough to allow Warren to wriggle inside. It certainly wasn't a normal chamber, and they'd guessed it was probably some kind of a small store room.

Not for the first time, Warren wished they had better illumination for their work. The Davy lamp gave more light than a candle, and was considerably safer than a naked flame, but it still wasn't particularly bright. The men weren't concerned about the possibility of explosions – which was the reason behind the creation of the Davy lamp, designed as a flame-proof light for use in mines – because there was no evidence of gas in the tunnels and chambers they were exploring. Nevertheless, a candle flame was easily extinguished by any sudden movement or even an errant draught, and they needed a reliable and constant source of light to see what they were doing in the utter blackness.

As his head emerged from the archway into the chamber Warren paused, repositioning the Davy lamp so that he could see exactly what lay ahead of him – and more importantly any loose rocks on the ceiling above which might tumble free – before he continued crawling forward.

The small chamber appeared to be very much like the others that the two men had forced their way into and already explored. He could see a low ceiling hacked from the rock, walls formed by patches of ancient masonry built into and around natural stone, and a floor of beaten earth. In a few places he could still see marks in the earth made by the unyielding soles of the sandals of the men who last worked in that dark and claustrophobic space, perhaps two millennia ago.

Satisfied that the ceiling wasn't about to fall on his head, Warren completed his transit of the archway and got to his feet, lifting the lamp above his head to provide the greatest possible illumination. The room was quite small, certainly a lot less spacious than many of the other chambers they had entered, perhaps twelve or fifteen feet square, the roughly hewn ceiling about seven feet above floor level. And, again like all of the other spaces they'd explored, there appeared to be absolutely nothing in it.

Ever since he'd arrived in Jerusalem three years earlier, Warren had been hoping to make a discovery that would justify the decision by the Palestine Exploration Fund to send him, rather than a professional archaeologist, to explore this ancient site. But though he and Birtles and the other men under his command had explored and mapped a fascinating underground maze, they'd found no significant artefacts of any sort. It was as if the intricate labyrinth of tunnels and chambers under the Temple Mount had been emptied centuries, or even millennia, earlier, stripped of any treasures that it might originally have held.

Warren walked around the perimeter of the small chamber, the glow of light from the Davy lamp dim, but adequate, because his eyes were well used to the gloom. He and Birtles actually found it quite painful when they finally re-emerged from the shaft at the end of each dig, and their eyes were suddenly subjected to the brilliant Mediterranean sunlight again.

'Anything in there?' Birtles asked.

Warren shook his head.

'Nothing yet,' he said, continuing to walk around the perimeter of the room. 'Oh, just a minute,' he added, 'this might be interesting.'

He stopped in one corner, where a natural fissure in the rock appeared to have been widened slightly. Warren could just make out the marks made by chisels on the sides of the opening.

He lifted the Davy lamp so that its light penetrated the cavity as far as possible, then shook his head in disappointment. It looked as if there was nothing inside the gap. He turned away and took another step, but then a sudden thought struck him and he turned back. There had been something in the fissure, a lumpy object in the centre that he'd assumed was simply rock, but which his subconscious mind had just recognized as perhaps being something else.

He pushed the lamp into the gap as far as it would go, jamming the metal case into a narrow crack at the top of the opening so that he would have both hands free. Then he reached out and touched the dark mass which occupied the centre and rear of the fissure.

The moment he did so, he felt a tingle of excitement, because what he was touching was neither cold nor solid, and it yielded slightly under his probing fingers. It appeared to be fabric of some sort, cloth or maybe thin leather.

Scarcely daring to breathe, Warren felt around in the cavity, pushing and pulling at the fabric as he tried to discern what, if anything, it was concealing. And almost at once he discovered it *was* covering something. That much was immediately clear, because he could feel a solid object underneath it. He needed to remove the cloth – the material was too thin to be leather – and his probing fingers eventually discovered a tiny tear in the fabric.

Warren checked that the Davy lamp was still securely positioned, then inserted his two index fingers into the tear and carefully began to pull the material apart. The ancient cloth didn't yield its secrets easily, the fabric giving way with the greatest of reluctance, but after a few seconds Warren had opened up the split in the cloth far enough for the tips of his fingers to touch the object it had been concealing.

It was clearly metal, but for a few seconds that was all he could tell. He was looking at a gently curved section of tubing which terminated in a much larger, rounded, bulbous and apparently ornate shape, and he had not the slightest idea what it could be. The metal appeared black in the faint illumination, either covered in paint or possibly simply displaying the encrusted dirt of the ages.

Warren rubbed his thumbnail along the piece of metal he'd exposed, and then caught his breath. Under the black coating, which he now thought probably was paint, his action had revealed the faint gleam of a dull yellowish metal, and his mind sprang to the obvious conclusion. He'd found a gold relic of some sort, a wonderful and valuable find.

But what, exactly, was it?

Carefully, he felt around inside the tear in the cloth, the tips of his fingers tracing the shape of the object. His sense of touch was telling him that it seemed to be shaped like a flower, a long stem with the head of the flower at its end. And that did make a kind of sense. Or rather, he realized a moment later, it didn't.

Warren knew quite a lot about Jerusalem and the Jewish religion. Before he had arrived in the Holy Land he had studied numerous books dealing with the history of the country. One of the most important treatises in Judaism was the Zohar, essentially one of the source documents of the Kabbalah, the sacred scriptures and teachings which explain the relationship between the divine architect of the universe and his creation. And the early part of the Zohar compared the Jewish people to a rose with thirteen petals. Could that be what he had found, a symbolic representation of that image?

But there was an obvious problem with that idea. Warren knew that the Zohar had surfaced comparatively recently, in the thirteenth century, in fact, in Spain, but it was believed to date from the period of the Second Temple, from between about 540 BC and 70 AD, because of the language it was written in, which was Aramaic. He was unsure when the chamber had last been used by anyone, but he would have been surprised if the footprints he could see on the earth floor had been left there less than two thousand years earlier.

So the date was about right, if the object he was exploring with his fingers *was* a carving of a rose. But one of the most fundamental and best-known tenets of Judaism was the prohibition on idolatry and graven images. The Jews simply didn't produce representations of anything, and they never had, not since the time of Moses. So that idea had to be wrong.

As his fingers continued probing, he wondered if the object was some later relic, something left under the Temple Mount by the Knights Templar or the Muslim invaders or some other group. But again that didn't accord with his researches. Anything found in these tunnels and chambers had most likely been left there by the Jews.

So what was it?

He again traced the curved metal with his fingertips, then felt further under the material as he tried to get a better idea of the shape of the entire object. He felt another flower-like object close to the first, and his fingers traced the 'stem' of metal that extended below it.

Warren shook his head. He had no idea what it was. He would have to drag it out of the crevice and examine it properly.

But as his hands closed around it, he suddenly gasped with shock, because in that single instant he knew exactly, without the faintest shadow of a doubt, what the object had to be.

'Oh, my dear God,' he muttered.

Outside the chamber, Birtles must have heard his sudden intake of breath, or his murmured invocation.

'Are you all right, sir?' he asked, his slightly muffled voice echoing through the gloom. 'Do you need any help?'

Warren needed time to think, just a few seconds, to decide what to do. And he needed Birtles to remain where he was.

'No, stay there,' he ordered. 'I'm fine. Just banged my knee on a rock, that's all. Give me a minute.'

Warren's mind was racing. If he was right – and the shape of the object that his fingers had traced beneath the material led to only one conclusion, as far as he could see – then what he'd found was at once the most valuable and by far the most dangerous relic that had ever been discovered anywhere in the Holy Land. He knew that if he simply dragged it out of the chamber and up to the surface, there was a very good chance that he and his men would be dead within twenty-four hours. But he couldn't leave it where it was. It was too important, and far too valuable, for him to just walk away from.

He had to make a decision.

'Did you find anything?' Birtles asked.

Warren paused for another second or two, weighing up the likely consequences of the action he was contemplating, and in that instant he made a decision, the repercussions of which, unknown to him, were to dominate much of his life from that point onwards. He couldn't simply leave the relic behind in the dark of that hidden chamber, but equally he couldn't permit anybody, not even his own men, to know what he intended to do with it.

So he replied to the corporal, comprehensively burning his boats behind him, but just possibly saving the man's life.

'No, nothing of any interest,' Warren said. 'It's just another empty chamber. I'll make a note of the location when we get out of here. In fact, let's head back now. There's nothing else we can do here for the moment.'

A few moments later, Warren emerged from the shallow opening and the two men began retracing their steps along the tunnel towards the vertical shaft that would take them back up to the surface.

The entire reason that Charles Warren was more or less living underground in Jerusalem was a woman. But not, it has to be said, just any woman.

In the summer of 1866, Warren had been instructed by his commanding officer to attend a meeting in a building on the Strand – in a bank, in fact – but the senior officers he was anticipating had been nowhere in evidence as he was escorted to the small private room on the first floor. There, already seated at a table and waiting for him, was an elegant lady who introduced herself simply as 'Angela'.

But that didn't matter, because Warren had recognized her immediately. His hostess was an aristocratic lady named Angela Burdett Coutts. She was a baroness, the daughter of the banker Thomas Coutts, who owned the building they were sitting in, and at that time she was the wealthiest woman in England. And

Warren had not the slightest idea what she could possibly want with a humble army lieutenant. That, at least, quickly became clear.

'I was simply appalled, Lieutenant Warren,' she began. 'The water tasted utterly vile, and I could not believe that our Lord Jesus might have had to drink such filth.'

The story, as 'Angela' told it, was simple enough. She had visited Jerusalem in 1865, the previous year, as part of a Grand Tour, where a commonplace and seemingly utterly insignificant event had taken place. It was a hot and sultry day, the baking air barely moving, and she had been given a drink of water by her guide, a drink that the man had drawn from one of the old cisterns that lay under the city. The water in the mug he offered was foul and stinking, and that had started her thinking.

'I was in the Royal City of David,' she went on, 'treading in the footsteps of Christ himself, and it occurred to me that if there was such foul water in one cistern under the old city, there must surely be other cisterns where the water is sweeter.'

Warren hadn't been entirely sure what she was driving at.

'You want me to go to Jerusalem and find the old water cisterns?' he asked.

'Of course not,' Baroness Coutts snapped. 'The water supply is irrelevant. But because there must be underground water storage tanks, there are probably also other underground structures, storerooms and passages and tunnels, and I want you to go to Jerusalem and explore them.'

She leaned forward and lowered her voice slightly.

'In particular, I would like you to explore under the Temple Mount and any other religious site that you can manage to get into. You're a surveyor, and so I expect you to be able to produce detailed maps showing exactly what lies underneath the old city. It would be helpful if you could also examine any writing or other evidence that you find which might clarify our picture of life in biblical times.'

'Surely you would be better to employ an archaeologist for such a task?'

Baroness Coutts shook her head decisively.

'If I was interested in obtaining detailed information about one very small area of Jerusalem, that would be the right course of action. But I'm not. I want somebody who can produce a map, as I've said, who will be able to find a way around any bureaucratic hurdles he might encounter, and a man prepared to employ any means necessary to achieve the objective. You, according to your senior officers, are such a man.'

'Very well. I will need to speak to my commanding officer,' Warren began. 'I will need to seek a leave of—'

'You will not,' Baroness Coutts interrupted. 'I have already been in conversation with the general, and he is entirely in favour of your undertaking this commission. As is Vicky, I might add.'

Warren nodded. He was intelligent enough to recognize a fait accompli when he was confronted with one. The 'Vicky' the Baroness had referred to was her best friend, a woman better known to the wider world as Queen Victoria. Whatever his personal feelings, he knew he had absolutely no choice in the matter.

'Very well,' he said again. 'I will prepare a list of the equipment I will need, and begin selecting the men who will accompany me.'

Warren had already made something of a name for himself by climbing and surveying the Rock of Gibraltar, which was one reason why the Baroness had chosen him. Shortly after this meeting in London, he was officially loaned for an indefinite period to the Palestine Exploration Fund, an organization set up by Baroness Coutts in 1865 with a donation of 500 pounds sterling, and his stated task was to research the archaeology and history of biblical Palestine, a vague and extremely flexible brief. In private, and during the course of a second and third meeting, the Baroness had delivered much more specific and detailed instructions: he was to investigate the site of the ancient Temple, Jerusalem's old fortifications, the City of David itself, and the authenticity of the Church of the Holy Sepulchre. But as she had indicated at their original meeting, she was especially interested in what lay under the ancient Jewish site of the Temple Mount, and that, she told him several times, was to be his highest priority.

And so, in February 1867, Warren – who was then aged only twenty-seven – had arrived in Jerusalem with Henry Birtles, a corporal in the Royal Engineers, who had assisted the lieutenant on the Gibraltar climb, two other corporals, a surveyor and a photographer, and some eight mules carrying all the equipment they thought they'd need.

The Holy Land and Jerusalem were then ruled by the Ottoman Turks, and because the permit to begin the dig – a document known as a *firman* – had not yet arrived from Constantinople, Warren had immediately justified Baroness Coutts's faith in him and used his initiative to get his expedition started as quickly as possible.

He'd asked the British consul to arrange for him to meet the pasha, the Turkish ruler of Jerusalem, to try to obtain his permission whilst awaiting the *firman*. Using his considerable powers of persuasion, Warren managed to convince the pasha to approve digging around the Haram es-Sharif or Noble Sanctuary, the Temple Mount. But Warren was strictly forbidden from conducting any excavations within the Haram, the third holiest site in the world of Islam, upon which stood both the Dome of the Rock and the Al-Aqsa Mosque.

That wasn't exactly what Warren had wanted, because he was in Jerusalem with Baroness Angela Coutts's most specific instructions still ringing in his ears, instructions which stated that his principal task was to explore the subterranean world that was believed to lie under the Temple Mount. But Warren was not the kind of man to be deterred by such a minor matter as a blanket prohibition.

He had come up with a scheme that would allow him to both apparently comply with the limited permission the pasha had provided for him, and at the same time satisfy the aims of the PEF. He surveyed the area, then employed local diggers to begin excavating a number of vertical exploratory shafts located some distance from the outer walls of the Temple Mount. Once one of these shafts had reached a satisfactory depth, he ordered his men to take over the dig and change direction, and to begin to excavate a tunnel which led straight towards the Mount. The work absolutely consumed Warren, who spent so much of his time underground that the people of Jerusalem nicknamed him 'the mole'.

A short time after they had reached the subterranean world under the Temple Mount, the *firman* – the permission to dig – finally arrived from Constantinople. But when he read it, Warren was dismayed to discover that his expedition had been given permission to dig almost everywhere, with the sole exception of all religious sites, which were of course the only ones he was interested in. He had hoped the *firman* would have allowed him to excavate the Temple Mount directly, rather than having to rely on his mole-like tunnelling activities, but instead of that he now had two separate permissions, both of which forbade him from doing what he was already doing. And what he, naturally, intended to continue doing.

The only good thing was that Warren now had a piece of paper he could wave around if anybody asked him if he had permission to dig in the area, and that would work perfectly right up until the moment when somebody asked to actually read it. But, fortunately, nobody ever had.

Warren's men drove numerous shafts into the ground around the Temple Mount over the next few months, sometimes hacking their way down through over a hundred feet of rubble and rubbish before finally reaching bedrock. Other shafts terminated in parts of existing underground systems: the area was a honeycomb of ancient caves and shafts and tunnels. The digging was both difficult and dangerous because of the unstable nature of the ground above them, the debris which formed the walls of the shafts frequently moving and occasionally crumbling away. Several times they had to dodge for their lives as falling stones tumbled down from above them.

Charles Warren knew from the start that he and his team couldn't openly dig anywhere on the Temple Mount, but he did manage to establish friendly relations with the guards and was able to examine both the Dome of the Rock itself and a part of the network of cisterns that was known to lie under it. In all, during both his legal examinations on the Temple Mount and his illegal excavations under it, he had established that there were at least thirty-four reservoirs hacked out of the rock there, of a variety of sizes, the largest holding some two million gallons of water.

He was the first person to explore beneath the Temple Mount in modern times. He was not to know that he would also be the last.

*

The morning after his discovery, Warren gave his team the day off, suggesting they take the opportunity to wash off the dirt of the expedition and enjoy what recreational facilities were offered by Jerusalem, which he knew were few and very limited. But at least they would be able to enjoy a decent meal or two, and perhaps even find a drink somewhere: the expedition camp was dry, with no alcohol being permitted there. Warren himself, he declared, would remain at the excavation writing up his notes and preparing a number of drawings showing the location of the chambers and passages and other features they'd explored.

Warren waited until everyone else had departed, then began work, writing up his notes, as he had said he would, and starting to prepare a drawing, which he displayed prominently on his desk. That would, he hoped, provide some kind of an explanation for his absence if any of the expedition members returned unexpectedly early. He would be able to say that he'd needed to descend into the shaft once again to check the dimensions of one or two of the chambers.

He pulled on his old digging clothes, then took two Davy lamps, three sacks, and a pick and shovel, and descended the shaft he and Birtles had used the day before. In a few minutes he'd retraced his steps to the low and restricted entrance to the chamber they'd found. There, he used the shovel to remove some of the earth that still partially blocked the doorway. The ground was hard-packed and difficult to even get the shovel into, but Warren persevered, driving the blade of the tool as hard as he could into the earth, the sweat running down his face and body as he did so.

As he worked, he wondered if the almost complete blocking of the entrance had been deliberate, if the ancient workers in these tunnels had known about the prize that lay within the cleft in the rock and had done their best to conceal not only the object within the chamber, but the entrance to the chamber as well. Most of the spaces he and his men had explored had been fairly open and much easier to get inside, but this one had been almost completely hidden. In fact, it was only a glimpse he'd caught of the corner of a piece of worked masonry that had indicated there was anything there at all.

Within twenty minutes he'd opened up the entrance far enough to allow him to slide into the inner chamber reasonably easily; more importantly, he hoped the gap would now be big enough to allow him to extricate the object he'd discovered.

Inside the chamber, Warren stood up and walked directly across to the opposite corner, where the cleft in the rock appeared as a dark vertical slash in the light from the Davy lamp. As he'd done before, Warren wedged the lamp into a narrow section of the cleft to allow him to use both hands. It was still quite difficult to see exactly how the object had been lodged in the opening, and for a few moments he debated about lighting a piece of magnesium wire to provide much greater illumination.

This was a technique that he and Birtles had used on many occasions during their explorations, the wire burning with a fierce white light. But the problem with doing that was that it would completely destroy his night vision for several minutes after the wire burnt out. In the circumstances, Warren thought, it would be better to just rely on the Davy lamp, which would provide a much dimmer, but reliable and continuous, illumination.

He stared into the opening at the bulky dark fabric, which at a casual glance still looked remarkably like a jumbled collection of rocks a couple of feet high, then reached out and seized it in both hands, lifting and pulling the material up and towards him, to try to uncover the object underneath.

That didn't work, and it was quickly apparent to Warren that the fabric wasn't simply covering the object, but was wrapped tightly around it. So then he grasped the section of metal which he had uncovered the previous day and began moving it back and forth, assessing the degree of movement available and trying to work out if it was jammed into the gap in the rock or simply lying at the bottom of the crevice.

It seemed to move relatively freely, and he realized that it was probably only the considerable weight of the relic that was preventing him easily removing it from its hiding place. In fact, it was quickly obvious that the object was actually standing upright, the heavy base resting on a flattened area of rock, and to him that made perfect sense, because now he not only knew exactly what the relic was, but precisely why it had been placed in that particular part of that specific chamber. The reason had been obvious to him that morning, as soon as he'd examined the maps and drawings he'd been making of the subterranean maze.

He seized the object with both hands, gripping it through the fabric, and began to lift it. It was an awkward manoeuvre, because he was having to stretch deep into the crevice, and use all the strength in his arms to move it at all.

But he managed it. Slowly, inch by inch, he manoeuvred the fabric-covered object out of the gap in the rock, taking care not to knock it against the sides, because he was desperate not to damage it.

When he'd got the object part of the way out, he changed his grip to seize it around the central shaft, which both confirmed his belief about what he'd found and made it much easier to lift and to manoeuvre. Then, when he'd lifted it completely clear of its hiding place, he lowered it gently to the earth floor, resting it on its base. Then he moved the Davy lamp so that he could see what he was doing. Warren had a folding knife in his pocket, but rather than risk scratching the relic, he decided to unwrap it, carefully unwinding the fabric from around it.

It looked as if whoever had secreted the object in the chamber had been just as concerned about keeping it undamaged as Warren, because he ended up removing a very long piece of linen, almost like a burial shroud, from around it, the material having covered and padded every part of the relic apart from the bottom of the base. He wadded up the cloth and replaced it in the crevice, and only then did he turn back and examine the object.

It didn't look particularly impressive, in part because of the dark paint which had been applied to its surface, perhaps in an attempt to conceal the material from which it was made. The workmanship was good, but he could still make out faint hammer marks on the metal, a kind of silent confirmation of the way it had reputedly been made. Although Warren knew exactly what it was, he'd never actually seen anything like it before. He knew, without the slightest scintilla of doubt, that the object he was looking at pre-dated Christianity by centuries, possibly by over one millennium, if the Bible was right. It was, at one and the same time, probably the most valuable single religious object ever created. So important was it, that virtually every citizen of an entire nation would happily kill just to possess it. And members of other faiths would just as readily kill to destroy it.

And as he stared at the black-painted relic, Warren's mind span backwards as he recalled what little he knew – and what little the rest of the world knew, in fact – about this most sacred of all religious artefacts.

Its blood-soaked history extended back to the period even before the wandering Israelites crossed the Jordan River, and it had been seized many times as a prize by victorious armies contesting ownership of Jerusalem and Palestine. Biblical sources suggested that in 586 BC, when it had already been in the possession of the Israelites for well over 500 years, it had been transported to Babylon by Nebuzaradan, the commander of Nebuchadnezzar's guard, who had been responsible for the destruction of the Temple of Jerusalem and the deportation of the people of Judah.

It had been restored to the Temple about forty years later, and then almost half a millennium later it was captured by the Greek ruler Antiochus Epiphanes when he sacked Jerusalem in 167 BC, killing forty thousand Jews in the process and selling another forty thousand into slavery.

Recorded, rather than biblical, history took up the story in the first century AD, when the relic was looted by the victorious Roman army, led first by Vespasian, and then by his son Titus, as the legions suppressed the Great Jewish Revolt. It was one of the most brutal conflicts in history. At the end of the long siege, Jerusalem had quite literally been surrounded by the crucified bodies of tens of thousands of Jews who had tried to flee from the beleaguered city. Estimates suggested that as many as 100,000 Jews died during the siege, and an almost equal number were captured by the Romans and marched in chains to Rome and elsewhere in the Mediterranean, to be sold in the slave markets.

The relic was carried into Rome, paraded in triumph with the other treasures of the Second Temple, then placed on display in the city's Temple of Peace, where it probably remained until the fifth century, when the city was sacked, first by the Visigoths under Alaric in 410 AD and then by the Vandals almost fifty years later. Historians' opinions were divided, but the consensus was that it had most likely been the Vandals who had seized the relic, carrying it off to their capital city of Carthage.

More spilled blood followed when Carthage itself was attacked by a Byzantine army under General Belisarius in 533 AD and, according to one contemporary source, a writer named Procopius, the object was later carried through the streets of Constantinople as part of the general's triumphal procession, a reprise of the events in Rome half a millennium earlier. Procopius had also claimed that the relic was then returned to Jerusalem, but no modern historians had been able to find any documents or accounts which lent support to this suggestion.

All this Warren knew. Well before he'd travelled to Jerusalem he'd made a study of the history of the region, so that he would properly be able to understand the significance of the ruins he would be excavating and the historic finds he and the PEF, and especially Angela Coutts, had hoped he would uncover.

And now, in the dark underground chamber, lit only by the dim light from the Davy lamp, Warren knew that Procopius had been right. The most sacred relic of the Jewish civilization, arguably even more important and significant than the Ark of the Covenant, had indeed been returned to Jerusalem.

People had been looking for it for at least one and a half millennia, and he'd found it, almost by accident, in a place where nobody had ever looked before and where he wasn't supposed to be.

And nobody knew anything about it except Warren himself.

Part One

Jerusalem

Chapter 1

1886
Mount of Olives, Jerusalem

They'd first broken the ground with very little ceremony. After all, the whole area had seen countless buildings erected, repaired, rebuilt and ultimately demolished over the centuries, and it was only one more church.

The builders of the new house of worship were familiar to the local inhabitants, although they were neither Jews nor Arabs. They were Christians, from one of the oldest extant religious groups, by tradition tracing their history back to the Apostle Andrew, although it wasn't until the end of the tenth century that Russian Orthodox Christianity came to prominence under Prince Vladimir I of Kiev, who adopted Byzantine Rite Christianity as the state religion. The Russian Orthodox Mission had only arrived in Jerusalem in 1858, so they were relative newcomers, but when the Russians had decided to build their own church on the Mount of Olives, it didn't seem to be in any way an inappropriate location.

The builders started work in 1886, intending to complete the structure within about three years. They found the stone box roughly eight feet below ground-level as they dug down into the hillside in preparation for creating the foundations.

Finding any kind of relic wasn't a surprise in view of the history of the area. Jerusalem had been fought over and built on since pretty much the start of recorded history, and the builders had known that there was a better-than-even chance that they'd find something – bones or relics of some sort – as they carried out their excavations.

When they first examined what they'd turned up with their picks and shovels, they thought it was most probably an ossuary, a bone box, and that immediately meant it was old. During the time of the Second Temple, between roughly 500 BC and the end of the first century AD, Jewish burial customs in and around Jerusalem had altered. They began using a system of primary and secondary burials. The corpse would first be laid to rest on a stone slab in a burial cave and then, when all the flesh had rotted from the skeleton, the bones would be removed, cleaned and then placed in an ossuary before being laid to rest again, this time permanently, in the same or sometimes another burial cave. The day of the second and final burial was an occasion which evoked both sorrow at the remembrance of the death, but also a celebration for the life of the deceased, and traditionally family members would join together and fast during the morning and then enjoy a feast in the afternoon.

For some reason, the custom of primary and secondary burials ceased to be followed in Jerusalem after about the end of the first century AD, and never gained much support among Jews living outside Israel. The foreman of the builders had been told about this, and about the other kinds of relics his men might encounter, and so he knew that if the object *was* an ossuary, it had to be approaching two thousand years old.

But he was far from certain that that was what he was looking at, because the stone box lacked any kind of an inscription, which most ossuaries did possess, simply to identify the deceased person whose bones had been placed inside the box. As far as the foreman could see, the stone box was devoid of markings of any sort.

And there was another odd feature. Ossuaries were normally fairly crude in their design, just an open-topped box hacked and chiselled out of fairly soft stone and topped with a stone lid that was equally simple and basic in construction. The lid of an ossuary was a covering, nothing more. Just a way of keeping the bones hidden from view.

But this stone box had obviously been fashioned with care, possibly by a trained mason, because the corners were sharp and precisely cut and the sides were flat. And the lid was a tight fit, which resisted his attempts to remove it. Not even the end of a chisel inserted into the narrow gap between the box and the lid succeeded in shifting it, and at that point he gave up trying, put the box safely to one side to show to the Russian church officials when they arrived at the site on one of their periodic inspections, and told his men to get back to their digging.

The task of overseeing the construction work on the new church had been entrusted to a local Father Superior, who in turn reported to his bishop. The Father Superior – his rank was virtually equivalent to that of a parish priest – was an elderly Ukrainian cleric named Anatoli Chenkovsky. When he arrived at the site the next afternoon, he was shown the stone box, and took it away for further examination in the privacy of his own home.

In his lodging, Chenkovsky placed the box on a table and studied it carefully. As the foreman had noted, neither the base nor the lid displayed any markings at all, and that was unusual. Then the Ukrainian took a small chisel and bent forward to stare at the thin gap between the lid and the top of the box, and saw something which he had certainly not expected.

There was a layer of some kind of sealant, a thin brown line, just visible between the body of the box and the lid, and it seemed to be that which was keeping the lid in place, not merely the tightness of the fit of the lid.

'Now why has somebody done that?' Chenkovsky wondered aloud, lowering the chisel to the table beside him, because the fact that the box was sealed changed everything, and especially what he would have to do about it.

Before he was sent to Jerusalem a year earlier, Chenkovsky had been given a number of instructions, orders which he was to follow in the event of certain circumstances arising. One of these sets of instructions had been given to him by his bishop in Moscow, but it had originated in a very different building elsewhere in the city.

In 1880, the Third Section of His Imperial Majesty's Own Chancellery had been replaced by a new organization with the almost equally unwieldy title of the Department for Protecting the Public Security and Order, in Russian the Отдѣленіе по Охраненію Общественной Безопасности и Порядка. In either language, this was something of a mouthful, and its name was quickly abbreviated to *Okhrannoye Otdelenie*, or the 'guard department', and was eventually simply referred to as the Okhrana. It was essentially the secret police force of the Russian Empire, and a part of the police department of the MVD, the interior ministry.

While most of its focus was inwards, towards the people of Russia, to counter left-wing activity and quickly suppress any forms of political dissent and terrorism, a significant number of the Okhrana's agents operated abroad, monitoring Russian émigré groups and keeping a close watch on their activities. The most important foreign location for Moscow was probably Paris, because it was believed that the French capital was a hotbed of Russian revolutionaries, but the Okhrana had eyes and ears in every country and city where a significant number of Russians lived, and that included Jerusalem.

As soon as Chenkovsky realized that he was looking at a sealed container, which might possibly contain an object or objects of either high commercial value or cultural significance, he knew there was only one thing he could do. He had no option but to turn over the stone box, unopened, to the man who had been introduced to him as the highest-ranking Russian official in Jerusalem, and who was also the local Okhrana agent, a former surgeon named Alexei Pedachenko.

Chenkovsky had met Pedachenko on a number of occasions, and had felt an instinctive dislike towards him. There was something about the man's eyes that spoke of a trace of madness – or at best of instability – somewhere in his soul, and Chenkovsky had never felt comfortable in his presence.

But he had no choice. He knew from past experience that Pedachenko's watchers kept the man very well-informed, and the priest suspected that news of the find in the foundations of the new church would already have reached the Russian's ears.

Chenkovsky had used a small donkey cart to carry the relic from the church to his home on the outskirts of the old town of Jerusalem, and he knew he would need the same or a similar form of transport to deliver the box to Pedachenko. With some difficulty, because the object was heavy and he wasn't a strong man, he managed to wrap the box in a length of material and tuck it away inside a cupboard. Then he locked the doors of both the cupboard and his house before venturing forth into the streets of the city to obtain the help that he needed.

The air was hot and still, stirred by not even the slightest of breezes, and Chenkovsky felt the sweat beading on his forehead before he'd covered more than a dozen paces. The old city was busy at that time in the afternoon, when the heat of the sun had abated somewhat and work began again. Around him, crowds of men, and a mere handful of women, walked with the leisurely pace which Chenkovsky had come to associate with Jerusalem.

People almost never ran, or even walked briskly there, simply because to do so meant that their bodies would pump out sweat which would soak into their clothing, and most seemed to wear the same clothes day after day. That was quite obvious from the smells which assailed Chenkovsky as he walked down the street, weaving his way through the crowd. It was a sour, rank odour overlaid with a complex array of sharper and more redolent scents, a heady mix of spices, cooked food, animal dung and other pungent smells which he had never been able to identify properly. Or had wanted to. It simply smelt of Jerusalem. Quite unmistakable, and very unattractive.

And the other thing that the Ukrainian knew he would always associate with the city was the dust. Anything that moved on the streets of Jerusalem, even a cat – and there were plenty of those – seemed to kick up a cloud of fine white powder which slowly settled back onto the ground, and which had a faint smell all of its own.

Then there was the noise. The almost-constant hum of conversation, of voices sometimes raised in anger or excitement, but more often simply talking, the guttural and unfamiliar sounds of Hebrew – a language which Chenkovsky spoke only poorly and haltingly – meshing into a distinct background clamour which again seemed inseparable from the old city.

Jerusalem was, in short, an assault upon all of a person's senses.

The Ukrainian eased his way through the crowds of people, his head swivelling from side to side as his eyes searched for a cart or barrow, his ears tuned for the distinctive rumbling of wooden- or metal-rimmed wheels moving over cobbles. At first, it seemed as if all the porters had deserted the area, but then, a few streets away from his house, he found a man with a hand-cart who had just delivered some bundles of cloth to a small shop, and hired him for an hour. That, he calculated, would be ample time for him to complete his task.

In fact, it took less time than he had expected. In just under forty minutes he was able to dismiss the labourer, as the door of a house inside the old city swung open to reveal Alexei Pedachenko's slim frame and somewhat delicate features.

'Come in,' Pedachenko instructed, and gestured to somebody standing behind him.

Two bulky men with flat, Slavic faces stepped past the Russian and out into the street, where they glanced in both directions before one of them bent down and, without apparent effort, picked up the stone box, still in its cloth covering, and took it into the house. Chenkovsky and the other man followed him.

Pedachenko led the way into a small square room which was dominated by a solid old wooden table, half a dozen chairs ranged around its perimeter. He pointed at one end of the table and the man carrying the relic lowered it carefully onto the bat-tered and scarred wooden surface.

With a flick of his fingers, he dismissed the two men, waiting until they had left the room and the door was closed behind them before turning his attention to Chenkovsky and the stone box.

'I was about to send those two men round to your lodgings,' Pedachenko began. 'I was concerned that you might have decided to neglect your duty and fail to tell me that this object had been discovered.'

The Russian's voice was soft, but sibilant with menace, and Chenkovsky felt a sudden tingle of fear. Despite Pedachenko's slight stature and delicate, almost effeminate features, the priest had heard about his propensity for sudden and devastating violence. He shook his head.

'No,' Chenkovsky murmured. 'As soon as I was able to examine it properly I knew that I would need to bring it to your attention. The only delay was finding a local man with the means of transporting the object to your house.'

Pedachenko stared at him with a kind of cold appraisal for several seconds, then nodded.

'Very well. What do you suppose it is? An ossuary?'

Chenkovsky shook his head. 'If it is a bone box, then it possesses some unusual features of interest and distinction. I feel it is something very different.'

As he spoke, the priest began removing the cloth which he'd wound around the box before transporting it to its present location.

'What features?' Pedachenko asked, as the stone box was finally revealed.

'This object has been much more skilfully made than all the other ossuaries that I have studied. More care has gone into its construction than is normal for an object that was never intended to be seen. The second burial that these Jews practise is a simple ceremony, and the bone box is usually quite crudely fashioned, because it will be placed in a cave and is not then normally looked upon again.'

The Russian studied the relic for a second or two, then stretched out his hand and ran his fingertips along the smooth side of the object.

'And the other features?' he asked.

'There is no inscription, no way of identifying the bones – if indeed there are any bones – which are inside the box. Again, the carving is normally simple and crudely done, but there is usually at least a name, and often a listing of the forebears of the departed soul. "Jacob, son of Joshua, son of Enoch", that kind of thing.'

'And you have never seen an ossuary without such an inscription?'

'There are some, yes, but they are not common. Then there is the size. This box is only about half as big as most of the ossuaries I have examined. In fact, I doubt if it's big enough to accommodate much more than the skull of an adult, or long enough to hold the leg bones.'

'Children die as well,' Pedachenko pointed out.

'Of course, but I'm sure that an ossuary for a child would be inscribed by the parents. It would be the last thing they would be able to do for their dead son or daughter, a final act of love and devotion. No, I don't believe that this is an ossuary of any description. And there is one other peculiar feature of this object that I wished to bring to your attention.'

Pedachenko looked at him keenly, and nodded for him to continue.

Chenkovsky bent forward slightly, until he could clearly see the gap between the box and the lid, and then he pointed at the grey-brown substance which sealed the space between the two components.

'I do not know what this is, or why it has been done, but it is clear that whoever deposited this object in the ground on the Mount of Olives felt it was important that the contents of this box be protected from the elements. Some kind of material, presumably an adhesive, has been used to seal the gap, to keep out dust and moisture and the creatures that burrow and tunnel in the ground.'

'So what do you think is inside it?'

Chenkovsky shrugged his shoulders and spread his arms wide.

'I have no idea. But I still maintain that the contents of this box are of importance. Or at least, they were of importance when the object was buried. Until we release the lid, we have no way of knowing whether or not they have any significance today.'

'Very well,' Pedachenko replied. 'Then our course is simple enough to chart. We must remove the lid and examine what lies inside this stone vessel, and then we will be able to determine our next move.'

The Russian turned away from the table and opened the top drawer on a small dresser which stood on one side of the room near the door. From inside it he removed a broad-bladed chisel and a heavy hammer, then turned back to the stone box. He slid the blade of the chisel into the gap at one end of the object and gave it a sharp rap. He withdrew the tool, changed his position slightly, and began repeating the same sequence of actions all around the perimeter of the lid.

As he drove the chisel into the narrow gap at the far end of the box, both men heard a faint sigh, like the distant breath of some animal or person, as the seal finally surrendered its millennia-old grasp on the lid.

Pedachenko produced a second chisel and handed it to Chenkovsky. Working on opposite sides of the stone box, they slowly began to lever the lid out of the recess into which it had been placed. Even without the adhesive effect of the sealant, it was a really tight fit. As soon as they were able to, they dispensed with the chisels and seized the lid with their fingers, rocking and jerking to release it from the ancient embrace of the worked stone.

With a sudden rush, the lid shifted one last time, and they were finally able to lift it away from the base and lower it to the table.

Then both men, their differences forgotten – or at least temporarily placed to one side – stood shoulder to shoulder at the end of the table and looked down into the interior of the stone box.

Chapter 2

Quite obviously, neither man had had the slightest idea what to expect. The box could have contained a treasure of some kind, an ancient relic fashioned from gold or silver, or studded with precious stones, but in fact it held nothing of that sort.

For the briefest of instants, Chenkovsky even thought it might be empty, but then immediately realized that made no sense at all. Nobody would go to the trouble and expense of fabricating the box and lid, sealing the container and then burying it with nothing inside it. The cause of that errant thought was that, at first sight, the stone interior of the vessel didn't appear to contain anything; but then he looked down at the base of the box and saw a flat object lying there, almost precisely the same colour as the interior of the stone receptacle into which it had been placed centuries earlier.

'What is it?' Pedachenko asked, glancing at the priest.

'I have no idea. May I?'

The Russian nodded, and Chenkovsky reached his hand down into the box and tentatively touched the object in the bottom.

He moved the very tip of his finger delicately over the surface, tracing a faint path in the thin layer of dust which had accumulated there. As he did so, a darker colour emerged from below the dust, a light brown, like tanned leather. And that, Chenkovsky realized an instant later, was exactly what they'd found. It was a piece of leather, or at least the cured skin of some animal.

'What is it?' Pedachenko asked again.

'I think it's leather, so it's most likely a codex.'

'A what? Do you mean some sort of code?'

Chenkovsky shook his head. 'No. A codex is a kind of book.'

He looked at Pedachenko, wondering how much the man really wanted to know. From what he had heard about the Russian, he knew he was driven by results and wasn't overly concerned with the details. But perhaps he should, at the very least, try and educate the man a little.

'A lot of the earliest forms of writing used clay tablets, and a kind of impressed script like cuneiform. That arose very early, perhaps around three thousand years before our Saviour was born. It was a very complicated language to decipher because of the huge number of different symbols and characters that can be created from that simple triangular shape.'

'Why was it called cuneiform?' Pedachenko asked.

'The name comes from the Latin *cuneus*, which means "wedge". The individual elements which made up cuneiform characters were wedge-shaped because they were usually impressed on wet clay using a length of blunt reed as a stylus, and the reed had a triangular cross-section.'

As he spoke, Chenkovsky extended both his hands into the stone box and gently grasped the object with the tips of his fingers to lift it out of the receptacle. He moved it over to one side, and just as gently lowered it onto the table, where both men could see it clearly.

'It looks like a book,' Pedachenko said, staring at the object. 'A very old book.'

'That's exactly what it is,' Chenkovsky replied. 'Cuneiform lasted for centuries, but it wasn't an ideal means of communication and recording, because impressing characters onto wet clay and then firing the tablet in an oven was a long and very cumbersome process. But when ink was invented, probably independently in many different countries at about the same time, writing techniques began to develop, and written languages evolved. Scribes no longer had to rely on shapes made by the end of a reed, but could produce the far more complex letters and words which were the precursors of the written languages we have today. To begin with, the medium they used to write on was either parchment or vellum, both materials derived from animal skins, so preparing it was still quite a long and expensive process.'

As he spoke, Chemkovsky took a handkerchief from his pocket and very gently began to clean the dust of the centuries from the cover of the codex.

'So what is this made of? Parchment?' Pedachenko asked.

'Possibly. I won't know until I open it.'

'Didn't they use papyrus here?'

Chenkovsky nodded, surprised that the Russian knew anything at all about the subject.

'You're quite right,' he replied. 'In Egypt and the eastern end of the Mediterranean, papyrus was used – in fact, it was probably invented almost five thousand years ago – but it, too, had its limitations, and one of them was that it was quite brittle, which meant it was only really suitable for scrolls, for lengths of writing material that could be rolled. Because it couldn't be folded, it fell out of use when the codex was invented.'

Pedachenko nodded, now staring at the object on the table and clearly only giving scant attention to the priest's words.

'So what is it, this codex thing?'

'That's what we're about to find out,' Chenkovsky said.

With great care, the priest lifted one side of the leather cover to open up the document.

'This is definitely parchment,' he said, 'and it looks as if it's very early.'

'Who invented it? This codex thing, I mean?' Pedachenko asked.

Again Chenkovsky was surprised that the man had any interest in the object, apart from whatever pecuniary or other advantage he thought he could gain from its contents.

'Nobody knows,' the priest replied. 'About two thousand years ago, some unknown scholar had the idea of folding sheets of parchment to form quires, which could then be attached, sewn or tied together, along one side, and that produced the first codex. Since then, nobody's had any better ideas, and all modern books are essentially codices, but today the pages are made of paper rather than parchment.'

'So how old is it? And what's in it?'

Chenkovsky shook his head as he examined the faded characters covering the first page that he had revealed.

'I don't know,' he replied. 'If I had to guess I would say this has been buried for at least a thousand years, probably longer, just because of where the stone box was found. As for the writing, I can tell you that it's Greek, not Latin or Aramaic or Hebrew. Hebrew, of course, is still used today here in Jerusalem, and was actually derived from the older Aramaic script. But because this is written in Greek, it probably means that it wasn't written by a Jew, but by an outsider, perhaps by a visitor to Jerusalem.'

Chenkovsky nodded, warming to his theme.

'And it obviously isn't Roman in origin, because if it was it would have been written in Latin, so possibly this was written by a Greek visitor to the country, or maybe it's a piece of Greek text which somebody thought was important enough to protect and seal away for perpetuity.'

Pedachenko snorted in disbelief.

'An important text,' he echoed. 'What scrap of ancient writing could possibly be important enough to seal in a box like this and then bury on a hillside?'

The dismissive tone of his voice was almost as irritating to Chenkovsky as the words the man had used.

'If I may remind you, our sacred religion was founded on precisely this kind of ancient text, texts which contain the very words uttered by our Saviour and authored by the Lord God Himself. And many of the most important such works were written in this language, in Greek.'

Pedachenko stared at the priest for a long moment, then smiled.

'You may keep your superstitions, old man,' he said. 'Just do not try to impose them on me, because I have no interest in such nonsense. All that concerns me is this book, this codex, and what it contains. Is it of value? What should we do with it? Throw it away? Or do we sell it? Or should we send it off to Moscow?'

Chenkovsky bridled again.

'I don't think that it is our property to sell or otherwise dispose of,' he replied.

'Then perhaps you can suggest who does own it,' Pedachenko said, with a slight smile.

Chenkovsky shook his head.

'That we may never know, but I hardly think we can just keep it for ourselves.'

'Of course we can, because the only people who even know this codex exists are the two of us. So if neither of us tells anyone, it will obviously remain our secret. And if anybody else does get to hear of its existence, I will know precisely where the blame lies. And what to do about it.'

For a moment, Chenkovsky didn't reply as he realized the precarious nature of his situation. More than one member of the Russian community in Jerusalem had reportedly disappeared without trace after crossing swords with Pedachenko. But still he felt a moral obligation to emphasize his concerns.

'But you must understand how important this could be,' he insisted. 'The New Testament of the Bible was written in Greek, not Hebrew. This is clearly an ancient document, and it could be an early version of one of the gospels, or perhaps even a completely unknown work that would provide crucial information about our Saviour.'

'Your Saviour, old man, not mine,' Pedachenko snapped.

He pointed at the codex lying open on the table in front of them.

'All we know about that so far is that it's written in Greek. Before you start making assumptions about it, why don't you at least translate some of the text so that we can find out exactly what we're dealing with?'

Chenkovsky nodded, and bent forward to look at the ancient relic. He took up his handkerchief again and gently, almost reverently, wiped all traces of dust off the open page. He stared down, his lips moving silently as he read the first few words, his right forefinger tracing a shaky path along the line of text.

Then he paused for a few seconds and looked up at Pedachenko, an expression almost of relief shading his features.

Chapter 3

1886
Jerusalem

'What?' the Russian demanded.

'I still don't know what this is,' Chenkovsky said, 'but I do know what it isn't. The first thing about it is the language. I was expecting this to be written in Koine Greek, which was used for about 600 years from roughly 330 BC, but it's not.'

'Koine Greek? What's that?'

'The word just means "common", that's all. But this is quite clearly Mediaeval Greek, the language which succeeded Koine Greek and only fell out of use about 500 years ago, when Modern Greek developed. And the second thing I've discovered is on this very first page. Just here there's a reference to a Roman – or more accurately to a Byzantine – general named Belisarius, and I happen to know that he lived in the first half of the sixth century. So whatever this codex contains, it's significantly later in date than any of the Gospels or other important Christian texts.'

'So you mean it's of no interest to you or that collection of ancient relics who run your church?' Pedachenko sneered.

'That is not exactly how I would have phrased it, but you're right. The contents of this text appear to be secular rather than religious, and so I doubt if my bishop would wish to take possession of it.'

'That's good, because I hadn't planned to offer it to him. Or to you, in fact. But you still haven't answered the question I asked you: what exactly is this codex? Who wrote it, and why?'

'That I don't know, and it will take me some time to get you the answers. My Greek is somewhat unused, and I will need to study a dictionary to produce a proper translation.'

Pedachenko shook his head.

'I don't need a word-for-word translation, or at least I don't think I will. All I want you to do is find out what the text says, what it's about, and if any part of it has any relevance to the present day. A secret – or whatever it is that the writer has put down in that codex – that was important in the sixth century is probably completely irrelevant today. I'm only interested if what he's saying could possibly be relevant to us, right here and right now.'

'May I take this back to my lodging, then?'

Pedachenko thought for a second, then nodded.

'Make sure you take care of it, and bring it back to me no later than tomorrow evening. Does that give you time enough?'

'As you don't require a written translation, yes. But what should we do with the stone box? The workmen at the site will know that I removed it.'

'Go to the church tomorrow and tell the foreman that we opened it but found nothing inside it, and that we will hand over the box to the authorities here in Jerusalem. I'll keep it here for a couple of days, and then you can deliver it as the representative of the church here in the city.'

As usual, Chenkovsky realized, the Russian was intending to

do nothing himself, simply issue a series of orders to his subordinates. But he was relieved that the codex was clearly of a relatively late date and could have no significance as far as his religion was concerned. If it had been a gospel or something of equal importance, Pedachenko could, and probably would, have made things very difficult for him.

A few minutes later, the priest took his leave, the codex wrapped in a length of cloth and tucked under his arm, and made his way back to the house where he lodged, on the outskirts of Jerusalem.

Once back at home, he prepared a simple supper of bread, cheese and olives, and allowed himself a glass of red wine as a small celebration, because he now knew that the contents of the codex could not be in any way significant to his faith. After he had finished, and washed the plates, glass and utensils, he lit an oil lamp which he placed on the side table in his small sitting room. He rummaged around in his bookcase for a minute or so, looking for the Greek dictionary which he was sure he'd placed there, and finally found it. The top of the book was dusty, like everything else in Jerusalem, and he cleaned it carefully before he placed it on the table next to the wrapped codex.

He removed the cloth from around the ancient tome, opened it at the first page and began reading the text, slowly and carefully, taking his time, and with frequent references to the dictionary beside him.

His first reaction to what he was studying was, paradoxically, disappointment. He supposed he'd hoped, subconsciously, that the buried codex would have contained some startling revelation about Jerusalem or its people, or even something significant about Christianity, despite its late date, but in fact what he was reading seemed to be little more than an account of the known history of one particular period of the Byzantine Empire. By the time he'd studied half a dozen pages, he also knew the original author's name.

The man who'd written the work was Procopius of Caesarea, which at least explained why the codex contained such apparently authoritative accounts of the campaigns of General Belisarius.

Chenkovsky had read quite a lot about Roman and Byzantine history – he was deeply interested in the history of the Mediterranean region and its people – and he knew that Procopius had accompanied the general during his various campaigns in the reign of the Emperor Justinian I, and had later become the most important and significant historian of that period of the sixth century, writing at least three books, two of them about Justinian himself and his activities.

Chenkovsky smiled to himself as he remembered the contents of the third, and much more controversial, book. Known as the *Secret History*, or the *Historia Arcana* in Latin, it had been essentially a detailed and scurrilous exposé of Justinian and his wife, the Empress Theodora. The existence of the *Historia Arcana* had been suspected for many centuries, and a copy was later discovered in the Vatican Library, the last secret and inaccessible repository of so many supposedly lost treasures, and subsequently published in 1632.

While Justinian was portrayed, among his other failings, as incompetent and cruel, Procopius reserved most of his venom for the Empress, describing her as, essentially, a sexually frustrated exhibitionist. According to the scribe, one of her favourite tricks was to lie on her back virtually naked – apart from a belt or girdle around her groin to satisfy Roman law which forbade complete nudity in certain places. Slaves would then scatter grains of barley over her naked body, after which specially trained geese would approach her and eat the grains one by one. It wasn't entirely clear what satisfaction the Empress Theodora gained from this exercise, but at least the geese got a meal out of it.

Whether these accounts were based on fact or had been wholly invented by Procopius was unknown, but the *Secret History* made interesting and salacious reading – Chenkovsky knew that, because he owned a copy of the book. But he wasn't familiar enough with the other books Procopius had written to know if the text he was reading in the codex was simply an extract from one of the man's other known works, or something completely new. And knowing whether it was a copy or an original didn't address the obvious and still-unanswered question: why had somebody thought it was important enough to seal in a stone box and bury deep underground on the Mount of Olives?

Because nothing that he'd read so far seemed in any way significant or important. The text didn't cover the entire period about which Procopius was known to have written. Instead, the first pages of the codex described the expedition led by Belisarius which had sailed to North Africa in the sixth century to attack the Vandal capital of Carthage.

The Vandals had sacked Rome almost one hundred years earlier, in 455 AD, and had been an ever-present threat to the Byzantine Empire after that date, because of the strategic location of Carthage on the African coast, which threatened maritime trade in the area. After a bitter six-month campaign, Belisarius had scored a decisive victory at the Battle of Tricamarum, and as well as removing the Vandal threat to maritime operations in that part of the Mediterranean, the

Byzantine Empire also managed to recover the lost Roman provinces located in North Africa.

It was another triumph for Belisarius, who had risen from being a humble foot-soldier and part of the bodyguard of the Emperor Justin I, and who had advanced through the ranks to command the Byzantine army in the East. And in recognition of his achievement in Carthage, he was rewarded with a Roman Triumph when he returned to his base in Constantinople. This was the last such Triumph ever recorded, a ceremonial parade through the streets where the spoils of war, the Vandal treasure, which included a host of objects looted from Rome some eighty years earlier, were displayed along with hundreds of captured prisoners, the latter normally destined for bloody and painful public execution in the arena shortly afterwards as the victors celebrated their success.

All this Chenkovsky knew. The details of Belisarius's African campaign were well known, both from the writings of Procopius himself, and from other contemporary sources. Nothing he had read in the codex was new to him, and he still had no idea why the document had been hidden in such an elaborate fashion.

After two hours, having read almost every word of the text, Chenkovsky carefully closed the cover of the codex again, then sat back and for a few minutes simply stared at the ancient document. Something in the text had to be of such crucial importance that sealing the codex in the stone box and burying it had been essential. Or, at least, somebody had thought it was essential some 1,500 years ago.

He had to be missing something, but he had no idea what it might be.

*

The following morning, he carefully wrapped up the codex again and walked back through the streets of Jerusalem to Pedachenko's house to deliver his report.

As he had expected, the Russian was not pleased with the priest's explanation.

'So what you're telling me is that this book, this really old book, is nothing more than the history of some ancient Roman battles in Africa?'

Chenkovsky nodded.

'That's correct. As far as I can tell, it was written by Procopius, perhaps as a part of his book *De Bello Vandalico*, the Vandal War, or it might possibly be a separate account which he wrote for some other reason. It describes the battles General Belisarius fought in Africa, and finishes with his triumphal return to Constantinople.'

'And nothing else?'

'Not really. Just some – I suppose you could call them administrative details – about Belisarius.'

'Like what?' Pedachenko demanded.

Chenkovsky shook his head.

'Nothing of particular significance. He was made sole consul in the year 535, which was really just a ceremonial post which harked back to the days of the original Roman Republic. And some medals were produced which honoured him, though as far as I'm aware none seem to have survived to the present day, so we only have Procopius's word for this.'

Pedachenko shook his head in irritation.

'That simply doesn't make sense,' he said, echoing Chenkovsky's own view. 'Why would anybody go to such trouble to bury a piece of text which must have been completely unimportant even when it was written? There must be something else in this codex, something you've missed. Could there be a code of some sort built into the text?'

'I doubt it,' the old priest replied. 'In those days codes were extremely basic, and normally just involved simple letter substitutions which were quite easy to decipher. And because that method of encoding produced text which made no sense, it was always very obvious if a code had been used. As far as I've been able to see, this text is grammatically accurate and contains no hidden meaning.'

'Then there must be something in the text itself,' Pedachenko insisted, 'some statement which means more than you've read into it. Forget the campaigns this Roman general conducted in Africa. Constantinople is much closer to home, to where we are now, and to where the stone box was buried. It has to be something to do with what happened after Belisarius came back.'

For a few moments, Pedachenko stroked his smooth and slightly receding chin thoughtfully. Then he nodded, as if he'd just come to a decision.

'I know I told you I didn't want a translation of the text, but I don't read Greek and I think I need to study that last part of the codex. Take it away again and write out exactly what this historian Procopius says about the events in Constantinople, after the battles. Word for word. How long will that take you?'

Chenkovsky shrugged. He'd anticipated that the Russian would probably want more information, and at least he wasn't going to have to translate the entire manuscript.

'Not too long,' he replied, 'because that's the shortest section of the text. Probably about four or five hours, something like that.'

'It probably didn't take you that long to go through the entire text,' Pedachenko pointed out.

'I know, but that was just me reading the Greek, trying to get a sense of what Procopius was saying. Translating every word of the last section and then writing it down will be a much longer and more complicated process.'

Pedachenko nodded.

'Then you'd better get started,' he said.

In fact, it didn't take Chenkovsky as long as he'd been expecting, because the account of Belisarius's return in triumph to Constantinople was really quite brief. Procopius had clearly been aware that, as an historian, his principal duty was to record as accurately as possible the major events of the period. The battles which had been fought on the hot and dusty sands of North Africa were clearly far more important than the celebrations which had followed those victories for the Byzantine forces.

After three hours, he had transcribed everything written in that section of the codex onto several sheets of paper, and then took another half an hour or so to read through his work, making sure that his translation was as accurate as possible.

And it was while he was doing that, checking each sentence word by word, that he came across a single phrase which he had read at least twice before, but the significance of which had escaped him until that very moment. Suddenly, he had an inkling of the reason why the codex had been considered so important, and possibly even why it had been buried in that particular location, on the side of the Mount of Olives.

He went back to the Greek text in the codex and carefully read the original sentence again, making sure that he hadn't misinterpreted it, or read into it something that wasn't there. Then he did the same for the sentences which preceded and followed it, but found nothing else which seemed to him to be as important.

Then he sat back in his seat and for a few minutes stared at the wall opposite, his gaze vacant and unfocussed. If he was right, and the assumption which logically followed from the text of that single sentence proved to be correct, the conclusion was literally awesome.

And that made him wonder about Pedachenko, and about the man's complete absence of faith, and about his greed. Should he tell the Russian at all, he wondered? Could he manage to pass off the codex as just an obscure historical relic, of no significance to the present day? But if he did that, Pedachenko might not believe him and might even give the codex to somebody else to translate, somebody who might also see the significance of that single sentence. And if that happened, then Chenkovsky guessed his own life might be forfeit.

Then there were the wider questions. The Jewish authorities would have to be informed, obviously, because they would need to do the work. And then there were the religious aspects to be considered. Chenkovsky shook his head, almost sadly. No, he reasoned to himself, he really had no option. He didn't like it, but he would have to tell the Russian what he'd found.

So this time, when he knocked on the door of Pedachenko's house late that afternoon, he had a faint, slightly worried, smile on his face.

Chapter 4

1886
Jerusalem

'So what does it mean?' Pedachenko asked. 'I can read what your translation says, but I still don't understand the significance of it. Isn't he just saying that the spoils Belisarius and his men looted from Carthage were stored away?'

Chenkovsky nodded.

'That's exactly what he's saying, because a lot of the treasure, the gold and silver and jewels, were valuable assets for the Byzantine Empire, and most of them had originally been stored in Rome itself, all the spoils of earlier battles which the Roman legions had won. The Romans used to display such captured treasures so that the ordinary citizens could marvel at the triumphs of their generals and legions. When Belisarius retrieved these objects, it was important to him, and to the emperor, that they be seen publicly, to emphasize the military might of the Eastern Roman Empire.

'You have to remember,' Chenkovsky continued, 'that Rome had been sacked twice in the previous two centuries, first by the Visigoths under Alaric, and then by the Vandals. Then the original Roman Empire crumbled and the balance of power shifted

east to Constantinople, then known as Byzantium. In almost all
respects, Constantinople was then the most important city in the
world, the emperor Justinian the most powerful ruler, and
Belisarius the most successful military leader. The success of the
North African campaigns simply underlined this, and the display of the treasures was a final reinforcement.'

'I understand all that, but unless I'm missing something, the
codex doesn't say where the treasure actually went.'

'You're quite right,' the priest replied, 'except for one single
item.'

He pointed at his translation, and at one sentence about
halfway down the page.

'This was what I wanted to show you. When I first translated
this, I was unsure how accurate my version was, and in particular I didn't know exactly what the writer meant by these two
words, because like a lot of words in Greek and other languages, they have multiple possible meanings.'

The words Chenkovsky was indicating were κάτω από.

'Those words, or even just κάτω by itself, can mean "below",
"beneath", "underneath", "lower" and so on, and in modern
Greek κάτω forms part of expressions like "under sheet" and
"the Netherlands", so it's a fairly imprecise word. But I think I
know which meaning the writer intended to convey in this particular sentence.'

The priest looked up at Pedachenko, then back down at the
paper. Then he read out the sentence he'd translated.

'So this passage reads: "And the symbol of the Jews he sent
back from whence it came to reside beneath – κάτω από – the
resting place of the divine presence until the end of days." If you
interpret that statement correctly, it's really very clear what he
means.'

Pedachenko frowned.

'It might be clear to you, old man, but it certainly isn't to me. It just sounds like the typical kind of meaningless nonsense that you hear spouted by priests of all religions. I suppose by "divine presence" he means God?'

Chenkovsky was well used to the Russian's complete lack of faith and sneering dismissal of every kind of religion, and didn't rise to the bait. Instead, he simply answered the question which the man had asked.

'Not exactly,' he said. 'In fact, I don't think that Procopius really understood what he was saying, because that sentence actually doesn't make sense. In the Jewish religion, there's a concept known as the *Shekhinah*. That's a word that can be spelt in several different ways when it's transliterated from the Hebrew expression.'

The priest paused for a moment, then took a pen and wrote a series of Hebrew letters – שכינה – on the page.

'That's the way the word appears in Hebrew,' he said. 'It's often assumed to mean a divine presence, God, if you like, but actually it doesn't. The word comes from a Hebrew verb meaning to settle or to inhabit, and so it actually refers not to God, but to the place where God lives, and that has a very special significance for the Jewish religion.'

Pedachenko looked at him expectantly.

'Get on with it,' he snapped.

'It's all to do with the Temple Mount, and the various buildings which have been erected on it over the centuries. According to the first part of the Hebrew Bible, the Five Books of Moses or the Torah, the first Temple was built on that site by King Solomon almost three thousand years ago to replace the portable sanctuary the Jews had used in the Sinai desert since the time of

Moses. A few years after its construction, Jerusalem was attacked by an Egyptian army under a pharaoh named Sheshonk, but it wasn't destroyed. Some of the damage was repaired, but it wasn't fully rebuilt for nearly one hundred years, and just over a century after that, it was attacked and badly damaged again when the Assyrians invaded. Then the Babylonians completely destroyed the Temple when they attacked the city about 150 years later. That building became known as the First Temple.

'Work on the Second Temple started after the Babylonian Empire had ceased to exist. According to surviving records, the structure was nothing like as elaborate or ostentatious as the earlier building, but it didn't fare much better in the troubled times which followed its construction. It was damaged several times by successive invaders, and was finally destroyed by the Romans in the first century, and no attempt was made to rebuild it.

'Then the forces of Islam conquered Jerusalem in the seventh century, and any opportunity to construct a Third Temple was lost after an Islamic shrine, the one we still see standing there today, the Dome of the Rock, was built on the site, along with the Al-Aqsa Mosque. The Temple Mount has remained in Muslim hands ever since that period, so the Jewish inhabitants of the city have lost not only the Temple, or rather the Temples, but also access to the sacred site upon which the two buildings once stood.'

'I did know some of that,' Pedachenko remarked, 'but I still don't see how that is linked to what it says in the codex.'

'It's all to do with the dwelling place of God,' Chenkovsky replied. 'The Jews are no longer allowed access to the Temple Mount, the location where they believe that their God used to reside. Even the fact that there are Islamic buildings on the site does not diminish, in their eyes, the importance of that place. As far as they are concerned, their God once rested there, and will be there again: they have always believed that one day there would be a Third Temple on the site. More importantly, they also believe that the divine presence can be summoned, if you like, whenever a certain number of worshippers gather together, and that the best and most important location for communicating with their God is the Temple Mount. And that, I think, is what this sentence in the codex is referring to.

'Elsewhere in his writing, Procopius states that some of the treasure that was removed from the Second Temple in Jerusalem by the Romans, under Vespasian and then his son Titus, when they crushed the Jewish Revolt, was returned to the city by Belisarius and Justinian. Some historians have rejected this suggestion because there was no independent confirmation that this had actually happened. I mean that no documents have been found here in Jerusalem or anywhere else which supported this contention.'

Chenkovsky pointed down at the codex again.

'I believe that this document is telling us that Procopius was correct, and that at least one of the treasures seized from the Second Temple was restored to this city. I think that is exactly what the expression "symbol of the Jews" means.'

Pedachenko was now clearly fascinated by what the elderly priest had deduced from his study of the codex, and a glint of greed had entered his eyes.

'So what treasure are you talking about? What were the treasures of the Second Temple?'

'The two most valuable and most important artefacts of all time: the Ark of the Covenant and the sacred menorah. And I think I know which one he was referring to, and exactly where it was hidden.'

Chapter 5

1886
Jerusalem

'Go on.'

Chenkovsky paused for a moment to collect his thoughts, then replied to the Russian.

'I don't think we're talking about the Ark of the Covenant, for two reasons. First, if the Ark ever existed, it would have been comparatively fragile, a wooden box, possibly made of acacia wood, and then covered in gold. The gold would have endured, obviously, but probably not the wood, and in my opinion if such an object had ever been created, it would probably not have survived to this day, or possibly not even to the time of our Saviour. Secondly, if the Ark had been a part of the treasure of the Second Temple, and had been seized by the Romans, it would presumably have been paraded through the streets of Rome when Titus returned to Italy in triumph. There is a frieze on Titus's triumphal arch in Rome which shows that parade, and as far as I am aware there is no object depicted there which could conceivably be the Ark of the Covenant. But what that same frieze does show, quite unambiguously, is the Jewish menorah.'

'Which is what? I've never heard of it.'

That didn't entirely surprise Chenkovsky. The depth of his superior's ignorance on most aspects of both religion and history was exceeded only by his blinkered bigotry.

'The menorah was a seven-branched lamp stand, handmade and beaten from solid gold. According to the Torah, the object was fashioned according to God's most explicit and detailed instructions to Moses. Because it was fashioned from solid gold, the relic would last for millennia, in fact it would survive forever, unless it was deliberately destroyed and melted down.

'The menorah is quite clearly shown on that arch in Rome, being carried in triumph through the streets, and contemporary records state that it was then placed on display in the city for several years. The probability is that when the Vandals sacked Rome, the menorah was one of the objects they seized, and that it was also a part of the Vandal treasure recovered by Belisarius when he captured Carthage. If so, what Procopius says makes sense. The menorah would have been carried back to Constantinople by the victorious army, and it is conceivable that the Emperor Justinian would have agreed to allow the relic to be returned to Jerusalem, if for no other reason than to keep the Jews quiet.'

'But surely if this relic was sent back to Jerusalem the Jewish population here would have rejoiced and placed it in some church or other prominent location, and it would have been guarded and protected there ever since?'

Chenkovsky shook his head.

'Not necessarily,' he replied. 'You have to appreciate that the Jews were treated very much as second-class citizens at this time. Their city had been conquered by the forces of Islam, and their most sacred site, the Temple Mount, had been corrupted – at least in their eyes – by the erection of two Islamic places of worship. If the menorah had been returned to Jerusalem openly, I believe that the Muslim authorities would have done their best to confiscate it, because it would have been far too dangerous for them not to do so.

'If they had suddenly been made aware that such a fundamentally crucial object had been found, a relic which would help to establish the historical reality of the Jewish faith and confirm some of the accounts recorded in the Torah, they would have been appalled. They would probably have seized the menorah and melted it down to become just another anonymous lump of gold which the Muslims would retain for themselves, and anyone in the Jewish community who knew about the relic would probably have been murdered immediately, to ensure that no word of the menorah's existence could ever leak out.'

'So what do you think happened?' Pedachenko asked, his eyes alight with the prospect of getting his hands on the relic. 'If it was brought here in secret, where would they have put it?'

'That's the crux of the matter. The Jewish authorities couldn't have risked the menorah being seen by anybody, Jewish or Muslim, because if that had happened, word would have got around very quickly, and the object would almost certainly have been taken from them. But they would also have wanted the ancient relic to be located somewhere that was appropriate for members of the Jewish faith.'

Pedachenko was getting more excited.

'Then where is it?' he demanded.

Chenkovsky smiled gently.

'They couldn't have put the menorah back onto the Temple Mount, quite obviously, so I think they did the next best thing.

They put it *under* the Temple Mount, in one of the tunnels or cisterns that we know exist in the rocks below it. I believe the relic was hidden there out of sight of everyone, but close enough to the location of the original Temples to satisfy the Jewish belief in the resting place of the divine presence. In fact, I can think of no better place for it to be hidden.'

'Then what was the purpose of placing the codex in the stone box and burying it?'

'I believe that was just a kind of insurance, if you like. Obviously, the Jewish people hoped that one day they would not be a conquered nation, subject to the laws of a race of invaders. I think they probably anticipated that eventually the Mount of Olives would be developed or perhaps excavated, and they buried the box there, in a direct line of sight to the Temple Mount, so that whoever found the box and the codex would make the appropriate connection.'

'So you think the menorah is still there today? Still buried somewhere under the Temple Mount?'

Chenkovsky nodded.

'If it had been found some time during the last fifteen hundred years, I'm quite certain that we would know about it. So, yes, I'm as near certain as I can be that the menorah is still lying hidden under the Temple Mount, in whatever tunnel or cavern is the closest to the original location of the Temple, and just a short distance from where we're sitting now. So what we have to decide is who we should tell about it,' Chenkovsky went on. 'Obviously we'll need to inform the Jewish authorities here, so that we can obtain permission to excavate the area to try to find it. Or help direct them to the most likely location.'

For a few moments Pedachenko didn't reply, as he worked out the best course of action he should take.

Then he stood up, placed his arm around the shoulder of the elderly priest and smiled at him.

'You have done very well, my friend,' he said softly, 'very well indeed, but I don't think we need trouble any of the Jews here with this matter.'

Chenkovsky stiffened as he heard what Pedachenko said, and in those few final instants of his life he realized how severely he'd underestimated both the Russian's greed and his ruthlessness.

With a kind of lethally casual grace, Pedachenko swept the priest's legs from under him and slammed his body, face-first, onto the unyielding edge of the wooden table. It was a killing blow, the impact crushing the front of Chenkovsky's skull, driving bone splinters deep into his brain. But actually, that wasn't what killed him. The force of the impact was so severe that his neck snapped a split second later, and he was dead before he hit the stone floor of the room.

The Russian bent down to ensure that his murderous attack had been successful, then concealed both the codex and the sheets of paper on which Chenkovsky had written out the translation. Only then, when he was completely satisfied that he had left no trace anywhere in the room of what he and the priest had been discussing, did Pedachenko wrench open the door and call out to his staff.

'Come here, quickly,' he yelled out. 'There's been a terrible accident.'

Chapter 6

April 1888
Jerusalem

The clang of steel striking steel was followed immediately by a sudden howl of pain, the sound loud and seemingly amplified both by the stone walls of the tunnel and the confined space in which the men were working.

'What happened?' another of the labourers asked, putting down his shovel and inching his way forward, bent almost double as he approached the rock face where his companion had been working.

The injured man didn't reply, just sat down with his back against the wall, his right hand cradling his left, which even in the dim light was clearly oozing blood. He just nodded towards the rock face on his right.

The second labourer moved forward until he could see what had happened. The hammer the man had been using lay on the floor of the tunnel where he had dropped it, but there was no sign of the steel chisel. Then he looked more closely at the rock face directly in front of him and saw a dark circular shape almost at eye level. He lifted the oil lamp to examine the mark, and in the flickering light he realized that he wasn't looking at some darker patch of rock, but at a hole. The blackness was the empty space on the opposite side of the rock.

Obviously his companion had been injured when he struck the end of his chisel, but instead of the tool striking hard rock, the chisel had shot straight through the stone at a weak point, and the steel head of the hammer had then smashed painfully into the man's left hand.

The labourer positioned the oil lamp where it gave the best light, picked up the hammer and his own chisel, placed the end of the steel blade a few inches away from the hole and gave it a sharp but controlled rap. Another piece of rock fell away, the hole now a ragged oval shape. He repeated the operation half a dozen times until he had widened the opening sufficiently to allow him to stick both his head and his arm holding the lamp into the open space they had just breached.

While he'd been increasing the size of the opening, the third and fourth members of the work party had moved forward to see what was happening.

'What is it?' one of them asked.

For a few seconds his companion didn't reply, then he turned round to face them with a smile on his face.

'There's another tunnel right in front of us,' he said, 'one of the old ones. Go and fetch the Russian,' he ordered. 'He will want to see this.'

Alexei Pedachenko had known from the start that it wouldn't be easy.

Two years earlier, when the old priest from the Ukraine had explained the significance of the codex to him, he'd known immediately that if there was the slightest chance of recovering the menorah, he would have to take it. He knew little about the

Jewish religion or customs and cared less, and saw the relic as nothing more than a meal ticket. If he could find it, he could live the rest of his life in luxury, because he was absolutely certain that the ancient relic would be worth a literal fortune simply on account of the value of the gold from which it was made, while its value as the most crucial religious icon of the entire Jewish faith was incalculable. How he would sell the object once he'd recovered it he had no idea, but he was quite sure that he would find a way. Buyers, he was certain, would be queuing up.

His first problem was much simpler: he had to work out a way of getting into the subterranean world that lay under the Temple Mount so that he could locate the chamber where the menorah had been secreted.

That, he knew, would be a difficult job. The one thing he certainly couldn't do was order a group of labourers over to the Temple Mount and tell them to start digging. All excavations in that area of Jerusalem had been banned, and the Muslim authorities had begun posting guards and sending out patrols to ensure that their rules were not broken. He couldn't even try to get into the tunnel systems at night, because night watchmen were also stationed around the Mount.

Even starting a tunnel some distance away wasn't feasible because of the impossibility of obtaining permission to excavate anywhere, and the equal impossibility of trying to dig such a tunnel covertly. An operation of that sort simply couldn't be carried out without somebody seeing what was happening and asking questions.

But Pedachenko was both resourceful and determined, and he knew that the answer lay in his grasp, simply because of the church.

The construction of the Russian Orthodox church involved a considerable amount of digging, and the whole operation had obviously already been approved by the authorities in Jerusalem. Fortunately for Pedachenko, the design of the church also included a crypt, which was one of the reasons why the digging of the foundations had penetrated so deep into the ground, and why the stone box had been found there.

For about a month after the unfortunate 'accident' to the Ukrainian priest, Pedachenko had bided his time and made his plans. And then he'd acted.

He recruited six local labourers, part of the gang who were working on the crypt of the church, and explained that he had a special mission he wanted them to assist him with. If they agreed, he promised them double their normal payment for working and a bonus at the end of the job, in return for complete silence about what they were doing. If he discovered that anybody outside that group of workers knew anything about his project, he promised that he would personally kill all six men. And such was the Russian's reputation even among members of the local community that he knew not one of the labourers would even breathe a word about what they were doing.

The concept of the job was simple enough, the execution rather more difficult.

Pedachenko had led the workers into the partially excavated crypt and ordered them to fashion an opening at one corner, an opening small enough to be concealed by wood or sacking from the view of any casual observer. From that point he instructed them to begin creating a small tunnel which would lead from the site of the church down the side of the Mount of Olives, under the Kidron Valley and then up towards the Temple Mount itself. The tunnel would need to be shored up at regular intervals, because the ground it was penetrating was earth and rubble rather than rock, but that at least meant that progress should be fairly fast until they reached the Temple Mount, which stood mainly on solid rock.

During daylight hours, the normal working day, they worked in the tunnel in pairs, the other four men continuing with the construction of the crypt and other parts of the church. At night, four men worked in the tunnel, one man digging his way deeper into the ground while the other three removed the debris, and used lengths of timber to support the tunnel.

The straight-line distance between the church and the Temple Mount was not very far, perhaps 500 metres or so, but because the Kidron Valley ran inconveniently between the two locations, the tunnel was a fairly major undertaking, not least because of the importance, and the associated difficulty, of following the contours of the ground. It had to be deep enough to ensure that people walking on the ground above couldn't hear the sounds of the picks and shovels, but not so deep that the workers lost their sense of direction. At least the horizontal bearing of the tunnel had been easy enough to establish, simply because the Temple Mount was so close to the Mount of Olives.

Pedachenko had been deeply asleep when the workmen hammered on his door but, as soon as he learned what had been discovered, he dressed quickly and followed the labourer through the silent streets of Jerusalem and over to the unfinished church standing on the Mount of Olives.

He descended to the crypt, pulled a heavy woollen cap on to his head as some protection against the projecting lumps of stone which studded the roof of the tunnel, and ducked inside the entrance. Both Pedachenko and the labourer who'd summoned him carried oil lamps to illuminate their path, and they made their way as quickly as they could along the narrow and constricted tunnel to the western end of the excavation. The flickering light from the lamps cast giant shadows onto the walls of the tunnel as they hurried along, bent almost double in the confined space, their feet slipping and stumbling on the uneven surface.

At the end of the tunnel, the other three men waited, two of them sitting quietly, leaning against the rough-hewn stone, the third one muttering and groaning as he did his best to attend to his injured hand.

As Pedachenko reached them, all three stood up and moved aside to let him pass. He stopped a couple of feet from the opening in the rock, which had now been widened and was high enough for a man to step through it, lifted his oil lamp and extended it through the hole and into the old tunnel that his men had breached.

The light, dim though it was, showed him exactly what lay in front of him, which was precisely what he had hoped to see.

The tunnel that his men had broken into looked both ancient and abandoned, the walls clearly displaying the marks of the picks and chisels which had hewn it from the solid rock, and also the blackening caused by the naked flames of the torches which workers in antiquity would have been forced to use to see their way.

Pedachenko studied the area in front of him, as far as the light from his lantern would allow him, then nodded in satisfaction. He had no idea where the tunnel began or ended, and at that moment he frankly didn't care, because he knew that he had achieved exactly what he had set out to do: he'd managed to break into one part of the tunnel complex which lay under the Temple Mount. No matter where the old tunnel led, he was quite sure that he would be able to find his way through the warren and reach his goal.

But first, he had to decide what to do about the workmen he'd used to achieve his objective, because now he had – he hoped – no further use for them.

Pedachenko would have preferred all six of them to be involved in a number of unfortunate accidents which would prevent them ever speaking about their work in the area. The dead simply couldn't talk, couldn't betray any secrets and, as far as the Russian was concerned, that was the ideal situation. But he was also aware that the deaths of six men, even the deaths of six simple labourers, would generate unwanted official attention on the church, their place of work, and that was the last thing he needed. Any organized search of the building would quickly reveal the tunnel entrance, and if that were to be discovered, his entire plan would be ruined.

It went against the grain, but he realized that the best thing he could do was pay the men what he owed them, including the promised bonus, and simply frighten them into keeping their mouths shut.

He stepped back from the opening and turned to face the four men who were waiting expectantly in the tunnel behind him.

'You have done well, my friends,' Pedachenko said, his face creasing into a smile. 'The discovery of this tunnel proves exactly what I had suspected, that there was a watercourse which ran from the Temple Mount to one of the springs in the valley below.'

That – the fiction that Pedachenko was trying to locate and map the ancient cisterns and watercourses which were believed to be located below and around the Temple Mount – was the justification he'd used when he'd recruited the six men. He'd impressed upon them the difficulty of excavating the ground directly because of the blanket prohibition which existed, and that had been the reason for his offer of increased pay and a bonus if they were successful.

'Thanks to you, I will now be able to map the whole of the tunnel system.'

He looked at each of the men in turn.

'Your work here is done. I will be at the church tomorrow afternoon, when work ceases for the day, and I will pay you what we agreed when you started this task. Please make sure that your two companions are there as well. And remember, do not speak to anyone of this discovery or of the work you did to make it possible. I will complete my mapping as quickly as I can, and as soon as I have completed that I will also pay you the bonus.'

'You said you would pay us a bonus when the job was finished,' one of the men pointed out, somewhat sourly.

Pedachenko nodded.

'You're quite right, but the job will only be finished when I have completed the mapping that I wish to do. That should only take me a matter of a few days, and then you will receive the money that I have promised you. But remember' – and here the Russian's voice seemed suddenly edged with steel – 'if anyone discovers the tunnel before I have finished, not only will you not receive the bonus, but your lives will be forfeit. I will kill each one of you myself. Let that be clearly understood. You will talk to nobody. Do you all understand that?'

Quickly, all four men nodded their agreement as Pedachenko again looked sharply at each of them in turn.

He hoped his entirely justified reputation for violence, and the promise of the bonus payment, would together be enough to force them to keep silent. In truth, he wasn't particularly concerned about them talking to their fellow workers: his concern was solely that the authorities in Jerusalem should not learn what he had been doing. But now that they had forced a way into the ancient tunnel system, he knew that within a few days, perhaps a week at the most, he would have found the treasure that he sought, and after that it wouldn't matter what anybody said or did.

'Just so long as we understand each other,' Pedachenko finished. 'Now you should all go to your homes and get some rest. You have done an excellent job, and I will see you at the church tomorrow afternoon, as we've agreed.'

Without another word, the four men picked up their tools, turned away, and began heading back down the tunnel towards the eastern end.

As soon as Pedachenko could no longer see or even hear them clearly, he again thrust his lantern through the opening into the ancient workings and feasted his eyes on the walls of the old tunnel. He was so close to finding the menorah that he felt he could almost reach out and touch it.

For a moment or two, he considered stepping into the tunnel and beginning his search immediately, but then he rejected the idea. He wasn't sure how much oil there was left in the lamp he was carrying, and the last thing he wanted was to suddenly be plunged into impenetrable darkness and have to try to feel his way out. Much better to prepare and equip himself properly, to return the following night with two or three oil lamps and whatever other tools he thought he might need to conclude his search.

He took a final look into the tunnel, then turned on his heel and started to retrace his steps eastwards towards the crypt and its hidden opening.

Chapter 7

April 1888
Jerusalem

The following afternoon, precisely as arranged, Alexei Peda-chenko arrived at the site of the church on the side of the Mount of Olives, ostensibly to check on the progress of the construction so that he could report back to his masters in Moscow. For several minutes, he discussed the work with the foreman of the gang, then took his leave. But he didn't go far, stopping a few dozen yards away from the building and taking a seat on a flat rock which offered a good view of the site.

He waited there as the workers began leaving, exchanging pleasantries with them as they walked past him towards their homes in the old city. The six men he'd recruited were the last to leave the site, apart from the foreman. They stopped near the Russian and talked together, waiting until the foreman had also walked away before approaching him.

Pedachenko stood up as the men approached and gathered around him in a loose circle. He handed over the additional money which he had agreed, and again reiterated his warning against speaking to anybody about what they'd been doing.

As soon as the labourers had gone on their way, the Russian

took a last look around the unfinished church and then made his way over to the Temple Mount.

Throughout the entire digging operation, he had kept an accurate note of both the tunnel's length and the direction in which it was heading. That afternoon, he'd spent some time checking the figures – it was a fairly simple geometrical calculation – and now he knew, with a reasonable degree of accuracy, where his men had broken through into the ancient workings.

He came to a halt on the ground below and to the south-east of the Temple Mount, and for a few moments just stared at the massive stone wall which supported the southern side of the Mount, and at the Dome of the Rock which reared above it, the rays of the evening sun seeming to make the massive golden dome glow as if illuminated from within.

People bustled around him, but Pedachenko ignored them, concentrating on his location, on the landmarks he had picked out, and trying as far as he could to ensure that he was standing on the ground above the entrance to the ancient tunnel. In his left hand, he held a small compass, a device he hoped would help him navigate his way through the underground labyrinth later that night.

Pedachenko regarded the Dome of the Rock almost with amusement.

He had never understood how any rational person could give a moment's credence to the idea of any kind of a god or supreme being, and it was a constant source of amazement to him that there were so many different religions in the world, all with different ideas and beliefs, and all with adherents who absolutely knew that they were right and that, by definition, all the other religions had to be wrong. Bloody wars had been fought for such beliefs, mostly in the name of some god or other who was believed to preach peace, and he had no doubt that other, equally bloody, wars would be fought in the future for the same reason. Personally, Pedachenko believed that human beings were simply a kind of highly evolved ape, the first creatures on the planet to have mastered the twin arts of communication and adapting their environment to suit themselves, rather than having to adapt or evolve to suit the environment. As far as he was concerned, man had no more need of any kind of a god than did a dog or a cat or a donkey or any other animal on the planet.

Churches and other places of worship were, to him, nothing more than a testament to man's folly and gullibility, and to the entirely erroneous belief that human beings were in some way special and different. Though it was undeniably true, he thought as he looked up again towards the Dome of the Rock, that some of these buildings were rather impressive.

He looked down again at his compass, checking the reading once more. One of the problems he knew he would face underground was that nobody actually knew where either the First or Second Temple had been located on the Mount. Most people seemed to be of the opinion that the Dome of the Rock had most likely been erected directly on top of the foundations of the Second Temple, in a deliberate attempt by the Muslims to obliterate all traces of the earlier building, but there were Jewish scholars, he knew, who had proposed slightly different locations.

The other side of the coin was that the people who had concealed the menorah in the tunnels beneath the Temple Mount would also not have known the precise location of the Temple, any such knowledge having been lost centuries earlier, and would probably have just positioned the relic in whichever tunnel or chamber they believed lay closest to the centre of the Mount. But the compass would certainly be a help. At least it would ensure that when he began his explorations in the tunnel system under the Mount, he would be heading in more or less the right direction. After that, it would simply be a matter of looking in every chamber and room he discovered until he found the object he sought.

Pedachenko took a final glance around him, then headed off towards his own lodging, where he'd instructed one of his men to prepare a good meal for him, because it looked like being a very long night.

Over five hours later, just after midnight, Pedachenko once again stepped inside the partially finished church on the side of the Mount of Olives. He'd seen nobody since he left the outskirts of the old city, and was confident that he was unobserved. He was dressed in a dark coloured flowing robe topped with an Arab headdress, a *keffiyeh* or *ghutrah*, which had almost replaced the turban in the area about half a dozen years earlier, to ensure that he blended in. If anyone did see him, the fact that he was wearing Arab dress, rather than the European-style clothes he wore every day, should serve to divert suspicion away from him.

In his hand, he carried a small brown leather case, inside which he had placed three oil lamps, their reservoirs filled to the brim, a spare bottle of oil, an airtight metal tin containing a dozen phosphorus matches and sandpaper to light them, and a piece of chalk. In themselves, these items were perhaps unusual, but not in themselves suspicious. The only other thing in the case was a large piece of sacking, which Pedachenko hoped would be big enough to conceal the menorah when he found it, but which he'd arranged in the case to keep the oil lamps and the bottle upright.

He had no tools with him, and he hoped he wouldn't need any. He expected that when he found the correct chamber under the Temple Mount, the menorah would be placed in an obvious position, perhaps even standing on a stone altar or a niche in a wall, and all he would have to do would be to wrap it in the length of sacking, tuck it under his arm and then retrace his steps back down the tunnel.

If he was wrong, and the relic was placed behind metal bars or secured in some other way, he would be able to examine it and decide then what tools he would need to remove it and carry those with him the following night. Time was on the Russian's side: if it took him a week or even two or three weeks to find and recover the menorah, it really wouldn't matter.

He opened the case, lit one of the lamps and then descended to the crypt. He lifted away the wood which concealed the tunnel entrance and stepped inside, removing his robe and head-dress moments later. Under his basic disguise he was wearing a pair of old trousers and a woollen shirt, clothes which would allow him the freedom of movement he would need in the cramped tunnels and chambers he would be exploring.

About ten minutes after he entered the tunnel, Pedachenko reached the point where it intersected with the ancient workings, and he immediately stepped through into the open space which lay in front of him. This tunnel looked as if it was a natural fissure in the rock, widened and expanded by the efforts of workmen perhaps two or three millennia earlier.

According to his compass, the old tunnel ran more or less north-east to south-west. Neither was exactly the direction he wanted to go – he knew from his measurements and calculations

that the Temple Mount lay to the north-west of his present position – but he turned to the right to follow that arm of the tunnel.
After about twenty metres, he encountered a branch and unhesi-
tatingly took the left-hand fork, pausing only to use the chalk to
mark a large cross on the side wall of the tunnel, because he had
no intention of getting lost in the myriad passages of the underground complex.

When he had visited the tunnel his recruited labourers had
been constructing – something he had done every couple of days
since his unauthorized project had started – he had always been
struck by how warm it was underground. But that, Pedachenko
now realized, must have been because of the very restricted
space, the fact that the tunnel wasn't very far underground and,
more prosaically, at least partly because of the heat generated by
the four men working together in such cramped conditions.

That thought had been sparked by the fact that the air in the
tunnel system he was now exploring was cool, if not cold. He
knew this had to be because the underground labyrinth was
both much deeper underground, probably under several feet of
rock, and simply because the tunnels and chambers were so
much bigger. Pedachenko guessed that the temperature would
probably remain constant for most of the year, the labyrinth
insulated from the heat of the sun by the earth and rock which
covered it.

In fact, it was quite difficult for the Russian to even get an
approximate idea of the size of the complex he was exploring,
because the light from the oil lamp cast only a fairly dim circular glow, which was barely bright enough to illuminate both
sides of the tunnel at the same time. He was having to proceed
slowly and carefully to ensure that he didn't miss any chambers
or junctions in the system. And also, of course, he was having

to mark the walls at regular intervals to ensure that he would be able to retrace his steps.

Alexei Pedachenko was not a nervous man, but the thought of being lost in that cold and pitch-black darkness, deep under the earth, was enough to send shivers down his spine. A short way down the tunnel he stopped for a moment and, just as an experiment, extinguished the flame of the oil lamp he was carrying. Even after he had allowed his eyes to get accustomed to the dark, he quite literally could not see his own hand in front of his face: the blackness was absolute. The relief he felt when he lit a match to rekindle the flame of the oil lamp was almost overwhelming.

And it wasn't just the darkness. It was, he knew, completely irrational, but the open spaces he was walking through seemed to simply swallow the sound of his footsteps, the noise not echoing or reverberating from the walls but simply dying away, like the sound of a stone dropped down a deep shaft. Every time he stopped walking and stood to listen, he heard absolutely nothing. Every noise he made, even the faint sighs of his breathing, seemed to be swallowed and deadened by his surroundings. There was no noise whatsoever. It was almost as if the very walls themselves soaked up everything. And the air – which had a musty and unpleasant odour, for some reason faintly reminiscent of decay – was absolutely still.

He shook himself mentally, and walked on, deeper into the labyrinth.

A couple of chambers came into view in the flickering light of the oil lamp, and he entered and carefully explored both of them in turn, but neither contained anything of interest. That was not entirely surprising, because he knew that he could not yet be under the Temple Mount itself.

He moved on through the darkness, the leather case clutched in one hand and the oil lamp held aloft in the other, stopping periodically to check his compass to ensure that he was still heading in approximately the right direction. The rough-hewn tunnel gave way to something more like a passageway, the sides reinforced with masonry, which in turn led into a large open space, the ceiling so high above him that he could barely see any of its details, or even make out its shape.

Pedachenko had been keeping a very rough count of his steps ever since he'd entered the ancient tunnel system, and now he estimated that he must have walked far enough to have passed under the southern wall of the Temple Mount and be somewhere close to his goal. He was still carefully marking the tunnel at regular intervals so that he would be able to find his way out again, but as he lifted the light close to the right-hand wall at yet another junction in the tunnel system, and prepared to mark another cross with his piece of chalk, he saw something which stopped him dead.

Almost exactly where he had intended to place his mark, there was already a chalked symbol on the wall. Not a cross, but an arrow, pointing in the direction he was walking. And that, Pedachenko knew immediately, could only mean one thing. Somebody else had been down there, inside the tunnel system, and probably fairly recently. The wall was slightly damp and chalk marks, he knew, degraded in the presence of moisture. Then he spotted something on the ground, an object which provided an immediate and irrefutable confirmation of his suspicion. It was the remains of a match, quite similar to those he was carrying in the airtight box in his case.

Pedachenko felt a sudden surge of doubt and despair. Had he been beaten to the relic? Or was it still hidden away in one of the chambers, overlooked by whoever had explored the tunnel system before him?

There was only one way to find out. He turned in the direction that the arrow was pointing, lifted his oil lamp above his head and began walking forward.

Almost immediately he saw the entrance to a chamber over to his right, crossed over to it and stepped cautiously inside. He'd seen evidence of a number of rock-falls in the tunnels since he'd stepped inside the old workings, and was keenly aware that if he suffered any incapacitating injury while he was underground – whether from a rock tumbling onto his head or even something as stupid as a broken ankle – the tunnels would become his tomb. Nobody knew he was there, and by the time any comprehensive investigation discovered the hidden entrance in the crypt of the church being built on the Mount of Olives and anyone traversed the cramped and claustrophobic tunnel to find out where it led, he would be long dead.

So he moved slowly and carefully, taking his time and making sure he could see where his next step would take him before he moved forward.

The chamber was, like all the others he'd investigated so far, a crudely hewn space cut from the rock, approximately square, and with a ceiling perhaps nine or ten feet high. It was also, as far as he could see, completely empty. He was looking for any niches cut into the rock walls or any other openings in which the menorah could have been concealed. But the walls he was looking at, though very rough and uneven, were completely solid. He made two complete circuits around the perimeter, raising and lowering the oil lamp to ensure that he was seeing the entire height of the walls, but without result. There was nothing in the chamber.

Pedachenko stepped back out into the tunnel, lifted the lamp above his head to ensure he could see where he was going, and continued his steady and methodical search.

Another rough-hewn entrance loomed up in the gloom, this one on the left-hand side, and he stepped across to it, checked that the roof looked solid, and then stepped inside. This room was a lot smaller, and with a much lower ceiling, and for a moment his spirits lifted, because on the opposite wall, almost in the centre, was a tall but narrow opening.

He lowered the oil lamp to make sure there were no obstructions on the floor, but it was just beaten earth and stones, then strode across to inspect what he'd seen. A few moments later, his shoulders slumped in disappointment. It was a niche in the rock, but it was entirely empty apart from a few slivers of ancient timber, possibly the remains of a shelf or perhaps even a box.

Pedachenko carefully inspected the rest of the chamber, but found nothing of any interest or significance. He turned back, retraced his steps to the entrance, and then resumed his slow and cautious progress deeper into the labyrinth.

In the next minute, he saw two things which concerned him. The first was another chalked arrow on the rock wall at about head height, and the second was the unmistakable signs of recent digging. On the right-hand side of the passageway, close to floor level, there were several pieces of masonry, apparently forming the top of an arch, the base buried deep in the earth below him. The opening below the masonry had clearly been deepened: soil and debris were scattered around the spot, and the space was big enough to allow a man to enter the hidden chamber, albeit only by crawling on the ground.

Of course, there was absolutely no way of telling whether or not the digging was recent. It could have been done the previous year or a millennium ago, but Pedachenko suspected the work was recent, and that was not good news for him.

He muttered a foul Russian curse, then bent down, slid the oil lamp through the gap, crouched down and crawled through the opening.

At first sight, the space didn't appear significantly different to any of the others. A simple chamber, hacked out of the rock in antiquity for some unspecified purpose, and then abandoned for centuries. The only small distinguishing feature was a crevice, possibly just a natural crack in the rock, in the opposite corner, not even as substantial as the niche he'd already inspected in the wall of the other chamber. It didn't look to him as if it was big enough to conceal something the size of the menorah.

The Russian walked over to it and lifted the oil lamp to illuminate the crack. At first, he thought there was nothing in the crevice at all, and the opening in the rock appeared to be just a natural fissure, not something man-made. Then he looked more closely and saw the unmistakable marks made by chisels or possibly hammers on the sides of the opening. It was a natural gap in the rock, but somebody, at some time, had clearly attempted to widen it for some reason.

He lowered the oil lamp to rest it on the flattened rock at the base of the crevice, but as he did so the lamp toppled backwards and he only just caught it before it fell onto its side. He looked more closely at the bottom of the opening, and stretched out his hand to touch it. Then it was obvious to him. What he had taken to be a layer of uneven rock was actually some kind of cloth, black with the dust of ages.

Pedachenko was no expert on fabrics, and even if he had been, in the dim light available to him it was doubtful if he would have been able to deduce anything useful about the material. But to him it definitely looked as if it was old.

Why would somebody leave a length of cloth in such an inaccessible chamber, he wondered. He grabbed the fabric and lifted it out of the crevice, placing the oil lamp on the ground as he did so, and looked at what he'd found. The material was thin, but very long, and he immediately wondered if it was perhaps a burial shroud. Maybe the chamber he entered had been used to prepare bodies for burial. Or possibly the ground he was standing on was a kind of underground cemetery. He could have been walking on a floor of bones. He didn't know enough about Jewish burial customs to know if that was even possible, but he thought it unlikely. The old priest had described a two-stage burial process, but he'd never mentioned the interment of bodies in a place like this.

Then another unpleasant thought struck him. The cloth he was holding his hands could have been a burial shroud, but it could also have been used to wrap something else, either to protect it from damage or to keep it hidden, or even both. Pedachenko dropped the cloth on the ground and stepped back to the crevice to carry out a thorough examination of the space. It was immediately obvious to him that there was nothing else concealed in the crack in the rock, because the sides and back of the opening were solid, but he looked closely, covering every inch of it.

And right at the top of the crevice he found something. It was a flake of paint – in fact it was a couple of scrapes of paint and some very faint scratches in the rock – where the crevice narrowed and its sides came together. It looked as if something, something metallic and painted a dark colour, had been jammed into the gap. He couldn't be certain, obviously, but an unpleasantly logical scenario was beginning to assemble itself in his brain.

If the cloth had been used to wrap up the menorah, and if it had been standing in that crevice, then a man investigating the chamber would probably have seen it. He would obviously have been carrying a lamp of some sort, and might very probably have forced that lamp into the gap so that it would be held in place to provide a steady light while he used both hands to examine what he'd found. It was a scenario that contained a large number of imponderables, but taken as a whole it all made a horribly logical kind of sense.

Pedachenko had trained as a surgeon, and had then worked as an investigator for the Okhrana. Both career choices meant that he was well used to making logical deductions based upon whatever evidence was offered to him.

He took a couple of paces away from the opening and looked around the room again, seeking any further clues and trying as far as he could to work out the probable sequence of events which must have occurred in the chamber, assuming that his initial deduction was correct. The menorah, he knew from what Chenkovsky had told him two years earlier, had been made of gold. That would mean it was heavy, obviously, and so if whoever had entered the chamber had found it standing in the crevice, and had then lifted it out, he would probably have put it down fairly quickly.

Pedachenko lowered his oil lamp to examine the floor close to the opening in the rock. And there he saw what he had hoped not to find. Right in front of him was a square indentation in the soil which formed the floor of the chamber, a place where some heavy object had clearly been put down. It wasn't difficult to work out what that object had most likely been.

And there was confirmation, of a sort, around that spot. He could see a number of footprints, but these weren't the imprints of the flat-bottomed sandals which he'd noticed at other locations in the tunnels. These shoes seemed to have separate heels and a faint pattern on the sole. In fact, those prints didn't look significantly different to those that his own shoes had made as he worked his way along the tunnels.

The conclusion was as obvious as it was unwelcome. Pedachenko cursed volubly in Russian for over a minute, then fell silent. He'd been beaten to the prize. The menorah had obviously been wrapped in that cloth, and whoever had found it had jammed his lamp into the narrowest part of the crevice while he removed the relic. It must have happened relatively recently: the match he'd found and the footprints he'd just discovered were proof enough of that.

For a few moments, the Russian debated whether he should check the rest of the underground complex, but then he shook his head. In his heart he knew that that would be a complete waste of time. There was nothing else he could do in the tunnels, because he was as certain as he could be that the menorah was long gone.

But that didn't mean that his quest had come to an end. He knew that the evidence he had discovered for the location of the relic, and for its subsequent removal, was largely circumstantial, but in his own mind he was as certain as he could be that it had been hidden in the tunnels under the Temple Mount, and that somebody had found his way into the ancient labyrinth, discovered the menorah, and then removed it.

But because there had been no statement – at least as far as he knew – in any country that the most sacred relic of the Jewish religion had been found, he was confident that the person who'd found it hadn't made his discovery public. And that implied that the finder had probably secreted the object away somewhere, either to organize the private sale of the relic or to arrange to have it melted down as gold bullion.

So the hunt wasn't over. What Pedachenko needed to do now was to find out the identity of the man who had beaten him to the prize, and then recover the menorah from him. Whatever it took to do that, the Russian was confident he could manage it, one way or another.

He would start his search the very next day, and discover the identity of anybody who was known to have carried out excavations of any sort in the vicinity of the Temple Mount. He was aware that digging in the area had been forbidden for some time, but Pedachenko already knew that an Englishman had been given permission to carry out some limited excavations near the site a few years ago, long before he himself had arrived in Jerusalem. He also knew that the man had been forbidden to dig on or under the Temple Mount, but that meant nothing. The English were a mongrel nation, lacking the purity and nobility of the Russians, and known to be devious and deceitful, and if the man had wanted to excavate under the Mount, Pedachenko was sure that he would have found a way to do so.

That man was probably the most likely culprit, but before he did anything else Pedachenko would make absolutely sure that his conclusion was correct, and check that nobody else had been near the site.

And then, Pedachenko promised himself, he would track down both the man and the menorah. He would take away the relic, which he believed was rightfully his, purely on the basis of the work and expense he'd already incurred in trying to trace it, and then he would arrange another accident. Another fatal accident, just to ensure that nobody would ever know what had happened or where the menorah had been found.

As he emerged into the crypt of the church, and despite what he'd discovered, Pedachenko felt strangely satisfied. He'd been cheated in this first move of the game, but now his course of action was obvious.

He almost relished the expectation of the hunt and the kill which were to come.

Part Two

London

Chapter 8

Thursday, 2 August 1888
London

That night, he'd had the nightmare again.

He was back in the tunnel system under the Temple Mount in Jerusalem, struggling along with the menorah, now wrapped in sacking, clutched in both hands as he headed for the vertical shaft that would take him back to the surface. But there were noises behind him, noises that were getting steadily closer. A scrabbling sound, like running feet, and a whispering and hissing as of many voices, growing louder. And then there were the clutching hands, the hands of Jews, Warren was sure, grabbing at his clothing while the horde of shapeless figures behind him muttered a simple and endlessly repeated six-word mantra: 'It is ours. Give it back.'

And then he was climbing the ladder, climbing up the shaft and away from the tunnel complex, but still he could feel the hands on his ankles and wrists, trying to pull him down, to pull him back into the darkness of the underground labyrinth. And the voices were louder, almost a shout. Why could nobody else hear them but him? And just as the grip of the bony skeletal fingers around his limbs finally stopped him moving upwards, and began to drag him slowly down, down into the depths and into the darkness from which he knew he would never be able to emerge again, he woke up with a yell of horror.

For a few seconds, he had no idea where he was, only an overwhelming sense of relief that he wasn't still in Jerusalem. The bedsheets were tangled around his limbs, and his arms and chest were clammy with sweat. He looked across the room at the connecting door, which gave access to his wife Fanny's bedroom, wondering if she had heard him call out, but there was no sound anywhere in the house.

Outside the window the sky was lightening to reveal what looked like the start of another fairly dull day in a fairly dull summer in London. According to his pocket watch on the stand beside his bed, it was just before 5.30 in the morning, and he knew that he would get no more sleep that night.

He glanced across to the chair which stood close to the bed, and upon which he placed a number of reports which he had been studying until late the previous evening. As he was now wide awake, Charles Warren decided that he might as well try and get some work done, because he had quite enough real problems to cope with, without dwelling on nightmares that were triggered by what had happened over a decade and a half earlier in Jerusalem.

He picked up the first report from the pile, opened it and began reading the terse official language. But even as his eyes scanned the typewritten notes, his memory took him back to the dark tunnels under the Temple Mount as he relived the experience once again.

There had, of course, been no clutching hands or whispering voices – they were merely a product of his imagination – and he had encountered no difficulty, apart from the sheer weight of the object, in hiding the menorah, now a shapeless bundle wrapped in the sacks he'd taken down the shaft, in the bottom of the largest of his personal trunks. Then he'd replaced his clothes and other belongings on top of it to conceal it from view.

He had known at the time that he was taking a tremendous risk in not declaring the object, but he'd also felt that admitting what he'd done and revealing what he'd found would be even more dangerous. Because Jerusalem was under the control of the Ottoman Turks, who of course followed Islam and barely even tolerated the Jewish religion, he had dared not announce his find to the pasha, the local ruler, because he feared that the man would most probably simply seize the relic for himself, and might even just melt it down for its gold content.

He had also been concerned for his own safety and that of his men, because they would clearly have been aware of the significance of the find, and would be inconvenient witnesses to whatever the pasha decided to do. The man might even have come to the conclusion that no witnesses at all would be the ideal solution, and have arranged for Warren and his men to be executed.

The only problem he then had to solve was how to get himself and his team, and of course the menorah, out of Jerusalem. But that conundrum was unexpectedly solved a few days later, when a second and completely unanticipated *firman* arrived from Constantinople, this one forbidding all further excavation. They obviously had no option but to pack their belongings and leave.

After his return to Britain, Warren had locked the menorah away in the large safe at his London home while he decided what to do with it. And in some ways that had proved to be a far bigger problem than finding the relic in the first place, because he really had no idea of the best course of action. He couldn't admit that he'd found the object and carried it back to Britain, because by any definition that would be regarded as stealing. He had too much respect for the relic and what it had meant in the past to the Jewish nation to even consider having it melted down for its bullion value alone. It was simply too important for that. And while he tried to make up his mind, the object sat behind the heavy steel door of his safe, having exchanged one dark and secure hiding place for another.

And then other factors had come into play, all of which had conspired to prevent him doing anything with the menorah, even if he had been able to come to a decision about it.

For several years after his return, he had been appointed to various domestic posts because his health didn't permit him to travel abroad: he had suffered considerably because of the cramped and insalubrious conditions he had encountered under-ground and, even if the prohibition on further excavations hadn't been sent, he would probably have had to leave the Jerusalem dig anyway, at least for a time.

And then, when he was finally fully recovered, he was imme-diately sent out to Africa. Then his career had blossomed, but he hadn't returned home for four years, until 1880, to become the Chief Instructor in Surveying at the School of Military Engineering, a post he held for a further four years. A year after that, he'd stood for Parliament, but hadn't been elected.

In 1886 he had been ordered to go back to the Middle East, when he was appointed commander at Suakin in the Sudan. But instead of the two-year tour of duty on the shore of the Red Sea he had been anticipating, within a matter of weeks after his arrival he was unexpectedly recalled to London.

A man named Sir Edmund Henderson had just resigned from

his job as the Commissioner of Police of the Metropolis – the Metropolitan Police – and Warren had been chosen as his replacement. Nobody, least of all Warren himself, seemed to have any idea exactly why he had been selected, as he had no experience of police work and was by training a surveyor. His single experience of criminal investigation had been a brief detachment to Sinai four years earlier, in 1882, to try to discover the fate of the missing members of an archaeological expedition led by a Professor Palmer. Warren had been successful – he found that the men had been robbed and then murdered, and he even managed to identify the perpetrators and bring them to justice – but that had been a military-style investigation, not a civilian police operation at all.

But Warren had no choice. His masters had decided his fate, and he had to obey.

And since then, he'd found himself, if not out of his depth, certainly encountering far more difficulties and problems than he could ever have anticipated.

And his core difficulty could be summed up in one single word: London.

The capital was a city of contrasts and a city in turmoil. The disparity between the small number of incredibly wealthy people and the grinding poverty of the masses was simply enormous. In the West End, vast armies of servants lived in huge houses, virtual palaces in many cases, catering to the needs and whims of both the nobility and members of the newly evolved merchant class – old and new money living side by side. But in the East End, entire families were forced to live in single unheated and largely unfurnished rooms in buildings which had no sanitation whatsoever, and frequently not even the luxury of one cold-water tap.

The city's history was dark, dank and depressing. Bubonic

plague had ravaged London in the middle of the fourteenth century, killing about two thirds of the inhabitants and, throughout the mediaeval period, the population never reached the level it had achieved when the Romans had been occupying Britain. The plague made four return visits in the seventeenth century, killing over 100,000 people, and in 1666 the Great Fire of London destroyed a huge area of the city. At this time, the Thames was little more than an open sewer, the streets were strewn with offal, excrement and rubbish, and the whole city teemed with feral dogs, cats, rats, mice, fleas and other pests. The stench was simply dreadful.

By the beginning of the eighteenth century, London's population had risen to about 300,000, roughly a tenth that of the country as a whole, which made it the largest city in Europe at the time. One reason for the growth was the expansion of the London docks and the growing importance of the city as a centre for maritime trade. Something like half of the ships serving Britain loaded or unloaded their cargoes in London. And allied with the development of the docks were the warehouses, factories and manufacturing facilities, housing, entertainment and shops that were directly or indirectly associated with this expansion.

And all these legitimate businesses were mirrored by what might be termed the darker side of the city: the slums, drinking dens and rampant prostitution which characterized the East End of London.

As trade increased so, inevitably, did crime. Sophisticated criminal gangs stole such huge amounts of cargo that in some cases they operated their own warehouse facilities simply to handle the vast quantity of goods they had obtained. The police were outnumbered and frequently outsmarted, and relied heavily on informers and turncoats as they vainly battled to combat the thieves. To make matters worse, the police force was largely corrupt, officers often working hand in glove with the criminals they were supposed to be apprehending, and in some cases actually participating in, or at the very least encouraging, the actions of the thieves.

The situation for the poor had deteriorated markedly with the series of Enclosure Acts which had handed over large tracts of land to wealthy landowners and prevented the peasantry from making use of areas which had historically been in common usage. Despite the fact that people were starving to death every day, England's farmers were at this time producing more than enough grain to feed everybody in the country, but instead of being distributed equably, a substantial proportion of the crop was turned into gin.

For the working – and far too often the starving – classes, gin became a part of their staple diet, and alcoholism a way of life. By the middle of the eighteenth century, figures suggest that there was one gin house in London for every seventy people, and in some parts of the city as many as a quarter of the houses sold the liquor. The annual consumption of the spirit in London exceeded seven million gallons, and some estimates suggest that as many as one in eight citizens died as a direct result of drinking alcohol. The death rate increased to about double that of the birth rate, and the average lifespan of a male dropped to less than thirty years.

Diseases, which included measles, scarlet fever, tuberculosis, tubercular meningitis, pleurisy, diphtheria, dysentery and whooping cough were endemic in London, and especially in the East End, and contributed to the high mortality rate. About one in every four children died before they were one year old.

By the end of the nineteenth century, the population of the city had surged to over four million, and crime was rife. The streets teemed with thieves, muggers, pimps, prostitutes and even pirates, and the East End had degenerated even further into a vast and squalid slum comprising an unholy mix of doss houses, churches, brothels, shops, slaughterhouses, pubs and poor houses.

The last resort for many was the 'spike' or workhouse. With nowhere else to go, a destitute man or woman could register either long term or just for a few nights in the 'casual ward'. But even getting inside was far from easy, as there were usually long queues for admittance, and the rules and routine were harsh. Any supplies of alcohol and tobacco were removed from the inmates, and families were split up, children being taken away from their parents and housed separately. Discipline was rigid, the food virtually inedible and the conditions insanitary in the extreme: in those workhouses equipped with the luxury of a bath, people were expected to bathe in the same tepid water used by as many as a dozen others before them. The regime was more like a prison than anything else, inmates being forced to perform the kind of tasks that incarcerated men and women would have regarded as hard labour, including breaking rocks and picking oakum – unravelling old ropes. The workhouse routine also prevented the inmates from finding work by refus-ing to allow them to leave until late in the morning, by which time all the available casual-labouring jobs would have been taken.

Children walked the streets barefoot and wearing rags. Baby farming was common, as was skinning, the seizing of a child too young to resist and removing and then selling his or her clothes.

Despite the Education Act of 1870, which made schooling

compulsory for children aged between five and thirteen, many families were unable to either pay the school fee – about one or two pence per week – or spare their children, simply because by the age of five most of them were already working and their small income was essential for the survival of the family. Those children who did attend school were taught only the basics: girls were expected to learn domestic skills and the boys the three Rs: reading, writing and arithmetic.

The principal form of entertainment for the masses was turning up at places like Tyburn – where Marble Arch now stands – to watch the frequent public executions. The Tyburn Tree stood in various forms for over 700 years, and in that time well over fifty thousand men, women and children died at the end of its ropes. Capital punishment was applied to a range of so-called crimes that was simply breath-taking, ranging from the theft of goods valued at less than one penny to consorting with gypsies, and neither age nor sex had any bearing on the punishment. Children under ten years old were executed just as frequently as male and female adults.

Unemployment was a major problem. At the London docks, some ten thousand men would appear each day although there were only about six thousand available jobs. In other locations, hundreds of men would compete, and frequently fight, for a small handful of positions. Women and children of both sexes were frequently forced into prostitution simply to survive, because the alternative was starvation and sleeping rough. At common lodgings, or doss houses, payment for a bed was by cash, and for many women selling their body for ten minutes on the streets would provide the few coppers they needed to pay for these most basic and appalling of accommodations.

A bed in a doss house – which meant just that, a bed, in a

large room that might be occupied by as many as sixty or
seventy other people at the same time – cost about four pence a
night, or slightly less than the price of a ticket on an omnibus
from Cricklewood to Oxford Circus. There were hundreds of
such doss houses in the East End, some licensed but most not.
Five shillings would buy a cheap room in a basic lodging house
for a week. A labourer in steady work and with a good job
could earn as much as three pounds a week, but most brought
home a lot less than this.

As well as what might be termed casual prostitution, there
were also women for whom this was their principal employment, their way of life. By 1870, there were estimated to be
1,200 full-time prostitutes operating in the Whitechapel area
alone, and more than sixty brothels. According to a contemporary source, in one street alone, in a line of thirty-five houses,
thirty-two were known to be brothels. In another area near
Whitechapel there were forty-three brothels housing over 400
'unfortunates' or 'fallen women', as prostitutes were then
known, some of them as young as twelve.

Homelessness was endemic, not least because the Artisans
and Dwelling Act of 1875 had seen many of the slum dwellings
demolished. But few of the working-class accommodations that
were intended to be erected in their place had been built. In
some cases the sites simply remained vacant, many for years,
and on other sites commercial establishments were built instead.
And some landlords of what replacement properties were built
were charging rents that put the accommodation out of the
financial reach of the very people for whom they were intended.

Perhaps unsurprisingly, the city faced an economic crisis,
which resulted in frequent demonstrations on the streets, especially in the area around Trafalgar Square, which was seen as

the symbolic location where the starving and homeless of the East End met the well-fed and wealthy inhabitants of the West End.

And all this was the reality at a time when Britain was far and away the richest nation on earth, and London seen as the greatest city in the world. By 1870, Britain's volume of foreign trade was four times greater than that of the developing United States, and also greater than that of Germany, France and Italy combined, and the British Empire was still expanding.

This, then, was the London that Charles Warren had been so unexpectedly appointed to police as its most senior officer. He had major problems to face, and not just because of conditions in the city: the police force he had inherited was incompetent, disillusioned and riddled with corruption.

For any man, even an experienced law officer, this would have represented a serious challenge, but Warren faced a number of additional difficulties. He didn't get on with his political master, the Home Secretary, and his attempts to introduce more military-style procedures into the police force, in an effort to instil a sense of discipline and root out corruption, met with considerable and continuing resistance.

The low point of his time in office had occurred on 13 November the previous year, at what became known as the Bloody Sunday demonstration in Trafalgar Square, a protest against coercion in Ireland, which Warren had ultimately been forced to break up. But he'd used overwhelming force against the 10,000-odd marchers: some 4,000 police officers, 600 mounted police and Life Guards, and three hundred infantrymen. At least three people were killed and hundreds injured when the policemen and troops waded in to disperse the demonstrators, using fists, boots, rifle butts and clubs.

Warren was vilified in the press over his handling of the incident, and in truth he could have managed the situation much better. After that, things quietened down slightly in the city, and for a time Warren began to think that the worst was over. His political masters apparently believed the same thing, because on 7 January 1888 Warren was awarded a KCB – Knight Commander of the Bath.

But, actually, Sir Charles Warren's problems were only just beginning.

Chapter 9

Thursday, 2 August 1888
London

A slim, dark haired man in his mid thirties leaned against one of the trees which lined Whitehall Place and stared across and down the street. At the far end, the imposing and completely unmistakable sight of the Houses of Parliament and Big Ben dominated the road. Most of the old Palace of Westminster had been destroyed in a serious fire in October 1834, and this new building erected in its place. The freestanding clock tower, which had already become something of a symbol of London and Britain itself, had been completed thirty years earlier, in April 1858, and the clock and bells installed the following year.

But it was neither the palace nor the clock which held the man's attention.

On the opposite side of the road stood a large and imposing building. The lower two storeys were constructed of white stone, with two further storeys above them, the whole surmounted by a roof of dark grey, almost black, tiles, itself studded by three rows of windows which indicated the presence of additional floors. The official address of the building, a former private house, was 4 Whitehall Place, but almost nobody

referred to it by that name, because the structure had two
entrances. At the rear of the building was a street called Great
Scotland Yard, on which the public entrance to the headquarters
of the Police of the Metropolis was located, and over the half
century that the police had been based there, the expression
'Scotland Yard' had become synonymous with both the building and the organization which occupied it.

Alexei Pedachenko had been waiting patiently in the street
for almost an hour, and had every intention of remaining there
for the rest of the day if necessary, because that afternoon he
wanted to see his prey.

In Jerusalem, it had taken him less time than he had expected
to confirm that the man who had carried out the excavations –
and they had been, by any definition, illegal excavations because
Pedachenko had seen the tunnels which had been created –
around and under the Temple Mount, was an Army officer
named Charles Warren. As far as he could tell from his researches
in Jerusalem, nobody else had done any digging, approved or
illegal, anywhere in the vicinity. That meant that Warren *must* be
the man who had taken possession of the menorah.

And as soon as he'd established that fact to his own
satisfaction, Pedachenko had contacted Moscow and advised his
superiors that for personal reasons he needed to be relieved of
his duties in Jerusalem for a period of twelve months. He reasoned that if he couldn't track down the menorah within that
period of time, he would probably never find it, and he was
trying to leave the door open so that he would be able to find
employment with the Okhrana again if his search failed.

If he succeeded, which he confidently expected to do, he
wouldn't care about ever working again, because he had already
calculated that the probable value of the gold from which the

relic had been fabricated would be more than enough to ensure that he would immediately be able to retire. And if he didn't need to sell the object as bullion, but could sell it as the ancient menorah of the Jews, then its value would be so high that he had no idea how to even begin to calculate it.

As he had expected, permission was granted very swiftly by Moscow. His career in the Okhrana had been highly successful to date, and he was confident that the organization would not want to lose him.

But even before that particular letter arrived in Jerusalem, Pedachenko had already set in motion a number of enquiries intended to find out where Warren was, and exactly what he was doing.

Because already he knew that the man was a serving officer in the British Army, the Russian had been prepared to travel to Africa or wherever else the Englishman had been posted, and that had been one of his major concerns. He had been worried that if Warren was serving on a campaign somewhere out in the field, perhaps in the African bush, he would almost certainly not have the menorah with him: it would have been placed in his bank or some other safe location pending his return. So when he discovered that Warren was not only in Britain, but was actually being employed in a civilian capacity in London, he guessed that both the man and the menorah would be easy enough to track down.

He'd arrived in London at the end of June, and spent a few nights in a modest hotel. During his career with the Okhrana, Pedachenko had used his position to accumulate adequate funds from a variety of illegal activities to which he had been paid to turn a blind eye, and could actually afford the very best of accommodation, but he had decided to maintain a low profile from the first.

Then he moved out into a comfortable furnished lodging near the centre of the city, not far from Charing Cross railway station. The building was a tall, five-storey residence, and Pedachenko took half of the ground floor, which comprised a small drawing room, a double bedroom, a tiny study and a very basic kitchen that was only a little bigger. The bathroom and lavatory were on the same floor, at the back of the house, and he shared these facilities with the lodger on the other side of the ground floor of the property.

And once he had established himself in the house, he set about locating his quarry.

The civilian job to which Warren had been appointed had come as a surprise to Pedachenko, and not an entirely pleasant one. He had expected the man to have been serving somewhere in the city in a military capacity, not heading a civilian unit. And he'd also realized that, with an entire police force under Warren's command, it might be a lot more difficult to achieve his objective than he had expected.

If the commissioner was always surrounded by squads of officers, simply getting close enough to him to pass him a message might have proved impossible. But that hadn't been the case: getting in contact with Warren was clearly not going to be difficult. Persuading him to hand over the menorah would, of course, be an entirely different matter, but after mulling over the problem for about a month, Pedachenko now believed that he had come up with a plan that would work. It was at once both crude and brutal – which appealed to the Russian's nature – but it would also prove to be exquisitely sophisticated and force Warren into an impossible position. That, at least, was Pedachenko's belief.

His inspiration, oddly enough, was an event which had occurred earlier that year, on 2 April, in Spitalfields, and which he had only found out about from reading an old newspaper he had discovered when he moved into his lodgings, and which he had then investigated further. It wasn't so much the event itself which had inspired him, but more the reaction of the people of the East End of London to it.

He had spent much of the intervening time walking the streets of the city, getting his bearings and identifying locations which he thought would be suitable if the new commissioner refused to accede to his demand from the start. Knowing something about Warren, he didn't expect the man to give in without a fight, and he was, in truth, rather relishing the struggle which he guessed was to come.

Pedachenko already knew where Charles Warren lived. He'd followed him back to his home address from Scotland Yard several times, sometimes on foot and occasionally in a carriage, and believed that he had established the man's routine with a fair degree of accuracy. He'd also done what he could to build as complete a picture as he could of Warren. He knew he'd been married since September 1864 to a woman named Fanny Margaretta Haydon, that he was a devout Anglican – a mark of the man's weakness, in Pedachenko's opinion – and was also a keen Freemason. That final piece of information had provided a further refinement he decided he could use to fuel the plan he was about to put into practice.

In fact, he'd had several ideas, but they were all variations on the same theme, a theme which he was quite convinced would eventually be enough to persuade Warren to hand over the menorah, because as far as he could see it would leave the man with absolutely no alternative.

Freemasonry was just one of the factors that he believed he could use, but that was one of the most important. Two other considerations were seemingly unconnected, but would actually, he knew, be crucial in the implementation of his plan. These were the appalling conditions in the Whitechapel area of London, and the presence in the city of a large Jewish community. Pedachenko thought he could use both of these elements to his advantage.

He glanced over to his left, towards the Thames, the water a dark and muddy brown and running swiftly, the smell of raw sewage rising from it unmistakable, even at that distance. Several barges, laden with goods, were manoeuvring around each other fairly close to the shore, the actions being accompanied by the yells and oaths which seemed inseparable from almost every kind of physical activity Pedachenko had observed since he'd arrived in London. The English, he had concluded, were a very noisy race.

And he noticed something else. Faint yellow tendrils of mist were beginning to appear over the water, and were already starting to spread to the streets around him. It looked as if the population of the city were to be treated to another evening of smog.

Which would be appropriate for the Russian's mood, if not, on this occasion, for the actions he had planned.

Pedachenko straightened up as he saw the main door of 4 Whitehall Place open, the private entrance used only by senior police officers, and the now-familiar figure of Charles Warren, dressed in civilian clothes instead of the dress uniform which the Russian had seen him wearing on a couple of occasions, appeared outside the building, carrying a leather briefcase.

Even if Pedachenko had not seen Warren before, he would probably still have been able to recognize him. The commissioner had not been perceived by any of the London newspapers to be doing a particularly good job, and he had frequently been caricatured in the press, the artists concentrating on his two most obvious distinguishing features: his large and well trained moustache, and the elaborate scarlet uniform he had had made for him when he had taken up the post, complete with cocked hat, epaulettes and a chest-full of medals, which had attracted a huge amount of ridicule.

He was talking to two other men, neither of whom Pedachenko had seen before, and in whom he had no interest whatsoever. After a few moments, Warren turned away, the other men turning back to re-enter the building whilst the commissioner strode into the street and hailed a hansom cab.

As the vehicle pulled away from the kerb, the iron shoes of the horse clattering on the cobbles, Pedachenko stepped away from his observation post and began walking in a leisurely fashion down the street. Warren, he knew, was almost certainly returning to his home, and would most likely remain in the property for the remainder of the evening, as he usually did. The Russian decided he would leave him alone for about two hours, then knock on the door and put the initial phase of his plan into operation.

And that would give him time to make his own preparations for his conversation with Warren, a conversation which he anticipated would be extremely brief.

Chapter 10

Thursday, 2 August 1888
London

The house which Charles Warren owned in London was a substantial four-storey property, easily big enough to accommodate his wife and family, two sons and two daughters. His position allowed him to employ a small domestic staff of just three people: a chambermaid, a cook and a butler-cum-footman named Thomas Ryan, a former soldier in Warren's regiment. Ryan was a kind of general factotum who essentially ran the house and supervised the other two members of the staff.

And it was this man who climbed the stairs to Warren's study early that evening and knocked respectfully on the door.

'Come.'

Ryan opened the door and stepped into the room. It was perhaps the most restful and certainly the most masculine room in the house, panelled in dark wood, one wall lined with open book shelves on which several sets of leather-bound volumes were positioned. The room itself was dominated by a large mahogany desk behind which Warren was seated in a comfortable dark wood-and-leather swivel chair, studying a typewritten sheet of paper. The job of the Commissioner of the Police of the

Metropolis did not end when he left Whitehall Place, and on most evenings Charles Warren expected to spend at least two or three hours studying paperwork and reports.

'What is it, Thomas?' Warren asked, looking across the room.

'You have a visitor, sir,' Ryan replied. 'He has no appointment, speaks good English but with a pronounced foreign accent, and claims to have information of vital importance. He refused to tell me his name or anything about the nature of that information, but he said that it was essential he passed it direct to you, to avoid what he called a catastrophe in the city.'

Warren smiled slightly.

'I really don't need another catastrophe, Thomas,' he replied, 'but I'm also not in the habit of speaking to people who call at my house unannounced and who will not divulge their names.' Warren paused for a moment. 'Do you think he's serious? I mean, he's not in drink or a lunatic?'

Ryan shook his head.

'I cannot speak for his state of mind, sir, but he struck me as being both sober and serious. Certainly there is no smell of gin or other liquor on his breath. And I feel that there is a quality of – I suppose *menace* is perhaps the best word – about him.'

Warren nodded.

'Very well, then. Where is he at the moment?'

'I have left him in the hall, sir, and instructed Annie to remain there with him.'

Warren doubted if the chambermaid would be an effective counter if the man proved to be dangerous, but in fact Ryan's actions made sense. He certainly didn't want a stranger to be roaming the house unsupervised.

'Is the drawing room free?'

'At present, sir, yes.'

'Good,' Warren replied. 'Put him in there and remain in the room with him yourself. I will be down in two or three minutes to speak to him.'

'Very good, sir.'

Ryan turned and left the room. As he did so, Warren took a key from his pocket and unlocked and opened the smallest drawer on his desk. From it he removed his personal firearm, a Webley Mark 1 revolver with a four-inch barrel, chambered for the heavy-calibre .455 Webley cartridge. It was the kind of pistol that would instantly end any argument, simply by one of the people involved producing it. The weapon was of course unloaded, but in moments Warren had opened the box of cartridges which he also kept in the drawer and loaded five of the six chambers, so that the firing pin would rest over a vacant chamber, for safety. He slipped the revolver into his pocket, left the study and walked down the stairs. On the ground floor he turned left in the hallway and crossed over to the door of the drawing room, which stood very slightly ajar, then pushed it open and stepped into the room.

Ryan stood on one side, his legs slightly apart and his hands behind his back, unconsciously adopting the 'at ease' position that had been so familiar to him in his earlier career as an infantryman. Warren registered his presence with a nod, then turned his attention to the second man in the room.

The visitor was standing on one side of the fireplace, which was already laid with kindling and coals in preparation for later in the evening, apparently completely relaxed, looking as if he'd just dropped by to see an old friend. He was slimly built, with dark hair, and was wearing a long black coat of an expensive cut. The buttons down the front were undone and Warren could see evidence of a neatly tailored suit underneath it. Whoever the man was, he clearly wasn't poor.

What Warren couldn't see, or at least not with any degree of clarity, was the stranger's face, because despite being in the house he was still wearing a soft hat, the brim pulled down low over his eyes, and almost all the rest of his face was hidden behind a bushy black beard that Warren immediately guessed was false. A rudimentary, but actually quite an effective, disguise.

'I am Charles Warren,' the commissioner began, introducing himself, 'and I understand from my man here that you have some information for me. Who are you, and what is it that you want to divulge?'

The stranger glanced across the room at Ryan, a still and silent witness, and shook his head.

'What I have to tell you is for your ears alone, Commissioner. It is a matter so sensitive that I dare not let any other person hear the details.'

Warren noted the accent and inflection in the man's voice. Although his English appeared to be virtually fluent, he guessed the stranger probably spoke Russian or one of the eastern European tongues as his first language.

'Thomas Ryan is a valued and trusted member of my staff,' he said. 'You may speak freely in front of him.'

Again the man shook his head.

'I think not. This does not concern your present employment here in London, but an event that took place some years ago. When you know what it is I am referring to, I am quite certain that you would not wish any other person to be a party to our discussion.'

A feeling of cold emptiness settled on Warren as he heard these words. Absolutely the only event in his past that still caused him any concern was the Jerusalem excavation and the events which had taken place at the very end of the dig. After all these years, and because he had taken care to leave no traces of what he had done in the tunnels under the Temple Mount, he had hoped that nobody would ever be able to deduce what he had found or done. But if his immediate guess about his visitor was correct, somebody, somehow, must have worked it out. So perhaps his reading of the man's identity was wrong. Perhaps he wasn't just some Russian, but maybe a Russian Jew, sent by the authorities in Jerusalem to recover the menorah.

And if that was the case, Warren knew that his career would effectively be over. He was already loathed by a large part of the population of the city he had been charged with policing, his relationship with the Home Secretary, Henry Matthews, was less than harmonious, and many of his subordinates would be absolutely delighted to see him removed from office. And if it ever came to public attention that he had not only stolen the most sacred icon of the Jewish people from its resting place while engaged in illegal digging in Jerusalem, but had also smuggled it out of the country, he would be reviled as a liar, a thief and a smuggler, and clearly a wholly inappropriate person to be London's most senior police officer. He would probably also be dismissed from the Army, in which he still held his commission as a senior officer, and of course lose his knighthood.

Whatever happened, he would have to deny all knowledge of the relic to this man, although it was actually in the house, safely stowed away in the safe in his study upstairs. That was all he could do. And that should be enough, because the one thing he did know was that there was no actual proof, no proof whatsoever, that he had even found the menorah, far less removed it from the caverns under the Temple Mount.

But it would obviously not do for Ryan to hear any of that conversation.

'Very well,' he said.

Warren walked a few paces to an easy chair, an occasional table beside it, and sat down. As he did so, he removed the Webley revolver from his pocket and placed it on the table within easy reach and in plain sight. Then he turned to Ryan.

'Thank you, Thomas,' he said. 'I think it might be best if you left us now. I'm perfectly capable of conducting this interview alone. Close the door on your way out and return to your normal duties.'

'As you wish, sir.'

When the heavy door of the drawing room had closed behind the manservant, Warren again directed his attention towards the stranger, who was still standing in precisely the same place as before, seemingly not in any way perturbed by the commissioner's production of the firearm.

'I hope,' Warren said, 'that you have some information of interest to me, because I do not like having my time wasted. First, what is your name?'

The stranger shook his head, and for the first time Warren could clearly see his eyes, cold and hard and unblinking below the brim of his hat.

'My name is not important,' the man replied, 'but for convenience you may call me Michael.'

'Well, *Michael*' – Warren emphasized the obviously false name – 'what do you want?'

'It's really very simple, Commissioner. When you were sent to Jerusalem by the Palestine Exploration Fund just over twenty years ago, you were forbidden, first by the pasha, and then by the *firman* issued by the Ottoman authorities in Constantinople, from excavating any religious sites in and around the city. Despite this, you practised a deception, ignored this prohibition, and excavated tunnels underneath the Temple Mount itself. That was bad enough, and there is no point in you denying that this took place, because I myself have inspected your excavations in Jerusalem and I have seen what you did. In fact, since I arrived in Britain I have discovered that you even had the effrontery to publish a book called *Underground Jerusalem* fourteen years ago, which described in some detail how and where you excavated.'

Warren nodded.

'What I did in Jerusalem is now a matter of public record. As you say, I've even written a book about it.'

The man who called himself Michael also nodded.

'Exactly. But what is not a matter of public record, or in your book, is what happened in the last few days of your excavation, before the second *firman* arrived from Constantinople which banned all digging in the area.'

'I have no idea what you're talking about.'

The visitor wagged his finger.

'I think you know exactly what I mean, Commissioner. I know what you found in that last chamber, the one with the very restricted opening, the chamber that lay under the very heart of the Temple Mount.'

'I have absolutely no idea what you're talking about,' Warren said again firmly, though the faint flicker in his eyes told a different story.

'It was wrapped in cloth,' the stranger continued remorselessly. 'Quite a long cloth which covered it completely, and which you left behind. It was placed in an alcove in the rock, an opening which was narrower at the top than the bottom. You were carrying a metal lantern, and you jammed that into the gap at the top of the crevice so you could see what you were doing when you lifted out the object. Once you'd got it out of the alcove, you placed it on its base on the ground behind you.'

For a few seconds, Warren didn't reply. He knew, knew absolutely without the slightest possibility of error, that he had been alone on that final expedition below the Temple Mount, despite the fact that the man in front of him had just painted a remarkably accurate picture of what he had done in that small chamber. It was almost as if there had been another person there, somebody who had noted down precisely what had happened.

But Warren had an analytical mind. He had been trained as a surveyor and as an army officer, and both careers had fostered the habit of clear, logical and rapid thinking. Because he knew he had been alone in the chamber, the stranger must have deduced what had taken place there from the clues that had been left behind. He remembered discarding the cloth which had enshrouded and protected the menorah, replacing it in the stone alcove. He had jammed his lamp into the narrow gap at the top of the crevice, so that he could use both hands to remove the relic, and in doing so he might have left scratches on the rock, or even a few flakes of paint. Finally, he had placed the menorah on the ground behind him once he had lifted out, and it was so heavy that it would probably have left an impression on the fairly soft soil which formed the floor of the chamber.

A clever man, he supposed, who knew what he was looking for and had examined the chamber with a critical eye and in a decent light, might have been able to spot these telltale clues and reconstruct the possible sequence of actions which had taken place there. In the same circumstances, Warren knew, he might

even have reached the same conclusion himself. And the fact
that he had been excavating around the Temple Mount had
been common knowledge in Jerusalem while he was there, and
no doubt after he had left the country. What he had written in
his book about the excavations would simply have confirmed
this man's suspicions.

Somehow or other, the bearded man – whose name Warren
knew certainly wasn't 'Michael' – had discovered that the menorah had been concealed in that chamber centuries earlier, and
had entered it either himself, or perhaps with a group of other
men, to retrieve it. When he had found that it wasn't there, logic
would suggest that the only person who could have removed the
relic was Warren himself, and that was why this stranger was
standing in front of him at that moment.

But there was, Warren knew absolutely, no proof at all that
he had done what this man was accusing him of, and he certainly wasn't going to admit what had happened. He was a
powerful man in London, with the resources of the entire
Metropolitan Police force at his disposal, and whatever this man
thought or believed really didn't matter to him.

In fact, at that moment Warren was more curious than concerned. He wondered again if he had been right in his initial
assessment. Was the man a Russian Jew? More importantly, was
he acting as a part of some kind of official or semi-official
group? Or, alternatively, might he simply be a treasure hunter,
seeking the menorah as probably the greatest of all the lost
treasures of history, out for what he could get?

Neither the stranger's stance nor his expression – or what
little Warren could see of it behind the beard – seemed to have
changed. That might suggest that he was not acting alone, and
that he had comrades either right outside the property or

waiting somewhere close by, perhaps ready to rush to his assistance if required.

Before Warren threw the man out into the street – and that seemed to him to be the most obvious and sensible course of action – it might be as well to find out who, if anybody, the stranger represented.

Warren picked up the revolver and held it loosely in his right hand, the threat of the weapon clear and explicit. He appeared to examine the pistol for a few moments, then looked up at the man standing a few feet away from him.

'I'm not going to dignify your preposterous allegations with a rebuttal. All I will say is that you are utterly mistaken in your belief. But before you leave my house, I would like to know your real name, and who you represent.'

Warren had supposed that his blanket denial would have produced some kind of a response from the stranger, but the man seemed to be entirely unmoved. His eyes still bored into Warren, but he remained apparently completely relaxed and comfortable, despite his situation and the weapon aimed loosely at him. All he did was shake his head, his gaze never leaving the commissioner.

'That is precisely the response that I had been expecting,' he said, his voice soft but laced with menace. 'As I told you before, my real name is not important. What is important is what I will do now. Sooner or later, you will hand over the menorah to me. Eventually, you will probably be pleased to do so, because only when that happens will the nightmare end.'

'What nightmare?' Warren asked, an unpleasant echo of the dream he'd had the previous night flashing into his memory.

'The nightmare which is about to engulf you. You will see me again, and you will also hear from me, and my actions will speak loudly and clearly on my behalf. I will leave you this piece of paper' – he took a folded sheet out of his pocket and placed it on the mantelpiece beside him – 'on which I have written an address. It is a warehouse in Bermondsey, on the south bank of the river. There is no point in any of your men watching the building, because I will not be going there. Or at least, not yet.

'For your part, when you finally decide that you will do what is right and surrender the menorah to me, you will kindly have it packed in a wooden crate and mark it with the instruction which I have also written on this page.'

The stranger smiled, or at least Warren believed that he did, though the thick beard made it impossible to tell for sure.

'I know that at this moment you are probably thinking that I'm a deranged lunatic, but I would suggest that you give the most serious consideration to me and what I have said to you. I know that you have the relic in your possession, or that you can retrieve it easily from a secure location, probably somewhere here in London. Your bank, perhaps. I also know that you have told nobody about it, otherwise the whole world would already be aware of what you found in that small chamber. Rest assured that I will tell nobody what you did, at least for the moment, because silence will help me, as well as helping you. But make no mistake. You will surrender the menorah to me. Not now, perhaps not even very soon, but eventually you will be pleased to hand it over.'

Warren simply stared at him, tightened his grip on the revolver and stood up to face the stranger.

'You must be a lunatic,' he said, 'and I will thank you to leave my house immediately.'

'I have no problem in leaving,' the man replied, 'and I wish you no harm personally. I only came here to deliver that message. But I do have two other things to say to you. They will mean nothing at all at this moment, but their significance will become very clear over the next few weeks. You are, I believe, a Freemason, and you will know well the commonest of all the symbols of that Craft, the mason's square and compasses. You should remember the shapes of those two objects, because that will provide a confirmation to you of both my resolve and my actions. And you should also remember who fabricated the menorah, and who rightfully owns it.'

And with that, the stranger stepped across the drawing room towards the closed door, Warren following him a few paces behind.

Despite the commissioner's instructions to him, Ryan was waiting outside in the hall, just in case of any trouble, and opened the door when he heard footsteps approaching across the wooden floor. Without a word, he turned, strode across to the front door of the house and opened that as well.

The stranger nodded his thanks to Ryan, then stepped through the door, walked down the stone steps which led to the pavement, turned to his left and almost immediately vanished from sight into the swirling smog.

'Who was he, sir?' Thomas Ryan asked, closing and locking the street door.

'To be perfectly honest, Thomas,' Warren replied, with a calmness that he really did not feel, 'I have no idea. He had no useful information for me, and in fact he ended up threatening me. I doubt if we'll see him back here again.'

Warren returned to the drawing room, stuffed the piece of paper the man had left into his pocket, then climbed the staircase back up to his study and resumed his seat at the desk, unloading his pistol and replacing it in the drawer. But for several minutes he didn't direct his attention back towards the report he had been reading. Instead, he stared at the opposite wall of the room, his eyes unfocused and blank. Ever since he had found and then removed the menorah, he had been half-expecting to hear a knock at the door and find that somebody, somewhere, had somehow managed to discover what he had done.

But he hadn't been expecting anything like the approach which had just been made to him.

He glanced at the paper he'd picked up. On it, as the stranger had said, was the address of a warehouse in Bermondsey. Below that were another few words:

The label is to read 'Consignor Charles Warren, c/o 4 Whitehall Place, London. Consignee Miss S. Winberg, to be collected." It is essential that your real name is on the label, for reasons that will be obvious to you. After delivery of the relic, no attempt is to be made to identify, apprehend or in any way impede Miss Winberg, or the circumstances which led to your decision to return the menorah will resume.

Warren read the words several times, then shook his head. Nothing about the events of that evening made sense. The instructions – if that was the right word – which he had been given were bizarre, though he could see the logic behind them. By insisting that Warren's name and official address were on the shipping label, the man was clearly doing what he could to ensure that the commissioner wouldn't dare try to seize both the relic and 'Michael' or the Winberg woman, who was presumably his accomplice, after she had collected the crate. If that happened, Warren would have no easy way of explaining how the ancient Jewish menorah, labelled with his name, had come to be in his possession in the first place, and his public disgrace would inevitably follow.

But that, of course, wasn't going to happen, because Warren had not the slightest intention of surrendering the menorah, and the veiled threat made by the stranger was too vague for him to give it the slightest credence. The single fact which was unarguable was that the foreigner – the Russian or Russian Jew or whatever he was – had somehow deduced what had happened in Jerusalem nearly twenty years earlier. But as far as Warren could see, there was nothing, not one single thing, which the man could do to threaten him or apply a single iota of pressure that would force him to surrender the menorah. The stranger had obviously been well-informed, but just as clearly he was deranged.

Warren looked again at the paper and the words written on it. He was about to screw it up and throw it away when he paused. Though he was convinced the man was mad and posed no threat to him, it might be as well to retain it, just in case. He unlocked one of the drawers of his desk, slid the paper inside and then turned the key in the lock.

Chapter 11

Friday, 3 August 1888
Central London

The house in which Alexei Pedachenko had secured his lodging faced east, and during the morning the drawing room was bright and cheerful, but was plunged into gloom as soon as the sun passed its zenith. In the afternoon, by far the best light was in the study, at the rear of the property, and this room offered a further advantage in that it was not overlooked by any other house, and no road or path ran near it. So the Russian could work in there without fear of anyone seeing what he was doing.

Though, in fact, his actions would have appeared to be innocent enough.

Spread out on the desk in front of him was a map of the East End of London, a map which he was studying intently. Pedachenko was a man who believed in the importance of thorough preparation, and he was not prepared to leave anything to chance. He needed to determine a good place to start his campaign, and that place had to be close to the centre of Whitechapel, because that district and neighbouring Spitalfields were the two areas in which he believed his actions would have the biggest and most public effect. But he also needed to allow for the subsequent events. He didn't want to go as far to the east as Mile End or Stepney, but he still wanted there to be a reasonable separation between each of the events he was planning.

Then he had an idea. He opened one of the desk drawers and took out a newspaper cutting from the *Daily News* of 6 April 1888 and read again the article which had been the inspiration for his plan. He jotted down 'Osborn Street' on a slip of paper and then turned his attention back to the map, looking for that location.

He found it quickly enough. Osborn Street lay just to the north of Whitechapel High Street and very close to the largest junction anywhere in the district, where Commercial Street, Leman Street, Commercial Road and Whitechapel High Street all met at a single intersection. It was as near to the centre of Whitechapel as made absolutely no difference, and would be as good a spot as any to begin his campaign.

Pedachenko smiled slightly, and nodded to himself. It was fitting, he decided, that he would start very close to the site of this incident, as a kind of silent and unacknowledged homage to the woman featured in the article.

He drew a rough circle around Osborn Street on the map. Anywhere within that area would be a satisfactory starting point for the first of the two triangles he planned to create. As a check, he then took a ruler and drew a narrow triangular shape, the apex of which lay a short distance to the west of the Cambridge Road and the left-hand base point in the centre of Spitalfields. That, he decided, would do very nicely. He would link the second, wider, triangle to the first, but the dimensions of that could wait until he had completed the first one.

He sat in thought for a moment as he considered the date.

The sooner the better, obviously, but he expected that the streets would be very busy over the weekend, and possibly on the Monday as well, because 6 August was a bank holiday. Nevertheless, that would be the date he would start looking. If he didn't find a suitable combination of circumstances that night, he still had plenty of time left. But he would also walk the area on both Saturday and Sunday nights, to ensure that he knew the warren of streets and alleys as well as possible, but also, and even more importantly, to work out the patrol route of the beat police constables, because in this venture timing was everything.

His campaign to force Sir Charles Warren to hand over the menorah would start within the week.

Pedachenko nodded in satisfaction, folded up the map and replaced it in the desk drawer. Then he opened another drawer and took out a heavy knife with a six-inch blade in a leather sheath, a second and smaller knife, also in a sheath, and a whetstone, and for the next hour he sat quietly at the desk, running the blade of first one knife, and then the second, up and down the whetstone until both were as sharp as he could get them.

When he was satisfied with his work, he cleaned both knives carefully and then replaced them in their respective sheaths.

He was ready. Unless he was thwarted for some reason, within four days he would have completed the first event he had planned. And then all of London would know about it.

Chapter 12

The public house was crowded, as it was almost every night of the week, but the crowds were even bigger because of the bank holiday. Every seat was occupied. Groups of people stood around the premises laughing and talking and arguing and, above all, drinking. The furniture in the pub was sturdy, basic, discoloured and badly scarred with scratches and gashes and tobacco burns, and the floor was covered by a fine layer of saw-dust to help soak up spilled drinks, blood, vomit and anything else that landed on it.

At one end of the long wooden bar a drunken soldier was singing loudly and entirely tunelessly to the enthusiastic accompaniment of his equally drunk companions. A small scuffle had broken out at the opposite end of the room between two pros-titutes who were arguing over a man who had passed out – or possibly even died – in the chair between them. Numerous other prostitutes, many of them already drunk and several virtually incapable, plied their trade around the room, moving from one man to another as they offered their services for the price of a drink or two.

In short, it was a typical night in a typical East End pub, and the Angel and Crown was virtually indistinguishable from dozens of others in the area.

Tucked away in one corner, sitting around a tiny wooden table, were four people. Mary Ann Connelly – better known to her friends and clients as 'Pearly Poll', a tall and somewhat masculine-looking prostitute who lodged in Crossingham's doss house in nearby Dorset Street – had her arm around the shoulders of a uniformed soldier, and the man had already agreed to meet her price. She was only waiting for her companion, Martha Tabram, sometimes known as Martha Turner, to complete her negotiations. Then they could do their business and move on to their next clients of the evening. Or have another drink, or even find somewhere to sleep.

Tabram was cheaply dressed, wearing a black bonnet over her dark hair, a long black jacket over a dark green skirt, brown petticoat, stockings and spring-sided – elasticated – boots. All her clothes, and especially the boots, were old and in very poor condition. She was about five foot three inches tall, thirty-nine years old, slightly overweight, and attractive by the somewhat liberal standards applied to her profession in those days.

She had been born Martha White on 10 May 1849, at 17 Marshall Street, London Road, Southwark, and had had a difficult childhood, her parents separating and then her father dying when she was only sixteen. She had been married at the age of 20, in fact on Christmas Day 1869, to Henry Samuel Tabram, a packer at a furniture warehouse. The couple had had two sons, but within six years husband and wife had separated, the root cause being Martha's heavy drinking.

For some three years afterwards, Henry Tabram had supported his wife financially, paying her twelve shillings a week in maintenance, but when he discovered that she had established a relationship with another man – a carpenter named Henry Turner – he had reduced the sum to only two shillings and sixpence.

She'd lived in the East End for some thirteen years, the last decade off and on with Turner, hence her alias as Martha Turner. But in August 1888, Henry Turner had lost his job and he and Martha were trying to eke out a living as hawkers, selling small articles such as needles, pins and trinkets on the street, and had for some four months been lodging in a house off Commercial Road owned by a Mrs Mary Bousfield. But they had left that property about four weeks earlier, without giving notice and owing rent money.

Martha's relationship with Turner, too, had suffered because of her habitual drunkenness, and the couple had split up at about the same time as they left Mrs Blousfield's premises. Since the break-up, Martha had been occupying a bed in a common lodging house at 19 George Street, Spitalfields, and was supplementing her erratic daytime income as a hawker with casual prostitution at night on the streets of Whitechapel.

'Come on, Emma,' Connelly muttered, using the familiar name she usually called Tabram. 'Must be nearly midnight, and I still ain't got the price of a bed.'

Tabram glanced over at her friend, but didn't reply, her attention fixed on the soldier sitting beside her.

'Sixpence too bloody much,' the man said, his voice slurred with drink. 'Give you three. Thas my best offer.'

'Four, then,' Tabram replied, reducing her price to clinch the sale. 'Four pence, and we can do it right now.'

'What, in here?' the soldier said, and burst out laughing.

'No. I know a place, just round the corner. Nice and private.'

'Right. Four pence. That right?'

Tabram nodded, drained the last swallow of gin from her glass and stood up. She needed to get the man outside, and get the business done, before he passed out in the bar and she lost her opportunity.

'C'mon, Poll,' she said, grabbed the soldier's left hand firmly, and began weaving her way slightly unsteadily through the throng crowding the pub. Connelly and the other soldier followed her lead, and moments later all four of them stepped outside to stand for a few moments on the rough pavement. It was about fifteen minutes before midnight.

'Where you two going?'

'I know a good spot in George Yard, nice and quiet.' Tabram said. 'What about you?'

'We'll go to Angel Alley,' Connelly said. 'It's not far. See you later.'

The two couples separated, Tabram leading her client, who seemed even more drunk and unsteady on his feet now that he was outside the building and in the open air, down Whitechapel High Street as far as the White Hart Inn. Then they stepped through a covered archway and turned into George Yard, a narrow alley oriented north–south which connected Whitechapel High Street to Wentworth Street. Angel Alley, the spot chosen by her friend Pearly Poll for the completion of her business with the soldier, actually ran parallel to George Yard, just a few tens of yards distant.

There were a number of premises, the George Yard Buildings, on the east side of the alley, and Tabram found a quiet corner easily enough. Most prostitutes wore no underclothes and routinely conducted their business in the open air, in any spot that offered even a bare modicum of privacy. Such couplings were clumsy, hasty and usually of short duration, and Tabram didn't anticipate that her present encounter would prove to be any different to the others she'd endured during that day.

But there was something she needed to do first, before she lifted her skirts and offered herself to the drunken soldier. She was well aware of the effect alcohol had on the male physique, one bit of it in particular, and if the man couldn't perform, that would be his fault, not hers. But if they were unable to complete the act, some of her clients had refused to pay, and she'd spent too much time talking the soldier into purchasing her services to just walk away now.

'Let me see the money,' she murmured, boldly rubbing her hand across the man's groin.

Her action produced a physical reaction she could feel even through the thick and rough material of the soldier's uniform, so she guessed he wasn't so drunk as to be incapable. But she still wanted payment in advance, just in case.

''Ere you are, you old trollop,' the soldier said, taking a few coins out of his pocket and handing four copper pennies to Tabram.

'A bit less of the "old",' she replied, swiftly checking that she'd been given the right money and then slipping the coins into one of her pockets. 'Now we've got that out of the way,' she added, 'I'm all yours.'

She reached down towards her knees and, with the ease that comes from long practice, pulled up her skirt and petticoat to expose her naked groin.

'All right like that?' she asked, spreading her legs wide and leaning back against the wall of the adjacent building. 'Or do you want me round the other way?'

'You'll do like that,' her client replied, sounding slightly more sober.

He looked down at her naked white flesh, unbuttoned his trousers and took a couple of steps forward.

Their coupling was brief, slightly painful because of the absence of any kind of lubricant, and unsatisfactory for both parties. As soon as it was concluded, the soldier stepped backwards and rearranged both himself and his clothes.

All Martha Tabram needed to do was drop her skirt and petticoat down again, and then she was ready for her next customer.

'That all right, love?' she asked, not caring in the least whether it had been or not.

'Yeah. Suppose so.'

'I'll be off then,' she said, turned and started walking back along George Yard to Whitechapel High Street.

Reaching the road, she loitered for a few minutes near the end of Angel Alley, waiting for Pearly Poll to reappear, but when she didn't, Tabram decided to wait for her in the White Hart Inn, at least until it closed. She found a seat near the bar where she had a view of the street outside the window, and bought herself a glass of gin. She had always been a heavy drinker, frequently consuming enough alcohol to cause fits.

She didn't see Pearly Poll on the street outside, and her fellow prostitute didn't enter the inn either, so Tabram continued drinking. By two in the morning, she was again out on the street, and had spent all the money the soldier had paid her.

Somewhat belatedly, her befuddled brain registered that she had no money even for a bed in a doss house, and that she needed to find another customer, or she would probably end up having to sleep on the street or in the minimal shelter provided by some doorway. She stared around, hoping to see a single man whom she could persuade to hand over money in exchange for her sexual favours. But the street seemed virtually deserted, the only people visible a man and woman turning off Whitechapel High Street into George Yard, presumably on their way home.

Tabram shook her head, leant against the wall of the White Hart Inn for a few moments while she got her bearings, then began staggering down the street in the general direction of the now-closed Angel and Crown pub. Perhaps, she thought, she might find someone down there.

But as she made her way along Whitechapel High Street, a figure seemed almost to materialize directly in front of her, stepping out of a doorway.

The man, for the figure was clearly male, was neatly and casually dressed, and Tabram immediately realized from a single glance at his clothes that he probably had money. Or at least, certainly more than enough money to buy her a bed in one of the nearby doss houses. And right then, that was her highest priority.

She stepped boldly over to him and took his arm.

'You lonely, my love?' she asked. 'Looking for some company, are you?'

The man looked her up and down for a moment, then nodded.

'I know just the place. Nice and quiet. Nobody'll disturb us.'

The man nodded again.

'It'll be sixpence,' Tabram added, as the two of them walked side by side towards the entrance to George Yard. The man reached into his pocket, extracted some coins and handed them over.

Tabram led the way through the covered passage and over towards the buildings on the east side of the alley where she and the soldier had briefly coupled some two hours before.

There was enough illumination in the alley for them to see each other reasonably clearly, and as soon as she reached what she considered the best spot, Tabram turned to face her client and lifted her skirt and petticoat.

'You like what you see, my dear?' she asked, attempting a coquettish smile which didn't quite come off.

The man, who still hadn't spoken a single word since they'd met, gestured towards the buildings they were standing beside.

'Don't you worry 'bout them,' Tabram murmured. 'Nobody about there this time o' night.'

Then an idea struck her, and she again took his arm and led him inside, into the building itself. There was nowhere suitable on the ground floor, so they walked up the staircase together and stopped on the first-floor landing.

'Even better in here, ain't it?' she said, looking at him.

The man nodded once more, then gestured for her to turn around, to face away from him.

That didn't bother Tabram. Many of her clients preferred a rear entry position, and on the streets and alleys where she plied her trade, and where she never had the luxury of a bed, it was often more comfortable for both parties.

She turned away from the man, then reached down to her ankles with both hands, intending to lift the skirt and petticoat again, but this time to expose her rear.

But before her fingers even touched the material of her skirt, something completely unexpected happened. The man reached over her left shoulder and wrapped a pad of some kind of material over her face and then, too quickly for her to utter even a single cry of alarm, pressed it hard over her nose and mouth, holding it there with both hands.

Behind Tabram, her assailant was operating with rapid and lethal efficiency, in precisely the way that he had planned. His weapon was simple enough. The cloth pad was simply a folded scarf, of the kind that many men wore around their necks, and which would arouse no suspicion if he was unfortunate enough to be stopped by a patrolling police officer. The other weapons which he carried were rather different, but he wouldn't use either of those until the woman had succumbed to the suffocating effects of the scarf.

Martha Tabram was struggling violently, fighting for her life, but because her attacker was behind her, her flailing arms never even touched him and the few kicks she landed with her heels on his shins had no effect. Even if she had been sober, it would have made no difference.

And as her convulsions diminished, her body beginning to shut down because of the lack of oxygen in her bloodstream, the man behind her added the finishing touch, removing his right hand from the pad and placing it on her neck, feeling for the carotid artery and then jamming his fingers into exactly the right place to stop the blood flow to her brain.

It was all over in less than two minutes, and there was barely a mark on Martha Tabram's body to show what had killed her. But that was going to change in a matter of seconds.

The man lowered the woman's body to the floor of the landing and quickly felt for a pulse. Finding nothing, he then stood up and looked around, checking that he was still unobserved.

Then he reached into his pocket and took out a heavy knife with a six-inch blade from a leather sheath. He moved to crouch beside the shoulders of the dead body, and drove the knife deep into her chest, ramming the heavy dagger through the victim's breastbone, causing a gaping wound which Tabram luckily could not feel. Even if she had not been dead before, that blow would certainly have killed her, as the point of the blade plunged straight through her heart. That was just to make sure she was dead.

Then he changed position, and his weapon, cleaning the blood off the blade using Tabram's clothing, and then replacing it in the sheath, before taking out his much smaller knife, which had a blade only about half the size of his main weapon. The other knife was simply too big and heavy for what he had in mind. He needed the lighter weight and more delicate blade of the small knife.

He bent down once again, roughly pulled the woman's skirt and petticoat up to expose her stomach and groin, and plunged the short but freshly sharpened blade into her naked flesh. And not once, but time after time, the blade carving a glittering arc through the gloom of the landing, droplets of blood cascading off the knife as it performed its grisly task, slicing first into her abdomen and then her throat, further desecrating her corpse.

Taking care to avoid getting any blood on his clothing, he delivered almost forty stab wounds, several of which, despite the fairly short blade, would have been instantly or ultimately fatal had Tabram still been breathing, before he finally cleaned her blood off his blade and replaced the knife in his pocket.

As he did so, Pedachenko smiled. He wondered if the police or the doctor would realize he'd used two very different knives in the attack and, if they did, if they would assume that the killing had been done by two men. He also decided, at that moment, not to bother using the small knife for the next one.

He could work more quickly and just as accurately with the heavy blade.

Then he stood up, again checked all around him, but could neither see nor hear any signs of life. He glanced down at the body of the prostitute. It was lying in a shadowed area of the landing, and would probably not even be noticed if anyone walked past it. He nodded in satisfaction, straightened his jacket which had become slightly dishevelled during his attack, walked down the stairs and disappeared into the night.

As he stepped outside the building, he muttered a single three-word sentence.

'Now it begins.'

Chapter 13

At about half past three that morning, a young cab driver named Alfred George Crow returned home from work. He lived in one of the George Yard Buildings and, as he climbed up to his lodging, he saw a figure lying on the first-floor landing, but the lighting was so dim that he thought she was simply another vagrant who had chosen that spot as her bed for the night.

At about 2.45, John Saunders Reeves, who was employed as a day labourer at the London docks and who was leaving for work at that hour because of the distance he had to walk, also saw her, but because of the better illumination in the building as the skies outside brightened with the approach of dawn, he saw the blood around her body and realized immediately that she was dead, or at least very badly injured.

Reeves rushed down the stairs and out of the building, looking for help. A few yards down the street, he saw the unmistakable shape of a patrolling police officer and ran over to him.

'There's a dead body,' he shouted, as he approached. 'In my building.'

The patrolling constable, PC 226H Thomas Barrett, left his

beat and followed Reeves back down George Yard and into the building.

'She's dead all right,' Barrett said, crouching down and giving the body a cursory examination. 'You stay here and make sure nobody touches her. I'll fetch a doctor.'

'You'd better be quick,' Reeves retorted. 'I've got to get to work, you know.'

When Barrett reached Whitechapel High Street, he blew his whistle to summon assistance, and when another constable ran up to see what the trouble was, he sent this man off to find a doctor, while he relieved Reeves on the first-floor landing. Barrett knew as well as anyone that being late for work any-where in London, but especially at the docks, was frequently sufficient cause for immediate dismissal, and he had no intention of causing Reeves any problems.

Dr Timothy Robert Killeen, who had his surgery at 68 Brick Lane, arrived at the scene at about 5.30 to examine the body. The sight that greeted him was shocking for its casual brutality. The woman was lying on her back, her legs spread wide, and her skirt and petticoat had been pulled up to expose her corpse from about the waist down, as if she had been engaged in sexual intercourse when she'd been killed. Her stomach and groin were covered in blood from what were clearly dozens of separate stab wounds.

'Looks to me like she was at it with a customer when he turned nasty,' Barrett suggested, as Killeen bent over the body.

'Perhaps,' the doctor agreed, 'though I don't see any obvious signs of recent connection.'

Killeen stood up and took a pace backwards, his eyes never leaving the body lying in front of him.

'There's nothing more I can do for her here,' he went on. 'We have to get the body moved to the mortuary as soon as we can.'

Before Barrett could reply, heavy footsteps sounded on the stairs below them, and a few moments later another police officer arrived at the scene.

'Not a good morning, doctor,' the new arrival stated, 'and certainly not for her,' he added, with a nod towards the mutilated corpse. 'I'm Inspector Reid, from H Division, Whitechapel. Any idea how long she's been dead?'

Killeen nodded a greeting.

'Based on the body temperature, I'd suggest about three hours, but it's difficult to be more accurate than that, because of the way she's been left unclothed, and the stone floor will have cooled the body as well.'

'So between about two and three in the morning, something like that?' Edmund Reid suggested. He was the so-called 'local inspector', or head of the Criminal Investigation Department, of the Metropolitan Police's H Division in Whitechapel, and a few minutes earlier he had been ordered to take charge of the investigation.

'Probably about then, yes,' Killeen agreed.

'And she's obviously been stabbed to death.'

Killeen paused for a moment before replying.

'I'm not entirely certain of that yet. She's certainly been stabbed, there's no doubt about that, but I can't see any defensive wounds, no cuts on her hands or anything of that sort, which could suggest that she was choked or strangled first, or maybe even hit on the head, and that these wounds were inflicted after death. I won't know for certain until I've performed the post-mortem examination. Have you arranged for a cart or an ambulance?'

Inspector Reid nodded.

'There's one on its way,' he replied. 'So it looks like she might have been killed before she was stabbed? That doesn't make a lot of sense to me, not unless we're dealing with the work of a lunatic.'

'Nor to me, Inspector, nor to me. And this is not what we're used to here.'

Oddly enough, despite the squalor, poverty and crime that were endemic in the Whitechapel area at this time, murder there was almost unknown. In the previous year, there had been eighty murders in London, but not one of them had occurred in Whitechapel. The mortality rate in the district was high, but the causes were enormously varied, including disease, starvation and accident, and assaults were by no means uncommon. But very rarely was a life ever taken there by violence.

The sound of iron-shod hooves sounded in the silence of the street outside, and Reid sent Barrett down the stairs to find out who it was.

The constable was back in a few seconds.

'It's a cart come to remove the body, sir,' he reported.

'Right,' Reid said. 'You start talking to the residents, Barrett. Somebody must have seen or heard something, in a building like this. Bring whatever information you find to me at the station.'

As Barrett walked away, two men made their way up the staircase, carrying an old and battered lightweight wooden coffin between them, its scratched and battered exterior showing the unmistakable signs of repeated use.

'There's no official mortuary here in Whitechapel,' Killeen said, 'so where are you taking her body?'

'I've already sent a constable to the workhouse in Old Montague Street. He'll arrange for it to be put in the deadhouse there.'

The deadhouse was a kind of makeshift mortuary attached to the workhouse, intended to accommodate anyone who died while they were resident at the establishment. It wasn't an ideal location, but it was the best they could do.

'I know where that is,' Killeen replied, nodding. 'I can do the post-mortem there.'

The two men watched as the bloody corpse was lifted off the stone floor and lowered into the coffin.

'If there's nothing else, Inspector,' Killeen said, 'I'll get back home for some breakfast. You're welcome to attend the post-mortem if you want, but otherwise I'll see you at the inquest.'

'I think it'll have to be the inquest, doctor, because I'll need to organize a search of the building and talk to the residents. I have to catch this man, and quickly.'

'A murder?' Charles Warren asked. 'Of a woman? Where? And what were the exact circumstances?'

It was the middle of the afternoon, and the commissioner had summoned one of the senior detectives on his force to provide him with a summary of the events which had taken place in Britain's capital city within the previous twenty-four hours.

'It happened in a place called George Yard, sir,' Detective Inspector Frederick George Abberline replied, standing in front of Warren's desk, then went on to explain the location in more detail, because he knew that the commissioner was unfamiliar with the layout of the streets in Whitechapel. And, in fact, with most of the East End of London. Warren's preferred stamping ground began in Mayfair and ended in Kensington.

'It's not actually a yard, sir, despite the name. It's a fairly narrow alleyway that runs between Whitechapel High Street and Wentworth Street.'

'Those names mean nothing to me, Abberline,' Warren snapped. 'For God's sake, man, show me on a map.'

The request was not unexpected – nor, the Detective Inspector had to admit to himself, entirely unreasonable – but as always it was the commissioner's attitude which made him bridle.

Like every other senior officer of the police force of the metropolis, Abberline knew that Charles Warren had no background in law enforcement, and frankly didn't know why the man had been appointed to the post he held, a question that he doubted the commissioner could answer either. And since Warren had arrived in London, he had made it very clear that he knew almost nothing about police work – some of the measures he had tried to impose made that perfectly obvious – and didn't much care for either his subordinates at Scotland Yard or his political masters. And this had translated into an attitude of autocratic aloofness, of snapping orders and expecting instant and unquestioning obedience, and that didn't sit well with the civilian officers under his command.

Abberline, in contrast, had been a police officer in London for almost his entire adult life. He was forty-five years old, five feet nine inches tall, somewhat overweight and balding, his bushy moustache and side whiskers accentuating, rather than concealing, this condition. He had served in the Metropolitan Police Force for twenty-five years, and had spent over half that time – some fourteen years – policing the streets of Whitechapel. It was an area he knew extremely well, where almost everybody knew him, and where most liked him because of his competence and experience, and his fair and even-handed attitude.

Abberline took a step to one side and picked up the leather briefcase he had placed on the chair. There were two chairs in front of Warren's desk but the commissioner had, absolutely typically, not invited the detective inspector to sit in either of them. He much preferred to see his subordinates standing in front of him, and preferably standing to attention, Abberline suspected, but he was never prepared to do that.

He opened the case, extracted a rolled map from it and then replaced the briefcase on the chair. He placed the map on Warren's desk, unrolled it and anchored the four corners with convenient objects: a paperweight, an ink pot and a heavy ruler which secured one side. The map had been cut out of a much larger sheet and showed only the Whitechapel district.

Abberline took a pencil from his pocket and pointed at an area almost in the centre of the map, the lead tip of the pencil tracing the line of a marked road which ran more or less south-west to north-east.

'That's Whitechapel High Street, sir,' he said. 'It's only a fairly short stretch of road because at the western end it changes into Aldgate High Street, just here, and to the east it becomes just Whitechapel Road.'

He moved the pencil down slightly to indicate another road running east-west.

'That's Commercial Road,' he went on, 'one of the main streets in the area. Wentworth Road is just up here' – Abberline pointed at a narrow road which was slightly north of Whitechapel High Street and ran parallel to it – 'and again that's quite a short road that starts at Middlesex Street, here, but only runs as far as the crossroads with Brick Lane. Over to the east, it turns into Old Montague Street.'

'Who the devil named these roads?' Warren muttered. 'It's a complete mess.'

Abberline assumed, correctly, that this was a rhetorical remark and didn't reply. Instead, he indicated two faint parallel lines which ran south from Wentworth Street.

'That is George Yard,' he said.

'And that's where she was killed?'

Abberline nodded.

'In fact, she didn't die in the street itself,' he added, 'but in one of the buildings – they're known simply as the George Yard Buildings – which line the alley.'

'I presume she lived there, then. Was she married? Did her husband do it?'

'At the moment, sir, we have no idea of the identity of the woman, or whether she lived in that building. Or whether she was married, of course. But because of where she was found, and the way her body was lying, the officer in charge of the case – that's Inspector Reid of H Division in Whitechapel – believes she was possibly an unfortunate who had entered the building in the early hours of the morning with a client and had been killed by him during or after connection.'

'She was a prostitute then?' Warren asked.

'That's what Reid believes, yes. Her body was found on one of the landings of the building, not inside a room, which suggests that she was probably not a resident there. But what is particularly alarming about this case is that the woman died as a result of a frenzied attack with a knife. We won't know all the details until the post-mortem is carried out, but Reid said that it looked as if she'd been stabbed as many as forty or fifty times.'

For the first time since Abberline had entered his office, Charles Warren looked shocked.

'The work of a lunatic?' he asked.

'We have no idea at this stage, sir, but it certainly looks like the killer was either a madman or somebody in the grip of an incredibly strong emotion. If she wasn't a prostitute but a respectable woman, I suppose it is just possible that the murderer could have been her husband, slaughtering his wife in a frenzy of anger for some slight. But at the moment Reid doesn't think that was what happened. Obviously we won't know for certain until we can identify the body.'

Warren nodded.

'Very well,' he said. 'Find out who she was as quickly as you can, and then catch this maniac. Keep me informed.'

Without another word, the commissioner turned his attention back to the reports on his desk.

When Charles Warren returned from work at 4 Whitehall Place that evening, he found a hand-delivered letter waiting for him on the table in the hall. He didn't recognize the handwriting at first, and the short message on the single sheet of paper inside the envelope meant nothing to him.

It was only when he took it up to his study and compared the handwriting with that on the note that the stranger had left for him that he realized they had almost certainly been written by the same person. The man who'd confronted him in his home was the murderer of this poor woman. The appalling realization hit Warren hard, though he knew there was nothing he could do about it. And the meaning of the message he had been sent was obscure in the extreme.

The text read: 'Remember the symbol. George Yard. The first of five and the first point of the first triangle. The apex is next.'

Warren studied the note and the envelope for several minutes, trying to decide what it meant, and what the killer was trying to convey, but no matter how he tried, it simply didn't make sense. Finally he locked it away in the same drawer as the original note and went into his chamber to dress for dinner.

*

'You seem a little distracted tonight, Charles,' his wife murmured, as she replaced her soup spoon in the bowl. Preparing a consommé was not one of their cook's greatest talents, but this evening she seemed to have done quite a good job.

Fanny Margaretta Haydon had married Charles Warren twenty-four years earlier, and knew him and his moods better than anyone else. She knew that he was unhappy in his work, because of the circumstances. He was used to the ordered and disciplined life of the army, and the haphazard – and above all *civilian* – organization of the Metropolitan Police was a constant source of irritation to him, not to mention the frequent arguments he had with the Home Secretary.

But he rarely brought these frustrations home with him, and tried as far as he could to keep the battles he had to fight in his office away from his wife and children. But this evening, Fanny could see very clearly that there was something gnawing away at her husband.

Warren smiled slightly from the opposite end of the long table where they habitually dined together.

'I'm sorry, my dear,' he replied. 'I've had a very trying day, I'm afraid, and I've got rather a lot to think about at the moment.'

Fanny looked at him with mild concern.

'Would it help if we talked about it?' she asked. 'Sometimes you've found that helps to clarify your problems.'

Warren shook his head.

'Thank you for making the offer, Fanny,' he replied, 'but it's not that kind of a problem.' He paused for a moment, then shrugged and continued. 'There was a particularly vicious murder of a woman in London last night, and the worry is that there may be a maniac on the loose.'

Fanny's hands flew involuntarily to her face in shock as he said this, but she quickly regained her composure.

'A maniac? Whereabouts – I mean, where was this poor woman killed?'

'Nowhere near here,' Warren reassured her. 'She was murdered in Whitechapel. And she appears to have been a person of no consequence, just an unfortunate, perhaps killed by an angry client.'

Fanny Warren nodded, somewhat reassured by this piece of news, but her face still pale and drawn.

'But still,' she murmured softly, 'that poor woman.'

In his study later that evening, Warren took out both notes again and puzzled over them for some time, wondering what he should do for the best. He and his family would shortly be leaving London for his annual leave, which they would this year be spending in the south of France, and for a few minutes he wondered if he needed to cancel or modify those arrangements. But then he shook his head.

The killing of some woman, most probably a prostitute, in London wasn't, in his opinion, anything like sufficient justification for him to change his plans, and would only result in questions being asked about the reason, questions which he would be completely unable to answer.

There had been an unmistakable air of menace about his unidentified caller, though Warren had never expected the man's veiled threats to be manifested in such a violent and dramatic way. Perhaps he should have obeyed his first instinct, simply shot 'Michael' dead in his drawing room and faced the consequences. He could easily have concocted a story about being attacked in his home by a deranged foreigner, and he knew Ryan would have backed him to the hilt.

But it was too late for that now, and the commissioner guessed that, having committed this brutal murder, 'Michael' would keep well out of sight. But, perhaps, the very fact that Warren had left the capital might stop whatever action the man had planned next. After all, while he and his family were enjoying the sun and taking the waters in Provence, they could have no idea what the foreign killer was up to in London, and it was at least possible that the man might do nothing more during his absence. Because the real purpose of the murder, he was certain, was to apply pressure on him, to make his position as the commissioner untenable, and to force him to surrender the menorah, and that Warren wouldn't do.

No, to continue with his leave exactly as he'd planned it was probably the best decision in the circumstances.

Chapter 14

Thursday, 9 August 1888
Whitechapel, London

From the start, it had been clear to Inspector Edmund Reid that the case would be difficult to solve, because the murderer had left no convenient clues to his identity, and at that stage he didn't even know the identity of the victim, knowledge which might conceivably provide a motive, and which might in turn generate a list of possible suspects.

'You mean nobody knows who she was?' Reid asked.

Constable Barrett shook his head.

'We've spoken – that's me and the other constables – to every tenant in that building and none of them have ever seen her before. Or at least, that's what they told us.'

'Do you think any of them weren't telling the truth?'

Barrett shook his head again.

'Not really, sir. It's the kind of building where people come and go all the time, and if this woman was an unfortunate she might well have used the premises in the past as a nice quiet spot to take her clients. But if she did, she'd have taken care to keep out of sight, and so it's quite possible that none of the residents would have ever seen her before.'

'You're probably right, Barrett, but that does leave us with a bit of a problem, because she wasn't carrying anything on her person that we could use to identify her. I suppose we'll just have to start looking further afield, try and find out if anybody's missing. And you told me that nobody heard anything either?'

'None of the people we interviewed heard a sound that night, sir. I find that difficult to believe, and I'm wondering if maybe one or two of them did hear a scream or a bit of a struggle, and decided not to get involved. But whatever the truth of that, none of the residents will admit to it.'

Reid muttered in irritation.

'And I'm sorry about the identity parades as well, sir,' Barrett added. 'I really thought they might have done the trick.'

'Well, if you couldn't identify him, you couldn't, and that's the end of it.'

In the absence of other ideas, one of the first things Inspector Reid had done that week was to arrange two identity parades.

Earlier on the Monday evening, before the murder had taken place and whilst patrolling his beat, PC Barrett had observed a uniformed soldier – he had been almost certain that the man was a private in the Grenadier Guards – loitering in the vicinity of the George Yard Buildings and had briefly questioned him. As result of this, later that day and on the following day, 8 August, Barrett had been sent to the Tower of London to attempt to identify the soldier he had seen, but had been unable to do so.

So two days after the murder had taken place, the police still had no idea who the dead woman was, far less why she had been slaughtered. And, of course, absolutely no idea of the identity of her killer. The investigation seemed to have come to a grinding halt almost before it had even begun, and Inspector

Reid was not in the best of tempers when he attended the inquest on the afternoon of 9 August.

This was held in the Library of the Working Lads' Institute on Whitechapel Road, and was conducted by the Deputy Coroner, George Collier, because the Coroner for the South Eastern District of Middlesex, Wynne Baxter, was on holiday in Scandinavia.

Alfred George Crow described seeing the shape of a woman lying on the landing, a woman he had assumed was sleeping, and John Saunders Reeves and PC Barrett explained the circumstances of the finding of the body and raising the alarm. The constable graphically described what he had seen on the stone landing, and particularly the position of the woman's limbs and the conclusion which he had drawn from that.

'My impression was that she had been engaged in sexual activity when the murder took place,' Constable Barrett said.

'And what evidence do you have for making that statement?' Collier asked.

'Her clothes were all pulled up, her skirts drawn up above her waist, and she was lying on her back with her legs wide apart. All of her private areas were exposed.'

Collier made a note, and then called for the medical evidence to be given.

Dr Killeen's evidence shocked the inquest into silence.

'Her injuries,' Killeen said, when he stood up to describe what he had observed, 'were simply appalling. I counted a total of thirty-nine stab wounds, mainly to her body but also to her neck.'

'Can you be more specific, doctor? Exactly where were these wounds?'

'Of course. She had been stabbed nine times in the throat and seven times in her lungs. She received two wounds to the right lung and five to the left. Her killer inflicted six stab wounds to her stomach, and five to her liver. Two of the blows penetrated her spleen, but only one cut into her heart. It was clearly a frenzied and extremely brutal attack.'

'Clearly,' the coroner echoed. 'And presumably several of these wounds could have been fatal. Could you determine which was the specific blow that killed her?'

Killeen shook his head.

'The stab wound to the heart would certainly have killed her within seconds, and the injuries to her lungs would have caused her death, though not quite as quickly. Several of her other injuries would have proved fatal without immediate medical treatment, and might possibly have still resulted in her death even if such treatment had been available. But in fact I am perfectly certain that none of these blows killed her.'

Collier paused in the act of writing a note and looked across at Killeen.

'I'm sorry, doctor? What do you mean by that?'

'When I examined the face of the dead woman, I found clear evidence of recent bruising, suggesting that some object had been placed firmly over her nose and mouth. This would imply that she was suffocated before the stabbing took place.'

'So you mean that all these other injuries were inflicted after her death?' the coroner asked.

'That is my conclusion, sir, yes. At the very least, I believe that she was certainly unconscious, but most probably dead, before the attack took place. I would have expected there to have been more blood at the scene if she had been stabbed while her heart was still functioning normally. And my contention is supported by the absence of any defensive wounds on the body. If she had been attacked by a man wielding a knife, I would have expected that she would have suffered injuries to her arms and hands as she tried to protect herself from him. But I found no such evidence, and the position of her body on the stone landing gave the impression of having been quietly laid down. There were no signs of a struggle having taken place.'

The coroner looked down at the notes he had made.

'In his evidence, Constable Barrett stated that he believed the dead woman had probably been murdered whilst participating in a sexual act. Did you find any evidence to support this conclusion?'

Killeen shook his head.

'I agree that the gross position of the body and the disarranged clothing suggested this, but from a medical point of view I found no signs that this had been the case. The woman had taken part in a connection earlier that day but not, as far as I could tell, immediately before her death.'

'So her killer was presumably not motivated by some kind of sexual impulse?'

'That, sir, I cannot say. I can only give as my opinion that this woman was not murdered during an act of connection, despite the appearance of the body when it was found.'

George Collier nodded, and thought for a few moments before continuing.

'So perhaps it is possible that the woman believed that an act of intimacy was about to take place,' he asked, 'and willingly took up the position in which she was found, but was then suffocated by her companion before being mutilated?'

'That is outside my area of competence, sir. I can only provide information of a strictly medical nature. But the sequence of events you have suggested is certainly possible.'

'Thank you, doctor. Are there any other matters which are relevant in this case?'

'There is one very curious feature which I noticed,' Killeen said. 'I have already explained about the various penetrating stab wounds which the victim suffered, but I feel I should also point out that these injuries were caused by two different weapons. The majority of the wounds were inflicted by a knife with a short and narrow but sharp blade, perhaps even a large penknife or claspknife. But the gravest injury on the body was caused by a much bigger and heavier weapon, something like a dagger or even a bayonet.'

The coroner stared at him for a moment before replying.

'Two weapons?' he asked. 'Are you suggesting that this woman might have been murdered by a gang, or at least by two people working together?'

Again Dr Killeen could not be certain.

'I can only say, sir, that I'm certain that two different weapons were employed in this attack. I cannot be sure that they were wielded by two different hands.'

When Inspector Reid gave evidence, the coroner was surprised to learn that the woman was still unidentified.

'So you still have no idea of the identity of this woman, Inspector?' Collier asked him.

'No, sir, I'm afraid we haven't,' Reid replied. 'She was not a tenant of the George Yard Buildings, and none of the residents there had ever seen her before, so we have to assume that she entered the building to seek shelter or for some other reason. She apparently had no business being where she was found.'

'Can you suggest what other reason she could have had for being there, Inspector?'

'We have to consider the possibility that she was an unfortunate, sir, in which case she might have been using the building for a tryst with a client, but at present we don't know if this was in fact the case.'

'And nobody in the building or anywhere else has recognized her face?' the coroner persisted.

Reid allowed himself a slight smile as he replied.

'In fact, sir, three women have positively identified the victim, but unfortunately they have all suggested entirely different names for her. I am confident that we will learn her identity shortly, probably through the press reports of the murder, but at this stage we still do not know who she was or what she was doing in the George Yard Buildings.'

In fact, one of the three women who had contacted the police had correctly recognized the dead woman as 'Martha Turner', the other name by which Tabram was known, but because of the conflicting testimony of the other two women, the police were still uncertain on this point.

At the conclusion of the inquest, the jury, entirely unsurprisingly, concluded that the unidentified woman had been murdered by a person or persons unknown.

Later that day, Inspector Reid had something of a stroke of luck. Another person came forward to the police who was not only able to supply the name of the victim, but could also clarify the sequence of events which had taken place that night.

That afternoon, Mary Ann Connelly – Pearly Poll – the prostitute who had been with Martha Tabram on the evening of 6 August, walked into the Commercial Street police station. She was taken to the mortuary where she immediately identified the body as that of her friend Martha Tabram, and provided a description of what the two women had been doing on the night of the killing.

'So you went off to find a quiet spot with your soldier while Tabram did the same with the other one? Is that right?' Inspector Reid asked her.

'I already told you that, didn't I?'

'I'm just confirming what you said. Do you think you would recognize either of these soldiers again?'

Connelly shrugged.

'Don't know that, do I? Might be able to, I s'pose.'

Inspector Reid was hopeful that 'Pearly Poll' would be his key witness, the person who would help him solve the case quickly. If she could identify either of the two soldiers who she and Tabram had been with that night, that might be all the evidence he would need to secure a conviction.

Unfortunately, his early optimism would prove to be almost entirely misplaced.

Chapter 15

'It's been almost a week since that brutal murder, Reid, and as far as I can see we know virtually nothing more about this killer and his motive than we did when the body was found. Is that a fair assessment of the situation?'

The commissioner was annoyed, and when Charles Warren was annoyed he never made any secret of it.

Inspector Edmund Reid, standing haplessly to attention in front of Warren's desk, could only nod.

'I thought you told me that the Connelly woman would be able to identify the man that Tabram went off with that night?'

Reid nodded again.

'That was my understanding, sir, but when it came to it she either couldn't or wouldn't do so. I had her taken to the Tower of London and to Wellington Barracks, and she viewed two identity parades of soldiers from the Grenadier Guards that I had organized especially for her. She saw nobody that she recognized at the Tower, but at Wellington Barracks she picked out two men who she said she was certain were the soldiers she and Martha Tabram had entertained that night.'

'There you are then. Presumably you arrested these two men?'

Reid shook his head.

'Obviously we questioned them both, and the first thing we checked was where they were on the night of the sixth, when the murder took place. Both of them turned out to have completely solid and unbreakable alibis, supported by several reputable people, so quite clearly she was mistaken. Either that or she was just being deliberately mischievous.'

Warren nodded.

'Do you think she was trying to mislead you? Are you even sure that she was speaking the truth when she identified the body as this Martha Tabram?'

'That is one thing about which we're quite certain, sir. The dead woman was definitely Martha Tabram, and we've had that confirmed by her estranged husband, a man named Henry Samuel Tabram who lives in East Greenwich. As far as Connelly is concerned, I think she rather regretted coming forward to the police in the first place, because ever since she made her initial statement she's become extremely unhelpful and evasive. In fact, she vanished from sight shortly afterwards, and we later discovered that she'd gone into hiding, and had moved in with one of her cousins who lives in a house in Fuller's Court, off Drury Lane.'

'Why do you think she did that?'

Reid shrugged his shoulders.

'She has no liking for authority, sir, because of her profession. Like Tabram, she earns most of her living from prostitution, and I think she's keen to avoid coming too much to the attention of the police. She probably thought that she could just identify Tabram's body and tell us what happened that night, and that would be the end of it. I don't think she reckoned with identity parades and all the rest of it.'

For a few moments, Warren stared down at the report on the desk in front of him, his eyes scanning the typewritten paragraphs. Then he looked again at Reid.

'So you got nowhere with Connelly. Did you find any other witnesses? Anyone who saw or heard anything suspicious that night?'

'That's the peculiar thing about this case,' Reid replied. 'That poor woman was murdered and then mutilated on the inside landing of a building where dozens of other people were sleeping – or perhaps even awake, at that time in the morning, and getting ready to leave for work – and not one of them was aware that it was happening. Either some of the residents *did* hear something but chose not to get involved, or the killer was apparently able to carry out the murder in complete silence, which I find difficult to believe. And nobody outside the building saw anyone enter or leave it, either by themselves or with Tabram. The killer seems to be a ghost, or at least able to act like one. It was as if he popped up at the scene of the crime, carried out the murder and then vanished just as silently and invisibly as he had appeared.'

Warren grunted with displeasure.

'And what else have you done?' he asked.

'We've just followed standard procedure, sir, because there's nothing else we can do. My men have been out and questioned everybody in the area, concentrating on those residents nearest to the scene of the crime, obviously, and we've learned absolutely nothing. Nobody there, apart from one or two of the drinkers in the local public houses, seems to have known anything about Martha Tabram, and the few people who had seen her in the area only knew that she liked her gin and was probably a prostitute. But there are a couple of other points that I think I need to acquaint you with, sir.'

'Go on.'

'This killing has shocked the residents of the East End, and especially Whitechapel. I had to station a constable by George Yard for a few days after the murder because of the crowds of sightseers who arrived there wanting to visit the scene. Some of them weren't satisfied with just seeing the building, either. They were determined to find their way inside and get a look at the blood-stained stones where the woman's body was discovered. I know Whitechapel is a pretty rough area, but we don't have many killings there, and so this has been quite a shocking event.

'And there's been another unusual happening as well. This week a group of about seventy local men held a meeting in Whitechapel and apparently decided that they needed to supplement our efforts in the district. They've formed a thing called the St Jude's Vigilance Committee. The idea is that about a dozen strong and fit men have been appointed to keep watch in certain streets in the area for two to three hours after eleven at night, looking out for anything suspicious. I've been told that the committee will be holding weekly meetings to discuss any activity reported by their watchers, which they will then convey to the police. Their idea is obviously to try to increase the safety of women on the streets of Whitechapel. I'm not keen on this kind of vigilante action, but there's not a lot I can do about it.'

Warren shook his head. His private fear was that if 'Michael' was apprehended in the act of committing another murder and then told his story in open court, Warren's own career might be over, despite the lack of evidence of what he had done in

Jerusalem. In fact, it would suit him very well if a group of unofficial Whitechapel vigilantes *did* interrupt a murder and kill the perpetrator, and he decided immediately to encourage that possibility.

'I don't think that having a number of extra pairs of eyes on the streets will do any harm, Reid. They could be a useful extra unofficial force in Whitechapel, just in case this murderer decides that one killing wasn't enough.'

'So you think he'll strike again, sir?' Reid asked.

'I don't know that, obviously,' Warren replied sharply. 'All I would say is that this murder appears to be completely without motive, as if the killer simply selected a victim at random and then slaughtered her. If that is the case, and Tabram wasn't murdered because of something she had done, or hadn't done, then there may well be more such horrific events to come.'

Ten minutes later, Edmund Reid left the commissioner's office and made his way down the stairs and out into the street. As he turned back towards Whitechapel, his thoughts were troubled. He hadn't regarded the murder of Martha Tabram as anything other than an isolated and most unusual event. The possibility that it could be the first of a series of such crimes had genuinely never even occurred to him.

And he was particularly disturbed by the commissioner's final comments. It was almost as if Charles Warren *knew* that there would be further murders. And that really made no sense.

In fact, Warren was already virtually certain that there would be more killings. He believed there would be a series of murders in the East End of London to demonstrate the incompetence of the police force and particularly that of the head of the organization, Warren himself. 'Michael' had clearly planned that the pressure would eventually build to such an extent that Warren would have no option but to hand over the menorah or resign in disgrace. The obvious, and in fact the only, way to prevent this from happening would be to catch the killer in the act, and ideally silence him permanently there and then.

But that would be difficult, perhaps impossible, because 'Michael' had absolute freedom of choice and complete freedom of movement. He could select the date and time of his next killing, the place where he would perform the murder and, of course, the victim, who would be some unfortunate woman who just happened to be in the wrong place at the wrong time. Warren could see no way of guarding against such an entirely random and essentially motiveless killing.

Even flooding the streets of Whitechapel with every police officer he could deploy wouldn't guarantee success, because the killer could simply wait until the operation was scaled down, or seize the opportunity presented by a distracted constable or some other circumstance. The reality was that he hadn't got anything like enough officers to patrol every street in the East End of London for every night throughout the hours of darkness.

But Charles Warren was pragmatic. His detectives had failed to find any clues to the identity of the killer of Martha Tabram, and there was obviously no way that the commissioner could suggest where they might look, simply because he didn't know, so the best chance of success was to wait for 'Michael' to strike again, and hope that the next time he would be more careless in his actions, or might even be seen during the commission of the crime.

Warren realized that this would inevitably mean the death of another prostitute in Whitehall, but he was prepared to trade the life of an 'unfortunate', or even the lives of several such women, to preserve his secret.

When he reached home that evening, there was another hand-delivered letter waiting for him on the silver tray in the hall. He recognized the handwriting immediately, and took it upstairs to his study before he opened it.

The message inside was short and cryptic: 'Time for the apex. You'll hear of my work very soon.'

Or perhaps I won't, Warren thought. If the killer struck in the latter half of the month, he and his family would be taking their annual leave in the south of France. At worst, Warren would return to the city to find that another killing had taken place in his absence, but at best the fact that the commissioner was away from England might possibly make 'Michael' stay his hand.

Only time would tell.

Chapter 16

Friday, 31 August 1888
Whitechapel, London

A few minutes after 3.30 in the morning, a cart driver named Charles Cross, who lived at Bethnal Green, was walking through Whitechapel on his way to work at Pickford's. The sun was still well below the horizon and the streets were dark and badly lit, but Cross was treading a familiar path, a journey which he made virtually every day.

His route took him along Buck's Row, which ran roughly parallel to Whitechapel Road, and was very busy during the day, being close to the London Hospital, Whitechapel train station, Spitalfields Coal Depot, and with numerous office buildings in the area, but at that time of the morning, it was completely deserted.

Cross was whistling softly to himself as he walked, a popular tune of the day, but as he neared the entrance to Brown's stable, the sound died on his lips. Something – or possibly someone – was lying in the narrow alcove by the stable door. He came to a halt a few feet away and stared down at the shape lying on the pavement.

It was clearly the figure of a woman, lying unnaturally still and silent. For a few seconds, Cross didn't know what to do, then he heard the sound of approaching footsteps, following the same route that he had taken on his way to work. He looked round and saw a man walking down the street towards him. He turned away from the woman and strode out to intercept him.

'Come and look over here,' Cross said. 'There's a woman lying on the pavement.'

The new arrival was a man named Robert Paul, also from Bethnal Green, who was another cart driver.

'Sleepin' it off, I s'pose,' Paul suggested.

But Cross shook his head. There was something about the unnatural stillness of the body of the woman, and her disarranged clothing, which to him implied that something much more serious had happened to her.

The two men crossed to where the body lay on its back, the skirts pulled up to the woman's stomach. Cross touched her hands, which felt cold and limp to him.

'No,' he said. 'I believe she's dead.'

'I'm not so sure,' Paul replied. 'I mean, her hands and face is cold, but I reckon she's still breathing.'

Neither man had a torch or matches or any other form of illumination, and so neither of them could see the woman's body clearly.

'Well,' Cross stated, 'whatever's happened to her, she needs a doctor, double quick. And look at her skirts,' he added, 'all rucked up like that.'

For the sake of modesty, they pulled down her skirt to cover her abdomen and legs, and then left the scene as quickly as they could to find a policeman. Within a few minutes they spotted Police Constable 55H Jonas Mizen at the corner of Old Montague Street and Hanbury Street.

'She looks to me to be either dead or drunk,' Cross said, as Mizen listened to their report, 'but for my part I think she's dead.'

Their duty done, both men left the area and hurried away towards their places of employment.

Constable Mizen ran swiftly down Buck's Row towards the scene of the reported crime, but in fact he was not the first to arrive.

Following his usual patrol route, the beat officer for that part of Whitechapel, PC 97J John Neil, had already discovered the body just a few moments earlier. As he bent to examine the shape on the ground, he heard the sound of another police officer's heavy footsteps and flashed his lantern to summon him. The new arrival was Constable 96J John Thain, who was patrolling past the end of Buck's Row.

'Here's a woman has cut her throat,' Neil said. 'Run at once for Dr Llewellyn.'

Thain left immediately, running down the Whitechapel Road to number 152, the home and surgery of Dr Rees Ralph Llewellyn.

Within a minute or so, Constable Mizen arrived beside the body as well, and Neil, who had taken charge of the scene because he was the first police officer to have arrived there, sent him away as well.

'You'd better get over to the station at Bethnal Green,' Neil instructed. 'We'll need an inspector here as quickly as possible, and an ambulance for the body.'

There was clearly nothing that Constable Neil could do for the woman, who he was quite certain was dead, so while he waited for either the doctor or some other police officers to arrive, he carried out a quick check of the immediate area, searching for possible witnesses. He questioned Walter Purkis, the manager of nearby Essex Wharf, but neither he nor his wife had heard anything suspicious during the night.

Shortly afterwards, Sergeant Kirby arrived on the scene, himself checked the body to confirm that the woman was beyond medical help, and then joined Neil in his search. Kirby questioned a woman named Green who was resident in New Cottage, the house right beside where the body had been discovered, but she hadn't heard anything either. In the meantime, Neil checked the roadway, looking for the marks left by the wheels of carts, but found nothing, suggesting that the woman had probably died where she had been found.

'So what do we have here, Constable?' Dr Llewellyn asked, as he strode up to the entrance to the stable at a little after four in the morning.

Constable Neil directed him straight to the body, and the doctor bent down to begin his examination.

In the light from the bulls-eye lantern held by the police officer, Llewellyn immediately saw that massive injuries had been inflicted to the woman's throat. As a rudimentary assessment of the time of death, he felt the temperature of her limbs. Her hands and wrists were cold, but her body and legs were still quite warm.

'I think she's probably been dead for no more than about half an hour,' he told Constable Neil.

Whitechapel was then beginning to come alive, and groups of spectators were starting to gather at the scene. Soon afterwards the police officers were joined by three horse slaughterers who had been working overnight in Barber's slaughterhouse in nearby Winthrop Street.

'Her throat's been cut but there doesn't seem to be much blood,' Neil remarked, staring down at the corpse.

'That's quite correct,' Llewellyn confirmed. 'I see very little around the body, which is not what I would have expected, given the severity of the wounds to her neck. The arteries appear to have been sliced completely through.'

Llewellyn stepped back from the body and glanced around at the police officers and the growing crowd of sightseers.

'Move her to the mortuary,' he instructed, his irritation obvious. 'She's dead, so there's nothing more I can do here. I will make a further examination of her there.'

With the better light afforded by the sunrise, it soon became clear that quite a lot of blood had soaked into both her clothes and her hair, and when the body was lifted off the ground to be placed in the coffin, a considerable amount of congealed blood was exposed underneath it.

There was a delay getting access to the mortuary in Old Montague Road, and it wasn't until after five in the morning when the keeper, Robert Mann, eventually appeared with the keys to open up the building.

The first person to examine the body was Inspector John Spratling, who had arrived at Buck's Row a short time after the body had been removed, and who had merely examined the place where the corpse had been discovered, and had then proceeded directly to the mortuary itself. He made a series of notes about the woman's appearance, estimated roughly what she weighed and her height, listed the clothes she was wearing and looked, without any particular hope of success, for any form of identification in her pockets. Then he slowly and carefully began to remove her clothes, examining each item as he took it off the body.

As he lifted away the woman's skirts to reveal her abdomen, he blanched and took an involuntary step back from the examination table.

'Oh my dear God,' he muttered, then stepped forward again to take a better look at what he had discovered, and saw for the first time the full extent of the wounds which had been inflicted on her. Up to that point, both he and Dr Llewellyn had believed that she had simply died from having her throat cut.

That was quite probably still the case, but there were far more injuries than either man had suspected. There was a massive wound on her abdomen through which some of her internal organs could clearly be seen, a number of other deep cuts running both across and down her body, and even a couple of wounds to her private parts.

'Constable,' Spratling called out urgently, as he again stepped back from the table on which the body was lying. 'Go at once to Whitechapel Road and request Dr Llewellyn to come here as soon as possible.'

Llewellyn appeared shortly afterwards.

'What is it, Inspector?' the doctor asked, as he approached the examination table.

Spratling pointed wordlessly at the extensive mutilations he had discovered on the woman's abdomen.

'I had no idea about any of this,' Llewellyn said. 'I thought it was just her throat.'

'So did I, when I saw her,' Spratling replied, 'and we were both wrong.'

Together the two men carried out a full and detailed examination of the body, and recorded all of her injuries.

'I can't be certain until I carry out the autopsy,' Llewellyn remarked, as he made his final notes, 'but it looks to me as if most of these wounds were inflicted post-mortem.'

Spratling nodded. Although he had no medical experience, he had been wondering about that himself.

'If you're right, doctor,' he said, 'this could well be the work of the same man who killed the Tabram woman about three weeks ago. That was another frenzied attack with a knife.'

'Possibly,' Llewellyn agreed, 'but as far as I recall, Tabram's throat was stabbed but it wasn't cut, so that's one difference between the two murders. Other than that, though, I would have to agree. This degree of mutilation is very rare. I can't recall seeing anything like this ever before, and to have two such killings in the same area in the same month – well, I'd be very surprised if both murders weren't carried out by the same person.'

As well as the examination of the body, Inspector Spratling and a number of other officers also made a careful study of the dead woman's clothes and possessions, mainly looking for some means of finding out who she was, but no obvious form of identification was found.

With the exception of her hat, which was a new straw bonnet in black and trimmed with black velvet, all her clothes were old and worn. She had been wearing a brown ulster coat with large buttons, a linsey frock, grey woollen petticoat, flannel drawers, brown stays, ribbed dark-blue woollen stockings and a pair of men's spring-sided boots.

'Nothing at all on this,' Spratling said, folding up the frock he had been examining. 'Anyone else found something?'

'This might be something, John,' Inspector Helson said. 'It's a bit washed out, but I can just about make out what it says.'

'What's that?' Spratling asked.

Helson showed him the petticoat which he had been examining.

'Just here,' he said, 'can you see it?'

Spratling bent forward to look at the faint laundry mark the other inspector had discovered.

'It says "Lambeth Workhouse, P.R.",' he said. 'That's the one in Prince's Road, isn't it? Mind you,' he added, 'she might have borrowed or stolen the petticoat, or got it from a pawn shop, but at least it'll give us somewhere to start looking.'

It was not uncommon for the lowest class of women to pawn items of clothing to raise money for food, lodgings and, most commonly of all, for drink. So it was always possible that the petticoat might have belonged to another 'unfortunate' who had lodged in that particular workhouse.

But at least they had some kind of a lead.

Chapter 17

Saturday, 1 September 1888
Whitechapel, London

Detective Inspector Abberline strode along the corridor in the Scotland Yard headquarters to one of the doors near the very end, paused for a few seconds to straighten his jacket and ensure that he looked as smart as possible, rubbed the toe of each shoe down the back of the opposite trouser leg to remove any dust, then knocked.

'Come.'

Abberline opened the door and stepped inside the office. With the commissioner away on leave, his ultimate superior was Superintendent Frederick Adolphus Williamson, who had been appointed Chief Constable (CID) by Charles Warren.

Abberline had a good idea why he had been summoned, because the corridors of the Metropolitan Police headquarters had been buzzing with the news of the third killing in the Whitechapel area in recent months, and most of the officers he had spoken to were already of the opinion that only one man had been responsible for the last two murders.

And that had added a new dimension to the situation. In most of the murder investigations Abberline had been involved in, it was usually clear from a very early stage who the perpetrator was, and why the killing had taken place. When a man was killed, if the murder hadn't been the work of his wife or female friend, it was usually the result of some kind of a business deal which had gone bad, or a revenge attack, or something of that sort. And when a woman died, the first person the police always interviewed was her husband or any close male friends.

But if the killing of Martha Tabram and the murder of the so-far-unidentified woman in Whitechapel early the previous morning were linked, then that suggested the killer might have been a stranger to both his victims and, if that was the case, Abberline frankly had little idea how best to proceed.

'It's this business in Whitechapel,' Williamson began. 'Have you heard about it?'

The detective inspector nodded.

'Everybody in the station has been talking about it, sir, and I've seen some of the statements by the constables who found the body and the officers who examined it in the mortuary. The story doing the rounds is that she was ripped up pretty badly, and that was confirmed at the inquest this morning. I asked for an adjournment to give us time to make some further enquiries, but Baxter, the coroner, wouldn't agree, and it'll resume on Monday morning.'

'What further enquiries? Do you have a lead on the killer?'

Abberline shook his head.

'Not yet, sir, no, but we'll be questioning residents and local tradesmen. Hopefully somebody in the area will have heard or seen something.'

Abberline hoped so, anyway, though the initial reports had all proved negative.

'I hope you're right,' Williamson said, in a discouraging manner. 'Have you identified the victim yet?'

'Not yet, no, but news of the murder spread very quickly after the body was discovered and a lot of people were on the scene even before the dead woman was removed to the mortuary, so the press got hold of the story almost immediately. According to the officers at Bethnal Green, several women came forward yesterday with the potential identity of the deceased, though none were absolutely certain. Several supplied information we could check, like their belief that the victim had been a lodger at the doss house at 18 Thrawl Street. That's being looked into now.

'There was also a bit of good work from Inspector Helson. He found a laundry mark on the petticoat the woman had been wearing, and that led him to the Lambeth Workhouse, and enquiries are also being made there at the moment. We're pretty certain we'll have her identified later today.'

'Who's working on the case at the moment?' Williamson asked.

'John Spratling – he was the first senior officer on the scene – and Joseph Helson are in charge,' Abberline replied. 'They're both from the Bethnal Green station, and they're both good, reliable men.'

'Good. Now, the newspapers are all over this already. Have you seen the latest editions?'

'Not today, sir, no. I've had other things to do. Attending the inquest and so on.'

'Let me give you a summary, then. There's already been speculation about the identity of the killer. Some of the papers are suggesting that she might have been killed by a rampaging gang, just like that murder earlier this year. You remember – a woman named Emma Elizabeth Smith was attacked on the street in Whitechapel and she later died from her injuries.'

'From what I've seen of this case, sir, that doesn't sound likely. There's no evidence that this woman was attacked by more than one man.'

'I agree with you,' Williamson said. 'But other newspaper reports are linking this latest killing only with that of Martha Tabram, and they're suggesting that both of these women were murdered by a single assailant who was working alone. I don't like the sound of that, though from what I've read so far, I think it might well be the truth in this case. I think we've got one man out there who's decided to target a particular class of woman.'

'You're referring to prostitutes, obviously.'

'Exactly,' Williamson said. 'I've got one of the first statements here. It looks as if the woman was almost certainly a prostitute, which would explain why she was out on the streets at that time in the morning. She was apparently killed by having her throat cut, but then the killer mutilated her body as well. Her injuries,' Williamson added, an expression of revulsion on his face, 'were apparently very severe.'

Abberline nodded again.

'They were, sir. It was clear from the evidence given at the inquest that she was ripped apart. And some of my colleagues agree with the newspapers. They also think that this murder might well be linked to Tabram's killing.'

Williamson grunted.

'It's bad enough that another "unfortunate" has been murdered in an area like Whitechapel,' he said, 'and the mutilations obviously add an extra dimension of horror to the killing. But the last thing we want is for people to get the idea that there's a murderer out there who's attacking prostitutes.'

'That might well be the case, though, and I suppose it might help clear some of them off the streets.'

Williamson looked at him sharply.

'I hope that was meant as a joke, Abberline. I'm well aware of the squalid conditions in Whitechapel. But if the people there believe that there's a multiple killer haunting the streets and hunting down women, we could have civil unrest on an unprecedented scale. We could see vigilante action, rampaging mobs attacking innocent men, and a complete breakdown of law and order in that part of London. At all costs, we must prevent that from happening.'

The superintendent looked down again at the handwritten report in front of him, then back up at Abberline.

'And that's why I'm sending you over to the Bethnal Green division to assist in solving this murder. We want you to coordinate the investigation. I'm also sending Andrews and Moore with you, so hopefully the three of you, working with those two local inspectors, will be able to solve this case quickly. This is to be your highest priority, Abberline. We must have a swift result. The commissioner will be expecting it.'

'You've been in communication with him, sir?'

'No, but he left orders that if there was another murder you were to be placed in overall charge of the investigation.'

Abberline was silent for a moment.

'Do you think he *knew* the killer was going to strike again?'

Williamson shook his head.

'Don't be ridiculous, Abberline. How could he possibly have known that?'

As he left the office, Frederick Abberline shook his head. That wasn't really an answer to the question he'd blurted out, and until the second murder had been committed, he'd assumed that the first had been just an isolated occurrence, a very unusual crime of passion, if you like. But it looked as if Charles Warren had predicted something rather different, and that was interesting. Maybe the commissioner wasn't the autocratic idiot that so many officers of the Metropolitan Police believed him to be.

Privately, Abberline believed he was being sent on a fool's errand to Bethnal Green. As far as he knew, there had been no witnesses to the murder, and no clues found at the scene, though it was always possible that the local investigating officers might have discovered something new that would help identify the perpetrator. The unfortunate reality, though, was that unless the killing had been witnessed by somebody, or the murderer had been seen running away from the body, they would have almost nothing to go on.

Most murders were solved in that way, by the killer being seen in the commission of the act, and being apprehended quite literally 'red-handed', with the blood of his victim still on his hands. The only other avenue likely to be open to the detectives was if somebody was known to bear a grudge against the victim, and even then there might be no proof that the man had actually committed the crime.

And despite his suggestion to Williamson about local enquiries, Abberline had already talked to both of the inspectors at Bethnal Green, and he knew that nothing had been found anywhere near the body to indicate the identity of the killer. He also knew that constables had been sent to check on all the premises around the scene of the crime, and the adjoining areas, which included Essex Wharf, the East London Railway, the District Railway and the Great Eastern Railway, had been searched for the murder weapon, bloodstains and any other clues, all without the slightest result.

Inspector Spratling had independently searched Buck's Row and Brady Street and had only discovered one small stain in Brady Street which might have been blood. But he was unsure of that conclusion, and even if he was right, the source might have been an animal or, if it was human in origin, it could have come from a fight in the street or from somebody completely unconnected with the murder.

As far as Abberline could see, the only thing that he and the other two detective inspectors – Walter Andrews and Henry Moore – would achieve when they got to Bethnal Green would be to irritate the local inspectors and other members of the force, and get in each other's way.

But he could hardly have said any of that to Williamson, because he knew that the Superintendent would probably have been acting on Warren's orders, orders written before the commissioner had left London, and possibly even supplemented by instructions sent over the telegraph from his holiday destination in France.

And Warren was famous – or perhaps infamous – for never accepting, or even listening to, suggestions from other members of the force, or indeed from anyone else. As well as being profoundly unpopular as a man, the commissioner also seemed able to alienate almost anybody by his autocratic and aloof attitude to his job. He was one of those people who didn't just believe that he was right: he *knew* that he was right, despite his almost total lack of experience of police work, and because he knew he was right, anybody who disagreed with him very obviously had to be wrong.

He was not an easy man to get along with.

Chapter 18

Sunday, 2 September 1888
London

Early that evening, Alexei Pedachenko, dressed in smart but casual clothes, left his lodgings to walk the streets in search of a newspaper vendor. He had been reading the press reports of the murders with a good deal of interest. Reading what the newspaper reporters said about the killings obviously wasn't the same as knowing the collective opinion of the Metropolitan Police Force, but it certainly gave an indication of the way that his actions were being perceived.

He bought every edition of the newspapers that he could find. And what he read was entirely to his satisfaction. There had now been three killings of women in the Whitechapel area – the murder of Emma Smith on the night of Easter Monday 1888, which had been nothing whatever to do with Pedachenko, but which had given him the idea for the killing spree upon which he had now embarked, and then Martha Tabram and the unidentified woman who he had chanced upon in the early hours of Friday morning – and all the newspapers had been quick to see the connection. It was front-page news in every paper that he bought.

Some of them were claiming to see a link between all three murders, suggesting that the killing of Emma Smith had been some sort of trial run for the two attacks carried out over five months later. Precisely how they could make such a connection, Pedachenko really didn't know, because it was perfectly clear from what he had read that the Smith woman had been attacked by a gang of men, men who had raped, robbed and then violently assaulted her, but none of whom had used a knife. And, of course, she had survived the attack long enough to explain what had happened to her, although she had died of her injuries shortly afterwards.

But the more sensible and responsible of the newspapers – if those two adjectives could ever be applied to a sheet of newsprint – had entirely discounted the first murder, and had instead concentrated their righteous indignation and fury on the unknown killer of Martha Tabram and the 'mystery woman' as one or two of them had referred to the latest victim. All of these newspapers had pointed out the similarities between the last two killings, concentrating on the idea that a knife-wielding maniac was loose on the streets of Whitechapel, and asking what, exactly, the Metropolitan Police were doing about it.

And that, Pedachenko agreed, was the question to which he himself wanted an answer: just what, exactly, were the police doing about it?

Charles Warren, as far as he knew, was still out of the country on his annual holiday. In fact, Pedachenko knew precisely when the man had gone, because he had watched from a discreet distance as Warren and his family had embarked in a cab outside the man's home and been driven away. Following the vehicle hadn't been difficult, and a short while later Pedachenko had observed his quarry disembarking at Charing Cross railway station and taking a train to Dover. The deduction that the commissioner was going on holiday hadn't been difficult, and Pedachenko had confirmed this information by following a group of plainclothes officers from Scotland Yard to a nearby public house and simply eavesdropping on their conversation.

The Englishman's action had irritated Pedachenko, who had intended to resume his 'work' shortly after his murder of the woman he now knew had been named Martha Tabram, but Warren's action had indirectly prevented him from doing so. The whole point of the Russian's campaign was to force the commissioner to accede to his demands, and he could only do that if Warren was in London and could be pressurized.

So Pedachenko had stayed his hand, waiting for his quarry to return. But when he'd heard that Warren might be away for at least a further week, he had decided to act anyway. Perhaps, he had reasoned, the best strategy wasn't to wait until the man got back after all, but instead escalate his campaign so that the commissioner would be faced with a massive public outcry once he did get back to London.

And on the Saturday morning, the previous day, the people of Whitechapel had woken up to the news that the unknown killer had struck again, and this time with greatly increased ferocity.

Pedachenko smiled to himself. The newspapers were working for him, helping his campaign and whipping up a wave of public indignation against the apparently inept police force. They were instilling not just a sense of fear, but something more like a feeling of raw terror in the minds of the people, and especially of the women, in Whitechapel, Spitalfields and the East End.

And that was exactly what he wanted Charles Warren to come back and face.

Chapter 19

Monday, 3 September 1888
Whitechapel, London

'Well, now we know who she is, or rather who she was,' Detective Inspector Frederick Abberline announced to the superintendent. 'In fact, we've pretty much got her life story now.'

He had been summoned back by Williamson from Bethnal Green late that afternoon to report in person on the progress – or rather the lack of it – in the murder enquiry. Unfortunately, despite exhaustive questioning by officers of everybody they could find in the area around Buck's Row, they had discovered absolutely no new or useful information. Nobody had seen the murder being committed, and nor had anybody seen either the victim or a man who could have been her killer arriving at or leaving the vicinity at the time that the murder must have been carried out.

'What was her name?' Williamson demanded.

'Mary Ann Nichols,' Abberline replied, 'spelt with one "l". She was another unfortunate, and some of the earlier reports were correct: she *was* lodging at a doss house in Thrawl Street. She was turned out by the house deputy early that morning because she couldn't pay for her bed for the night.'

Abberline consulted his notes.

'We managed to track down her estranged husband, and he gave us a lot of the background information, and some of the women we've talked to have filled in the gaps. She was born here in London in August 1845, and her maiden name was Mary Ann Walker. In 1864 she married a man named William Nichols, who was a printer's machinist and worked for a firm named Perkins, Bacon and Company at Whitefriars Street in the City. They lived first on Trafalgar Street in Walworth and then in Peabody Square, Duke Street, Lambeth, and had five children, but the marriage failed in 1880.'

'Why?' Williamson asked.

'That's not entirely clear, sir. There was a bit of a domestic problem because Mary Ann's father accused William of infidelity. He claimed William was having it off with the nurse who had been present at the birth of their last child, but William denied that absolutely. He says that the couple separated because of Mary Ann's drinking. That, and the fact that she had deserted him on numerous occasions.'

'And do you believe what he's told you?'

Abberline shrugged.

'I don't think it's important whether I believe him or not,' he replied, 'because I don't think her early history has got anything at all to do with what happened to her. But William struck me as a decent man, so I think he was probably telling me the truth. He claims he supported Mary Ann with a weekly payment of five shillings until 1882, but then he discovered that she was living with another man, and also working as a part-time prostitute. Because she'd taken up with somebody else, William was no longer legally obliged to pay her an allowance, and so he stopped giving her any money. Of course, that meant she hadn't a lot of option but to continue selling her body on the streets if she wanted to survive.

'She was in the Lambeth Workhouse from April 1882 for nearly a year, then went to stay with her father for a few months. Afterwards, she moved in with a blacksmith named Thomas Stuart Drew, who lived in York Street in Walworth. When they broke up, Mary Ann went downhill even further. She spent time in three different workhouses, and early this year a couple of our constables arrested her for sleeping rough in Trafalgar Square, and she was put back in the Lambeth workhouse.

'According to a woman who knew her, she then took a job as a domestic for a couple out in Wandsworth, but left the job after a couple of months.She returned to the East End and almost immediately went back on the streets. For the first three weeks in August she shared a bed in a lodging house at 18 Thrawl Street, Spitalfields, with an elderly woman named Emily or "Nelly" Holland.'

'Did this Holland woman supply all this background information for you?'

Abberline shook his head.

'Oddly enough, no. She didn't have much idea of the woman's history, but we managed to find another source. Anyway, after a while Nichols moved out to another lodging house in Flower and Dean Street. But Holland's evidence is important, because she was probably the last person to see her alive.'

'At the lodging house, I suppose?' Williamson asked.

'No, it was much later than that. Nichols went out drinking that night, and was thrown out of a pub called the Frying Pan in Brick Lane when it closed. She went back to the Thrawl Street lodging, but she'd drunk whatever money she had and couldn't pay for a bed and so the house deputy turned her out at about half past one in the morning. She told him she'd soon be back with the money, and asked him to keep her bed for her.

'You must have heard about the fire that broke out that day down at Shadwell Dry Dock?' Inspector Abberline asked, an apparent non sequitur.

Williamson nodded.

'Yes. It wasn't too serious, I gather, but it attracted a lot of attention. What's that got to do with it?'

'Nothing, really,' Abberline replied, 'except that Nelly Holland decided that she wanted to go and take a look at it, and she met Nichols on the way back. Holland was heading for Thrawl Street, and saw Nichols on the corner of Osborn Street and Whitechapel Road. According to her, it was exactly half past two by the chimes of the clock on St Mary's Church, and the two women talked together for a few minutes. According to Holland, Nichols was drunk, but she claimed that she'd had a good day, earning her lodging money three times over, although she had then obviously spent it all on drink.

'Holland suggested that she should come back with her to the Thrawl Street lodging house, but Nichols refused. The last Holland saw of her was when she staggered off along the Whitechapel Road, heading in the general direction of the London Hospital. And of course, Buck's Row is down that way too.'

Williamson nodded slowly.

'So she was presumably out looking for another customer to raise the money for her bed when she met her killer?'

'That's what it looks like, sir, yes.'

'Who identified her body?'

'As I told you this morning, the Bethnal Green station officers had had a few reports that she'd lodged at the Thrawl Street doss house, and a couple had said that she shared a bed there with Nelly Holland. So Holland was picked up and asked to identify the body. She obviously recognized her, but she only knew the woman as "Polly", which didn't help us very much. There was no identification in her clothes, but the detectives had followed up on the laundry mark that was found on her petticoat. They visited the Lambeth workhouse, and one of the inmates there, a woman named Mary Ann Monk, was taken to the mortuary. She identified the body of the victim as Mary Ann Nichols, and told us that she had stayed at the workhouse until May this year, and she knew quite a lot about the woman's history.'

'And I suppose nobody saw or heard anything?' Williamson enquired sourly. 'At the scene of the crime, I mean.'

'There were no eyewitnesses, no,' Abberline replied, 'but one person did claim to have heard something. A woman named Harriet Lilley, who lives in Buck's Row itself, at number 7, told one of the constables that she'd heard whispering, or perhaps a muttered conversation, outside her property at half past three, and then what sounded like moans or gasps of pain. She says she woke up her husband, but then the 3.30 train went past and neither of them heard anything else. And they didn't bother going outside, or even to the window, to have a look. Noises like that aren't exactly uncommon in Whitechapel.'

'So at least that gives us a precise time for the murder.'

'That's true, sir,' Abberline agreed, 'but it's not much help, and we already knew fairly accurately when it had been committed, because of the report from the beat constable, PC John Neil. He walked down Buck's Row on his regular beat at 3.15 and saw nothing unusual, so Nichols must have been alive then. Half an hour later, at fifteen minutes before four, he walked that route again, but the body had been found about five minutes earlier by a couple of men leaving home to go to work. So we know she was killed within that twenty-five minute interval, and all the report from the Lilley woman does is suggest that the murder took place at almost exactly 3.30. If the killer had known Neil's patrol route and timing, you would even expect him to carry out the murder at that time, because that would be when the constable would be as far away as possible from Buck's Row. So, as I said, it's not that much help. Of course, if the Lilley woman had bothered to get out of bed and investigate what she'd heard, it might have been a very different story.'

'Are you serious about that, Abberline? Do you really think the murderer timed his killing based upon a police officer's patrol route?' Williamson asked.

'I don't know, sir. All I'm saying is that, if he didn't know when the constable would be walking down Buck's Row, he was very lucky to pick the time he did to kill Nichols. But if you want my hunch, sir, I don't think we're dealing with a man who's just some common thug. There've been two killings so far in Whitechapel that are probably the work of this man, and there are only four common factors that I've been able to identify.'

'Four factors? What four factors?'

'First, the victims were both unfortunates, prostitutes. Second, according to the doctors who examined their bodies, they were both killed – or at least both were mutilated – by a knife. Third, the killer might as well have been invisible, because nobody's seen even a trace of him. And, lastly, there's no apparent motive. These women had nothing of value on them, no money or jewellery or anything like that, so we can rule out robbery. They weren't related to each other, so I doubt if there's some family involvement, no jealous or embittered husband or relative, nothing like that, and they were unfortunates, so they don't look like crimes of passion either. The only thing each of these women had was her life, and that's what the killer took from them.

'If we were dealing with some typical thug, I think somebody would have seen him at the scene of one of the murders, lurking about, carrying out the killing itself or leaving the area. But this man is clever. It's as if he times his attacks so that the area is deserted, and chooses a spot where he won't be seen doing his work. That suggests he's either an intelligent man, or he's just been incredibly lucky, and I believe it's most likely the former.'

Williamson nodded thoughtfully. He didn't disagree with anything Abberline had said.

'What about the victims?' he asked. 'Apart from them being prostitutes, is there any other common factor there? Do you think he selects them beforehand and entices them to the spot he's chosen for the killing, or does he pick them at random?'

Abberline shook his head. 'Finding a whore in Whitechapel isn't difficult at any hour, sir. He probably locates a good spot and then picks the first suitable woman who wanders along. If there's anyone else nearby, I expect he waits until the coast is clear and then attacks the next unfortunate he sees. I doubt if he'd risk talking to one of them beforehand, because there'd be too much chance of somebody seeing them together and remembering what he looks like. I think he just waits for the right moment, and then gets to work.'

'I don't think "work" is quite the right word for you to use in this situation, Abberline,' Williamson pointed out. 'We're talking about the brutal murders of women here, not some type of casual labour.'

The detective inspector nodded.

'I know, sir, but when you look at the conditions in White-chapel and other parts of the East End of London, you can't help feeling that in some ways these women are better off dead. To be turned out of a doss house because she hadn't got the four pence needed to pay for a bed has to mean that she was completely destitute, probably owning little more than the clothes she was wearing at the time. Obviously I condemn what this man is doing, but if you consider the overall situation in London, you could almost argue that he's performing a public service.'

'I hope you keep that kind of view to yourself, Abberline. These women, these unfortunates, are just as entitled to our protection as the richest and most elegant ladies in the West End of the city.'

That, Williamson knew, as well as any other senior officer, was the official view of the situation, and the view that he was required, as a member of the Metropolitan Police, to promulgate. Privately, he agreed with Abberline. He'd visited Whitechapel and other slum areas of the city and had been appalled at the conditions he had found. The filth, poverty, unemployment, rampant sickness, and above all the absolute lack of hope and of any way for the people to improve their lot, had sickened him. In many cases, he knew that the people he had seen really were better off dead, harsh though that view was.

Abberline took a sheet of paper out of his pocket and glanced at it for a moment.

'What's that?' Williamson asked.

'The notes I made during the autopsy on Nichols, sir. It was performed by a Dr Llewellyn, who has a surgery in the Whitechapel Road, not far from Buck's Row. He was the doctor called to the scene of Nichols's killing by PC Thain. He described the injuries to the woman's body, several of which could have been fatal, but actually weren't, because she was already dead.'

'Because her throat had been cut, you mean?'

'Not necessarily, sir. One of the things Dr Llewellyn noticed was that there was bruising on Nichols's face which he thought could either have been caused by a blow, or by pressure. He also stated that her face was swollen, and that there was less blood at the scene than he would have expected if the cause of death had been the severing of the arteries in the neck.'

'So how was she killed?'

'He wasn't certain, sir, because of the extensive wounds to the body, but he thought she might have been asphyxiated, and that that was the cause of death. Then, when the killer began his mutilation, there would be less blood from the wounds, which would reduce the chance of him getting any of it on his clothing, though his hands would probably have been covered in blood.'

Abberline looked back at his notes.

'When I heard that,' he went on, 'I contacted the doctor who'd been called to examine the body of Martha Tabram, a man named Killeen. He also noticed bruising on that victim's face, which could have been consistent with her being asphyxiated, either by a man's hand covering her mouth and nose, or by the use of a pad of material. So I think the killer first subdues them, or more likely kills them, by asphyxiation, and then uses his knife when they're dead. That method of operation, plus the fact that there's no evidence he has any kind of sexual relations with them, either before or after the killing, suggests a very cold and determined man, not an opportunist killer, and he certainly doesn't seem to be motivated by any kind of sexual impulse.'

'So what do you intend to do now?' Williamson asked.

'I'm going to continue working with the detectives at Bethnal Green, as you instructed, unless you have some new orders for me, sir.'

The superintendent shook his head.

'No,' he said. 'Do what you can there. Make sure that you find out everything about the victim that you are able to. Check that the local detectives have knocked on every door near the scene of the killing, and talked to everybody who was in the area that night. I just can't believe that nobody saw anything.'

'They've already checked everybody, but I'll go through the statements they took again, just to make sure that they didn't miss anything.'

'Good.'

'So apart from that, is there anything else you want me to do at the moment, sir?' Abberline asked.

'No, not for the present. You'd better get back to Bethnal Green. Obviously, if you find anything significant or important that you think I should know about, let me know as soon as possible.'

'Very good, sir,' Abberline said, then stood up and left the office.

Chapter 20

Friday, 7 September 1888
Whitechapel, London

The Metropolitan Police had not had a good week. There had been three brutal murders in Whitechapel since the beginning of April, one certainly the work of a gang of young thugs, but the other two apparently carried out by a single, sadistic and virtually invisible killer. Unsurprisingly, the London press had continued to take a very keen interest in the killings, and even more interest in the continuing and obvious inability of the Metropolitan Police to solve the crimes and catch the perpetrator.

Initially, some newspapers had speculated that all three murders had been the work of the same man or men, but by the time that details of the killing of Mary Ann Nichols had become widely known, almost all the papers had begun subscribing to the view that the first murder was so different in character to the second and third killings that a different group of people, with the emphasis on the plural, must have been responsible for Emma Elizabeth Smith's killing. By the end of that week, Smith's murder was old news, and reporters from all the papers were convinced that a single deranged individual was haunting the streets of London, stalking prostitutes, and then brutally despatching them with his knife.

And what was also becoming clear was that a very different mood now prevailed in the Whitechapel area. The first reaction of the local residents to the killing of Emma Elizabeth Smith had been curiosity, as much as anything, because murder was such a rare crime in that part of London. Then, when Martha Tabram was found slaughtered, probably many people believed that it was likely she had had a disagreement with a client, possibly involving the payment for her services, or even the nature of those services, and had paid the ultimate price for not delivering the goods, or perhaps for delivering goods which did not meet the client's expectations.

But with the killing of Mary Ann Nichols, everything had changed. Now everybody knew that prostitutes – and possibly other women, respectable women, as well as unfortunates – were at risk from the lone killer lurking somewhere in their midst.

One of the local papers – the *East London Advertiser* – expressed the change in feelings almost poignantly. The editorial read: 'The crowds of people which have since daily assembled at the scene of the murder have been reduced to a condition of almost abject terror. They have talked almost in whispers, and a panic-stricken cry has gone up from the inhabitants and tradesmen in the neighbourhood of Buck's Row for more police protection.' Another paper, the *Daily News*, noted that: 'Very rarely has anything occurred even in this quarter of London that has created so profound a sensation.'

And there was another component to the stories printed in the newspapers which added a further dimension of horror to the two killings.

The inquest on Mary Ann Nichols had opened the day after her murder, on 1 September, and had been presided over by the Coroner for the South Eastern District of Middlesex, Wynne Baxter. The senior Metropolitan police officer in attendance was Detective Inspector Frederick Abberline.

The inquest began with identification evidence supplied by a very tearful and emotional Nelly Holland, and also by William Nichols, the dead woman's estranged husband. Then the inquest moved on to a description of the finding of the body of the victim outside the entrance to the stable in Buck's Row. This was provided by the two cart drivers – Charles Cross and Robert Paul – who had first found the body, but who had been uncertain whether the woman was alive or dead.

Then Constable 97J John Neil took the stand to describe his own separate discovery of the dead woman on his regular beat, and the actions which he had taken immediately afterwards.

But the bulk of the police evidence was given by the senior officer who had been placed in charge of the case, Inspector Joseph Helson. He began with a description of the victim.

'The victim's name was Mary Ann Nichols,' he said. 'She was forty-three years old, a short woman with brown eyes, dark-brown hair turning grey, and she was missing five of her front teeth.'

He went on to describe the clothes that the dead woman had been wearing, and confirmed the actions which he had taken at the scene when he had arrived at Buck's Row.

'Were you able to form an opinion as to what the victim might have been doing in that part of London in the early hours of the morning, Inspector?' the coroner asked.

Helson shook his head slightly.

'Obviously, sir, we cannot be certain, but from the information we have been given by people who knew the victim, and from her dress and appearance, we believe that she was a member of the lowest possible class of so-called "unfortunates". It appears that she was forced into prostitution simply by her desperate economic circumstances, and had been reduced to selling her body for the price of a bed in a doss house, because she had no other way of raising the necessary funds.'

'And if this supposition is correct, Inspector,' Wynne Baxter continued, 'it would be your opinion, I presume, that the reason this unfortunate woman was in the vicinity of Buck's Row was that she was seeking a client to raise the money she needed to purchase a bed for what was left of that night?'

'That is what we believe, sir, yes.'

'And if she was unsuccessful in her quest, then presumably she would have been forced to sleep on a pavement somewhere?'

'That is correct, sir.'

But it was the medical evidence given by Dr Llewellyn, who had been called to examine the body found in Buck's Row, and who had also carried out the autopsy, that was to send shockwaves through London's population.

'Please state your name and qualifications for the benefit of the jury.'

'My name is Rees Ralph Llewellyn, and I am a medical doctor with a surgery at a number 152 Whitechapel Road.'

'And can you please describe what happened on the morning of Friday, the 31st of August this year, Dr Llewellyn?'

'Of course. At approximately twenty minutes to four that morning a man who identified himself as Police Constable 96J John Thain knocked on my door and summoned me to the scene of a suspicious death – in fact he told me that a woman had been found with her throat cut – in Buck's Row. I got dressed as quickly as I could and made my way there, arriving at the address at about four o'clock in the morning. When I arrived, I was directed to the body of a woman which I noted was lying beside the closed entrance door of a stable. I carried out an initial examination on the spot, and determined that life was extinct.'

'And you then made arrangements to have the body transported to the mortuary?' Wynne Baxter suggested.

'Those arrangements were made by the police, sir, but otherwise that is correct.'

'And did you then carry out a post-mortem examination?'

Llewellyn nodded.

'But I should also add that later that same morning I was urgently summoned to the mortuary by Inspector John Spratling. He had not been present at Buck's Row when I was at the scene and before the body was removed, but he had inspected the corpse at the mortuary afterwards, and he was both surprised and concerned at what he had found. You will understand, sir, that I was unable to carry out a full examination of the corpse at the scene. I was summoned there merely to confirm that the victim was dead, a fact which was self-evident in view of the injury to her throat. But the inspector, when he had begun removing the woman's clothing in an attempt to find some means of identifying her, had discovered that although her throat had undoubtedly been cut, her torso had also been savagely mutilated. I carried out a cursory examination of the body with him at that time, and later carried out a post-mortem.'

Wynne Baxter made a number of notes on the paper in front of him.

'Now can you please tell the jury exactly what injuries you found on the body.'

Llewellyn turned slightly to face the twelve men who comprised the inquest jury.

'The wound which would undoubtedly have been fatal was to the woman's neck. Her attacker had sliced the blade of his knife through her throat twice. The first cut was on the left-hand side of her neck, just below the line of the jaw, but after cutting for only about four inches, her attacker then made a second and longer circular incision, all the way around her neck. The force behind the second cut was so great that it reached her vertebrae, and severed all the other tissues of her neck. Both of these cuts were made from her left-hand side to her right, suggesting either that the attacker was right-handed and standing behind her or, more likely, that the wounds were inflicted while she was lying on the ground by a person kneeling at her right-hand side.'

'Just a moment, doctor,' the coroner interrupted. 'We have already heard from the police evidence that there was comparatively little blood found at the scene. Surely if the arteries in her neck had been severed there would have been a very considerable outpouring of blood?'

'I was coming to that, sir, but you are quite correct. The arteries were severed – in fact, she had almost been decapitated – but the blood loss was comparatively modest. When I examined the woman's face during the post-mortem, I noticed extensive bruising around the nose and mouth, and it is my belief that she was suffocated before her killer wielded his knife. It is certain that she would have been unconscious before her throat was cut, and very probably already dead, and it is for that reason that there was so little evidence of blood around her body. There was also a complete absence of defensive wounds on her hands and arms, which again suggests that she was unconscious or dead before the mutilations were carried out.'

'And can you describe these mutilations?'

Llewellyn looked down at his notes to refresh his memory before he replied.

'The principal wound was to the front of her abdomen. Her attacker had driven the knife into the left-hand side of her body and then dragged the blade downwards with a sawing motion to cut through the skin, subcutaneous fat and muscle as far as her groin. He then made a number of other slashes, some quite deep, across her abdomen, and also drove the point of the knife twice into her genitals.'

His calm recitation of the appalling injuries Mary Ann Nichols had suffered silenced the inquest.

'I also examined the victim's clothing at the mortuary, and I believed that her killer probably cleaned the blood from the blade of his knife on her clothes before making good his escape from the scene.'

'Thank you, Dr Llewellyn. Was it, in your opinion, a frenzied attack, or do you believe that the killer was working to some kind of plan?'

Llewellyn shook his head.

'That I cannot say, sir, but it was certainly an extremely brutal assault. Could I also add that this attack must have taken place in almost complete darkness, and I am certain that the murderer would have been carrying out these actions in great haste because of the possibility of discovery. I therefore believe that he must possess a certain amount of rough anatomical knowledge.'

'Do you mean to suggest that the assailant could have some form of medical training?'

'Not necessarily,' Llewellyn replied. 'Rather, I am suggesting that he would have the same degree of knowledge that would be possessed by, for example, a slaughterman or a butcher or anyone else with some experience of the internal organs of either human beings or animals.'

Wynne Baxter nodded.

'In this regard, doctor, I'm inclined to agree with you.'

The verdict of the inquest jury was entirely predictable – murder by person or persons unknown – but it was the closing remarks made by Dr Llewellyn in his evidence, remarks that had then been endorsed by the coroner, which were the most sensational, even if they were immediately widely misreported.

Suddenly, and without any real evidence, the people of Whitechapel seemed to assume that the killer was a doctor, a healer of the sick somehow gone bad, and the fear quickly spread of a sinister figure in black haunting the cobbled and smog-laden streets, and lurking in the gloomy shadows of Whitechapel, clutching a medical bag which contained the sharpened steel weapons of his lethal trade.

And this idea was given added force when the people of Whitechapel realized that the site of Nichols's murder was only about one hundred yards from the looming bulk of the London Hospital. Within a very short time, anyone who was seen carrying anything like a medical bag through the streets was regarded by the residents with enormous suspicion, and in some cases such men were harassed and followed.

But they were all, of course, entirely innocent.

Alexei Pedachenko read the latest newspaper reports with interest. The way that suspicion had fallen on members of the medical profession amused him, but at the same time he acknowledged the essential truth of what the doctor had reported at the inquest and what the newspapers were now saying because he was, by training, a surgeon, though he hadn't practised that particular trade for many years.

He had planned on waiting a little longer before he acted again, because he'd expected that it would have taken the newspapers rather more time to whip up the feelings of hysteria and fear which were now clearly prevalent throughout Whitechapel. But he sensed that the time was right to strike again, to fuel that hysteria, which would in turn place even more pressure upon the commissioner when he returned to London – a return that was now imminent. And if he made the next killing as spectacular as he could, that might force Warren's hand almost immediately.

If it went according to plan, Pedachenko hoped he might be able to leave Britain, with the menorah, within the next couple of weeks.

Chapter 21

Saturday, 8 September 1888
Whitechapel, London

Annie Chapman had been born Eliza Anne Smith, probably in London, in about 1842 or 1843, though her date of birth was uncertain. Commonly known as 'Dark' Annie Chapman, she was also occasionally referred to as Annie Sivvey or Annie Sievey, a reference to the trade followed by her common-law husband, who was a sieve maker and also known, because of his profession, as Jack Sievey. For the previous two years, she had also had an on-going relationship with a man named Edward or Ted Stanley, who was a bricklayer's labourer.

She had been married in May 1869 to a man named John Chapman, who was a coachman in Windsor, and the couple set up home in Bayswater, and then moved to Berkeley Square. By 1881 they had moved out of London to Clewer in Berkshire. They had two daughters, one of whom had died in 1882 of meningitis at the age of twelve, while the other lived in France, and a crippled son who was in a charitable school. The marriage had then failed, the breakup probably initiated by the family tragedies, but then fuelled by Annie Chapman's intemperate drinking habits – she was particularly fond of rum – though her husband was also a heavy drinker.

Chapman wasn't an 'unfortunate' in the usual sense of the word. She was actually only an occasional prostitute, a woman who didn't take to the streets unless her financial situation left her with no other viable option. She was not a physically attractive woman, being fairly stout, and quite short, only five feet tall, with curly dark-brown hair beginning to turn grey, a fair complexion, blue eyes and a distinctive large and thick nose. She was also missing two teeth from her lower jaw – dental hygiene was rudimentary even in the best areas of London.

She had spent the previous years living in the Dorset Street area of Whitechapel in various doss houses, and for the last few months had been a resident of Crossingham's Lodging House located at 35 Dorset Street. People who knew her described her as a quiet and friendly woman, comparatively refined bearing in mind her disadvantaged situation, who was quite well spoken, almost never used bad language, and was generally thought to be very respectable.

After her separation from John Chapman, Annie had been in receipt of a regular allowance from him of some ten shillings every week, but this payment had ceased abruptly in December 1886, when he died suddenly. The loss of this quite substantial source of income hit Annie Chapman hard, when she realized that in the future she would have to support herself through her own efforts. As her separation from the sieve maker occurred at about the same time as John Chapman died, it's possible that her appeal to Jack Sievey disappeared along with her allowance and the measure of financial stability that this had provided for the couple.

In an attempt to raise money, she embarked on a number of

different ventures, including selling matches and flowers in the streets as a hawker, and making various items of crochet work, antimacassars and the like, which she would attempt to sell around the Dorset Street area. Her sister claimed that Annie had recently asked to borrow a pair of her boots so that she could walk from London down to Kent to try her hand at hop-picking.

She was, by most accounts, a decent, hard-working and industrious woman, at least when she was sober. She was also a regular visitor to a Friday market in Stratford where she would offer for sale whatever items she had available. But a perhaps inevitable consequence of her raising money on a Friday was that she would usually be drunk on the following day.

Early in the afternoon of Friday, 7 September, Chapman had returned to 35 Dorset Street and asked the deputy if she could sit in the kitchen for a while.

'You can stay here for a short time, Annie, but you know the rules,' the deputy, Timothy Donovan, replied. 'And where have you been all this week?'

'I've been in the infirmary. I haven't been well, and I don't feel well now.'

What Annie Chapman said to Donovan was actually true, and she hadn't been making an appeal to his good nature, not that such an appeal would be likely to sway the deputy. The rules in lodging houses in those days were simple, rigid and inviolable. If a person didn't have enough money to pay for a bed, they would be turned out into the street in the early hours of the morning.

The fact was that Annie Chapman had just spent several days in the infirmary after having been involved in a brawl with a woman named Eliza Cooper, who was another hawker, and who also lodged at 35 Dorset Street. The argument had started over a piece of soap which Annie had borrowed from Cooper and given to her companion Ted Stanley for him to wash with, and this apparently simple and inconsequential loan had culminated in a vicious fight at the Britannia public house on the corner of Dorset Street and Commercial Street.

That encounter had left Annie with a number of bruises and a black eye, and she was still feeling very unwell, but not just as a result of this confrontation. According to her friend Amelia Farmer, Chapman had been looking pale and weak for several days.

It would later be determined that she was actually seriously ill, possibly even dying, from a disease which was affecting the membranes of her lungs and also her brain. It's uncertain precisely what the disease was, but it was most likely tubercular meningitis, or maybe, bearing in mind her part-time occupation, meningovascular syphilis.

Possibly because of the fight with Eliza Cooper, but most likely because she'd been in and out of the infirmary, Chapman hadn't stayed at the lodging house for the last week of her life, but was seen elsewhere in the area by friends and acquaintances.

Amelia Palmer had met her in Dorset Street on 3 September, a few days after the brawl, and Chapman told her she was thinking about going hopping – hop-picking – down in Kent.

Palmer also saw her on the following day near Spitalfields Church, when Annie Chapman again complained that she was feeling extremely unwell and thought she might even go and stay in the casual ward at the local workhouse for a few days.

'I'm desperate, Amelia,' Chapman said at their meeting. 'I've got no money, no money at all, and I haven't eaten or drunk anything all day. It'll be the spike for me if I can't sort myself out soon.'

The threat of the workhouse was enough for Palmer to do what she could for her friend. She took out two pennies and handed them over to Chapman: that small sum was all she could spare.

'Here, Annie,' she said. 'Take this and at least get yourself some tea. All I ask is that you don't use it to buy rum.'

On 7 September, Chapman was in and out of the lodging house for most of the day, and had clearly obtained money from somewhere, because she spent at least some of the time drinking.

Amelia Palmer again saw Chapman in Dorset Street at about five in the afternoon. Palmer was surprised that her friend hadn't travelled to the Stratford market as she usually did every Friday, but Chapman said she still felt too ill to do anything. They parted for the last time some minutes later.

As she walked away, Annie Chapman said: 'I must pull myself together and get some money or I shall have no lodgings.'

At about 11.30 on the evening of Friday, 7 September, Timothy Donovan, the Crossingham's Lodging House deputy, spoke to Annie Chapman in the kitchen of the doss house. Shortly after midnight, she was seen in the kitchen by another lodger in the premises, a painter named William Stevens, and at about half past one in the morning, Annie Chapman was again in the kitchen, chatting to other lodgers and eating potatoes.

Concerned about her payment for a bed, Donovan spoke to her again.

'I need your rent money, Annie, if you're going to stay here tonight. Have you got it? It's eight pence, as you know.'

Donovan noted at the time that she seemed to be intoxicated, but was not completely drunk.

'I haven't got it,' Chapman replied. 'I am weak and ill and have been to the infirmary.'

A few minutes later, Donovan sent John Evans, the night-watchman at the lodging house, to ask her again for the lodging money, but shortly afterward Chapman herself appeared in the deputy's office.

'I haven't got the money, not enough to pay for a bed. But I'm going out now and I'll make enough to pay for it twice over. You'll see.'

Donovan was unsympathetic.

'Look, Annie, you're not looking very good and you've told me you're not feeling well. But I know you've had enough money today to buy gin or other spirits. Don't you think, in your condition, that you'd have been better using what you had to pay for your bed instead of buying drink?'

But Chapman seemed unconcerned and in good spirits.

'Don't you worry about me,' she replied. 'I know what I'm doing. I'm going out now, but I'll be back soon, so don't let anyone else buy my bed.'

At about two in the morning she walked out of Crossingham's Lodging House, wearing old and grubby clothes comprising a black figured jacket and black skirt, and a brown bodice and lace boots. The night-watchman, John Evans, watched her as she headed down Little Paternoster Row into Brushfield Street and then saw her turn towards Spitalfields Church.

But for over three hours, Chapman had no luck in finding a client, and by 5.25 she was making her slightly unsteady way down Hanbury Street. As she did so, she became aware of a man standing on the pavement outside number 29, some yards in front of her.

To say that the area was rundown was a grotesque under-statement. Most of the crumbling and disease-ridden four-storey houses had been built in the second half of the eighteenth century, at a time when that part of London had been prosperous and the citizens – many of them Huguenot silk-weavers – very affluent. But by 1888, the buildings had fallen into a state of almost total disrepair, grimy, decaying and literally falling to pieces, each with a larger population of rats and mice and other pests than human beings. It was one of the worst areas in the whole of Whitechapel, and that meant in the whole of London.

Nobody else seemed to be about and Chapman was getting desperate, not having found any clients at all in the previous three hours. That was why she had, as one last throw of the dice, decided to try the Hanbury Street area.

The man in front of her had a beard and was of slight build. He didn't look threatening in any way – he certainly didn't resemble the black-clad fiend carrying a doctor's bag who was popularly believed to be the murderer – and was dressed in good-quality dark clothes and wearing a deerstalker hat.

Chapman realized that he was probably her last chance of earning enough money to buy herself a bed for what was left of that night, and so she boldly strode straight across to him.

'Are you looking for a bit of business, love?' she asked him.

The man looked her up and down, and then nodded.

'I might be,' he replied softly, in accented English. 'What are you offering?'

Chapman recognized that he was a foreigner, which didn't bother her, and that fact also allowed her to hike up her price.

'Whatever you want, my dear. I've seen it all and I've done it all. I can give you whatever you want for eight pence.'

Eight pence was the price of her double bed at the lodging house.

'Will you?' the man replied.

'Yes.'

At that moment, a woman named Mrs Long appeared from the darkness and walked past the two of them, close enough to overhear the last two sentences of their conversation. Then she continued on her way.

The bearded man looked thoughtfully at her retreating figure for a few seconds, then back at the woman standing in front of him, and handed over some coins.

Annie Chapman reached out, took his arm, and led him confidently around to the back of number 29 Hanbury Street, where she knew that there was a quiet and dark backyard. She was very familiar with that area, which was only about a five-minute walk from Dorset Street. In the yard, she turned and led him across to the fence which divided number 29 from the next door property, 27 Hanbury Street, and then bent forward to lift up her skirt and petticoats.

But even as she did so, some intimation of danger must have crossed her mind, for as the man reached out towards her face, a pad of cloth held in his right hand, she suddenly called out: 'No!'

That was all she had time to say.

Chapter 22

Saturday, 8 September 1888
Whitechapel, London

Number 29 Hanbury Street had been leased by an elderly lady named Amelia Richardson who operated a small business from the premises, manufacturing packing-cases, and let out the remaining rooms in the property to lodgers. She had both long- and short-term tenants – a few had been there for as long as twelve years – and several of them worked in the Billingsgate and Spitalfields markets and left the building for their day's work in some cases as early as one in the morning. Even the late risers were usually walking out of the premises by about four or five.

Altogether, the building was occupied by no less than seventeen people, and both the passage between it and the adjoining property, and the yards located at the rear of the row, were known to be frequently used by local prostitutes for their assignations with their clients. Sometimes, these women had been found entertaining men actually inside the building, the doors to which were normally left unlocked because of the large number of people who lived there and the almost constant stream of traffic in and out of the building. But none of the local 'unfortunates' had ventured down into the back yard that night, or at least not at that time, and despite the number of occupants of 29 Hanbury Street, nobody in the building apparently saw or heard anything unusual.

One of these residents was a man named John Davis, who had had a largely sleepless night, lying awake in bed with his wife, on the top floor of 29 Hanbury Street. He'd dozed until the clock in the tower of the Spitalfields Church struck 5.45 and then got up, ready for another day's work at Leadenhall Market. Davis was a carman – a driver of a horse-drawn carriage or a tram – and at about six that morning he went out into the backyard of the building to start walking to his place of employment. Almost immediately he saw a lumpy shape lying close beside the fence.

In the predawn darkness, he was unable to see exactly what the object was, and so he strode across to the fence to get a better look.

What he saw was a sight that would be etched into his brain for the rest of his life. It was the body of a woman. She was lying flat on her back, with her head very near the steps which led up into the property, and Davis saw at once that she was dead, not least because a section of her intestines had been pulled over her left shoulder.

He stumbled backwards, shrieking with fright, and ran out of the yard and into the street to get help.

Out there in the street were two men – James Green and James Kent – who worked for the Bayley brothers at 23A Hanbury Street, another manufacturer of packing cases, and walking along the road nearby was a box maker named Henry John Holland. All three men were startled by the sudden appearance of a small and elderly man, who moved with a pronounced stoop, and who burst out into the street with wild eyes, yelling and screaming at the top of his voice.

Davis saw the three men in the street and calmed down slightly, recognizing that they could help him.

'You men,' he shouted, 'come here!'

The three of them followed Davis along the passage until the body came into view, and then stopped, transfixed by the scene in front of them.

'Dear God,' Green muttered. 'What kind of a fiend could do such a thing?'

Holland took a couple of paces forward, then stepped down into the yard to examine the body.

'What are you doing?' Davis called out. 'Don't touch her.'

'Don't worry, I won't. I just want a closer look.'

Holland strode over to where the corpse lay, while the other three men remained close to the back door of the house, staring down at the horrific sight. Then he retraced his steps.

'It's a woman,' he announced, unnecessarily, 'and she's dead. We need to find a police constable, as soon as we can.'

Davis and the three men left the premises, splitting up so that they would be more likely to find a patrolling constable quickly.

The first officer to arrive at the scene was Inspector Joseph Chandler, who had been on duty near the corner of Hanbury Street and Commercial Street, and by the time he arrived a size-able crowd had already gathered in the passage and around the rear door of the building. In view of the state of the body and the appalling mutilations, none of the spectators seemed inclined to approach it closely.

Chandler did his best to clear away the onlookers, then turned his attention to the dead woman. In the terse and almost clinical words of the official report he wrote later, he stated that in the backyard he had 'found a woman lying on her back, dead, left arm resting on left breast, legs drawn up, abducted, small intestines and flap of the abdomen lying on the right side of the right shoulder, attached by a cord with the rest of the intestines inside the body; two flaps of skin from the lower part of the abdomen lying in a large quantity of blood above the left shoulder; throat cut deeply from left and back in a jagged manner right around the throat.'

It was immediately obvious to him – to anyone, in fact – that the woman was dead, but Chandler still had to go through the motions. As soon as the first police constables arrived on the scene, he issued appropriate instructions to them.

'You there,' he instructed, 'go at once ask and Dr Phillips to come here as quickly as he can.'

As the first constable turned and ran off into the darkness, Chandler turned to a second man, and ordered him to run to the local police station to request additional officers and also to arrange for an ambulance to be sent to the premises.

More constables quickly arrived, and Chandler was able to take further measures.

'You two men. Get rid of all those gawking spectators and clear the passage. I don't want to see anybody anywhere near this yard who isn't a policeman or a doctor, understand? And some-body find me a coat or something to cover up this poor woman.'

One of the constables returned a few minutes later with a length of sacking, which he and Chandler then placed carefully over the body of the dead woman, for the sake of modesty.

Dr Phillips, a courtly and old-fashioned surgeon who was extremely popular with officers on the force and very competent in his work, arrived on the scene at about half past six. He listened carefully to what little information Chandler could supply him with, then had the sacking removed so that he could examine the corpse.

The moment the length of sacking was lifted up, Phillips drew in a sharp breath as he saw the body for the first time.

'I can tell you that she's definitely dead,' he murmured, with a weak attempt at humour.

'I think we already knew that, doctor,' Chandler replied. 'Can you give us an estimate of the time of death before we have the body removed?'

Phillips bent down beside the mutilated corpse and carried out a perfunctory examination, which consisted of little more than feeling the temperature of her limbs and what was left of her torso.

'Because of the state of the body and the conditions in this yard,' he said, 'I can't be certain, but a good guess would be two hours, perhaps less. The body temperature would have dropped quickly, because of what has been done to her, and she's lying on cold stones as well.'

'So not earlier than 4.30 this morning?' Chandler asked.

'Yes, very approximately,' Phillips replied. 'There's nothing else I can do for her here, so we might as well arrange to have the body removed. Could you have it taken to the Whitechapel Workhouse Infirmary Mortuary, please? It's in Eagle Street, and I can do the autopsy there.'

The ambulance arrived a few minutes later, and the two men watched as the corpse was manhandled into a battered coffin shell – a lightweight wooden box used for collecting bodies – and placed in the back of the vehicle.

'Is there anything else I can do here, or will I see you at the post-mortem?' Phillips asked.

'Actually, doctor, there is,' Chandler replied. 'Before we get any more spectators and police officers trampling their way through this yard, could we search it, just the two of us?'

Phillips nodded agreement, and the two men quartered the yard, conducting a thorough search as they looked for the murder weapon – though Chandler was not optimistic about finding that – or any other clues. In the vicinity of the location where the body had been found, they discovered about half a dozen spots of blood on the rear wall of the house, and a number of other smears and patches of blood nearby. None of that was entirely surprising.

But they also found a piece of muslin cloth, a pocket comb in a paper case and a small toothcomb. These objects appeared to have been the contents of one of the victim's pockets, and presumably had either been placed on the ground or had fallen from her clothing.

Close to where her head had lain, they also found a part of an envelope that contained two pills and the back of which bore the words 'Sussex Regiment', while the other side displayed the handwritten letter 'M' and 'Sp' – possibly the start of the word 'Spitalfields' – and a postmark in red which was 'London, Aug. 23, 1888'.

They also found a number of other objects during their search, including a piece of flat steel, an empty nail box and, close beside the water tap in the yard, a leather apron which was saturated with water.

During the commotion which had followed Davis's discovery of the body in the back yard of the property, numerous other residents of the building had appeared on the scene, including the man's wife, who came down to find out what was going on. She nearly fainted when she saw the state of the body, and later talked to a reporter.

She said: 'The poor woman's throat was cut, and the inside of her body was lying beside her – quite ripped open.'

The last clause of her sentence was a prophetic foretaste of what was to come, and of the name that would later be applied to perhaps the most notorious serial killer of all time.

Chapter 23

When Detective Inspector Abberline walked into the Bethnal Green police station that morning, he found the place in an uproar.

'There's been another one, Fred,' Inspector Moore called out to him as Abberline stepped in through the main door. 'And this one's a hell of a lot worse than anything we've seen before. She's been totally butchered.'

That was the last thing Abberline wanted to hear.

'Where?' he demanded shortly.

'Hanbury Street. In Spitalfields.'

'Who's got it?'

'Joseph Chandler was the first on the scene.'

'Right,' Abberline said. 'As soon as he gets back here, tell him I want to see him, with a full report on what he found there. You and Andrews can sit in on it as well. This has got to stop, right now. And let me have a note as soon as you can of exactly where the body was found.'

There wasn't a great deal of available space at the Bethnal Green police station, and all three of the Metropolitan Force inspectors – Abberline, Andrews and Moore – were sharing a tiny office in the back of the building that was really only designed for a single occupant, or at the most two people. It was separated from the adjacent office by a thin wooden partition, upon which Abberline had pinned the largest-scale map of the Whitechapel and Spitalfields districts of London that he could find. On it, he had marked the locations of the two prostitute murders which had so far taken place – Martha Tabram and Mary Ann Nichols – in red ink with the dates below them. Just to complete the picture, he had also marked the place – oddly enough very close to the site of the killing of Martha Tabram – where Emma Smith had been fatally attacked by the gang of thugs. But this notation was in blue, because Abberline could see no connection between this killing and the later two murders. The later *three* murders, he amended silently to himself, as he pushed the door open and stood for a moment glancing at the map.

There was a brisk double tap on the open door behind him, and a uniformed constable handed him a slip of paper.

'Thanks,' Abberline said, and looked at what was written on it.

The note was short and to the point. It read 'Unidentified woman. Body found at 29 Hanbury Street.'

Abberline nodded to himself, picked up a pen from the desk, located the site of the murder on the map, marked it with a red cross and added the only piece of information he had to hand at that moment, which was the date of the killing. The name, he hoped, would follow in due course.

Inspector Chandler appeared about half an hour later, looking harassed, which was entirely unsurprising.

'It's a bad one this, Fred,' he said by way of greeting, his voice angry but subdued, almost as if he was in shock, which was probably not far from the reality of the situation. 'I've never seen anything like this before. Whoever did it totally gutted her.'

Abberline nodded, and spotted his two colleagues, Andrews and Moore, approaching the office down the corridor outside.

'We need to find a bigger room, Joseph,' he said. 'We won't all fit in here.'

Chandler led the way to a small conference room down the corridor, pushed open the door and stepped inside. A table was positioned in the middle of the room, and there were six chairs ranged around it.

'This should do us,' Abberline remarked, as the four officers pulled out chairs and sat down. 'Right, Joseph, tell us what you found at Hanbury Street this morning.'

Inspector Chandler nodded, took a notebook from his pocket and in grim, subdued tones explained what had happened in the early hours, and what he'd seen when he arrived at the site of the latest killing.

'I've never seen anything like it before,' he concluded, echoing his previous statement to Abberline. 'This time, he hadn't just killed her and cut her open: he'd gutted her like a pig and pulled out most of her intestines, as well as cutting off flaps of her skin.'

There was a horrified silence around the table as the three seasoned detectives absorbed this piece of information.

'I know this will sound ridiculous,' Chandler added, after a few seconds, 'but it almost looked to me as if the killer had been preparing her body. You know, the way a butcher prepares an animal for the table, cutting out the intestines and all the other stuff that you don't eat to leave the bone and muscle, just the empty carcass.'

For a moment, Abberline and the other two officers just stared at him.

'You don't mean you think the murderer was planning to *eat* some part of the woman, do you?'

Chandler shook his head.

'I really don't know, Fred. I can't believe that any killer, no matter how depraved he might be, would do that. I'm just telling you what I saw, and what it looked like to me.'

Again there was a brief silence in the conference room, before Abberline spoke again.

'I think you might be right, Joseph, at least in one respect.'

'You're not saying that you think this man is a cannibal, are you?' Moore asked, his voice betraying the disgust he was feeling.

'No,' Abberline replied, 'but there is another way of looking at what he did. I know Joseph has described exactly what he found this morning, and I also know exactly how the four of us feel about this, the same way that any normal person would feel when confronted by this kind of brutality. And perhaps that's the real point here.'

'I don't understand what you mean,' Andrews said.

'Bear with me. Look, we've all had exactly the same reaction to this killing. We're all absolutely disgusted by it. I'm beginning to wonder if this man's motive isn't just the taking of human life, or even the mutilations which he performs on the dead body – and everything I've seen about this case so far suggests that the women are dead before he starts work on them, which I suppose has to be some kind of a blessing – but something else. I think he's deliberately setting out to shock people, and that's his plan. That's why he's doing it.'

Chandler nodded slowly.

'I see what you're driving at. You mean it's not the victims who are important – I'm sorry, that's not quite what I mean. Obviously these women are important, just as the life of any woman, or any man for that matter, is important. But what you mean is that for this killer, they're almost incidental. What's important for him is the way the corpse looks once he's finished with it.'

'That's it exactly,' Abberline said, 'and if I'm right, that gives us a real problem. It means there's absolutely no point in investigating the victims, and trying to identify anybody in their lives who might have a motive for killing them, because we won't find anyone. We won't find anybody simply because there's nobody there. This is an unknown man killing somebody that he's never met before. It's a stranger killing another stranger. And that means there's really no point in us even finding out who the women were – although obviously we will do that – because it's utterly irrelevant.

'This man, I think, is picking his victims completely at random. So far, they've all been prostitutes, but that's only because he strikes in the early hours of the morning and the most likely women to be on the streets at that time of day are unfortunates. But any woman, of any class, walking alone in Whitechapel or Spitalfields late at night, could become the next victim. The woman he chooses is just something he can use to express himself, if you like, the way a painter can turn a blank canvas into a masterpiece. This man is using his victims to make a statement. It's as if he's trying to send a message to somebody.'

That was such a radical way of looking at the seemingly motiveless and completely unconnected murders – unconnected apart from their being carried out by the same perpetrator – that for several seconds none of the other officers responded.

Finally, Andrews broke the silence.

'A message, Fred? But a message to whom?'

Abberline smiled bleakly.

'That's the problem, of course. I have absolutely no idea.'

Chandler closed his notebook and looked across the table at Abberline.

'If you're right,' he said, 'then you're really also saying that there's nothing we can do about these murders. The killer could strike again, at any time, anywhere in the East End of London. Even if we put a constable on every street corner – and don't tell me we can't, because I already know we haven't got enough men to do even a tenth of that – there would still be no guarantee we'd catch him. He can just wait until the street's quiet and nobody's looking, grab a single woman and drag her into a dark corner somewhere, and do his business with her. The first we'd know about it would be when some man on his way to work sees the body.'

Moore and Andrews both nodded their heads: the logic of the situation seemed inescapable.

'That's not a bad summary of the situation, Joseph,' Abberline said, 'but I'm not giving up on this. There must be *something* we can do to catch this maniac.'

Chandler reached into another pocket and pulled out a newspaper.

'I have no idea what we can do about it,' he said, 'but whatever plan you want to put into effect, Fred, you'd better do it soon. I picked up this newspaper on the way in to the station here. The press are all over this latest murder already.'

'The *Star*, Joseph?' Andrews asked, with a small smile, as he recognized which newspaper Chandler was holding. 'I thought you were more of a *Telegraph* man.'

'I am, but the people of Whitechapel aren't reading the *Telegraph*. They're reading the *Star* and newspapers like it, and that's what matters.'

Chandler placed the newspaper on the table in front of him.

'Let me read you the first section of the editorial,' he said, 'and then you can tell me what you think: "London lies today under the spell of a great terror. A nameless reprobate – half beast, half man – is at large, who is daily gratifying his murderous instincts on the most miserable and defenceless classes of the community. There can be no shadow of a doubt now that our original theory was correct and that the Whitechapel murderer, who now has four victims to his knife, is one man, and that man a murderous maniac." Not exactly reassuring for the unfortunates of Whitechapel, is it? I don't like the way the reporter has described it, but I have to say that I can't really argue with what he's said.'

'It's three murders, not four,' Abberline pointed out. 'I'm quite sure that that this killer had nothing to do with the death of Emma Smith.'

'True enough,' Chandler agreed. 'I think the *Star* is about the only paper left that thinks her killing was the work of the same man, but three or four, or thirty or forty for that matter, I still don't see how we're going to catch him. And when the other newspapers come out, they may use different expressions and describe the killer in different terms, but I don't think there's much doubt that the *Star* pretty much sums up the feelings of the people of Whitechapel, and especially of the women. They really think there's a kind of man-beast out there, picking them off, one by one.

'And the other thing,' he went on, 'is that the crowds have already started to gather all around Hanbury Street. When I left, there were already hundreds of people milling around the area, trying to find the exact spot where the murder had been committed, and I passed hundreds more on my way back here. I've ordered extra uniformed constables to the area to try to keep some kind of order, because I think we could easily see fights breaking out, maybe even a riot.'

Again there was silence for a few moments as Chandler finished speaking. Then Abberline took a folded sheet of paper out of his pocket and looked at what he'd written on it.

'I had worked out a kind of plan,' he said, 'but I think what you've told us this morning, Joseph, has rather scuppered that. I kept on thinking that there must be some connection between the victims, that they all knew each other or something of the sort, and that the killings were revenge or retribution or something else that linked them. But now I think it's very clear that that's not the case, and that what we're looking at is essentially a random, almost a motiveless, crime. This man doesn't care who he kills, or even when or where he kills them. All he's interested in is putting the corpses on display, if you like.'

Abberline glanced around the table at his fellow officers.

'You all know how limited our resources are. If any of you have got any good ideas about where we go from here, I'd very much like to hear them.'

Chapter 24

Monday, 10 September 1888
Whitechapel, London

On the Saturday, news of the murder spread quickly through the crowded tenements of Whitechapel, and crowds began to gather in the area shortly after dawn.

Frightened, anxious, agitated or simply angry people assembled outside the site of the murder in Hanbury Street, while other groups congregated near the mortuary where the body had been taken. Police stations in the area also attracted crowds, and the Ten Bells pub located on Commercial Street, where it was popularly believed that Chapman had taken her final drink, was packed. But it was Hanbury Street, the scene of the atrocity, where most people assembled.

The crowds grew so large, quickly numbering in the thousands, that many of the local businesses were forced to close, and police officers had to make frequent forays into the street to try to disperse them to allow normal road traffic to pass. According to *Reynold's Newspaper*, the streets 'swarmed with people who stood about in groups and excitedly discussed the details of the murder. Great anxiety is felt for the future. While the murderer is at large, they cannot feel safe.'

And it wasn't just the people of Whitechapel who had assembled in Hanbury Street. According to other reports in the press, people had travelled there from all over London. According to the *Standard*, 'thousands of respectably dressed people visited the scene,' and these allegedly included 'two prominent members of the peerage.'

Perhaps predictably, the natural sense of enterprise of the Londoners soon began to assert itself. A number of costermongers quickly arrived and set up their stalls in the streets and began doing a roaring trade selling fruit to people in the crowd, and some of the residents of 29 Hanbury Street seized the opportunity to make some easy money, and began charging eager spectators one penny a time to look at the actual murder site. According to contemporary accounts, several hundred people paid this fee before the police managed to stop it. At a small waxworks nearby, the owner splashed red paint over one of his displays and immediately began attracting crowds of eager spectators, all of whom paid the admittance fee to view his 'reconstruction' of the killing.

Then the rumours began to circulate. One of these stated that the murderer had daubed a message on the wall of the house stating that: 'I have now done three, and intend to do nine more and give myself up.' A different version of the same rumour suggested that the message read: 'This is the fourth. I will murder sixteen more and then give myself up.'

Yet another report claimed that a woman had been murdered behind the London Hospital, though nothing was found there, and when a young woman began moaning that the so far unidentified victim had been her mother, she attracted immediate sympathy from the crowds of spectators, none of whom thought to ask how she could possibly know the dead woman's name. But it was soon established that she was deluded, and she ended up in a violent struggle with a police officer. An ambulance heading towards the hospital was pursued by crowds, and hundreds of people ran to the Commercial Street police station when another rumour started to the effect that the murderer had been caught and taken there. In fact, the prisoner in question was simply a common thief.

The killer was seen everywhere. Any man who didn't appear to be entirely normal in his dress, or his conduct, or his actions, was immediately assumed to be the murderer. Innocent passers-by were attacked by mobs. A slaughterman with a few spots of blood on his hands was followed by a group of men from a pub, where he'd stopped to take an innocent drink. And there were the inevitable braggarts who, for whatever reason, either claimed to be the killer or to know who he was. Men with knives and suspicious looks abounded, and even the most respectable of men were suspected of being the faceless murderer.

The London newspapers were quick to exploit the situation. The evening papers sold out in record time, and large crowds gathered outside the newsagents waiting for fresh supplies to be delivered. People who had obtained copies quickly found themselves surrounded by groups of men and women eager to hear the latest news.

Even respectable papers like the *Telegraph* were not immune from the hyperbole which dominated the news. On the following Monday, the paper featured an article which discussed a baleful prowler haunting the dark streets and alleys of Whitechapel and the East End, and talked of 'beings who look like men, but are rather demons, vampires.'

And then things took an unexpected turn in Hanbury Street.

During the second half of the nineteenth century, the Jewish population of the East End of London had increased enormously, and it was estimated that in the Tower Hamlets district alone there were probably almost fifty thousand Jews, and around two thirds of this number lived in Whitechapel. Hanbury Street in particular, along with several other neighbouring roads, had a very high concentration of Jewish residents.

Although some of the Jewish residents were fairly prosperous, a very large proportion of them lived in poverty, and their situation was made worse by the attitude of the English residents of the area. They regarded the Jewish community with deep suspicion because they were, by definition, foreigners and therefore strange.

The Jews were also seen as a source of competition in the employment market, and were thought to be taking jobs that rightfully belonged to the English workers in the area. There were other bones of contention as well, including the charge that Jewish manufacturers concentrated on producing shoddy and cheaply made goods which were then sold in the various shops and markets for much less money than good-quality products from English manufacturers.

More pertinent to the recent events in Whitechapel, it was also known that the Jews had bizarre and – to English eyes – unnatural habits, such as the ritual slaughter of animals as part of their food preparation, a method of killing which involved slitting the animal's throat. As far as many of the local residents were concerned, it was only a short step from the slaughter of animals to the slaughter of 'unfortunates', and the news of the murder of Annie Chapman provoked an immediate violent wave of anti-Semitic feeling.

Clearly, the spark which had kindled this particular fire was the latest killing, but more particularly the belief, expressed consistently, loudly and frequently by the crowds of concerned and frightened East End residents, that the latest murder had been so brutal and the mutilations so gross and horrific that no Englishman could possibly have perpetrated it. And, because of the very large Jewish population in the area, it was therefore deemed logical to assume that the killing had been performed by a Jew.

The inevitable result of this piece of tortuous illogic was that the crowds began threatening, and in some cases attacking, any Jews they found on the streets. Fortunately, there was still a heavy police presence in the area, and the few fights which broke out were quickly brought under control, and nobody was seriously hurt.

There was a further superstition, which also gained ground around this time, that any Jew who had enjoyed carnal knowledge of a Christian woman would be required, in accordance with the laws promulgated in the Talmud, to afterwards kill and mutilate her as a form of atonement for his 'sin'. Some people even began quoting selected passages from this book to 'prove' the case and assert, at least by implication, that the Whitechapel murderer was very obviously a Jew.

Another result of the anti-Semitic feeling was a peculiar obsession which appeared to be shared by all three interested groups in London – the press, the residents of Whitechapel and, to a lesser extent, the police. They had all become fascinated by a Jewish cobbler who had somehow acquired the nickname 'Leather Apron'. Cobblers, of whatever race or religion, commonly wore such a garment, so the soubriquet was hardly unique, though it was undeniably appropriate. This man very quickly achieved an almost mythic status, and in the process became, in the eyes of the people, a virtual embodiment of fundamental evil.

The newspapers were quick to exploit the story. On both the fifth and sixth of September the *Star* had printed lurid articles which were clearly designed to capture the public imagination. The first of these bore the headline:

"LEATHER APRON"
THE ONLY NAME LINKED WITH THE
WHITECHAPEL MURDERS
A NOISELESS MIDNIGHT TERROR
The Strange Character who Prowls About Whitechapel
After Midnight – Universal Fear Among the Women –
Slippered Feet and a Sharp Leather-knife

The headline was enough to send shivers of fear down the collective spines of the Whitechapel prostitutes, though the stories themselves were noticeably devoid of facts, and appeared to be little more than a collection of rumours, half-truths and complete fabrications. 'Leather Apron' was allegedly a Jewish slipper-maker who had decided to embark on a second career by threatening prostitutes and demanding money from them.

But it wasn't just the *Star* which printed such material, and the other London papers were quick to join in. A report in *Lloyd's Weekly London Newspaper* contained a typical description of 'Leather Apron', similar to those in most of the other periodicals. It stated that: 'His expression is sinister and seems to be full of terror for the women who describe it. His eyes are small and glittering. His lips are usually parted in a grin which is not only not reassuring, but excessively repellent.' The paper went on to describe him as 'a Jew, or of the Jewish parentage', and as a 'slip maker' but asserted that his principal trade was blackmailing women late at night, a statement that cried out for clarification, but which the reporter did not elaborate upon. He was also believed to carry a sharp knife which 'a number of women have seen' but, strangely if he really was the 'Fiend of Whitechapel', he had not apparently attacked anybody with it.

His most alarming characteristic for the prostitutes of Whitechapel, however, was that he never made any noise when moving about, and the first indication most women had of his presence was when he materialized right beside them. He was also apparently frightened of men and ran away the moment any male approached to assist one of the ladies he was presumably blackmailing and, according to one paper, he also had the extremely unusual, not to say anatomically unlikely, habit of walking without bending his knees.

On Monday, 10 September, public concern over the alleged activities of the man nicknamed 'Leather Apron' had reached such a level that Detective Inspector Abberline, who was still waiting to be officially confirmed as the senior officer in charge of the investigation into the series of murders, knew he had to do something about it or anti-Jewish riots would be quite likely to rage through the East End. And the odd thing was that the police already knew the identity of 'Leather Apron'.

Abberline called in one of the detective sergeants at the police station, a heavily built man with dark hair and a luxuriant moustache named William Thick, and told him what he wanted him to do.

'Are you quite sure about this, sir?' Thick asked. 'I thought we'd already looked at this man and decided he didn't have anything to do with these killings?'

'We have, we did, and he doesn't, Sergeant,' Abberline replied, his voice resigned and flat. 'We know that he's innocent, but my concern is that if we don't bring him in, we could find that some of the local citizens in Whitechapel will decide to do our job for us. And if that happens, this man might not survive. So this is as much for his benefit and safety as anything.'

A short time later, a small group of police officers walked into Mulberry Street, off Commercial Road East, led by Detective Sergeant Thick. He knocked on the door of number 22, which was opened by a Polish Jew who was dark and thickset.

'We want you,' Thick stated, as his opening gambit.

'What for?' the Pole replied.

'You know what for. You will have to come with me.'

'Very well, sir. I'll go down to the station with you with the greatest of pleasure.'

The Pole's name was John Pizer, and he was the man who had – for reasons nobody was ever able to clearly explain – acquired the nickname the 'Fiend of Whitechapel', and who was otherwise known as 'Leather Apron'. But far from being the very incarnation of evil, he was an insignificant little man of thirty-eight years. He was short, standing only about five feet four inches tall, and of unpleasant appearance, at least according to the *East London Observer*, with thin and cruel lips.

Under Abberline's guidance, the police went through the motions in an attempt to satisfy public opinion. Pizer was placed in an identity parade, and entirely unsurprisingly none of the women who had alleged that they had been molested by 'Leather Apron' recognized him. Several people who knew him attested to his good character, and it was easily established that he had unbreakable alibis for the times when Nichols and Chapman had been murdered.

Despite this unequivocal proof of his innocence, Pizer continued to be harassed for the rest of his time in Whitechapel, and on one occasion was physically attacked on the streets.

The edition of the *East London Observer* for 8 September had described the events in and around Hanbury Street as 'A Riot Against the Jews', and attempted to bring a measure of reason to the situation, pointing out that since Jews began returning to England in 1649, only two members of that race had been hanged for murder. The article went on to say that: 'There is something too horrible, too unnatural, too un-Jewish, I would say, in the terrible series of murders for an Israelite to be the murderer.'

Despite this, anti-Semitic sentiments continued to linger in the East End of London for several months afterwards, and this caused sufficient concern within the Jewish community as a whole for it to offer a financial reward for the capture of the man who would shortly become known as 'Jack the Ripper'.

Alexei Pedachenko had, as usual, bought all the weekend papers, and all those published on Monday morning as well, and had consumed every word about his latest killing, searching for information.

When he had been making his plans to begin this killing spree, he had decided to establish a series of ground rules, so to speak, to ensure as far as possible that he would never get caught. And unfortunately, during his latest attack, he had broken almost every one of them.

The sudden appearance of the woman pedestrian, walking down the street behind him, and passing so close that he could probably have reached out and touched her, had been entirely unexpected and a very unpleasant surprise. With hindsight he knew that what he should have done was to just walk away. Make some excuse and leave the prostitute alive. Maybe he should even have gone through with the transaction he was pretending to negotiate with her, though the mere thought of copulating with such a female filled the Russian with shuddering horror.

But what he certainly shouldn't have done was what he did in fact do: he shouldn't have killed her. Absolutely the only saving grace was that the prostitute had been standing with her back to the wall, which meant that, because he was facing her, the only part of his body that the woman pedestrian could have seen with any clarity was his back. If she'd seen his face, that would have been an entirely different matter. And the reports he had read in the newspapers seemed to confirm that the police still had no accurate description of him to go on. All the pedestrian had been able to supply was a rough word picture which included his approximate height and build, and the clothes he had been wearing, clothes that Pedachenko had already disposed of.

Even that very rough description concerned him. He had expected that, as soon as he had accomplished two or three murders, the female population of Whitechapel and Spitalfields would be placed in a state of extreme alertness, and would be very suspicious of strangers. But he hadn't anticipated that anyone would actually see him about his work, except the woman he had selected as his victim, and obviously she would be in no position to talk to anyone once he'd finished with her.

So next time, if there had to be a next time – which, of course, depended upon what Charles Warren now did – he knew it would be necessary to change his tactics. The latest killing and the brutal mutilation which had followed it meant that any man – whether he appeared to be respectable or not – who approached a lone prostitute on a deserted street late at night would immediately arouse suspicion, and he'd find it much more difficult to carry out his work. He would have to devise some way of allaying the fear that such an encounter would produce, and that wouldn't be easy.

Chapter 25

Friday, 14 September 1888
Whitechapel, London

The inquest into the death of Annie Chapman was held on the Friday following her killing, and was attended both by a large crowd of spectators and by several officials, including Inspector Abberline as the senior investigating officer.

Chapman had quickly been identified by Timothy Donovan, the deputy of Crossingham's Lodging House at 35 Dorset Street. He stated that he had known her for almost a year and a half, during which time she had operated as a prostitute, and that for about the previous four months she had been a lodger in his doss house, the common term for a lodging house. He also confirmed the circumstances of the last evening when he'd seen her alive.

When the collection of evidence moved on to the discovery of the body, one of the first witnesses called was Mrs Amelia Richardson, who held the lease for the entire premises. When she was questioned about the presence of a dead prostitute at her property, she claimed that she had often in the past turned such women out of her yard when they appeared there with their clients.

But her son John fuelled a certain amount of speculation when he claimed in his later evidence that they had also often had prostitutes 'working' on the first-floor landing of the building, a practice, he said, that had been going on for years.

His mother was visibly less than impressed with the suggestion that her property had been used for immoral purposes, especially as she was known to hold weekly prayer meetings there, but John Richardson didn't waver and stuck to his story.

'But you did recognize this woman, Mrs Richardson?' the coroner asked her.

'I did, sir, yes. I did not know her well, and I did not know her name, but I recognized her as the dark woman that used to come around with cotton and crochet work.'

'So you knew her as a hawker, rather than as an unfortunate?'

'That is so. I might also add that I frequently bought such goods from her, not because I needed the products she was selling, but because of my charitable nature.'

And it was certainly true that Annie Chapman did act as a hawker as well as a prostitute. But this suggestion made for much less exciting copy for the newspapers than the alternative explanation that Mrs Richardson had recognized Chapman as a prostitute who had previously used parts of her premises for her liaisons.

But it was the medical evidence for which everybody at the inquest had been waiting.

Dr George Bagster Phillips, the man who'd been called out to the scene of the killing at Hanbury Street, and who had later performed the autopsy at the Whitechapel Workhouse Infirmary Mortuary, delivered his statement in as calm and dispassionate a manner as was possible, but there was no mistaking the sensational implications of the report he had to give.

He began by explaining to the coroner's court why the circumstances of the autopsy had been far from ideal.

'When I arrived at the Whitechapel Workhouse Infirmary Mortuary in Eagle Street, I discovered that the body had already been stripped of its clothing and partially washed. This was unfortunate, because it would have destroyed any clues which the killer might have left upon the body,' Phillips stated.

By now, following the murders of Martha Tabram and Mary Ann Nichols by a knife-wielding killer, the people of London, and especially the residents of Whitechapel, had probably come to expect that the victim's throat would have been cut and that there would be other wounds to the body. In this respect, they were not to be disappointed, but Dr Phillips had far more to explain.

'Moving on to what I witnessed at the scene of the crime, let me start by describing the gross position of the body. The victim's left arm was placed across her left breast, and her legs had been drawn up with the feet resting on the ground. I noted that the knees were splayed outwards, into a position which implied at least the possibility of sexual contact or connection.'

'Did you find any evidence that such a connection had taken place?' the coroner asked, interrupting him.

'No, sir, I did not. Her face was quite swollen and turned to the right, and the tongue, which was very swollen, was protruding between her front teeth. I might also add that, unusually for a person of her class, Annie Chapman's teeth were in very good condition.'

But nobody at the inquest was particularly interested in the dead woman's dental hygiene.

Phillips then went on to describe some of the other injuries to the corpse.

'The body was terribly mutilated. Her throat had been deeply cut by a very sharp knife. The incisions reached right around the neck and penetrated the tissues all the way down to the spinal column.'

'And was that, in your opinion, the cause of death?'

Phillips nodded.

'Almost certainly,' he replied. 'The cause I have noted in my report was syncope, the failure of the heart to continue working due to a massive loss of blood. And this loss, of course, was caused by the major arteries in the neck having been severed.'

He went on to describe the bruising to the face and the very swollen tongue, both of which he believed were consistent with the woman having been asphyxiated, which in this case had probably been enough to render her unconscious, but had not been sufficient to kill her.

'I also discovered that there were abrasions to the ring finger of her left hand, though these clearly had nothing to do with the cause of her death. I understand from enquiries made by the police that the victim was known to always wear two brass rings, a wedding ring and a keeper, on that finger. These abrasions suggested to me that these rings had been removed by force, presumably by the murderer.'

'Were these rings of any value?' the coroner asked. 'Is it possible that the motive of the killer could have been robbery rather than murder?'

'I do not believe so. The woman could simply have been rendered unconscious and the rings removed then. It would not have been necessary for her to be murdered in order to take them. And they were, to the best of my knowledge, of little or no value.'

'And what of the other mutilations to the body?' the coroner asked.

But Dr Phillips was noticeably reluctant to provide a detailed answer to this particular question.

'It is my understanding that the purpose of this inquest is solely to determine the cause of death, and I have already covered this in my previous evidence. I can say that there were further mutilations, but these had no bearing upon the manner of death of the victim. There is however, one more fact that I feel I should bring to your attention. The whole of the body was not present, the absent portions being from the abdomen. The mode in which these portions were extracted showed some anatomical knowledge.'

Despite further questioning, Dr Phillips would not be moved from his position.

The coroner then turned his attention to the evidence supplied by the police, and in particular whether any clues of any sort had been discovered at the scene.

'I regret to inform you that we have recovered no useful evidence or clues from the scene of the crime,' Inspector Abberline stated, in answer to the question. 'Various objects were discovered in the yard of the property, but all of these were unhelpful to our investigation. We discovered a leather apron there, but it was uncontaminated by blood and appeared to have been in the yard for some time. This was subsequently confirmed by Mrs Richardson, who advised us that she had found the apron in the cellar, covered in mildew, and had washed it thoroughly under the tap in the yard before leaving it out there to dry off.

'Mrs Richardson also stated that she owned both the length of steel and the nail box which we found there. That only left the few items which it would appear the killer had removed from the victim's pocket, or which had possibly fallen out of it. So far they have yielded neither information nor clues to either the identity or the motive of the killer.'

'I understood that there was part of an envelope which displayed the stamp of the Royal Sussex Regiment?'

'That is true, sir,' Abberline responded, 'and to begin with we were hopeful that it might shed some light on the identity of the perpetrator, but it did not. One of my colleagues, Inspector Chandler, visited the regiment to compare pay-book signatures with the writing on the envelope, but he was unable to find a match. He subsequently learnt that the Lynchford Road post office stocked a supply of the envelopes which were for sale to the general public, and an inspection of the remains of the envelope showed that the one found beside the victim had been franked at that very post office and not inside the barracks.'

Clarification of this matter came from another witness, a man named William Stevens. He was a painter who sometimes lodged at 35 Dorset Street.

'I saw her in the kitchen at Crossingham's Lodging House on the afternoon of the seventh of September,' Stevens began, 'and we fell into conversation. She told me that she had been to the hospital and had been given two bottles, one of medicine and the other of lotion, and a box of pills. She showed me these items, but the box which held the pills fell all to pieces as she showed it to me. We couldn't repair the box, and so she wrapped the two pills which had been in it in a piece of paper which she picked up from the floor of the kitchen. I saw the paper clearly, because she was wrapping up the pills right in

240 **Jack Steel**

front of me, and I am certain that the envelope which the police showed me was identical to that piece of paper.'

But the inquest did produce three witnesses who at least supplied some information, including evidence which cast doubt upon the time of the murder which had been estimated by Dr Phillips, and one of whom clearly saw the murderer with his victim just a few minutes before the killing took place.

Amelia Richardson's son John was thirty-seven years old. He didn't live on the premises, but at John Street in Spitalfields, where he worked in the market as a porter. But he also assisted his mother with her packing-case business. Following the theft of some tools from the cellar of the house, John Richardson had been in the habit of checking the security of the door in the mornings after he left his home and before he walked on to his place of work.

'I arrived at the building at about a quarter to five on the morning of the eighth of September,' he began, 'and as is my habit I walked through to the backyard of the house to check that the door to the cellar was locked.'

'And was it?' the coroner asked.

'Yes, sir, it was. But I didn't leave immediately. One of my boots was hurting my foot, so I sat down on the steps at the back of the house and took out my knife to trim a piece of leather from it. It didn't take me very long to do this, and then I continued on to the market.'

'While you were sitting on those steps did you see anything unusual in the yard?'

'No, but if the body of that poor woman had been there, I would certainly have seen it. The police inspector has told me exactly where it was found, and it was only a few inches away from where I was sitting.'

'What time did you leave the premises?' the coroner asked.

'I doubt if trimming the leather took me more than five minutes, so I probably left at about ten minutes before five.'

The coroner nodded.

'Thank you, Mr Richardson. That evidence will be very helpful in determining the time at which the murder must have been committed.'

The second witness was a woman named Elizabeth Long who was the wife of a cart minder called James Long. Just after half past five that morning, she had been walking along Hanbury Street and saw a man and a woman talking together near number 29. She was certain of the time because she had heard the Black Eagle Brewery clock in Brick Lane strike the half-hour a few seconds earlier.

'And you saw these two people clearly?'

'Yes, sir. The woman had her back to the property, so I could see her face, and I am certain that that woman was the same person whose body I was later taken to see in the mortuary.'

'Can you describe the man who was with her?'

'He was standing facing the woman and so he had his back towards me and I didn't see his face. He looked to me as if he was aged over forty, and he seemed to have a dark complexion and a foreign appearance. He was quite smartly dressed, wearing a brown deerstalker hat and I think a dark coat, though I cannot be certain of the colour. I would describe his appearance as shabby genteel.'

'Were you able to hear any part of their conversation?' the coroner asked.

'Yes, sir, I did. As I passed the two people, the man said "Will you?" to the woman, and she replied "Yes". I heard nothing after that as I continued on my way along the road.'

The third witness at the inquest was Albert Cadosch, the carpenter who lived next door at number 27 Hanbury Street. He related how he had gone outside at about half past five that morning and had heard voices in the yard of the adjacent property.

'Could you make out what they were saying?'

'Not really,' he replied. 'The only word I am certain I heard was "no".'

'What did you do then?'

'I went back indoors, but then I came out again a few moments later. I didn't hear the voices any more, but I did hear a thump, as if some object had fallen against the fence between the two properties.'

'Did you look over the fence or stay in the yard any longer to listen?'

But Albert Cadosch was clearly a man who possessed no sense of curiosity whatsoever.

'No, sir,' he answered. 'I left the building to walk to work.'

Abberline and Chandler walked back from the inquest together.

'Anything strike you as a bit odd about that, Joseph?' Abberline asked, as they walked down the street.

'I suppose you mean why did Dr Phillips refuse to say anything about the mutilations to the woman's body?'

'I'll be having a word with our police surgeon over that later, because we need to find out as much as we can about this killing. No, it was something else that Phillips said.'

Chandler glanced at him enquiring.

'What do you mean?

'The time, Joseph, the time. When you told me what had happened that night, you said that Phillips was quite certain that the killing had taken place about two hours before he examined the body, and he was at the murder scene at about half past six in the morning. That puts the time of the murder at half past four in the morning, maybe even earlier.'

Chandler nodded.

'That's right,' he agreed. 'That's what Phillips said today in his evidence, that her death had occurred at about 4.30.'

'That's precisely my point. Phillips was basing his estimate on the approximate body temperature of the dead woman, and you told me that he didn't even use a thermometer but just felt various parts of the corpse with his hands. Probably not the most accurate way of working out the time of death.'

'But Phillips has got years of experience and he's a police surgeon. I think he knows his stuff.'

'On most things, maybe,' Abberline agreed. 'But just look at the other evidence, and the other timings. Elizabeth Long is certain that she saw Annie Chapman standing outside 29 Hanbury Street at almost exactly 5.30 in the morning. She'd just heard the brewery clock strike the half-hour. And she positively identified the body in the mortuary as the same woman that she'd seen.'

Chandler shrugged.

'Maybe it struck half past four, not half past five. She could have been mistaken.'

'If it was just that one witness, if it was just Elizabeth Long, then you could be right. But Albert Cadosch was also quite certain about the time, and so was John Richardson, as you'd expect, as both men were leaving home at the same time they did every day to walk to their places of work. And if Richardson's account is accurate – and we've absolutely no reason to believe that it isn't – it's simply impossible that he could have sat on the steps in the yard trimming a piece of leather from his

boot with the mutilated body of the woman lying on the ground
less than a foot away from him.'

'So what are you saying?'

'I'm simply saying that, despite all of his undoubted experience and competence, on this occasion Dr Phillips has simply
got the time wrong.'

Chapter 26

Friday, 14 September 1888
London

Charles Warren had returned from his holiday in France to a capital city in a virtual state of siege, but with the enemy already within the walls, a faceless maniac who was intent not just on killing women, but also on hideously mutilating their bodies after death.

And, as the last killing had clearly shown, he was also removing body parts as revolting souvenirs of his work. Despite the curious reticence shown by Dr Phillips at the inquest, it had quickly became common knowledge in London that Chapman's womb, the upper part of her vagina, most of her bladder and a section of the wall of her belly, including her navel, had been removed from her body, and from the scene. This added yet another dimension to the horror that was afflicting the city.

In the whole of London the only person who had any idea of the identity of the murderer was Warren himself, and even his knowledge was incredibly scanty, far too slight to permit any search to begin for the killer, even if the commissioner had wanted to do so. A middle-aged man, possibly a Russian, and using the alias 'Michael', was little enough for even the most talented and committed detective to go on.

Three women – four if you included the unfortunate Emma Smith in this wretched total – had now been killed in the White-chapel area, and the one thing Warren was quite certain about was that there would be more deaths before the year was out. And though he regretted that the women had been killed, at least on an intellectual level, he found he was still able to adopt a profession-ally detached attitude towards what was going on. In truth, he was far more concerned about the effect the killings were having upon the population of London and on the reputation of the Metropolitan Police, than in the facts of the deaths themselves.

In his personal opinion, the slaughtering of a handful of des-titute and probably diseased prostitutes – brutal and hideous though their killings had been – was of no significance whatso-ever when compared to the importance of the menorah, the most sacred relic of the entire Jewish religion. Warren knew that almost any number of murders of that class of person would not be compelling enough to make him accede to the demands 'Michael' had made and hand over the relic. But if the killer had selected middle- or upper-class women, women of his own class, Warren knew that his attitude would of necessity have been com-pletely different.

He spent that morning going through his correspondence at home, intending to proceed to his office in Scotland Yard after lunch. Among the routine letters and tradesmen's accounts he found two hand-delivered letters, the handwritten address now easily recognizable. Before he opened them he called Ryan up to his study.

'These letters,' he asked, holding up the two envelopes. 'When did they arrive?'

'While you were away, sir,' Ryan replied, stating the obvious, 'and each time during the afternoon. The first one arrived on the 31st of August and the second on the 8th of September. I was actually here in the hall when the second one was delivered, and I did glance outside to see who had left it.'

'Who was it?'

'A common street urchin, sir. I assume that he had been given the letter and a penny to deliver it. But before I could open the door and question him, he ran away from the house.'

Warren nodded.

'If it happens again, do your best to catch the urchin and get a description of the man or woman who recruited him for the task.'

'I'll do my best, sir, but those young lads can certainly run.'

Warren waved his dismissal and Ryan turned on his heel and walked out of the study. As soon as he was alone again, Warren slit open the first envelope with a paper knife, extracted the sheet of paper it contained and read the message.

Like the previous communication he'd received, it was both brief and cryptic. It read: 'Second of the first three. Apex of the compasses. First the triangles, then the star.'

Two things immediately struck him. The first was simply the timing, which was nothing more than another confirmation to him of what was going on. He had received the first letter immediately after the killing of Martha Tabram, and it was too big a coincidence to be accidental that the second communication had arrived at his home straight after the second murder. He was quite certain that the sender of the letters was also the killer roaming the streets of East London, just as he was quite certain that the murderer was the stranger who had demanded that Warren hand over the menorah to him.

The second point was the reference to geometrical shapes: triangles and a star, which had meant nothing to him until that moment. He realized that the only thing that they could refer to was the physical location of the murders, the places where the bodies had been found.

As a part of his preparation for taking on the job of Commissioner of the Police of the Metropolis, Warren had purchased a number of maps of London, in order to provide information about the vast area that he would he required to control. And, as a trained surveyor, he was very used to working with maps of all types and descriptions.

On one side of his study was a map cabinet, a handsome piece of furniture made of walnut, which contained about a dozen shallow, but long and wide, drawers, each holding maps of various scales which covered different areas of London. The third drawer down held maps relating to the East End, and Warren sorted through these until he found one which he hoped would serve the purpose. He had already cleared his desk, and laid the map out flat on the polished wood surface, anchoring the four corners of the sheet with paperweights and other objects to hold it in place.

He looked carefully at the map, which was monochrome, grey-black markings on a white background, and selected a pen containing bright blue ink. Then he shuffled through a pile of reports until he found the one he was looking for, the summary prepared by Detective Inspector Edmund Reid of H Division of the Metropolitan Police, the division covering Whitechapel, who had been in charge of the investigation into the death of Martha Tabram. He scanned the type-written sheet until he found the precise location where the body had been found, in George Yard, off Whitechapel High Street. Then he took his pen and marked that spot on the map with a neat cross, adding the name 'Tabram' and the date of the murder – 7 August – beside it.

The report on the killing of the second woman was on top of the other papers, and he quickly read the appropriate section again, to identify the place where she'd been murdered. That location, too, he marked on the map with a small cross, adding the date and the name Nichols. Finally, he took a long ruler and drew a line between the two crosses, a line which he noticed was aligned almost perfectly north-east to south-west.

As an afterthought, he referred to another one of the early reports, this one dealing with the killing of Emma Elizabeth Smith, and marked that location on the map as well. Strangely enough, that mark fell precisely on the line he'd already drawn, but that had to be a coincidence, because the Metropolitan Police already knew that Smith's killing had been the work of a gang of youths and young men, and had been different in all respects from the two subsequent murders. Apart from anything else, Smith had been able to explain exactly what had happened to her, although she had then fallen into a coma and had died in hospital the following day.

Warren looked back at the two cryptic notes he'd been sent by the foreigner who'd called himself 'Michael'. The first read: 'Remember the symbol. George Yard. The first of six and the first point of the first triangle. The apex is next.' The second was a good deal shorter: 'Second of the first three. Apex of the compasses. First the triangles, then the star.'

Both mentioned a 'triangle' and the 'apex', and the second 'compasses'. As a trained surveyor, Warren was very familiar with the use of compasses, and the more he looked at the two notes and the map he'd prepared, the more disturbingly obvious the meaning became.

'Michael' had obviously decided not only to put pressure on Warren, as the head of the Metropolitan Police service, by killing prostitutes on the streets of Whitechapel, but he was also clearly trying to suggest that there was some sort of a Masonic component to the murders. That much was clear from the repeated reference to the 'compasses', because a set of compasses, along with the square, was the best-known of all the Masonic symbols, and the two shapes together formed the badge of the organization. That was a second threat to Warren, or at the very least another way of putting pressure on him, because he was known to be an enthusiastic Mason.

And it looked to Warren as if 'Michael' was also going to try to implicate the large and diverse Jewish community in London, because of the last sentence on the second note. The only obvious interpretation of that line – 'First the triangles, then the star' – was to the Star of David, the symbol of the Jewish faith which was itself formed by two overlapping triangles.

He leant back in his chair, his eyes fixed on the line he had drawn across the map. The location of the killing of Emma Smith *had* to be a coincidence. The place just happened to fall on the same line as the places where Martha Tabram and the second victim had died, nothing more. But Warren was quite certain that these three killings had been perpetrated by 'Michael', and that the murders of Martha Tabram, Mary Ann Nichols, and now Annie Chapman, would not be the last. The note had said as much, very clearly. The second killing had been positioned at the apex of a ghastly triangle, and that meant that the location of the third murder would have completed the shape.

And that, Warren suddenly thought, might give the police a way of catching the perpetrator, if he was definitely attempting to create recognizable geometric shapes on the ground by killing prostitutes in specific locations. The line between the first two murders ran almost exactly south-west to north-east, and Warren knew perfectly well the approximate angle between the two legs of the pair of compasses on the Masonic symbol. In order to replicate that on the ground, the next killing – the third murder which had already been committed – would have occurred either due west or due south of the location of the second killing. And it would have to have been about the same distance away as the separation between the first and second murders.

He picked up the police report from his desk, noted the precise location where the body had been found, and then turned back to his map. He took up his pen and ruler, marked the new spot with the name 'Chapman' and the date, and then drew a line between 'Nichols' and 'Chapman'.

As he'd expected, the place where Annie Chapman's body had been discovered was almost due west of the site of Nichols's killing, and about the same distance from it as the second body had been from where Martha Tabram's corpse had been discovered.

Hideous though the concept was, the murderer had done precisely what he had set out to do. He had replicated on the ground, with these three brutal killings, the shape of one of the two ancient pieces of equipment which together formed the symbol of the Masonic movement.

It was time to look at the last note sent by 'Michael'. His left hand, Warren noted almost dispassionately as he reached for the second hand-delivered letter, was trembling slightly.

Chapter 27

Friday, 14 September 1888
London

'We're being crucified in the press,' Detective Inspector Andrews murmured, as he flicked through the pile of newspapers in the tiny back office at the Bethnal Green police station.

The papers spanned the previous week, ever since the discovery of the butchered body of Annie Chapman in Hanbury Street, and in all that time the stories of the London murders hadn't moved from the front pages of virtually every paper.

Andrews picked up a selection and addressed the other two detectives sitting in the cramped back office.

'These are all from this week,' he began. 'This is the *Pall Mall Gazette*. Their headline is "A Fourth Woman Foully Mutilated". *Reynold's Newspaper* calls it "Another Fiendish Murder". And it's not just the cheap papers either. This is the *Observer* from the beginning of the week. "Yesterday morning the neighbourhood of Whitechapel was horrified to a degree bordering on panic by the discovery of another barbarous murder of a woman at 29 Hanbury Street." Even *The Times* has got in on the act, though obviously its report isn't quite as sensational.

That just says: "This latest crime even surpasses the others in ferocity." Which is true, but obvious.'

'Typical of *The Times*,' Moore commented.

Andrews grunted and picked up another newspaper from the pile in front of him.

'All those reports,' he began, 'just deal with the murders, and that's at the core of most of the stories.'

'You'd expect that,' Abberline chimed in. 'As far as I know, Britain has never seen such a series of murders before, certainly not with the degree of mutilation that's been inflicted on these poor women. And that's the other component. The women of Whitechapel, and especially the prostitutes, obviously, think they're under deliberate attack by a ruthless and faceless enemy. To make matters worse, a lot of the papers still seem to think he might even turn out to be a doctor, a man who's supposed to save lives, not take them.'

Andrews nodded, then spoke again.

'As I said, those just talk about the murders, but there are now an awful lot of articles complaining about how inept the Metropolitan Police force is proving to be. I know this one is only a minor newspaper, but I think the reporter has hit the nail firmly on the head.'

'Which paper is it?' Moore asked.

'It's the *East London Advertiser*. The leader states that the police "have no basis to go on. They do not even know the kind of class from which to select the criminal. They have not a single notion of his whereabouts. They do not know his motive, except so far as our guessing psychologists have enabled them to decipher it. He has left no material trace, and practically no moral trace." What they're saying, in short, is that this killer is essentially invisible, and we're never going to catch him. And a bit further down in the same article, the reporter says "what is likely to happen is this: there will be more murders, and the ruffian's heels may be tripped by chance, if not by the foresight of the police." And that's more or less what we've decided, isn't it? We've got no way of knowing where or when he's going to strike next, and no clue about who his next victim will be. So our best hope is that some patrolling constable or a Whitechapel resident will manage to see him – or, even better, catch him – in the act, because as far as I can see there's nothing else we can do.'

'Oh yes there is,' Abberline countered. 'I agree with what you say, but we can still fall back on good old-fashioned police work, and I've already given instructions to the officers here to start making detailed enquiries in Whitechapel. I've organized some extra men from Scotland Yard to help out – both uniformed and plainclothes – and they're going to have to visit every doss house – and there are over 200 of them – within about half a mile of the murder site, and question everyone they find in them, both staff and residents, as well as undertaking all the normal house-to-house enquiries which have been going on ever since the body was discovered.'

'And do you think that will achieve anything?' Andrews asked.

'Frankly, no. It's as much an exercise to show the people of Whitechapel and Spitalfields that we're doing something to try to bring this man to justice. I doubt very much whether any of the information they collect will help us in our enquiries, just because of the type of man we're looking for. He may not even live in the area. In fact, if it was me doing these killings, I'd find myself a nice cosy billet somewhere well away from Whitechapel and only go there when I wanted to do another one.

That way, there'd be no clues to find anywhere in the district; and I'd be quite surprised if our mystery killer didn't think the same way, because whoever this man is, he's certainly not stupid.'

Abberline reached into his desk drawer and pulled out a couple of sheets of paper.

'Just while we're all here,' he went on, 'I've had a few more suggestions sent in by concerned members of the public.'

Both Andrews and Moore smiled at this. The two men had studied dozens of letters sent to the Metropolitan Police about the Whitechapel murders, and many of them had contained ideas that were simply ridiculous. Perhaps the most ludicrous was the suggestion that they should place spring-operated female dummies in certain areas of Whitechapel, dummies which would then in some way leap into action and grasp hold of anyone who touched them. The correspondent had unfortunately failed to suggest any way in which such mechanical traps should be made, or where they should be positioned.

'Right,' Abberline said, 'we've got the usual crop of silly ideas, but there are a couple that might be worth considering. The first one is really simple. This man has suggested that we issue all our beat constables with rubber soled boots, because he makes the point that you can hear a police constable coming long before he's in sight, just because of the tramping sound of his hobnailed boots. In fact, I've had a word with the officers working out of here, and several of them have already begun doing something about this, nailing strips of rubber on the soles of their boots to cut down the noise. I'm going to make this an official request, but obviously it will take some time to get new boots issued.

'Another letter writer thinks we should try to improve the

lighting in the back streets of Whitechapel, which is undeniably a good idea, but it would take months, maybe even years, before the whole area could be improved, and I'm hoping to catch this man a lot sooner than that.'

'Anything else?'

'Yes. The last idea actually ties up with something I've been thinking about ever since the killing in Hanbury Street. I think we're all agreed that conventional police work isn't going to catch this man, just because of the way he seems to work. So we need to think about doing something different, of trying to come up with a completely different approach.'

Abberline selected another letter and held it up.

'This man is on the right track. He's suggesting we recruit women to act as police officers and become decoys. We send them out into the streets of Whitechapel in the early hours of the morning, and hope that one of them gets chosen by the killer.'

Andrews and Moore looked horrified at the suggestion, and Abberline smiled at them.

'Now obviously we can't even think about doing that. It's not appropriate for women to serve in the police force and, even if it was, I wouldn't be prepared to subject female officers to that kind of danger. But we do have quite a lot of young constables, men in their early twenties who could perhaps pass for women at night, in the poor illumination of Whitechapel. And this is something I think we should try. I want you two to take a look at the constables working out of this station and try and pick out half a dozen or so who might be suitable. Try not to pick any with moustaches, obviously. I'm not going to order them to do this – it will be on a volunteer basis only – but if they agree, we'll get them out onto the streets as quickly as possible.'

'You'll arm them, I suppose?' Andrews asked.

Abberline nodded.

'Definitely. This man is too dangerous to take any chances with. Each constable who volunteers will be issued with a small fully loaded revolver – a British Bulldog or something of that sort – which he will keep in the outside pocket of whatever dress or skirt we can find for him to wear. Plus he'll have his whistle to summon assistance. What I'm hoping is that our killer will see one of these "unfortunates" and approach him. And then we'll have him.'

'Actually, Fred, that's a pretty good idea. Using an apparent prostitute as bait on the streets might just draw him in. We'll just have to hope that our decoys don't get too enthusiastic and start shooting holes in innocent clients.'

The three men chuckled at Moore's comment.

'One other thing,' Andrews said. 'On that note, I've heard a few reports that some of the regular prostitutes in Whitechapel are now carrying weapons – mainly knives, I think – for their own protection.'

Abberline shook his head.

'That might make them feel better, but I think the chances of any woman, and especially a malnourished 40-year-old unfortunate, being able to take on this man and come off best, even if they are carrying a knife, are pretty slim. Whoever he is, our murderer is fit and strong and determined, and I think he'll make short work of anybody like that who stands up to him.'

Chapter 28

Friday, 14 September 1888
London

Warren opened the second envelope and extracted the piece of paper it contained, expecting another cryptic message. He wasn't disappointed, though the two sentences on the page were longer than those he'd received before. The third note from 'Michael' read: 'The northern end of the base of the first performs the same function for the second. The interlocking square and compasses, base to base and slightly distorted.'

Warren switched his attention back to the map on which he'd marked the location of the three killings. It wasn't a perfect triangle, in that there was a very slight difference between the lengths of the two longest sides, but it was close enough, and if the killer was trying to create the shape of the Masonic compasses on the grimy streets of Whitechapel, he'd actually done a fairly good job.

He knew that 'Michael' was just playing with him, picking the time and the place and the victims to suit his own timetable and purpose. And if it was the last thing Warren ever did, he was determined to find the man and bring him to justice. He would only rest easy when he saw his adversary dangling from the end of a rope at Tyburn Tree. But it would be even better, he rationalized, if the man could be killed in the commission of another murder, because the last thing Warren wanted was for the murderer to have the opportunity to stand up in court and explain precisely why he had been carrying out these appalling crimes. If that did happen, he would just have to hope that what the man said would be dismissed by everyone as the ravings of a lunatic or homicidal maniac. But first, of course, the police had to catch him.

Only when 'Michael' was dead would Warren feel safe. And then he realized something else. If he'd stayed in London, if he hadn't gone on leave to France, and had made the same deduction about the triangular shape a couple of weeks earlier, he could have flooded police officers into the two most likely areas for 'Michael' to strike, one to the west of the site of Nichols's death, and the other down to the south.

But even then the problem would have been predicting the 'when' as much as the 'where'. There had been over three weeks between the killings of Tabram and Nichols, but only eight days had then elapsed before the murderer took Annie Chapman's life. Even if Warren had deduced approximately where 'Michael' would strike again, the third murder would very probably have taken place before the commissioner could have got his men into position, because he wouldn't have expected the man to strike again for at least another week or ten days.

And now, Warren knew, he'd missed his opportunity, because 'Michael' had completed the shape of the first triangle with his third killing. The bodies of Tabram and Chapman marked the two ends of the base of that geometrical shape, and Nichols the apex.

It was some small comfort that his deduction had been right

about the area that the man chose for his third killing, even if he would probably have guessed wrong about the timing.

Then there was, he knew, another problem which was rather more pertinent. Although Warren was effectively in charge of the Metropolitan Police, he would still need to produce some reason, some reason that made sense, for issuing orders for his officers to concentrate their efforts is in one particular area of Whitechapel. And what he certainly couldn't do was explain that he believed the murderer was positioning his victims in the shape of a Masonic symbol, because everyone from the Home Secretary downwards would immediately assume that he had lost his mind.

Even if they did believe him, they would obviously wish to know upon what evidence he was basing his theory, and he certainly wasn't prepared to admit that he had met the man he was convinced was responsible for the killings, or that this man was trying to persuade him to hand over a Jewish religious relic of incalculable importance and value which he, Warren, had stolen from underneath the Temple Mount in Jerusalem.

If at all possible, 'Michael' was going to have to be silenced without being given the chance to explain anything to anyone.

The way Warren read it, the third note suggested that the location of Chapman's corpse would, in due course, come to indicate one end of the base of the *next* triangle – which, it was obvious, 'Michael' was intending to represent the mason's square from the Masonic badge. The only difference between the two triangles would be the angles, because the angle at the apex of the square had to be ninety degrees – that was what a 'square' meant – whereas the angle of the apex of the compasses on the badge was about forty-five degrees.

On the Masonic symbol, the ends of the compasses overlaid

the ends of the square, and so if you replaced the two objects with triangles of the same shape, you ended up with two triangles overlapping each other, base to base, just as 'Michael' had suggested in his note. The problem was that he could choose almost anywhere for his next killing, and Warren had no way of predicting where it would be, except in the most general terms. If he assumed that the killer would be trying to describe on the ground a similar sized triangle to the first one he had created, then the base of the second shape would have to be considerably longer than that of the first, simply so that the angle at the apex of the new triangle could be ninety degrees, or close to it.

If that were the case, and if the triangles were to intersect each other, then that could suggest that the next killing would take place in the districts which lay to the south of Commercial Road and to the east of Leman Street, perhaps even as far out as Shadwell. The problem was that without any other indication of the likely location, that was far too big an area for Warren to cover with police reinforcements. He simply didn't have enough men to make that a viable option.

He had, he realized, only one possible option, and he didn't like it at all.

He would have to wait for the next killing, wait for 'Michael' to strike for a fourth time. That would provide him with two of the points which would define the shape and size of the next triangle. From that he could work out the approximate position of the apex, and this time he would make sure that no matter how long it took, that area of Whitechapel would have more policemen stationed in it than ever before during the hours of darkness.

This time, he knew he had to succeed because, despite his personal view that the lives of the 'unfortunates' were of no particular value, that was not a sentiment likely to be shared by the residents of Whitechapel, and especially not by the women. And if the Home Secretary ever discovered what was going on, Warren would at best be dismissed from his post in disgrace, and at worst end up in the dock at the Old Bailey charged with God knows what. Even if that didn't happen, Warren knew that if he couldn't stop the murders he would definitely have no option but to resign just to stop the carnage.

He looked at the map for a few minutes more, measuring the angles and calculating distances, and trying to work out how to handle the problem. Then he picked up the map and returned it to the chest on the other side of the room, closing the drawer and locking it securely. Though there was nothing on it which even hinted at his somewhat bizarre theory, he certainly didn't want Ryan or anybody else to see what he had been working on.

Chapter 29

Friday, 14 September 1888
London

Charles Warren had sat down with his wife Fanny for a somewhat rushed lunch.

'Do you really have to go in to work this afternoon, Charles?' she asked. 'I mean, surely it can all wait until Monday. Or even tomorrow?'

Warren shook his head.

'I wish it could, Fanny, but I'm afraid it can't. There've now been three very similar killings in London, and I simply have to go in to the office to review what's happened and find out what progress has been made in identifying the perpetrator of these horrific crimes.'

As soon as he'd finished his meal, Warren left his house in a cab to travel to Scotland Yard, and once he'd skimmed through his correspondence and read those reports which dealt with the two most recent killings, he summoned Detective Inspector Abberline and demanded an up-to-date progress report.

Unfortunately, the inspector had very little to tell him which Warren hadn't already gleaned from the written statements he had just seen. The reality was that despite the three brutal murders, the police still had no idea of the identity of the killer, because as far as Abberline had been able to discover, he had left no clues of any sort at any of the murder sites, and nor did they have the slightest clue as to the man's motive. Or at least, no clue that seemed to make sense. The only definite common factor linking the three victims was that they had all been 'unfortunates', and that hardly offered much in the way of motive.

So unless the so-called 'Fiend of Whitechapel' was simply a lunatic who, for some twisted reason of his own, had decided to clear the streets of the district of prostitutes – and the three murders had certainly achieved that, at least to some extent – then there had to be some other reason for the murders. And the only reason that Abberline had been able to come up with didn't really make sense, even to him.

The Inspector was still convinced that they were dealing with an intelligent and organized man who had some very clear purpose in mind, and that was the view that he had just expressed to the commissioner.

'These certainly aren't crimes of passion, in my opinion,' he continued. 'Although the killer is targeting prostitutes, it's clear to me that he has no sexual interest in them. I think he has chosen them as his victims just because women are obviously easier targets than men, and of all the classes of women in Whitechapel, the ones he's most likely to find wandering the streets by themselves in the early hours of the morning will be prostitutes.'

'Are you saying the killer is picking on prostitutes just because they're convenient?' Warren demanded.

'If you like to put it that way, sir, yes. They tend to walk the streets by themselves, or occasionally as a couple but, because of the nature of their work, they will inevitably at some point find themselves alone with a man in some secluded spot. And when they're engaged in the act itself, they're obviously at their most vulnerable because they're offering their unclothed bodies to a stranger. So as long as this man doesn't appear to be either deranged or murderous when he first approaches these women, they'll probably be quite happy to go off with him, with the tragic consequences that we've already seen.'

Warren sat in thought for a few moments before he replied.

'What you say does make sense, Abberline. I can see how the killer is able to lure these women to quiet spots where he can carry out his ghastly crimes, and why they would be prepared to accompany him. But do you think he's working to some kind of plan, or is he just wandering the streets in a random fashion, looking for a suitable victim?'

Abberline paused for a moment before he replied, wondering if he should even suggest the idea that he and Chandler had come up with to the commissioner. Then he shrugged and decided he would: what had he got to lose?

'I don't think these attacks are random, sir. As I said before, I think this killer is an intelligent man, and I'm sure he's got some very specific reason for doing this. It's almost as if he's trying to send a message to somebody.'

Abberline's conclusion, suggested so casually, almost as an afterthought, was so inspired and accurate – the idea that the killings were virtually incidental to the murderer's real intention – that it took Warren's breath away, and he struggled for a few moments to recover his composure.

'Are you feeling all right, sir?' Abberline asked.

Warren nodded.

'Of course I am. Why do you ask?'

'You just look a little pale, sir, that's all.'

'I'm fine. Can you justify that statement? What message – as you put it – can this man possibly be trying to send? And to whom?'

'I have no idea. I'm just trying to explain things the way I see them.'

'Well, don't,' Warren snapped. 'I'm only interested in the facts of this case, not in your interpretation of them. So unless I'm very much mistaken, you have no clues to go on. You have no eyewitnesses to any of the killings, no sightings of the killer arriving at or leaving the scenes, apart from this Long woman, who saw the back view of a man talking to the last victim – a man who might not necessarily have been the person who killed Chapman. In short, you still have no idea at all who the murderer of Chapman might be, only that he is possibly or probably the same man who slaughtered Tabram over a month ago and then Nichols three weeks after that.'

Abberline nodded. He couldn't dispute anything Warren had just said because it was entirely accurate. The reality was that they still had absolutely no idea of the identity of the killer, and no obvious way of finding out.

Warren was silent for a few moments, trying to decide what to say and how to say it. Then he nodded and looked up at Abberline.

'I have a feeling,' he said, 'that this man hasn't finished in Whitechapel just yet. I think that there'll be at least one more murder.'

Abberline looked surprised. Having chastised him just minutes earlier for discussing his personal feelings and suppositions about the murders, it seemed a little unfair that the commissioner was now doing precisely the same thing. But he supposed that different rules applied when you were actually running the Metropolitan Police force, rather than simply being employed as a detective inspector within that force. On the other hand, what Warren had just said matched his own views on the subject.

'I think we need to be seen to be taking the initiative in this matter,' Warren said. 'I will make sure that there's an increased police presence in Whitechapel in the hours of darkness until further notice. And later on, I might order extra officers to cover specific parts of the East End of London.'

'Which areas, sir?' Abberline asked, clearly puzzled. 'Do you mean you have some idea where he might strike next?'

'Of course not,' Warren snapped. 'I was just thinking that, if we made certain areas too dangerous for him to operate in, because of the sheer number of officers on patrol, we might be able to drive him to a part of the city where people would be more likely to see and apprehend him.'

To Abberline, that sounded a weak argument at best. In view of the high population density throughout the East End, he doubted if Warren's plan would achieve anything at all, because there were just too many people there. How could anybody spot a potential murderer in the crowded streets, even if the police officers operated after midnight, when the crowds thinned dramatically? And the initiative clearly lay with the killer. He could decide when, where and how to approach his next victim, and as far as Abberline could see, there was nothing they could do about that.

Even if they drafted in dozens of extra officers, all the killer had to do was move to an area where there were fewer police. Or he could simply wait until the extra officers were withdrawn: clearly, a massive police presence on the streets of

Whitechapel could only be sustained for a fairly short time, if only for reasons of cost.

'We'll do nothing for the moment,' Warren said, 'apart from starting the extra patrols in Whitechapel and Spitalfields, and obviously you'll be following up on any clues that do come to light. But be prepared to act quickly if I do decide to mount an operation in certain areas.'

Abberline nodded, still puzzled by what Warren had said.

'Anything else?' the commissioner asked.

For a moment, Abberline hesitated, wondering whether he should tell his superior about his plan to have male constables wearing female clothes walking about the streets in Whitechapel in the early hours of the morning, and then decided that that probably wasn't a very good idea. He couldn't see Warren agreeing with it, and in any case Abberline had only the faintest hope that it might produce any results. He'd keep that part of his strategy secret for the moment.

'No, sir,' Abberline murmured, and then took his leave.

After the detective inspector had left, Warren locked his office door, opened the document case he had brought with him from his home, and took out the notes he'd been sent by 'Michael' and the map of Whitechapel which he had been working on. The more he had studied the documents, the more convinced he had become that he knew what the man intended to do next. What he didn't know was when or exactly where the next murder would take place.

He also had no idea of the personal circumstances of the adversary he was facing. He didn't know if 'Michael' was prepared for a prolonged campaign of murder in London, or if he was intending to escalate the timescale in an attempt to force Warren to hand over the menorah. But the dates of the first two killings had been on the seventh and then on the 31st of August, a gap of twenty-four days, which suggested that 'Michael' was in no particular hurry.

On the other hand, it was of course possible that he had delayed carrying out the second and third attacks simply because Warren had left London for his annual leave. In fact, the more he thought about it, the more that seemed to him to be the most likely explanation. And perhaps he had then decided to resume his campaign to provide maximum embarrassment for the commissioner immediately after his return.

Or the reason might be much simpler. Maybe he hadn't been able to find a suitable victim in the right place at the right time, but that was probably the least likely explanation of all, in view of the number of prostitutes who wandered the streets of Whitechapel and Spitalfields every night.

The fact that it had taken him over three weeks to carry out the killings of Martha Tabram and Mary Ann Nichols, but only a further eight days to add Annie Chapman to his list of victims meant that Warren really had no idea when the next murder might take place.

And, as far as he could see, there was nothing that he could do to prevent the next killing from occurring. He would just have to wait until 'Michael' struck again, and then try to identify the most likely location for the next murder. And afterwards he would deploy all the additional police officers he could spare to cover that area for as long as it took. Then, perhaps, his men might get lucky and catch 'Michael' in the act.

It wasn't much of a plan, but it was all he had.

Chapter 30

Wednesday, 19 September 1888
Whitechapel, London

The reticence, or wish to avoid sensationalism, on the part of Dr
Phillips at the inquest into the death of Annie Chapman could
not be allowed to endure. For perfectly obvious reasons, the
police – at the very least – needed to know exactly what the
killer had done to the body. They knew that several of her
organs were missing, because that information was already
common knowledge, but clearly they needed the details of the
mutilation. And so, five days later, on 19 September 1888,
Phillips was recalled by the coroner. He was told he had to provide all the further evidence in his possession about the
post-mortem mutilations, evidence which he had omitted to
deliver on the first day of the inquest.

But before he began speaking, Phillips consulted the coroner,
Wynne Baxter, and together they decided that the court should
be cleared of women and children, because of the evidence he
was about to give. And after the press had heard all the details
of the mutilations, they would voluntarily decide to omit that
portion of the evidence from their reports on the inquest, deem-
ing it unfit for publication.

Phillips took the stand and, in a clear and dispassionate tone of voice, he described what else had been done to Chapman's body by the killer.

'After the victim's abdomen had been cut open,' he stated, 'her intestines were partially removed from the abdominal cavity and positioned by the killer on her shoulder. Then her uterus, most of her bladder, and the upper section of her vagina were entirely removed from the body.'

'Before you describe these mutilations any further, Dr Phillips,' Wynne Baxter interrupted, 'can you please give us your professional opinion as to the degree of medical knowledge evidenced by the murderer. Were these organs removed with care by somebody who knew exactly what they were doing, or did the killer just rip open the woman's abdomen and cut out her internal organs at random?'

The doctor paused for a few moments before he replied.

'Before I give my opinion on that specific question, sir, I would like to emphasize the circumstances in which these mutilations must have taken place. The killer would have been working in almost complete darkness, and performing his actions by feel alone on a fresh and fully dressed corpse, and had quite obviously been in danger of discovery at any moment. He would therefore have been working as fast as possible, and it is probable that these mutilations must have taken him no more than a few minutes to perform.

'Because of all these factors, it is my considered opinion, as I said previously, that the perpetrator must have possessed considerable anatomical knowledge because none of the adjacent structures had been damaged during this dissection and the removal of these organs. No trace of these parts could be found, and the incisions were cleanly cut, avoiding the rectum, and dividing the vagina low enough to avoid injury to the cervix uteri. Obviously this was the work of an expert – of one, at least, who had such knowledge of anatomical pathological examinations as to be enabled to secure the pelvic organs with one sweep of a knife.'

This statement induced an immediate buzz of excited conversation in the public gallery of the coroner's court, and the newspaper reporters present immediately began taking copious notes.

When the murmuring had died down, the next question to be asked by the coroner was entirely predictable, and the answer perhaps even more sensational than what had gone before.

'Are you suggesting, Dr Phillips, that the perpetrator of this hideous crime was a doctor?'

'That, sir, I cannot say,' Phillips replied. 'But whoever it was, he clearly possessed both extensive anatomical knowledge and considerable surgical skill. I myself could not have performed all the injuries I saw on the woman, and effect them, even without a struggle, in under a quarter of an hour. If I'd done it in a deliberate way, such as would fall to the duties of the surgeon, it would probably have taken me the best part of an hour. The whole inference seems to me that the operation was performed to enable the perpetrator to obtain possession of these parts of the body.'

This apparent confirmation that the Whitechapel murderer was very probably a doctor, confirmation supplied by no less a personage than Dr George Bagster Phillips, the divisional police surgeon and a very experienced medical man, caused an immediate uproar in the court, which the coroner took some minutes to silence.

These statements made by Phillips immediately served to

confirm some of the rumours which had already been circulating around Whitechapel. The killer was probably a doctor, and he had now begun taking souvenirs – body parts – from the ravaged corpses of his victims.

'Finally, doctor, could you provide any information about the weapon used in the attack?'

'It is difficult to be specific,' Phillips replied, 'because all I have to assist me in answering this question are the cut marks left on the corpse. But in my opinion, the instrument used was probably similar to the knives employed by surgeons in post-mortem examinations. This would be the correct weapon for the killer's purposes, possessing a long and sharp blade which is also very rigid. Two other possibilities are a slaughterman's knife, which serves much the same function as a post-mortem knife, or possibly the kind of knife used by the porters at Billingsgate and other markets to clean fish.'

The additional information now having been obtained by the coroner, the inquest was formally closed.

'A word with you, Dr Phillips, if I may.'

Phillips turned to look at the questioner as he walked out of the building and recognized him immediately.

'Detective Inspector Abberline, isn't it?' he asked.

'Yes. It's just a small matter I wanted to raise with you, but there's a minor discrepancy between your estimated time of the death of the last victim, Annie Chapman, and the evidence of some of the other witnesses.'

Phillips looked slightly put out by the suggestion that any part of his evidence should be questioned, no matter how obliquely.

'Which witnesses?' he demanded.

'One woman actually saw a person she later identified as the victim talking to a man in the street at half past five in the morning, one hour after your estimated time of death of 4.30. A neighbour heard noises coming from the area where the body was later found a few minutes after that, and the son of the woman who rents the house actually sat down in the yard, almost exactly where the body was found, at about a quarter to five. So my question to you, Dr Phillips, is this: could you have been mistaken in your estimate? Could the body have cooled down more rapidly than normal in the open air, especially in view of the dreadful mutilations which had laid open her abdomen?'

Phillips muttered something inaudible under his breath, then nodded slowly.

'I have to confess,' he began, 'that I was unaware of any of these witness statements. After I'd given my evidence at the first inquest, I left the building. If what you say is accurate, and if these three witnesses are being truthful, then it is very clear that my estimate should not be relied on. When I examined the body I tried to take into account all the factors that you mentioned, but it is certainly possible that the body might have cooled faster than I had expected.'

Abberline nodded.

'Thank you, doctor. That was all I wanted to ask you.'

'Was any of my testimony today of any help to you, Inspector?'

'At this precise moment, Dr Phillips, all information is valuable. The problem is that no matter what information I seem to collect, and we have now amassed a very considerable amount, none of it seems to even suggest who the murderer might be. Good day to you, sir.'

*

Jurisdiction over Hanbury Street was the responsibility of H Division – the Whitechapel Division – of the Metropolitan Police, where the Criminal Investigation Department was headed by Inspector Edmund Reid. He was the officer who had conducted the investigation into the murder of Martha Tabram, but he had left London temporarily and was on his annual leave. So responsibility for that continuing enquiry, and for that of the murder of Annie Chapman, now fell upon the shoulders of Inspector Chandler, and Detective Sergeants Leach and Thick.

Accordingly, Acting Superintendent West requested that Detective Inspector Abberline be formally deputed to head the Tabram and Chapman murders, as he was already leading the investigation into the killing of Mary Ann Nichols. In his official request, West stated exactly why he had specifically asked for Abberline's assistance:

'I believe he is already engaged in the case of the Buck's Row murder which would appear to have been committed by the same person as the one in Hanbury Street.'

In fact, Abberline had been instructed that very morning to take an active part in the Chapman murder investigation, an instruction which simply confirmed what he was already doing, along with the other two Metropolitan Police detective inspectors who had been seconded to the Bethnal Green station, Andrews and Moore.

Chapter 31

Wednesday, 19 September 1888
London

It was with this gruesome new evidence to hand, and with another matter which he wanted to discuss, that Inspector Abberline sought a further appointment with the commissioner, a request which Warren granted with a certain amount of reluctance.

Warren had been singled out by the press and frequently vilified in the newspapers for his force's failure to make any progress in identifying the killer, and he had proved himself to be an extremely accommodating target of such attacks, being aloof and autocratic. He also consistently displayed a complete and seemingly wilful lack of understanding of the situation in Whitechapel, and especially of the realities of daily life in that most depressed and desperate of London districts.

Warren had been appointed Commissioner in 1886, and almost from the first had begun to alienate the people of London. His force had arrested an entirely innocent woman for soliciting during the 1887 Jubilee Day Festivities, and his attitude to the mistake was entirely unsympathetic and completely unapologetic. And after the 'Bloody Sunday' fiasco in November of the same year, almost every English newspaper, from the radical end of the spectrum represented by publications like the *Star* and the *Echo*, all the way to the conservative papers such as the *Daily Telegraph*, began attacking Warren and his methods. And as if that wasn't enough, Warren also had frequent arguments and disputes with the Home Secretary, Henry Matthews, the Police Receiver, Richard Pennefather, and the head of the Criminal Investigation Department, James Monro. In fact, there were remarkably few people employed by the Metropolitan Police with whom he had anything that even approached a satisfactory working relationship.

One journal, the *Pall Mall Budget*, even went so far as to print a satirical letter purporting to have been penned by Warren:

Notice to Murderers: The following is a proclamation which, it is said, will in the future largely diminish the number of undetected murders: I, Charles Warren, hereby give notice that from and after this date, all the loyal subjects are required, with the view of aiding the police in the discovery of crime, to leave on the body of any person they may have murdered their engraved or printed address card, or failing this, a paper with full name and address legibly written. Constables will be in attendance night and day at all police stations to receive murderers desiring to give themselves up. A list of the stations may be had on application. Scotland Yard, September 1888.

He was also noticeably reluctant to even listen to any new ideas or suggestions for methods to help catch the killer, and it was that characteristic which Abberline found most difficult to deal

with. In his opinion, the type of killings was new, the murderer
was operating in a fashion which had never been seen before,
and to combat this situation the Metropolitan Police needed to
be innovative in its approach to the crimes. That was what
Warren seemed completely unable to grasp.

Inspector Abberline knocked on the commissioner's door,
then opened it and walked into the office. He knew how important smartness and discipline were to the man sitting behind the
desk in front of him, and he made a conscious effort to march,
rather than walk, across the office. Once he reached the desk he
stopped. There were two chairs positioned there, one on either
side of where he was standing, and he hoped that this time
Warren would ask him to sit down in one of them, because his
feet were already aching from the distance he'd walked that
morning.

'Sit down, Abberline,' Warren instructed, and the detective
inspector sank gratefully into the chair on his right.

Warren was studying a handwritten report, which suggested
it was a new case, as he normally preferred his paperwork to be
typed.

'I'm busy, Abberline,' he said finally. 'So what is it?'

'I thought you ought to know, sir, that we've finally managed
to find out from Dr Phillips exactly what else the murderer did
to Chapman's body after he'd killed her. Phillips and the coroner insisted on the court being cleared of women and children
before the doctor would speak out. And it was pretty gruesome
stuff.'

Warren nodded for him to continue.

Abberline described the mutilations in some detail, including
the positioning of the woman's intestines on her shoulder and
the removal of some of her organs.

'What particularly concerns me about this,' Abberline finished, 'apart from the fact that we still have no idea who the killer is, is that we're now dealing with four unsolved murders, if you include the killing of Emma Smith, and the mutilations are escalating in their violence and ferocity. Martha Tabram was simply stabbed – stabbed many times, that's true, but there was no mutilation as such. But Mary Ann Nichols was cut about quite badly, and Annie Chapman was simply butchered: there's no other word for it.'

'Get to the point.'

'The point is that I believe we're dealing with a very intelligent man who is also extremely cunning and clever, but one who's probably insane, or at least whose mental state is likely to be deteriorating. There will be more killings, of that I'm certain, and I've no doubt that the butchery will get even more grotesque. But I also think that the murderer is working to some kind of a timetable, almost, that he's following a predetermined plan. And he knows exactly what he's doing and where and when he'll carry out his next attack.'

Warren shook his head.

'We know all that, Abberline,' he snapped. 'We discussed it before, if you remember.'

'I thought you needed to know the details,' the inspector replied, 'but there's another matter which is troubling me. Rightly or wrongly, the perception on the streets of Whitechapel is that the police either don't care about catching this murderer, or that they're simply unable to do so.'

'That's a wholly unreasonable attitude,' Warren said. 'I want nothing more than to see this man dancing on the end of a rope.'

'I know, sir, but I'm just telling you what the people are

saying. And not just what they're saying: it's also what they're doing. After the last killing, another group of tradesmen in Whitechapel decided to set up their own vigilance committee under a man named George Lusk, and they intend to ask the Home Secretary to issue a reward for information that could lead to the arrest of the murderer.'

'Matthews will never agree to that,' Warren said.

'Perhaps not, but Lusk told me that if he didn't, then the committee would offer its own reward, and the Jewish community has already done the same. I've even heard that some of the officers from H Division in Whitechapel are raising money towards the same end.'

Warren sat in silence for a moment, considering the information Abberline had given him.

'Offering a reward is probably not a bad idea,' he conceded eventually, 'despite what the Home Secretary will almost certainly say, and I suppose that having even more groups of people out on the streets of Whitechapel searching for this man might well help us catch him.'

'I can't agree with you about that, sir,' Abberline replied. 'We've already had cases where entirely innocent men have been followed, sometimes chased and even on a few occasions physically attacked by mobs who believed they had found the killer. I really do not wish to see groups of vigilantes roaming the streets of London. That will undermine the work of the police, reduce public confidence in our efforts to catch this man, and could lead to assaults on innocent members of the public, and maybe even worse.'

'I'm not interested in your opinion, Abberline. You've already told me that you have absolutely no idea who this man is or why he's going around Whitechapel killing prostitutes, and as

far as I can see that situation isn't likely to change in the immediate future. If the local people want to organize groups to try
to protect their womenfolk, I don't have a problem with that. In
fact, I think it's a good idea. Tell your men to remember that
they are supposed to be finding this murderer, not obstructing
these vigilantes.'

'I still don't like this, sir.'

'I don't care what you like or don't like, Abberline. You will
follow my instructions. Is that clearly understood?'

Abberline nodded, obviously still unhappy with Warren's
decision, but knowing there was nothing he could do to change
the commissioner's mind. He'd just have to hope that no innocent men ended up lying dead on the pavements of Whitechapel
because of attacks by an uncontrolled mob of armed and angry
residents.

After Abberline had left, Warren stood up, walked over to
his office door and turned the key in the lock. Then he opened
one of the drawers of his desk and took out the map of
Whitechapel upon which he had plotted the locations of the
killings, and for several minutes just stared at it, hoping for
inspiration.

All he could be certain of was that, assuming 'Michael' made
good on his threat – and Warren had no reason to doubt the
man's resolve, because he knew exactly why he was doing it –
the next murder would probably be committed somewhere near
Commercial Road, and most likely somewhere to the south of
it.

He would have to take a chance, he decided, and begin concentrating the efforts of his officers in that area, and just hope
for the best. He looked again at the map, and made his decision.
He would order increased patrols and all the extra officers he

could spare to operate in the area bounded by Commercial Road to the north, the railway line to the south and between Leman Street and Cannon Street. Without any additional information, that was the best that he could do. And he would order the extra patrols to begin that very night.

Chapter 32

Friday, 28 September 1888
Whitechapel, London

Charles Warren would never know whether it was the increased numbers of police officers on the streets in the area he had selected, or for some other reason, but since the killing of Annie Chapman almost three weeks ago, no other murders had been reported in the Whitechapel area. He began to wonder if 'Michael' had met with an accident, had given up or had left the city, or if there was another explanation for the cessation of his murderous activities.

By the end of the month, both because of the lack of any further atrocities, and also the escalating cost, he'd had to scale back his extra patrols. The number of police officers on the beat returned to more normal levels, and were again concentrated in the areas where the earlier killings had taken place.

On the streets of Whitechapel, the tension began to ease as night succeeded night and the pale light of morning failed to reveal another mutilated corpse. The feeling in the area was that the killer was still out there, somewhere, and that his knife was still sharp, but for some reason he had stopped his campaign.

Life went on, and the 'unfortunates' continued to ply their trade in a slightly more optimistic, though still very cautious, frame of mind.

The story of the Whitechapel murderer began to fade from the front pages of the newspapers, though speculation about the killer's identity and motive continued to be the subject of articles and stories.

But all that was about to change.

On 27 September, a somewhat stained envelope was received at the Central News Agency in London, addressed to 'The Boss, Central News Office, London City', and postmarked the same day.

The writing on the envelope appeared to be the product of an educated hand: the capital letters were clear and precise, written in a copperplate script, and the lowercase letters were consistent in shape and size. The writer had even indented the left-hand edge of each line, and used a double indent for the word 'Office' when there was insufficient space to write the word on the same line after 'News'.

The letter inside was dated 25 September 1888 and, like the envelope, was addressed to 'Dear Boss'. It also appeared to have been written by an educated person, from the appearance of the handwriting, though the text itself contained a number of punctuation and grammatical errors. The full text of the letter read:

> 25 Sept: 1888
>
> Dear Boss,
>   I keep on hearing the police
> have caught me but they wont fix
> me just yet. I have laughed when

they look so clever and talk about
being on the <u>right</u> track. That joke
about Leather Apron gave me real
fits. I am down on whores and
I shant quit ripping them till I
do get buckled. Grand work the last
job was. I gave the lady no time to
squeal. How can they catch me now.
I love my work and want to start
again. You will soon hear of me
with my funny little games. I
saved some of the proper <u>red</u> stuff in
a ginger beer bottle over the last job
to write with but it went thick
like glue and I cant use it. Red
ink is fit enough I hope <u>ha. ha</u>.
The next job I do I shall clip
the ladys ears off and send to the
police officers just for jolly wouldn't
you. Keep this letter back till I
do a bit more work, then give
it out straight. My knife's so nice
and sharp I want to get to work
right away if I get a chance.
    Good luck.
               Yours truly
                Jack the Ripper
      Dont mind me giving the trade name

And below that, written vertically under the rest of the text, was
a short postscript:

wasnt good enough
to post this before
I got all the red
ink off my hands
curse it
No luck yet. They
say I'm a doctor
　　　now <u>ha ha</u>

Suddenly, the 'fiend of Whitechapel' had a name, and it was a name that fitted him and would endure.

This was not the first letter which had been received by either the police or the newspapers purporting to have been written by the Whitechapel murderer, and it was certainly not to be the last, but what marked this letter as being unusual, and what ensured that its contents would eventually receive the widest possible distribution, was the signature. The name 'Jack the Ripper' was so hideously appropriate as a description of the perpetrator of the murders which had been committed in the East End of London that it quickly caught on.

Soon everybody would be talking about 'Jack'.

What was obvious to everyone who saw the letter was that there was no guarantee whatsoever that it had been written by the murderer, and almost immediately a strong suspicion grew that it had actually been written by a journalist intent on reviving a good story that was seen to be flagging. People pointed out various inconsistencies in the text, the way that some sentences were perfectly correct grammatically, while others contained unusual forms of words, and the fact that the writer had obviously known enough grammar to correctly write 'knife's' and 'I'm', but had also used the incorrect contractions 'shant', 'dont' and so on. This could not, it was argued, be the work of a man who was only partially literate. More than anything else, the letter looked as if had been written by someone who was undeniably literate but who was trying to make the letter appear to have been written by such a person.

One aspect of the letter which did suggest it might have been sent by the murderer, by Jack himself, was the statement that he would 'clip the lady's ears off' his next victim. And if this action were to be performed on the subsequent killing – assuming, of course, that there would be another murder – it would go a long way towards proving the letter's authenticity. There was also the somewhat enigmatic statement about him doing 'a bit more work' in the near future, which was a clear statement of intent.

The newspaper editor who had received the letter hung on to it for a couple of days, and then forwarded it to the police. But in accordance with the stated wishes of the writer, for the recipient to 'keep this letter back till I do a bit more work', no statement or report was published in the press or elsewhere stating that the letter had been received, so the only people who knew about it were the police themselves and those people at the Central News Agency who had seen the document.

Inevitably, the letter ended up in front of Detective Inspector Abberline, and as soon as he received it, he showed it to the other senior detectives.

'That's a great name for the killer,' Chandler said. '"Jack the Ripper" says it all, really. It's exactly what he does.'

'I'm more interested,' Abberline murmured, 'in your views on the letter itself. Do you think that it really was sent by the murderer, whatever his chosen name is, or is it just another hoax?'

'I really don't know,' Chandler said frankly. 'If it *was* sent by the killer, I don't quite see why he's writing to the newspapers. And don't forget that we've had dozens of letters supposedly sent by the murderer, both at Scotland Yard and at the other London stations, and the newspapers have probably had hundreds by now. If you want my opinion, I think it's probably a hoax, and the only reason the Central News Office has sent it to us is because of the signature. My guess is that within a day or two we'll see headlines about this "Jack the Ripper" in all the papers. It's just too good a name for them not to use it.'

Chandler glanced back at the letter.

'And another thing,' he added. 'This doesn't look to me like it's been written by an uneducated hand. The most likely author of this, I reckon, is some bored newspaper reporter who's trying to drum up a bit more interest in a story that's nearly died.'

Abberline nodded.

'I think you're probably right, and I agree about the name. I'm sure the papers will pick up on it, but I don't suppose for a moment we'll hear any more of this. I think – I hope, anyway – that the murders have stopped. After all, it's now been nearly three weeks since the last one.'

But within a matter of hours after the police at Scotland Yard received the letter, the threat implied within it was to be executed. Not once this time, but twice, and in the same night.

Chapter 33

Friday, 28 September 1888
Whitechapel, London

Alexei Pedachenko had come to a decision, but before he implemented it, he decided to carry out one final test to confirm that the deception he had in mind was necessary. Although he had carried out no further attacks on prostitutes in Whitechapel since he'd killed Annie Chapman on 8 September, he was very aware that there were eyes everywhere. The police presence in the area was still heavy, and he'd read all about the rewards now on offer for information leading to the capture and conviction of the Whitechapel murderer, and about the efforts of the various vigilance committees and freelance patrols that were now operating in the district as well. And every time he walked the streets of Whitechapel late at night, he was very conscious of the watchful and suspicious eyes which followed his every move.

It was also obvious that Charles Warren had deciphered Pedachenko's simple clues and worked out the approximate area where the next killing would be likely to occur. The Russian had seen the extra uniformed police officers and the hard-faced men who he assumed were plain clothes detectives around Cannon Street. And although the numbers had been considerably less on the last couple of occasions he had scouted the district, there were still too many people out there for him to feel comfortable about what he was going to do.

Walking the streets as he had been doing would be too dangerous for the next event – or rather the double event – which he had planned. Some kind of a disguise was absolutely necessary, and he thought he knew what he was going to do, but first he would try one last experiment.

That evening, he dressed in his smartest clothes, placed a top hat on his head and checked his appearance in the mirror before he left his lodging to ensure that he looked as respectable and gentlemanly as possible. Then he ventured out into the dark streets of the late evening on the edge of Whitechapel.

He promenaded along streets and roads and alleys, looking for a single woman. He was not, on this occasion, intending to do her any harm. He was only interested in observing her reaction to his presence.

Just before midnight, he saw a person who he thought would be suitable. A woman, probably in her mid thirties, carefully but poorly dressed, walking along a street directly towards him.

He glanced around quickly, but there was nobody else in sight.

As he approached her, he could see that she was sizing him up, and already appeared nervous. Then he stepped in front of her and blocked her path completely, raising his top hat in salute.

'Good evening,' he said, an innocent enough greeting, but the effect on the woman was dramatic.

She shrank back visibly from him, her head swivelling in all directions as she looked about her vainly for help.

'Please, sir,' she muttered, 'please don't hurt me, sir. Please, sir. Please just let me pass.'

Pedachenko smiled at her and nodded.

'You're out very late, I must say,' he said. 'Why is that, may I ask?'

'I'm a respectable woman, sir, and my husband is in the hospital. I've just been to visit him, and now I must get back home to my children.'

She could even have been telling the truth, but there was no mistaking the tremor of fear in her voice and the terror on her face. That alone was the confirmation that he sought.

'I mean you no harm,' he said. 'My only concern in stopping you was to give you some advice. This has become a very dangerous area for a woman alone. I understand your position, but I would suggest that you visit your husband during the hours of daylight, because walking by yourself at night might give some people the wrong idea about why you are here.'

He reached into his jacket pocket and pulled out a piece of paper which he held out to her.

'Here,' he said, 'take this for your trouble, and as recompense because I know that I frightened you. And for your part, although you will not know how, you have helped me as well.'

Her hand trembling visibly, the woman reached out and took the folded piece of paper from Pedachenko, who doffed his hat to her once again, and then walked on.

Behind him, the woman stared at his retreating figure, then unfolded the paper and looked at it. It was something that she had heard about, but had never seen before, and had certainly never expected to hold in her hands or to own.

The piece of paper was a Bank of England five pound note.

Chapter 34

Elizabeth Stride, sometimes known as Long Liz, was Swedish. She'd been born on 27 November 1843 in a town named Torslanda, not far from Gothenburg, and christened Elisabeth Gustafsdotter. In October 1860, she moved to the Carl Johan parish in Gothenburg and began working there as a domestic servant for a man named Lars Fredrik Olofsson, but had moved on to the Cathedral parish in February 1862, and was still working there as a domestic. Then things began to go wrong for her, because three years later the Gothenburg police registered her as a prostitute, and the following month she gave birth to a stillborn baby girl. Later that year, in October, she was living in Östra Haga, just outside Gothenburg, and was twice treated in a special hospital for venereal disease, an almost inevitable consequence of her degraded lifestyle.

She arrived in London in February 1866, either simply to visit the country, or as a domestic servant – at different times she had told both versions of the story – and registered as an unmarried woman at the Swedish parish in London, and later at the Swedish Church in Prince's Square, St George-in-the-East. In

1869 she married a carpenter named John Thomas Stride at that same church. She was then living in Whitechapel at 67 Gower Street, and Stride's home was at Munster Street, near Regent's Park.

Very little is known about her marriage, except that it failed, and her situation deteriorated further, being admitted to the Poplar Workhouse in March 1877. That same year, she was treated in the Whitechapel Workhouse Infirmary for bronchitis, and when she was discharged she was sent from there into the workhouse itself. Afterwards, she lived for most of the time at the lodging house at 32 Flower and Dean Street. Her husband, John Stride, died on 24 October 1884 in the Poplar and Stepney Sick Asylum at Bromley.

From 1885 to 1888 she lived with a dock labourer named Michael Kidney, for some of that time at 35 Devonshire Street, off Commercial Road, but by the end of September she had moved back to the lodging house at 32 Flower and Dean Street, the address she had used intermittently for about six years.

She was attractive for a woman in her mid forties, and most people who knew her thought she looked a lot younger, some even believing that she was in her late twenties. She was thin and stood only about five feet three inches tall, so 'Long Liz' was probably a reference to the shape of her face, which was long and thin, the features somewhat sharp and pinched, at least partially caused by her various missing teeth. Her hair was curly, and dark brown, almost black, and her eyes light grey.

According to both her neighbours and the deputy at the Flower and Dean Street lodging house, a woman named Elizabeth Tanner, Stride was a clean, sober, quiet, hard-working and good-natured woman who earned a living as a charwoman, doing cleaning and other domestic duties. She was also a skilled seamstress, often working for the Jewish tailors in the area: she spoke Yiddish as well as her native Swedish, and was fluent in English, which she spoke without an accent.

But perhaps the people who talked about Elizabeth Stride were being either polite or generous in describing her as 'sober', because it was common knowledge that she had a serious drink problem. She had been arrested on several occasions for being drunk, and had made frequent appearances at the Thames Magistrates' Court on charges relating to her drinking. She was also known to sometimes use the alias 'Annie Fitzgerald' when arrested, perhaps in an attempt to preserve what was left of her reputation.

It seems likely that in Whitechapel 'Long Liz' worked only occasionally as a prostitute, presumably when she was short of funds and when other employment, such as charring or needle-work, was unavailable for one reason or another. The watchman at her lodging house told a reporter that 'when she could get no work she had to do the best she could for her living', the implication of which statement is reasonably clear.

Her relationship with Michael Kidney was somewhat stormy and sometimes violent, as both parties habitually sought recourse to alcohol, and separated quite frequently. In April of the previous year, Stride had even charged Kidney with assault, but had then failed to appear at the court to prosecute the charge. The final breakup occurred in the last week of September when Stride again returned to the doss house in Flower and Dean Street, telling friends there that she and Kidney had quarrelled again.

On Saturday 29 September, Stride worked for a few hours at the doss house, cleaning two of the rooms, and earned the sum of sixpence for her efforts. But instead of immediately paying for her bed that night with this money, she left the building and went with the deputy, Mrs Tanner, to the Queen's Head public house, located on the corner of Commercial Street and Fashion Street, which was one of her usual haunts, to enjoy a drink together.

They returned together to the lodging house at about 6.30 that evening, and then separated, Stride heading for the kitchen while the deputy went elsewhere in the building. At about seven, a barber named Charles Preston, another lodger at the premises, saw her in the kitchen, dressed ready to go out, and the doss-house charwoman, Catherine Lane, confirmed this.

She stated that Stride had given her a piece of green velvet material to safeguard for her until she returned, and at that time Stride was certainly in funds, because she showed Lane the sixpence which she'd been paid by the deputy for cleaning. At that time she still had not paid for her accommodation for the night, but it was quite common for lodgers to only hand over the money immediately before they went to bed, often in the very early hours of the morning.

Exactly where she went after leaving the lodging house is unknown, but the probability is that Stride spent some or all of the money that she possessed on drink, because during the rest of the evening, several different people claimed to have seen her in the area at various times, always in the company of a man, or more accurately of men. These were presumably clients she was servicing to raise the funds which she then needed to pay for further drink and her night's lodging.

At about eleven that evening, she was seen by two men in another pub, the Bricklayers Arms in Settles Street, in the company of a man, presumably another client. Three-quarters of an hour later, she was seen with a different client in Lower Berner

Street, and at about half past midnight a police constable saw her in the same area with a male who did not match the descriptions of either of the men previously seen in her company.

Fifteen minutes after that, Stride was seen standing by a gateway in Berner Street when another man approached her. A brief altercation occurred, and the man tripped her up and threw her down onto the pavement before running away.

It had been, by any standards, an eventful evening for Elizabeth Stride. She had serviced a number of clients, had drunk far too much alcohol, and then been attacked by a potential customer. But she had no option but to stay out a little longer because she still needed more money.

So at about ten minutes before one on that Sunday morning, she had taken up a new position near the International Working Men's Educational Club at 40 Berner Street. This was a socialist organization mainly patronized by Russian and Polish Jews, and which published the Yiddish journal *Der Arbeter Fraint*, 'The Worker's Friend'. She'd only been there for a few minutes when she saw an unwelcome figure approaching her.

Another woman, another 'unfortunate', was strolling along the pavement directly towards her and that, Stride decided, simply wouldn't do. She still needed a few more coppers for the night, because she hadn't just been lifting her skirt for strangers. She'd also been interspersing her work with drinking sessions in nearby pubs, and a lot of the money she'd earned had already been spent. So the last thing she wanted was any competition for the last few remaining men – and potential clients – on the streets.

As the woman approached, Stride stepped forward to confront her.

'Oi, you,' she said, 'don't you stop anywhere along here. This is my patch, so you can just piss off out of it. Find somewhere else to sell yourself.'

The woman looked at her, but didn't reply, just continued her steady progress along the pavement.

Stride stared at her, wondering who she was, because she didn't think she'd seen her before, and she knew many of the other 'unfortunates' in the area by sight if not by name.

'You're new here, aren't you? But it doesn't matter. Just keep walking down the street and there won't be a problem.'

But the woman didn't seem to have any intention of walking past. She had altered course very slightly and was heading directly towards where Stride was standing.

'I ain't kidding, you know. Mess about with me, and you'll be sorry.'

The woman smiled in the gloom, and as she did so Stride realized there was something unusual about her, though she couldn't put her finger on exactly what it was.

And then things happened very quickly.

The approaching woman reached out her hand towards Elizabeth Stride's shoulder, as if to reassure her. But the instant her fingers closed around the multi-coloured striped silk handkerchief Stride was wearing around her neck, the woman's grip tightened suddenly and dramatically.

In moments, Stride found herself fighting for breath, and for her life, her hands grabbing ineffectually for the handkerchief which was pulled tight around her throat. Her attacker was dragging her backwards through the gates which adjoined the Jewish club and into the dark open space – Dutfield's Yard – which lay beyond. Stride tried desperately to scream, but the pressure of her own handkerchief around her neck was choking her and preventing her from making a sound.

In her last moments of consciousness, Elizabeth Stride belatedly realized exactly what had seemed unusual about the woman who had approached her on the street. It was the fact that the 'woman' was actually a man.

Pedachenko maintained the pressure around the neck of his victim, even after she had passed out, this time making absolutely sure that she was dead before he pulled the knife out of its sheath.

He was desperately trying to avoid getting any blood on his new disguise, because he only had a couple of female outfits that he could use. He'd found the dresses and other garments in various pawn shops outside Whitechapel, never buying more than one item each time, but his problem had been finding clothes that fit him, because he was both bigger than, and a different shape to, most women.

When he was certain that the woman was dead, he swiftly cut her throat, the trademark wound which he had decided to inflict on each victim following the killing of Martha Tabram. Then he wiped the blade on her dress and replaced the weapon in its sheath. This one he wasn't going to mutilate, because that night, for the first time, he was going looking for a second victim, and with her he intended to take his time.

This first corpse, he was sure, would be found quite quickly, because there was clearly some kind of an event taking place in the club next door. That would obviously concentrate all the police resources on that one spot and provide him with an ideal opportunity to carry out the second killing without being disturbed.

And there was another reason for carrying out the two killings on the same night. Charles Warren, Pedachenko knew, was not a stupid man, and would certainly have been very well aware of the geometric shapes which were being formed by the positions of the corpses. As the second triangle would represent the square of the Masonic symbol, the location of the third murder, the apex of the triangle, would be very easy to predict.

If Pedachenko did not complete that triangle that very night, he guessed that Warren would flood the western part of Whitechapel with police officers and keep them there for the foreseeable future. And that would severely hamper the Russian's plans. So it had to be done tonight.

Moments later, Pedachenko strode out of the yard and back into Berner Street. He deliberately took small steps, so as to appear more female, as he walked north towards Commercial Road, where he turned left, heading back towards the centre of Whitechapel. He had already decided that he would find his second victim of the night somewhere near Fenchurch Street, due west of Berner Street, and that would complete the shape of the second triangle.

With that geometrical shape completed, and if Charles Warren still hadn't capitulated and handed over the menorah, it would be time to move on to the second part of his campaign, to implicate the Jews and suggest that all the killings had been performed by a member of that community.

And Pedachenko had a very good idea about how he could start that particular story circulating in the area.

Chapter 35

Sunday, 30 September 1888
Whitechapel, London

At about one o'clock in the morning a hawker of jewellery named Louis Diemschutz arrived at Dutfield's Yard with his pony and cart to unload his unsold wares before taking the animal to its stable in George Yard, off Cable Street. As he passed through the double wooden gates, which were only rarely closed because the yard was in almost constant use, Diemschutz stated that his pony shied towards the left, away from some object on the ground.

He stopped his cart, climbed down and attempted to find out what the obstruction was. It was too dark in the yard for him to see clearly, and so he struck a match. By its flickering light he saw enough to identify the figure of a woman, lying on the ground.

Diemschutz was a member of the Jewish club – in fact, he was the steward – and as soon as he'd calmed down his pony he went into the club where he met his wife in the dining room on the ground floor.

'Let me have a candle, will you?' he asked.

Somebody handed one to him, but before he returned to the yard outside, he explained the reason he needed it to the people in the room.

'There's a woman lying in the yard,' he said, 'but I cannot say whether she's drunk or dead.'

Diemschutz returned to the yard, accompanied by a young tailor machinist named Isaac Kozebrodski, and, with the better illumination afforded by the candle, the two men confirmed that what Diemschutz had seen was the dead body of a woman. His wife, who had followed him as far as the door, also saw the body and noticed blood all around it. She was of a nervous disposition, by Diemschutz's own account, and immediately emitted a sharp scream which alerted all the other members of the club that something had happened.

As soon as they were certain that the woman was dead, Diemschutz and Kozebrodski both ran out into the streets to try to find a policeman. They turned right out of the gates and then left into Fairclough Street, yelling out 'Police!' as loudly as they could. They ran as far as the T-junction with Grove Street and then turned back.

A man named Edward Spooner, a horse-keeper, was standing with a female companion outside the Beehive Tavern on the corner of Christian Street and Fairclough Street, and stopped the two men as they ran back past him.

'What's going on?' he asked.

'There's another woman been murdered,' Diemschutz replied. 'In a yard in Berner Street.'

Spooner left his companion and ran down the street with the other two men to Dutfield's Yard. When they arrived there, they found that a small crowd of people had gathered around the body. Edward Spooner stepped forward and lifted the chin of the dead woman, and for the first time they could all see the gaping wound in her throat.

In the meantime, another club member named Morris Eagle had also heard the shouts of alarm and commotion in the yard, and as soon as he had ascertained the cause he left the premises with a companion in search of a police officer. But where Diemschutz and Kozebrodski had turned south out of the yard, he went north, towards the much busier Commercial Road, and there he found PC 252H Henry Lamb and another constable.

'Come on. There has been another murder!' Eagle called out.

'Where?' Lamb replied.

'Berner Street.'

The two police officers returned to the scene with him. After they'd inspected the body, the other constable left immediately to summon a doctor.

Constable Lamb took charge of the scene, but he obviously needed further assistance, and as quickly as possible.

'Mr Eagle,' he asked. 'There is no one else I can ask to do this, so could you please run to the Leman Street police station right away. Tell them what has happened here and ask them to send an inspector as quickly as they can.'

Eagle agreed, and left the yard immediately. The Leman Street station was only a few streets over to the west, and it didn't take him long to get there.

The alarm was quickly raised. A telegram was sent to the Commercial Street police station at 1.25 that morning, and Detective Inspector Edmund Reid, now back from his annual leave, immediately set out for Berner Street, arriving there at about 1.45, by which time Chief Inspector West, Inspector Pinhorn and a number of other officers from Leman Street were already present.

PC Lamb, who had remained on the scene, stated in his report that the deceased 'was lying on her left side, and her left arm was slightly under her body. The right arm was across her breast. She looked as if there was no struggle, and she'd been quietly laid down.'

The first doctor to arrive was Frederick William Blackwell, who lived at 100 Commercial Road, not far from the northern end of Berner Street, and he got there at 1.16 by his own watch, but his assistant Edward Johnston had already been accompanied by the police constable to the scene of the crime.

'The doctor will be here directly,' Johnston had told Constable Lamb, 'but if I may I will start to examine the body myself.'

Lamb immediately gave his permission and, while Johnston was carrying out his preliminary examination, the police officers had the gates to the yard closed, which meant that a crowd of almost thirty people was trapped inside, exactly as intended.

They were a mixed bunch, comprising the tenants of adjoining premises, members of the club itself, and several people who just happened to have been passing and had been attracted by the commotion in the area. As well as detaining the group of potential witnesses, Constable Lamb then went into the club to check all the rooms, looking for evidence of bloodstains, the murder weapon or any other clues, a task that would be repeated several times that day.

The police examined the hands and clothes of all the people who had ended up in Dutfield's Yard, searched their pockets for weapons, took statements from them and recorded their names and addresses. Nothing suspicious was found, and all the people questioned were allowed to return home or continue about their business. Later that morning, the yard was also examined by both the doctors and the police a number of times in a further search for the murder weapon or other clues, but without result.

When Dr Blackwell arrived, he confirmed the physical description of the victim supplied by Constable Lamb, and then carried out his own examination of the body.

'There's a very large incision on the victim's neck,' he stated, 'and there's a length of chequered material, probably a hand-kerchief or scarf or something of that sort, which has been pulled extremely tightly around her throat.'

'Can you tell us how long she's been dead?' one of the police officers asked.

'Not for very long,' Blackwell replied. 'I estimate that she was killed between about ten minutes and half an hour before I arrived here.'

Dr George Bagster Phillips, the divisional police surgeon, had been summoned to the Leman Street police station at about twenty past one that morning and sent on from there to Dut-field's Yard.

When he arrived, he also examined the body and made a note of the victim's injuries. He agreed with the approximate time of death which had already been proposed by Dr Blackwell.

One oddity noted by both doctors was that the dead woman had died clutching a package of aromatic sweets, intended to sweeten the breath and known as cachous, in her left hand. This suggested that her murder had been very rapid indeed.

'There's nothing else we can do here,' Phillips said, when he had completed his examination. 'As soon as the ambulance arrives, she can be transferred to the mortuary at St George's.'

The vehicle arrived at the scene within the hour, and the body of the victim, who was still unidentified, was delivered to the mortuary shortly after four in the morning. Sometime after half past five, following a brief visit to the scene by Charles Warren, Police Constable Albert Collins arrived with a mop and a bucket of water to wash away all the bloodstains from the yard, and then the last of the police officers left.

Inspector Reid had followed the ambulance to the mortuary and examined the body of the dead woman there, carefully recording his observations. He estimated that she was about forty-two years old, five feet two inches in height, with dark-brown curly hair and a pale complexion. Her eyes were light grey, and her upper front teeth were missing. She was wearing a long black jacket trimmed with black fur and decorated by a single red rose and a piece of maidenhair fern, an old black skirt, a dark-brown velvet bodice, two petticoats of light serge, white stockings and a white chemise, a black bonnet and a pair of elasticated boots.

As usual, there was nothing on her person to suggest her identity, and her only possessions appeared to be two handkerchiefs, a thimble and a length of wool on a piece of card. Details of this evidence, scanty and inconclusive though it was, was sent by telegraph to all London police stations in an attempt to hasten her identification.

But, inevitably, the murder of the woman who would later be identified as Elizabeth Stride was quickly overshadowed by other, and even more brutal, events elsewhere in the city.

Chapter 36

Catharine Eddowes had been born on 14 April 1842 in Graisley Green in Wolverhampton, the daughter of a tinplate worker named George and his wife Catharine, and was one of eleven children. In 1843 the family moved down to London, but the young Catharine later returned to Wolverhampton, where she obtained a job as a tinplate stamper. This didn't last too long, and when she lost her job after stealing from her employer, she began living with her uncle in Birmingham, but after a few years she met a former soldier named Thomas Conway in the city and lived there for a while before they moved south to London in 1881, to a house in Lower George Street, Chelsea.

Conway is something of a mystery, with doubts surrounding almost everything about him, including his name. He had apparently served in the 18th Royal Irish Regiment, in which he had enlisted under the name of Thomas Quinn, and which paid him an army pension after he'd left the service. He also worked as a hawker to earn additional income, and had tattooed his initials – TC – onto Eddowes's left forearm.

He never married Catharine, though she had three children

by him, two boys and a girl, but then her drinking habits became so disruptive that soon after they arrived in London she was forced to leave the family. According to her sister Elizabeth, Conway was almost as bad with regard to drinking, and frequently beat Catharine when he was drunk, though Catharine's eldest daughter, Annie, had a very different story to tell. She claimed that her father was actually a teetotaller and had left her mother only because of her persistent drunkenness.

But whatever the actual reason for their separation, Catharine left and within a year she had met a new partner at a common lodging house named Cooney's at 55 Flower and Dean Street, in Spitalfields. His name was John Kelly, while Eddowes went by the aliases of Mary Ann or Kate Kelly and Kate or Catharine Conway, after her two successive common-law husbands. Her official occupation was as a hawker of matchboxes and other small items on the street, but she was probably making far more money by resorting to casual prostitution. By this time her relationship with Thomas Conway had deteriorated to such an extent that he did his best to make sure that Eddowes didn't know where either he or their children were living.

She'd had a break from the crowded streets of Whitechapel in August and September 1888, having walked out to a village named Hunton, near Coxheath in Kent, where she, Kelly and a woman named Emily Burrell and her partner were employed picking hops. At this time, 'hopping' was extremely popular, and as many as 80,000 itinerant labourers, principally from London, would travel down to Kent for the season, which ran from August to September. When the two couples parted on the way back to London, Burrell gave Eddowes a pawn ticket for a flannel shirt, which she thought would fit Kelly.

On 27 September the two of them reached Whitechapel, but the money they'd earned from their work was soon spent. At Maidstone, Kelly had bought a pair of boots from a shop in the High Street, and Catharine Eddowes purchased a jacket, but when they arrived in London they had no money left at all, and were forced to spend the night in the Shoe Lane Workhouse, in the 'casual ward'.

The following day, Eddowes did some kind of a job that earned her sixpence, but they needed more than that to pay for a double bed at Cooney's Lodging House in Flower and Dean Street, so they split it between them, Kelly taking four pence to pay for a single bed at Cooney's while Eddowes went back to the Shoe Lane Workhouse, where she would have to perform some hard and repetitive manual work, and endure a sermon or two, in exchange for her bed and a plate of indifferent food.

On the morning of 29 September, she was thrown out of the workhouse for some infraction and immediately went round to Kelly's lodging. Because they had no money or food, they decided to pawn Kelly's boots, which raised the sum of two shillings and sixpence at a shop named Jones at 31 Church Street. Eddowes and the barefoot Kelly then bought tea and sugar and a little food, and they had a simple breakfast together in the kitchen at Cooney's.

They remained there at the lodging house until about two in the afternoon when Eddowes told Kelly she intended to walk to King Street in Bermondsey that afternoon to try to obtain money from her daughter, Mrs Annie Phillips. Annie had married a Southwark-based gunmaker and was comparatively well off. Kelly was concerned for her, precisely because of the recent murders, and begged her to be careful, and to come back early. Eddowes replied that she could take care of herself, but promised that she would be back by four in the afternoon. Kelly stayed at Cooney's for the rest of the day, and at about eight o'clock that evening he bought himself a bed and remained in the building for the rest of the night.

Catharine Eddowes didn't meet her daughter that afternoon, because the two women had parted on bad terms and Annie hadn't told her mother that she had moved from King Street the previous year and was then living in Dilston Grove, Southwark Park Road. But without any doubt Eddowes managed to obtain funds from somewhere, probably by prostitution, because at about half past eight that evening she was arrested by PC 931 Louis Robinson outside 29 Aldgate High Street for causing a disturbance, and was clearly drunk. Robinson sought assistance from Constable 959 George Simmons, and together they took her to Bishopsgate police station in Wormwood Street, where she gave her name as 'Nothing' on being charged. The station sergeant, a man named James Byfield, locked her in a cell so she could try to sober up.

By one in the morning she had recovered her senses sufficiently to be released from the cell, and was then allowed to leave the station. The releasing officer was PC 968 George Hutt, who had come on duty at 9.45 and who had checked on the prisoner frequently during the evening.

She was questioned again before she was allowed to leave, and this time she gave her name as Mary Ann Kelly, and her address as 6 Fashion Street, Spitalfields. As Eddowes left the station she asked Constable Hutt the time, to which he replied that it was too late for her to obtain any drink. When she walked out of the building, she said 'Good night, old cock' to Hutt, then turned left and began walking back towards Aldgate and

Houndsditch, though for her to return to her lodging she should have turned right.

It's possible that her earlier promise to John Kelly, a promise which she had comprehensively broken, was troubling her, because when Constable Hutt had spoken to her shortly before her release, and had told her that it was one o'clock in the morning, she had said: 'I shall get a damned fine hiding when I get home then.' That may have been the reason why she decided to remain out on the streets, or perhaps try to find some other place to stay rather than returning to the lodging house where she knew Kelly would be waiting for her, either awake or asleep.

Half an hour later she was seen loitering in Duke Street, near the entrance to Church Passage, with a man she probably hoped would provide her with the funds she needed to pay for a bed that night. Three Jewish businessmen – Harry Harris, Joseph Hyam Levy and Joseph Lawende – were just leaving the Imperial Club, located at 16–17 Duke's Place, and saw the two figures, but only Lawende, a cigarette dealer, took much notice of them and even he later declared he would not be able to recognize either of them again, though he did supply the police with a vague description of the man. Then the three businessmen separated to return to their own homes.

After only a couple of minutes' conversation Eddowes realized that her potential client was lacking either the money or the inclination – or possibly both – and turned away in irritation.

She walked down Church Passage and into an open space named Mitre Square. Almost as soon as she stepped out of the covered passageway she saw a figure walking slowly across the square from the direction of Mitre Street. Eddowes snorted in disgust, because it was a woman, and that meant she would probably have to sleep rough, in a doorway or some other sheltered spot, because apart from the man she'd just walked away from, the only other people she'd seen on the streets since she'd been released from custody had been policemen, and approaching one of them would just ensure her a quick trip to another cell somewhere.

As she walked along beside the buildings which lined the side of the square, the other woman turned and headed towards her, reaching her just as Eddowes paused beside a fence with a door which gave access to an adjacent yard, owned by a firm of general merchants named Heydemann and Company.

'Bloody quiet night, love,' she said to the stranger, immediately identifying her as another 'unfortunate', simply because of the way she was dressed and the fact that she was walking by herself in the backstreets of Whitechapel at that hour of the morning. 'No trade anywhere.'

The other woman nodded and moved closer, then stepped right beside her, never saying a word.

Catharine Eddowes turned slightly to face her, but by then was too late.

Pedachenko clamped the pad of cloth firmly over Eddowes's nose and mouth, instantly silencing her, and ignored the struggling woman's thrashing arms and legs. He knew from past experience that she would be still within about a minute.

It actually took a little longer than that, but just under two minutes after he had reached the side of the prostitute, she was lying flat on her back on the pavement, her clothes pulled and cut away from her body to expose her abdomen and groin, and Alexei Pedachenko was just beginning his bloody work.

But even after he'd finished with the unfortunate, Pedachenko had two more tasks to perform. First, he intended to up his game, to put even more pressure on Charles Warren, and to leave him and the people of Whitechapel an unequivocal message about what he intended to do next.

And then there was something else he had in mind which would serve to greatly increase the already heightened level of terror in the East End of London, a further refinement which followed on almost naturally from the extensive butchery which he had visited upon his latest victim. But he needed to make careful preparations first, and he also needed to decide exactly who should be the recipient.

But that, perhaps, was the easy part.

Chapter 37

Sunday, 30 September 1888
Whitechapel, London

Police Constable 881 Watkins of the London City Police had walked through Mitre Square at about half past one, a few minutes before Catharine Eddowes had stepped into it, and PC James Harvey walked up Church Passage from Duke Street at roughly 1.40 and looked into the square, but did not enter it as all appeared to be quiet there.

At about 1.45, PC Watkins again walked into the square as a part of his normal patrol route, approaching it from the Mitre Street entrance, and immediately saw a huddled shape on the pavement over to his right. He crossed to it and saw at once that it was the dead body of a woman. And not just dead. As Watkins later described the sight to one of the newspaper reporters, 'she was ripped up like a pig in the market. I have been in the force a long while, but I never saw such a sight.'

Watkins called out for help and ran across the square to attract the attention of George Morris, a watchman for the company of Kearley & Tonge, which owned the buildings located on the two opposite sides of the square.

'For God's sake, man, come out and assist me. Another

woman has been ripped apart,' he called out, when Morris opened the door to him.

'All right. Keep yourself cool while I light a lamp.'

Watkins led Morris over to the corner of the square, where he clearly saw the mutilated body of a woman.

As Morris explained later: 'I saw a woman lying stretched upon the pavement with her throat cut, and horribly mutilated. I then left the constable, Watkins, with the body while I went into Aldgate and blew my whistle, and the other officers soon made their appearance. The whole shape of the woman was marked with blood upon the pavement ... she was so mutilated about the face that I could not say what she was like.'

The two officers Morris summoned were Police Constables James Harvey and James Thomas Holland. As soon as he'd been told what had happened, Holland went immediately to 34 Jewry Street, Aldgate, and at 1.55 he summoned a local doctor named George William Sequeira, who pronounced life to be extinct virtually as soon as he saw the body.

Some ten minutes after Watkins had discovered the dead woman, Inspector Edward Collard, based at the Bishopsgate police station, was informed of the killing, and set the wheels in motion.

Police surgeon Dr Gordon Brown was instructed to go at once to the crime scene, and arrived at Mitre Square at approximately 2.18 in the morning. He also examined the body to confirm that the woman was dead – though this would have been blindingly obvious to even the most uneducated layman – and to assess the injuries which had been inflicted on the victim. Dr Brown made a pencil sketch of the corpse on the spot, and also noted that a section of the apron the woman had been wearing had been cut off and removed from the scene.

The normal procedure followed by the police was for all corpses to be removed from the streets as soon as possible after death had been pronounced, and accordingly the body was swiftly transported by a horse-drawn ambulance to the City Mortuary in Golden Lane.

There was one very important difference between the latest killing and the earlier murders, but it had nothing to do with either the killer or the victim, only with the location, because Mitre Square fell within the boundaries of the City of London. Then, as now, the City had its own police force, which was responsible to the governing corporation. The investigation into the killing in Mitre Square, and the search for the man responsible, was directed by Major Henry Smith, who was the Acting Commissioner, and entrusted to Inspector James McWilliam, the head of the City Detective Department.

McWilliam was woken in the early hours of the morning to be told that yet another murder had been committed in London, and this time within the City boundaries. He dressed and proceeded initially to 26 Old Jewry, the City Detective Office, arriving there at about 3.45. He remained there only long enough to telegraph what information he had about the killing to Scotland Yard and then left the building to go to Bishopsgate Street police station, and from there on to Mitre Square itself. When he arrived at the scene, Detective Superintendent Alfred Foster, Inspector Collard, Major Smith and several other members of the force were already present.

Although the City of London Police had not been involved in the Whitechapel murders up to that point, because they had all occurred outside their jurisdiction, the force had certainly not been unaware of what was happening in the capital, and had actually instituted additional patrols along the eastern areas of

Jack Steel

the City boundary. In fact, almost one third of the available officers had been instructed to don plain clothes and keep a close watch on any woman suspected of being a prostitute, and on any male and female couple seen in the area. And while the killing was taking place in Mitre Square, three City detectives had been patrolling the streets just a short distance away.

The first detectives to appear at the scene were these same three City officers. They were Detective Sergeant Robert Outram and Detective Constables Edward Marriott and Daniel Halse, and they were told about the killing a couple of minutes after two in the morning. All three went immediately to Mitre Square.

Once they had satisfied themselves that a murder had been committed, they split up and headed out in different directions in an immediate search for suspects, stopping and questioning anyone they met, but without tangible result. When Inspector McWilliam arrived at the scene, he reinforced the actions already being taken and also instituted searches of nearby lodging houses.

But the murderer appeared almost ghostlike, seemingly able to materialize seconds after a patrolling policeman had left the scene, find his victim and accomplish his ghastly task, and then vanish once again. The killing in Mitre Square demonstrated his seeming invisibility in a spectacular fashion, as quickly became very obvious when the initial statements were taken and analysed.

PC Watkins had walked through the square and found it deserted at approximately 1.30 in the morning. Eleven or twelve minutes later, PC 964 James Harvey had inspected the square from Church Passage but did not actually enter the area, and neither saw nor heard anything suspicious. And then, at roughly

1.45, Watkins returned on his routine beat to find the mutilated corpse lying on the pavement. Neither man had seen either the killer or his victim enter the square, and nor had they seen anyone leaving it.

And it wasn't just the police officers on street patrol who had failed to hear or see anything. There were two nightwatchmen employed in Mitre Square that night. George Morris was working only a few feet inside the premises of Kearley & Tonge's office building, where the street door was standing slightly ajar. Morris was a former Metropolitan Police constable, and had actually looked out of the door a very short time before he was alerted to the murder by Constable Watkins.

The nightwatchman employed by Heydemann and Company was stationed at the rear of the premises in a room which overlooked the site of the murder itself. His name was George Clapp and he heard no sound that night, and saw nothing suspicious. There was also a City Police officer named Pearce, who lived in Mitre Square itself, at number 3, the windows of which property gave an excellent view of the murder site on the opposite side of the square. But Pearce and his wife slept through the entire incident.

So that night, two murder investigations were in progress in the East End of London by two different forces, the Berner Street killing being handled by the Metropolitan Police, and the murder in Mitre Square by the City force.

But there was one more completely unexpected surprise in store for the investigating officers of both forces that night.

Chapter 38

Sunday, 30 September 1888
Whitechapel, London

A few minutes before three o'clock, PC 254A Alfred Long was patrolling in Goulston Street, and peered into the entrance hall of numbers 108 to 119 Wentworth Model Dwellings. There, sodden with blood, he discovered a section of a woman's apron.

Long stared about him looking for any other signs of violence, another body or a weapon or any other suspicious object. He found nothing of that sort, but he did see something very different. The bricks which formed the wall on the right-hand side of the open doorway were black, and on them, written in white chalk, were the following words, written in cursive script:

> *The Juwes are*
> *The men That*
> *Will not*
> *be Blamed*
> *for nothing*

At the end of the first line was the barely visible word 'not' which had clearly been written but then erased by the writer.

Neither PC Long nor PC Halse, who arrived shortly after-wards, was in any doubt about the meaning the writer of the script intended to convey. It was a clear attempt to cast suspicion upon the Jewish community as a whole, and to suggest that one of their number was responsible for the Whitechapel murders.

Constable Long searched the staircases, but found nothing else. He summoned the constable from the neighbouring beat, told him to guard the entrance to preserve the piece of writing and also watch anyone who entered or left the building, and then took the section of apron to the Commercial Street police station, where he gave it to the duty inspector. Long arrived there at a few minutes after three in the morning.

Unsurprisingly, within a very short time the area around Wentworth Model Dwellings was busy with officers from both the City and the Metropolitan forces. Detective Constables Hunt and Daniel Halse went together to the Leman Street police station and then on to Goulston Street. They inspected the chalked message and then separated, Halse remaining at the scene to guard the message while Hunt returned to Mitre Square to report what had been discovered.

Inspector McWilliam had arrived at Mitre Square by the time Constable Hunt reached it and listened with interest to what the officer had to say.

'Good work, Hunt,' he said. 'One more job for you. I'll organize a photographer and get him down there as quickly as I can to record that message. You go back to Wentworth Model Dwellings. When you get there, you and Constable Halse are to search the buildings for anyone or anything that might be connected with this murder.'

The search was conducted by Hunt and Halse as McWilliam

had instructed, but no suspicious individuals, objects or clues were found anywhere there.

But despite the order given by Inspector McWilliam, no photograph of the written message was taken, and for that decision, ultimately, the Commissioner of the Metropolitan Police, Charles Warren, was responsible, even though it actually wasn't his idea.

News of the double murder had been transmitted to Warren at his home in the early hours of the morning, and for the first time – he had not visited any of the other murder scenes since the reign of terror in Whitechapel had begun – he decided to attend in person. Warren arrived at the Leman Street police station shortly before five, where Superintendent Thomas Arnold of H Division explained to him the circumstances of the two murders and also what had been discovered in Goulston Street.

'I have already ordered one of my inspectors to proceed to the scene with a bucket and sponge, and to wait there until I arrive. I feel very strongly that we should wipe this message off the wall as soon as we can, and certainly before the daily activity starts in that area.'

'Erase it?' Warren asked. 'It could be an important clue. It should be photographed at the very least.'

'I don't believe there's enough time to do that, sir,' Arnold replied. 'My concern is with the possibility of civil unrest in that district if any of the residents see that message and realize exactly what it is implying.'

'Which is what, exactly?'

'You've seen the text, sir. It's a very clear indication that the Jews of Whitechapel are responsible for the murders perpetrated by the killer we now know as Jack the Ripper. The fact that the blood-soaked missing section of the last woman's apron was found directly below the message proves beyond any doubt that it was written by her murderer. It's a crude attempt to throw us off the scent, and to throw suspicion onto an entire community. I fear that if the contents of the message become generally known, we could face a riot in the area, either one orchestrated by the Jews themselves, or by groups of English people manifesting their anti-Semitic feelings. Remember the problems we had with the "Leather Apron" situation.'

Warren didn't reply for a few moments, mulling over what Arnold had just said. In fact, despite his apparent reluctance to have the message obliterated, he was absolutely determined that no record of it – or more accurately, no record of the handwriting – should be allowed to survive. He definitely wasn't going to permit a photograph to be taken, just in case at any time in the future the handwriting on that message could be recognized as being the same as that on the letters which 'Michael' had sent him. He also made a mental note to burn all of the correspondence he had so far received from the man, and just to make a copy of the actual words he had used.

'I understand your views, Arnold, but I think I should be the one to make that decision. I will accompany you to Goulston Street.'

Superintendent Arnold was later required to explain his recommendation to the Home Office, and the relevant section of his later written report read: 'in consequence of a suspicion having fallen upon a Jew named John Pizer alias "Leather Apron" having committed a murder in Hanbury Street a short time previously, a strong feeling existed against the Jews generally and as the building upon which the writing was found was situated in the midst of a locality inhabited principally by that sect, I was apprehensive that if the writing were left it would be the means of causing a riot and therefore considered it desirable that it should be removed.'

And in reality Arnold had a point. There had been such an outburst of anti-Semitic rhetoric and actions in Whitechapel after the killing of Annie Chapman that he feared the consequences if the contents of the chalked message became public knowledge amongst either the Jewish or the Gentile communities in the East End or, even worse, in both, especially when the citizens of London learned the details of the two murders which had taken place that night.

Warren had listened carefully to Arnold's recommendation, despite having already decided exactly what he was going to do about it. In his written report, he later stated that it was 'desirable that I should decide this matter myself, as it was one involving so great responsibility whether any action was taken or not.'

Accordingly, when he left the Leman Street police station, he and Arnold proceeded first to Goulston Street, after which he planned to continue on to Berner Street, the site of the first murder that night.

The two senior officers arrived at the location of the chalked message in Goulston Street shortly before 5.30, to find officers from both the City and Metropolitan forces in attendance. Warren inspected the writing – written in a hand that was unpleasantly familiar to him – and decided that it had to be obliterated immediately. When he announced his decision, the only dissenting voice was that of Daniel Halse, the City of London Detective Constable, who wanted it to remain, at least long enough for Major Smith to see it, but he was both outranked and outside his jurisdiction and he knew it.

'Sir, couldn't we just rub out the top line and leave the rest?'

he suggested. 'This looks like a valuable clue to the killer, and I'm sure that Major Smith would want to inspect it.'

Warren shook his head and pointed out of the doorway, where the group of men was clustered around the chalked message, and gestured into the street beyond.

'We can't take the risk, Constable. It's already starting to get light and people are out there walking the streets. If any of them see and read what it says here, we could find ourselves in the middle of a riot.'

Warren turned to one of the Metropolitan Police constables standing in the hallway.

'Use that bucket and sponge, and clean that wall completely. I don't want to see a single white mark left on it anywhere.'

By half past five, the chalk message had been deleted from the wall

The last clue from Goulston Street was the section of bloodstained apron. Although there was little doubt about what it was and where it had come from, it was passed on to Dr Phillips. When he placed the piece of material against the rest of the apron found on the body from Mitre Square, it was a perfect match. There was therefore no doubt that the section of apron had been removed from the body by the killer after he had finished his mutilation, and had afterwards been placed in the entrance of the Wentworth Model Dwellings.

There was of course no absolute proof that the chalked message had been written on the wall by the murderer, but the obvious presumption was that it had been, and none of the officers involved seriously doubted that this was the case.

Once the message had been obliterated, Charles Warren drove on to Dutfield's Yard, off Berner Street, the site of the first murder of the night, and then continued to the headquarters of the City Police in Old Jewry. There, both Inspector McWilliam and Major Smith told him that his action in deleting the message had been a bad mistake. Smith would later describe this in writing as both a 'fatal mistake' and an 'unpardonable blunder'.

But Charles Warren was perfectly content with his action. A possible link between him and Jack the Ripper had been permanently eliminated.

As he had expected, and feared, when Charles Warren returned to his home later that morning, there was another handwritten and hand-delivered letter waiting for him on the hall table.

As soon as he stepped inside the house, Ryan apologized to him.

'I'm sorry sir,' he said, 'but I simply never saw this letter arrive. There was no knock at the door, and it was only when I was walking through the hall that I saw it had been delivered.'

Warren didn't reply, just picked up the sealed envelope and carried it upstairs to his study.

Before he even opened it, he first collected the previous missives he had received from 'Michael', wrote down on a clean sheet of paper exactly what each of them said, and the dates on which they had arrived, then took the originals and their envelopes over to the fireplace set in one wall. He screwed up the letters, placed them in the grate, then lit a match and touched the flame to the paper. When they had been entirely reduced to ash, he used the poker to crumple them into dust.

Only then did he slice open the latest letter from his nemesis, take out the note and read it.

It was composed in the same cryptic style which he had become used to, but was significantly longer than any of the previous messages. The text read:

Not an exact square, but almost. The symbol of the Masons, the two triangles completed. A reminder on the cheeks of the last one. Now we start with the star of the Jews. Two more triangles and six points. Look out for the kidney. The next one will be worse, because I will take my time. You can stop this whenever you want. Just follow my instructions. You have a month.

As he had done before, Warren copied out the text onto the sheet of paper and then consigned the original to the flames.

Then for several minutes he simply sat at his desk with his head in his hands, trying to decide what he should do.

Chapter 39

Monday, 1 October 1888
Whitechapel, London

'Do we know who they were? Or even what they were? Either of them?'

The mood in the small conference room at the Bethnal Green station, a room which Abberline had commandeered once he had officially been appointed to run the investigation into the multiple murders, was subdued. Everything had been quiet in Whitechapel for over three weeks, and Abberline and the other officers had privately begun to hope that the reign of terror was over, and that – for whatever reason – the unknown killer had ceased his hideous rampage. But the events which had taken place over the weekend clearly demonstrated that this was not the case.

'We don't have their names yet,' Detective Inspector Chandler replied. 'We're working on it.'

Chandler was still acting as their link to the officers of H Division, and was working very closely with Abberline and the other two Metropolitan Police detectives.

'And as you'd expect,' he continued, 'neither woman was

carrying any sort of identification. As for what they were, I suppose it makes sense to assume that they were both unfortunates, just because they were walking alone through the East End in the early hours of the morning.'

'God, what a mess,' Abberline muttered. 'And to kill twice in the same night. That shows he's getting bolder.'

'Not necessarily,' Andrews objected. 'The location of the first murder in – where was it again, oh yes, Dutfield's Yard – seems to have been fairly busy, lots of people coming and going. So I think he may have intended to only carry out one murder, but before he could finish the job and do whatever butchery he had in mind, he heard somebody approaching and legged it.'

'Maybe.' Abberline sounded far from convinced. 'But even if you're right and he was disturbed, I still think it shows a very bold approach to then go off and carry out a second killing. The other alternative is that, precisely because Dutfield's Yard *was* such a busy place that night, he deliberately just killed the woman because he knew that would immediately become the focus of all the police activity, and then set out to find his second victim in the belief that all of our efforts would be concentrated on that one part of London.'

'You could make the case either way, I suppose,' Chandler said, 'but in fact the place he picked for the second killing had quite a large police presence in it. I've already talked to the beat officers who were on duty that night, and as far as I can work out the murderer would have only had maybe ten or fifteen minutes at best to find, kill and mutilate the second woman. If this idea of a first killing to attract the attention of the police to one location so that he wouldn't be disturbed during the second murder is right, then I would have expected him to pick somewhere a lot quieter, with far fewer police patrols.'

Abberline nodded. That aspect of the double murder had been bothering him as well. Then another thought struck him.

'I think the way he's carried out the murders in the past shows that he's perfectly capable of finding a victim, killing her and then mutilating the body in a very short space of time, even when we've known that there are patrolling constables nearby. We've seen that already. I'm just beginning to think he might be a lot cleverer than we've supposed up to now.'

'What do you mean?'

'I'm wondering if he picked the location of the second murder quite deliberately, simply because it lies within the boundaries of the City of London, and he knew that that would mean a different police force would be handling the investigation. Maybe he thought that would lead to confusion over jurisdiction and allocation of resources, and that's why he took a chance and picked on that woman.'

'Well you're right about one thing, Fred, we do know that he's quite happy to take his chances. Of course, the other side of the coin is that perhaps that woman was the only one he had found walking the streets, and the location didn't matter to him. He might not have even known he'd crossed the boundary into the City.'

'We could argue this back and forth for the rest of the day,' Abberline said, 'and it wouldn't get us anywhere. Whatever his motive was in carrying out these two killings, and in picking those particular locations, that probably isn't going to be much help in tracking him down. We have to concentrate on the facts that we have available to us, and this time the killer seems to have left us with a lot more to go on than previously.'

'You mean the message and the bloody apron?' Chandler said.

'Exactly.'

'I suppose there's no doubt that the piece of apron was cut from the clothing of the second victim?' Andrews asked.

Chandler shook his head.

'None at all. I've already had that confirmed by Inspector McWilliam, who was at the mortuary at the time. James McWilliam,' he added in clarification, 'is the head of the Detective Department of the City of London Police.'

'So it's beyond any doubt that the man who discarded that piece of bloody cloth in the entry way to the building in Goulston Street was also the man who killed the second victim. And, unless we've got it completely wrong, the first woman as well,' Abberline said. 'And, at least by implication, he was also the person who wrote the message on the wall. The message that the Commissioner of the Metropolitan Police, Sir Charles Warren, was so keen to erase.'

The senior inspector's tone of voice showed his irritation almost as clearly as the words he used.

'You're closer to Warren than any of the rest of us,' Moore said. 'Have you got any idea why he did that? I know the message was a bit cryptic, but having a copy of something written in the killer's own hand could have been a lot of help to us.'

'I have no idea,' Abberline replied. 'I know he said at the time that he was concerned that some of the local residents – and by that he obviously meant members of the local Jewish community – would see what had been written and that might have led to riots or at least civil unrest. He's got a point about that, I have to concede, but I still don't understand why the message was wiped off the wall so quickly, before it could even be photographed. I can't see any reason why the officers on the spot couldn't have put up some kind of a screen in front of the message, and there were enough of them to make sure that none of the locals could come into the entry way. It seems to me to have been an extremely foolish decision, verging on crass stupidity.'

'McWilliam felt exactly the same way,' Chandler said, 'and he told me so yesterday. And his boss, Major Smith, told him that in his opinion Warren's decision was idiotic.'

'But at least we know what the message said,' Andrews pointed out. 'That's something, surely.'

'I agree, but I don't think it gets us very far. It's just a kind of rant against the Jews, but even that's not entirely clear,' Abberline said. 'According to the report by Constable Long, the word "Jews" was spelt incorrectly, and there was an extra word at the end of the first line which whoever wrote it had rubbed out, but it was still just visible. So the complete message would have read "The Juwes are not The men That Will not be Blamed for nothing", which doesn't make a lot of sense to me.'

Abberline wrote out the message in capital letters on a sheet of paper, then stood up, walked across to the wall on which he'd had pinned the Whitechapel map with the locations of the murders – now six in all, including that of Emma Smith – marked on it in ink, and pinned the sheet to the wall beside the map. Then he walked back to the table and sat down.

'It's a triple negative,' he pointed out, 'so the original message seems to be saying that it's not the fault of the Jews. But by rubbing out the first "not", he's turned it into a double negative, and that changes the meaning completely. You can shorten the message "The Juwes are The men That Will not be Blamed for nothing" to just "The Juwes are The men That Will be Blamed". I assume that when he wrote the word "not" on the first line, he hadn't quite worked out what the rest of the message would say, and when he stepped back to look at it, he realized he needed to change it.'

'It's still a very complicated expression, though, isn't it?' Chandler asked. 'If he wanted to blame the Jews, why didn't he just write "The Jews did it" or something obvious like that?'

'I think,' Abberline said, after a pause while he collected his thoughts, 'he's trying to show us that he's an educated man, not some common thug, which is why he used such a complicated sentence construction. And according to Long, the writing was done in an elegant and cursive script, the kind of script you'd expect a gentleman, a well-educated gentleman, to use. And that makes me wonder why every word in the message is spelt correctly, apart from the most important word of all: "Juwes". I've already done a bit of checking, and as far as I've been able to find out that's not a known spelling of the word "Jews" in any language. Any ideas?'

'It could just be an alternative spelling, I suppose,' Chandler suggested. 'I happen to know that quite a lot of the locals – those who can read and write, obviously – spell the "Jewry" in "Jewry Street" as "Juwery", probably because that's how it sounds when you say it.' He spelt the name out to the other detectives. 'It's not that big a leap from "Juwery" to "Juwes", is it?'

'That's an interesting idea,' Abberline agreed, 'and it does make a kind of sense. I can't believe that a man who can correctly spell "blamed" and "nothing" wouldn't know how to spell "Jews", so maybe what he's trying to do is to show us that he's a local, that despite being educated, that's the way somebody from round here would spell the word. Though if that *is* what he's intending, I still don't quite understand why. Anyway, I don't think the message is going to help us very much, and as Warren wiped off the wall before anybody else saw it, at least we aren't facing some kind of Jewish insurrection over it.

'The other thing I find interesting about this,' Abberline went on, almost as an aside, 'is that on the first and only time that Commissioner Charles Warren bothers to turn up at the scene of one of these murders, the only thing he does is obliterate the one clue that we've so far found that could help lead to the murderer's identity.'

The other three men stared at him.

'What are you saying, Fred?' Andrews asked.

Abberline gave an enigmatic smile.

'I'm not saying anything. I just think it's interesting, that's all. The other thing which is still a mystery to me is why the murderer is sending us messages at all. Why should he be trying to implicate the Jews in what he's doing? Because that seems to be his intention, I can only assume that he himself isn't Jewish.'

'Unless it's a kind of double bluff,' Chandler suggested, 'and he thinks, by leaving a message blaming the Jews for the murders, that we'll think he's a Gentile, but he's actually a Jew himself.'

'Like I said before,' Abberline responded, 'all this is just speculation, and it isn't going to get us anywhere. We have to get back to basics, to ordinary police work. None of our decoy constables have been approached yet, obviously, but it's probably worth keeping them on the streets for a while longer, just in case. About all we can do now is the usual house-to-house enquiries and interviews of anybody known to be in the area – in either area, I mean – when the murders were committed. But this time I want more than just house-to-house. I want hand bills printed and delivered to every property in the area. I want everybody in Whitechapel and the East End of London to know that we're making every possible effort we can to catch this man.

'And I don't know about you three,' he finished, 'but I'm not holding my breath waiting for any good news at the moment.'

Chapter 40

The first of the two post-mortem examinations to be held was
that of the mutilated body discovered in Mitre Square, and that
was conducted during the afternoon of Sunday, 30 September,
by Dr Frederick Gordon Brown.

In the meantime, the police were trying to discover exactly
who the victim was. To begin with, it looked as if the identification of the dead woman wouldn't be easy. She appeared to be
about forty years of age, was about five feet tall and quite slim,
with dark brownish hair and hazel eyes.

Her clothes yielded no obvious means of identifying her,
being uniformly dirty and old, and in fact were a strange mix-
ture, featuring a man's white vest and a pair of men's laced
boots, a black coat edged in imitation fur, and a dark-green
chintz skirt, as well as numerous undergarments which included
a dark-green alpaca skirt and a ragged blue skirt, a grey petticoat and a white calico chemise. In common with many other
members of her profession, she carried no identification and
wore no drawers.

The state of her clothing was so poor that it was felt she

could almost have been a vagrant, or at best an occasional resident in one of the numerous doss houses in the Whitechapel area. Her meagre possessions included a white handkerchief and a few other pieces of material, a couple of clay pipes, two tin boxes containing sugar and tea respectively, a table knife and a teaspoon, a cigarette case, an empty matchbox and a handful of other objects of little or no worth.

'I don't know if this might be important,' Dr Brown said as he looked at the dead woman's left arm.

One of the attending police officers, Sergeant Jones, immediately stepped forward and looked down to where the doctor was indicating.

'That might help, yes,' the officer said, staring fixedly at the limp forearm.

Somewhat faded, but just visible, was a tattoo which formed the initials 'TC' in blue ink.

'Could be her initials, I suppose,' Jones said, 'or maybe they're the initials of her husband. Either way, it's something to be going on with, along with those two pawn tickets we found at the scene.'

A small mustard tin had been discovered beside the body, and Jones had picked it up and examined its contents. Inside he'd discovered two pawn tickets, one for a pair of men's boots, which had been pledged in the name of Jane Kelly of 6 Dorset Street on 28 September, and the other for a man's flannel shirt, pledged by Emily Burrell of 52 White's Row on 31 August. And in both cases the pawnbroker was Joseph Jones of 31 Church Street, Spitalfields.

At the time, these had both looked like good solid clues, but as soon as the investigation began there were problems. The first discovery the police made was that there was no number

'52' in White's Row, and nobody named Jane Kelly was known at 6 Dorset Street. It looked as if they were going to be no help at all.

But ultimately it was these two pawn tickets that led to the murdered woman being identified. Because of the huge swathe of publicity surrounding this murder, and the description of her possessions being prominently listed in most of the newspapers, late in the afternoon on 2 October a labourer named John Kelly walked into the Bishopsgate Street police station.

'It's this woman what's been murdered,' he began. 'It could be my Kate.'

Kelly explained that his common-law wife, Kate Conway or Kate Kelly, with whom he had lived at Cooney's Lodging House at 55 Flower and Dean Street for the previous seven years, had disappeared the day before the murder took place.

It was the first positive step in the identification process: a man who might well have known the dead woman. He was taken to the City Mortuary that day, and immediately identified the body. The following morning, 3 October, he assisted detectives in locating Mrs Eliza Gold, Kate's sister, who also immediately confirmed the identification of the dead woman, naming her as Catharine or Kate Eddowes.

At the inquest into her death, held on 4 October at the City Mortuary in Golden Lane, it was the medical evidence which was the most sensational, as it had been with the previous killing of Annie Chapman.

Dr Brown took the stand and began describing what he had discovered during the post-mortem examination, findings which simply substantiated and elaborated upon his original medical report, which he first read out to the inquest jury, and which summarized the sight which had greeted PC Watkins that night.

'The body was found on its back,' Brown stated, reading from his report, 'the head turned to left shoulder; the arms by the side of the body as if they had fallen there, both palms upwards, the fingers slightly bent; a thimble was lying off the finger on the right side; the clothes torn up above the abdomen; the thighs were naked; left leg extended in line with the body; the abdomen was exposed; right leg bent at the thigh and knee; the bonnet was at the back of the head; great disfigurement of face; the throat cut across; below the cut was a neckerchief; the upper part of the dress was pulled open a little way; the abdomen was all exposed; the intestines were drawn out to a large extent and placed over the right shoulder; they were smeared over with some feculent matter; a piece of about two feet was quite detached from the body and placed between the body and the left arm, apparently by design; the lobe and auricle of the right ear was cut obliquely through; there was a quantity of clotted blood on the pavement on the left side of the neck, round the shoulder and upper part of arm, and fluid blood-coloured serum which had flowed under the neck to the right shoulder, the pavement sloping in that direction; body was quite warm; no death stiffening had taken place; she must have been dead most likely within the half hour; we looked for superficial bruises and saw none; no blood on the skin of the abdomen or secretion of any kind on the thighs; no spurting of blood on the bricks or pavement around; no marks of blood below the middle of the body; several buttons were found in the clotted blood after the body was removed; there was no blood on the front of the clothes; there were no traces of recent connection.'

'Very well, doctor. Now could you please describe the full extent of the mutilations which were inflicted on the body.'

Brown referred to his notes before he replied, and then provided a brief list of the major injuries he had discovered, and his reply also confirmed another rumour which had already begun circulating: a suggestion that yet again the killer had removed some parts of his victim's body as grisly souvenirs.

'The abdomen had been sliced open using an upwards cut,' he said, 'a cut which ran from the groin to the breast. The liver had been stabbed and cut several times. The groin showed evidence of both cuts and stabs. A large part of the intestines had been cut away from the body and about two feet of the colon had been separated entirely. The left kidney and a part of the womb had been sliced off and removed. The entire womb had not been extracted, and a stump about three quarters of an inch in length remained, but the kidney had been entirely detached and removed. I should add that this procedure required a good deal of knowledge as to its position, because it is apt to be overlooked, being covered by a membrane. It had been carefully taken out and removed, and the murderer clearly possessed both a knowledge of the location of the organs which overlaid it and the way of removing them.'

This bombshell, and Brown's cold and clinical description of the mutilations inflicted on the woman, silenced the court for a few moments.

'I should also add,' he went on, 'that these were not the only injuries. The woman's face had also been targeted by her killer. He cut a line into each of her eyelids and carved two inverted 'V' shapes into her cheeks. He inflicted a large cut below her mouth and across the bridge of her nose, and he also removed the tip of her nose and the lobe of her right ear.'

He then moved on to more specific details about the manner of the woman's death.

'The absence of blood at the scene was, in my opinion, because the victim had first been asphyxiated. This means that her heart would already have stopped beating before the knife was used to cut her throat and perform the post-mortem mutilations on her body. Because she was already dead, there would have been little blood flow from the severed veins and arteries.'

Inevitably, in view of what Brown had described about the mutilations to the body, the coroner asked the same predictable question.

'You've told us that the individual who carried out these mutilations possessed a high degree of surgical skill. Could he in fact have been a doctor, for example?'

Dr Brown chose his words with some care when he replied, keenly aware of how inflammatory the suggestion was.

'I cannot answer that with any degree of certainty, sir. What I can say is that the murderer must have possessed both some surgical skill and a fair degree of anatomical knowledge. I am basing this conclusion upon the way in which the woman's left kidney had been removed. It required a great deal of knowledge to have removed the kidney and to know where it was placed.'

'Knowledge that a doctor would obviously possess,' the coroner suggested.

'That is true, sir. But such a knowledge might also be possessed by someone in the habit of cutting up animals, someone like a butcher or a slaughterman, or perhaps even a hunter, as well as somebody who had undertaken medical or surgical training.'

Among the other witnesses, the nightwatchman George Morris was unequivocal in the evidence he gave, both to reporters and at the inquest. Because of his police training, he was particularly alert, and had even hoped the murderer would appear in Mitre Square.

'It was only last night,' he said, 'that I made the remark to some policeman that I wished the butcher would come around Mitre Square, and I would soon give him a doing, and here, to be sure, he has come and I was perfectly ignorant of it.'

'Did you hear anything at all that night?' the coroner asked him.

'Yes, sir. As I always do, I heard the heavy footsteps of every patrolling police officer who entered the square throughout the night.'

'But you heard nothing else?'

'No, sir. I'm absolutely certain I heard no other noise, no cry or other sound, during the whole of that night.'

Chapter 41

The post-mortem of Elizabeth Stride had been carried out on Monday, 1 October in the St George's Mortuary and, because of the interest and alarm which were surrounding the series of murders in Whitechapel, on this occasion both the doctors who had attended the scene of the murder conducted the examination.

Dr Blackwell carried out the autopsy procedure himself whilst Dr Phillips noted down his comments and findings. For at least a part of the time, Dr Reigate was also in attendance, as well as Edward Johnson, who was Dr Blackwell's assistant and had been the first medically trained person to see the body in Dutfield's Yard. In the search for clues and other information, this time it was the doctors themselves who stripped the clothes from the corpse and examined them.

The cause of death was not difficult to ascertain, as the wound in the neck had partially severed her left carotid artery and the windpipe. No marks were found on the throat to indicate strangulation, but it was noted that the silk scarf Stride was wearing around her neck had been pulled very tight.

'This could possibly be how the killer first incapacitated this woman,' Dr Blackwell suggested. 'If he seized this scarf and pulled it tight around her neck, perhaps by twisting a loop in it so that it acted as a garrotte, that would both incapacitate the woman and allow the murderer to pull her backwards off her feet, and possibly all the way down onto the ground. And when she was lying flat and helpless, he would be able to deliver the fatal wound to her throat.'

'As a possible scenario,' Phillips agreed, 'that does make sense. What about the cut itself, the wound to the throat. Do you believe that could have been administered by somebody who possessed anatomical knowledge?'

Blackwell paused for a moment before he replied, then lifted the dead woman's chin up and back so that he could examine the wound more closely.

'That is more difficult to say,' Blackwell replied, 'because it is only a single wound. But I see no signs of hesitation or fumbling in the use of the knife, and I think that whoever did this is certainly accustomed to use a heavy knife. And from the position of the cut, I think it would be fair to say that the killer must have possessed at least some degree of medical knowledge.'

Dr Phillips agreed with his colleague, and would later tell the coroner at the inquest that 'there seems to have been some knowledge where to cut the throat to cause a fatal result'.

The autopsy was one thing, but while the doctors were making their painstaking examination of the corpse, the identity of the victim was still unknown.

The hand of fate then dealt the police a wild card – or perhaps more accurately a joker – in the form of Mrs Mary Malcolm. She lived at number 50 Eagle Street, Red Lion Square in Holborn, and was the wife of a tailor. On the evening of 1

October, she visited the mortuary and asked if she could see the body, which she'd explained could be that of her sister, Mrs Elizabeth Watts.

'Now I'm not so sure about this,' she said, as she stared down at the corpse. 'I think it might be her but because there's only this gaslight in here, you see, I can't make her out very clearly.'

'But surely,' the sergeant who had accompanied her to the mortuary asked patiently, 'you can recognize the face of your own sister?'

'Well, it's not that really. I think it's her face all right, but you see Elizabeth has a crippled foot – it's her right foot, actually – and I don't think that this woman suffers from that problem.'

'So this body has your sister's face, but not her feet. Is that what you're trying to say?'

'I suppose it is, really. Look, I'd better come back tomorrow when it's daylight and I'll be able to see better.'

'I think that's a very good idea,' the sergeant said, escorting her to the door of the St George's Mortuary.

Nobody at the police station seriously expected to see the woman again, but she did, as promised, return the following morning. In fact, she went to the police station and the mortuary twice. On her first visit to inspect the body again, she said she was unsure of the identification, but on her second appearance she was absolutely certain.

'Oh, yes,' she said brightly. 'That's definitely Elizabeth.'

'You are sure now, are you?' the same sergeant asked, with a certain degree of world-weariness.

'Quite sure, because of this small black mark here on her leg. That's an old adder bite that she got when we were children.'

'So despite the fact that you've explained that your sister has a crippled right foot, and that this body does not, you're still certain that this is Mrs Elizabeth Watts?'

'Yes,' Mrs Malcolm said, still sounding confident, but slightly less so than she had a minute or so earlier.

'Now what can you tell us about her?'

'Well, she's rather fallen on hard times,' Mrs Malcolm said, now apparently treading on firmer ground. 'She's lived in a number of East End lodging houses, and I've been supporting her in a small way for about the last five years.'

'What do you mean by "supporting her"?' the sergeant asked.

'We had this arrangement, you see. We would meet every Saturday afternoon at four at the corner of Chancery Lane, and I would give her what money I could afford. But the thing is that last Saturday she didn't appear, and that night, well, I can tell you I had the strangest dream, and a sort of premonition thing that something terrible had happened to her. And then when I heard about the murder I was quite sure that that's what it was.'

Unlikely though her story sounded, the police had no option but to call her as an identification witness at the inquest, simply because she still claimed to be certain about the identity of the dead woman.

At the inquest, held on the afternoon of Tuesday 2 October, Mrs Malcolm reaffirmed her identification of the body as that of her sister, and provided a number of statements which cast her sibling in a fairly dim and unattractive light.

'I mustn't speak ill of the dead,' she said, 'but I happen to know that my sister was several times arrested by the police for being drunk and disorderly, but that's not the worst of it. Once I heard a knock on the door and when I opened it I discovered that she'd left a naked baby on my doorstep for me to look after.'

The coroner looked somewhat bemused by this unexpected accusation.

'At the moment, Mrs Malcolm, we're concerned only with the identification of the body. So let me ask you again: you are quite certain that it is your sister Mrs Elizabeth Watts?'

'Oh, I'm quite sure,' she replied, 'because of the adder bite, you see.'

The fundamentally inconclusive identification and rambling statements made by Mrs Malcolm failed to impress either the police or the coroner, and their doubts were confirmed a short time later when the real Mrs Elizabeth Watts, who had married a brick-maker named Stokes and was then living in Tottenham, reported to the police. Her right foot was indeed crippled, the result of an accident, but in all other respects the story told by Mrs Malcolm was the purest fantasy. The two women had not in fact met for years, and Mrs Stokes was understandably aggrieved at the tall tales her sister had been telling about her.

But despite the best efforts of the imaginative Mrs Malcolm, the real identity of the victim of the Whitechapel murderer was fairly quickly established. Her name was Elizabeth Stride, she was Swedish by birth, and had been living at 32 Flower and Dean Street, a common lodging house.

Her past was something of a mystery and, just like the severely deluded Mrs Malcolm, she clearly had a fairly vivid imagination. She had repeatedly claimed to friends and acquaintances that she had lost her husband and two of her children in the sinking of a pleasure steamer named the *Princess Alice* on the Thames.

This was a genuine disaster and had occurred on 3 September 1878, when the vessel collided with a steam collier named the *Bywell Castle*, and sank with the loss of over 600 lives. In the struggle to escape the sinking ship, Stride claimed that a man clambering up a rope ladder directly in front of her had kicked her in the face, an action which knocked out her front teeth.

In fact, the whole tale was made up by Stride, perhaps in an attempt to gain sympathy – and possibly more tangible benefits – from people that she talked to. The reality of both her life and the death of her husband were markedly different.

Once the dead woman had been identified, all of her friends and acquaintances were questioned by the police during the days following her murder. In fact, working under the orders of Inspector Abberline, the police would make strenuous efforts to identify anybody who might have some reason for wishing Stride dead, as well as those who might have seen or heard something on the night of the killing. Every house in Berner Street would be visited and, again at Abberline's instigation, some eighty thousand pamphlets were sent out to the owners and occupiers of properties in the surrounding area requesting information, these being followed up by house-to-house enquiries.

The wording on the handbill read:

POLICE NOTICE
TO THE OCCUPIER

On the mornings of Friday, 31st August, Saturday 8th, and Sunday, 30th of September, 1888, Women were murdered in or near Whitechapel, supposed by some one residing in the immediate neighbourhood. Should you know of any person to whom suspicion is attached, you are earnestly requested to communicate at once with the nearest Police Station.

Metropolitan Police Office, 30th September, 1888.

The questioning also extended to the Thames Police who interrogated sailors from ships berthed in the docks or on the river, while Metropolitan Police officers questioned butchers and slaughterers, and such diverse groups as Greek Gypsies and cowboys working at the American Exhibition. All the common lodging houses in the area were also visited and some two thousand residents questioned.

But this very obvious activity did little to quell the growing unrest in the East End of London. Shortly after the 'double event', a rally was held in Victoria Park, which about a thousand people attended, to call for the resignation of Sir Charles Warren as Commissioner of the Metropolitan Police, and of Henry Matthews, the Home Secretary. Neither man, of course, responded to these calls.

But the murder of Elizabeth Stride differed in one important respect from the three which had occurred previously, in that for the first time the police had witnesses who had seen something that might help identify the killer. Two men in particular – PC 452H William Smith and a Hungarian man named Israel Schwartz – each believed they might have actually seen the murderer.

PC Smith had been allocated a long and circuitous beat that took him almost half an hour to cover, and which included Berner Street. He had walked down that road at about half past midnight on the morning Stride was killed, and had seen a man talking to a woman he later identified as Elizabeth Stride. He noticed the red rose decorating her coat, and was able to confirm that the two people had been close to where Stride's body was later found, although they were on the opposite side of the street from Dutfield's Yard.

Israel Schwartz's evidence was far more sensational. He told the police that he had walked into Berner Street at about a quarter to one that morning, and as he approached the entrance to Dutfield's Yard he had seen a woman standing near the yard entrance, and had watched her as she was accosted by a man who tried to pull her into the street. She resisted, and the man had then thrown her down onto the pavement.

'Then the woman screamed three times, but not very loudly,' he explained, 'and as I approached them I saw another man standing watching on the opposite side of the street.'

'What was he doing?' the inspector asked.

'He was lighting a pipe,' Schwartz replied, a somewhat unexpected answer.

'Then what happened?'

'The man with the woman saw me approaching and called out "Lipski".'

That was a name which could be interpreted in a number of different ways, as the inspector knew very well.

'I was not certain what to do,' Schwartz continued, 'and so I turned around and walked back the way I had come. Then I noticed that the other man, the man who had been lighting his pipe, was following me, and so I started to run. I ran as far as the railway arch and then looked behind me, but the man was no longer in sight.'

The first difficulty was that it wasn't clear whether or not any connection existed between the two men Schwartz had seen. The second man could easily have been an innocent bystander, just like Schwartz himself, who had then decided to leave the scene and had simply chosen to follow the same route as Schwartz. The fact that this second man followed Schwartz for only a short distance suggests that this might have been the case. If he was an accomplice, and the other man had in fact been the murderer, it would be reasonable to assume that he would have caught up with Schwartz and either killed or beaten him badly to ensure that he would not act as a witness against them.

When Schwartz later viewed the body of Elizabeth Stride in the mortuary, he identified her as the woman he had seen being attacked, and was able to give quite accurate and detailed descriptions of the two men he had seen in Berner Street. But what Schwartz could not say was whether or not the man attacking the woman was in any way connected with the person on the opposite side of the street.

The description given by Schwartz was similar, but certainly not identical, to that provided by PC Smith. The height of the man he'd seen was different, as were certain aspects of his build, his dress and the colour of his moustache, but most of these discrepancies could be explained away fairly convincingly as being caused by nothing more than the circumstances of the sightings by the two men.

On a dark street, a brown moustache would look very much like a black one, and height is particularly difficult to estimate unless there is some object whose dimensions are known in the near vicinity. But perhaps the most important single factor was that the police officer saw a red rose on the front of the woman's coat, and Schwartz positively identified the body in the mortuary as that of the woman he had seen. So at least the police could be certain that both witnesses had seen the victim, even if it was never entirely clear if either man had seen the murderer.

The use by the man Schwartz had seen of the name 'Lipski' was the subject of much debate. The name was well-known in the East End of London at this time, because the previous year a Polish Jew named Israel Lipski had been executed for the murder of a woman called Miriam Angel. So it was possible that the man seen by Schwartz had been speaking ironically, perhaps suggesting that he was going to do a 'Lipski' on the woman he was with. In other words, that he was going to murder her.

On the other hand, that name was common among the Jewish community in the area, and so it was possible that his companion – if indeed the man with the woman had some kind of relationship with the man standing on the opposite side of the street – might have been named Lipski, and was simply being addressed as such.

A third possibility was that, following the trial and execution of Israel Lipski, the word had to some extent entered the language as a slang term for a Jew, and so it was also conceivable that the man hadn't been calling out to his companion at all, but was addressing Israel Schwartz himself, who had an unmistakably Jewish appearance.

Other witnesses were identified as a result of the house-to-house search, and one – a labourer named William Marshall – claimed he had seen Stride with a man somewhat similar in appearance to the description supplied by Smith and Schwartz. But his sighting occurred well over an hour before the killing took place and in that time she might have been approached by, or have approached herself, numerous different men, so his evidence was hardly considered significant.

And, perhaps inevitably, some witnesses came forward who weren't witnesses at all, just people who decided that the time had come for their fifteen minutes of fame, and who relished their brief instant of celebrity status.

The most notorious of these was a fruit seller named Matthew Packer, who when first interviewed by the police stated categorically that he had neither seen nor heard anything on the night of the murder, and was unaware that the event had taken place until the following morning when it became common knowledge in the area.

Two days later, he was telling an entirely different story to anyone who would listen, claiming that he had not merely seen the murderer, but had overheard a conversation between the killer and his victim, and had then sold him half a pound of black grapes. This sale apparently took place, depending upon which account is relied upon, at 11 p.m., 11.30 p.m., 11.45 p.m. or midnight and he had closed his shop at 10 p.m., midnight, 12.15 a.m. or 12.30 a.m. The man to whom he sold the grapes also changed his appearance and age, ranging from a youthful 25 to between 30 and 35, all the way up to a predictably vague 'middle-aged'.

It is perhaps significant that Packer's account became increasingly detailed and specific as the monetary reward for information leading to the capture of the murderer grew to several hundred pounds, and as the newspapers began reporting details of the sighting by Israel Schwartz. Packer was also only too happy to oblige newspaper reporters by confirming whatever it was they were fishing for.

When a reporter from the *Evening News* suggested in passing, and entirely without foundation, that it was possible that the Whitechapel murderer's voice might have an American twang to it, Packer immediately replied: 'Yes, now that you mention it, there *was* a sound of that sort about it.' Presumably if the reporter had suggested that the killer sounded as if he'd come from Wales or Scotland or even Outer Mongolia, or had three legs, Packer would have agreed with that as well.

And then there was a lady named Mrs Fanny Mortimer who, though she was entirely truthful in her account and invented nothing about the events of that night, unwittingly added one important detail to the legend of Jack the Ripper, a detail that became inextricably linked to the 'Fiend of Whitechapel'.

Mrs Mortimer lived at 36 Berner Street, just a short distance down the street from Dutfield's Yard, and had been standing outside her house between half past midnight and one in the morning when Elizabeth Stride was killed, so she was in an excellent position to see anyone entering or leaving the premises. When she was later interviewed by the police, she was adamant that she had noticed nobody passing through the gate in either direction, so she was of no assistance in providing a description of either the murderer or his victim.

But what she had seen was a man aged about 30 and wearing dark clothes who walked down Berner Street carrying a black shiny bag. This figure had come, not from Dutfield's Yard but from Commercial Road, and so clearly could have had nothing whatsoever to do with the murder.

The man in question walked into the Leman Street police station a couple of days later, where he was cleared of any suspicion of involvement in the crime. His name was Leon Goldstein, he lived at 22 Christian Street and was a member of the International Working Men's Club and when he was seen by Mrs Mortimer he had been returning home after leaving a coffeehouse in Spectacle Alley. His bag, which he showed to the police at the time, was found to contain nothing but empty cigarette boxes.

But the fact that a man had been seen in the vicinity of the killing carrying a black bag was widely published in the newspapers and this, coupled with the existing and widespread fear that the murderer could be a doctor, reinforced the belief that the black bag contained the deadly tools of the killer's trade, and this accessory then became an even more inseparable part of the image most Londoners already had of the Whitechapel murderer.

Chapter 42

When residents of Whitechapel awoke on the morning of Sunday, 30 September, news of the 'double event' was already coursing through the streets, and crowds of fascinated and horrified people began making their way to one of the two murder sites.

Both Mitre Square and Berner Street had been cordoned off by the police, but this made no difference. Thousands of people advanced on both locations, assembling outside Dutfield's Yard and in the streets around Mitre Square. At one point during the day, Berner Street was choked with spectators, so many people, in fact, that even crossing the road was almost impossible. Any vantage point was quickly identified, and people fortunate enough to have a window in their property overlooking either site were quick to take advantage of the unique opportunity, opening the windows wide and arranging seats in front of them which they could rent to eager and ghoulish spectators for a few minutes at a time.

Tradesmen – costermongers and the like – set up their stalls and barrows in the area to supply food and drink to members of

the crowd. And because everybody was both fascinated and horrified by what had occurred, the demand for further information
was irresistible. Newspaper vendors were able to sell every paper
they had, and several editions were reprinted throughout the day
as the newspaper publishers attempted to cope with the demand.
Groups of people gathered around anyone with a paper and listened eagerly as details of the brutal murders were read out to
them. This was due in part to the shortage of newspapers, but
also because many residents of the East End of London were illiterate and could neither read nor write, so they depended upon
the news being imparted to them verbally.

Large crowds gathered at both Berner Street and Mitre
Square not just on the last day of September, when news of the
murders was fresh, but for several days afterwards. What was
particularly noticeable was that when dusk fell the badly lit
streets virtually emptied of both men and women, and those few
people who were prepared to risk their lives by walking the
streets where Jack the Ripper hunted his prey, tended to stick to
the very limited areas which had proper street lighting.

The lodging houses and workhouses reported greatly increased
occupancy as fear of the killer took hold of the lowest classes of
women, and in some cases the doss house deputies turned a blind
eye to those 'unfortunates' who did not have enough money to
rent a bed for the night, and either allowed them to sleep for free
or at the very least let them take shelter in the kitchen. Other
deputies were less sympathetic, and without remorse turned out
dozens of women to face the terrors of the night.

Many prostitutes armed themselves, concealing knives about
their persons as a last desperate means of defence should they
meet the Ripper. Others stayed together in groups, clustering in
doorways or anywhere else that offered any kind of shelter from

the elements as they waited for dawn to break and for the danger to pass.

But it wasn't just the prostitutes who were affected by fear of the serial killer. Respectable and better-off men and women began to avoid travelling to or through the East End of the city if it could be avoided. Tradesmen inevitably began to feel the effects of the loss of custom. One report stated that the volume of trade in the area had dropped by almost a half in the previous month. The situation grew so grave that over 200 traders from Whitechapel would later request that the Home Secretary increase the number of police officers patrolling the streets of the district in an attempt to restore confidence.

Their statement said: 'The universal feeling prevalent in our midst is that the Government no longer ensures the security of life and property in East London and that, in consequence, respectable people fear to go out shopping, thus depriving us of our means of livelihood.'

Both the police and the residents of the district were plagued by the inevitable crop of fantasists and jokers who began carrying knives about the place so that they could impersonate the killer by brandishing their weapons in front of terrified women. Fear of the unknown killer was so great that a number of deaths resulted, with both men and women taking their own lives either out of fear that the murderer was pursuing them, or because of – in the case of at least one of the men – an entirely misunderstood belief that the police were convinced that he was the Ripper.

But in the midst of all the fear and uncertainty, certain types of trade blossomed, principally the newspapers. And alongside the newspapers appeared broadsheets, written especially to provide information about the killings, some of which were produced in verse format, and which could be sung to the tune of popular songs of the time. Sellers of knives and swordsticks and similar weapons did a roaring trade among residents of the area.

Omnibuses and cabs brought crowds of eager sightseers from the more affluent parts of London to tour the dirty and squalid streets of Whitechapel, visiting the murder sites and perhaps allowing the tourists to catch a glimpse of a few of the 'unfortunates' whose fellows had become the chosen prey of Jack the Ripper. Pavement artists depicted the killings in brilliant colour to astounded gasps from spectators.

Providing access to the murder sites continued to be profitable once the police had left the area, and many residents took advantage of this interest, including the International Working Men's Club in Berner Street, which began charging admission to spectators eager to inspect the scene of the killing of Elizabeth Stride in Dutfield's Yard.

But it wasn't all about making money off the back of the killings. Throughout the East End, there was a huge groundswell of sympathy for the sad and desperate victims of the Ripper.

The funerals of the dead women attracted enormous crowds of people, and several received a far more elaborate burial than they would have been granted had they simply died in their beds of natural causes, the funerals being paid for by others. Members of the press attended as well, to report the details to their readers, and the London papers received large numbers of letters from the more affluent residents of the capital, letters which in the main called for social reform, for better policing of the area and for an end to the slum conditions in the East End which, many writers seemed to believe, were a contributing part of the problem and which might even have spawned the shadowy and ghostly figure of Jack the Ripper himself.

Just after 1.30 in the afternoon on Monday, 8 October, Catharine Eddowes's funeral cortège began the journey from the Golden Lane Mortuary to the City of London Cemetery in Ilford. Her body lay in an elm coffin bearing a plate which gave her name in gold letters, carried in an open hearse, this being followed by a mourning coach containing the chief mourners – four of Catharine's sisters and John Kelly – behind which was a brougham carrying members of both the national and local press.

The route was lined with spectators, in some places so many that the pavements were completely choked with them. Other people leaned out of windows to watch the procession, and others even climbed onto the roofs of houses along the route to get a better view. The police were forced to clear a way through the streets to allow the funeral procession to continue its journey.

It took almost two hours before the coffin eventually arrived at its last resting place, where hundreds more people had already assembled to witness this sad final chapter of Catharine Eddowes's life. The service at the graveside was performed by the Reverend Dunscombe, the chaplain of the cemetery, and the undertaker, George Hawkes, covered the cost of the funeral himself.

Chapter 43

Tuesday, 9 October 1888
London

That morning Charles Warren sat in silence in his office at Scotland Yard and studied in detail the two post-mortem reports written by the doctors who had carried out the procedures on Elizabeth Stride and Catharine Eddowes. It was a small consolation, but it seemed clear to him that the Stride woman had barely suffered at all, death coming upon her so quickly that she hadn't even released her grip on the packet of cachous she had been holding. And apart from the deep wound in her throat, her body had apparently not been touched by the killer.

The murder of Catharine Eddowes was of course very different in almost every way. Again, Warren believed that the woman had been killed very quickly, and he was quite satisfied that all of the mutilations had been inflicted post-mortem, when she would have been past feeling. But that was hardly the point. It was bad enough that a faceless and unidentified killer was stalking the streets of Whitechapel murdering prostitutes, but it was the mutilations that had really grabbed the attention of the public. And, if the last note he'd received from 'Michael' was to be believed, the next murder would be infinitely worse than anything that had gone before.

And the report on Eddowes clarified one thing Warren hadn't understood. A line in the message had read 'A reminder on the cheeks of the last one', which only made sense when he studied the autopsy report and noted the doctor's statement that the killer had carved two inverted 'V' shapes into the cheeks of the dead woman. 'Michael' was again taunting him, providing a visual symbol on that victim of the two triangles or V-shapes which he had already described on the ground with the locations of his victims.

The only good thing was that the one person to whom that particular mutilation made any sense was Charles Warren himself, and he had no intention of explaining it to anyone else.

He was also concerned by another line in the last note he had received from the killer. One reason he had asked to see the reports was because of the short statement 'Look out for the kidney', and he had been entirely unsurprised to discover that Catharine Eddowes's left kidney had been removed in its entirety from her body. The obvious and unpleasant conclusion was that 'Michael' had taken it away with him, and presumably intended to do something with it that would serve to further embarrass the Metropolitan Police and alarm the residents of Whitechapel.

Although Warren was still relatively unconcerned about the deaths of the women themselves – after all, they were only unfortunates and frankly of little concern to anyone, in his opinion – he had been unexpectedly moved by the sight of the body of Elizabeth Stride lying in the mortuary. For the first time since the killings had begun, Warren had seen at first hand the result of the work of his nemesis, and it had been something of a shock. Intellectually, of course, he knew exactly what had been happening to these women, but it had produced very different emotions in him when he had seen the corpse of that woman.

But although he was still absolutely determined not to hand over the menorah, he knew that, somehow, the killings were going to have to stop, and he was really beginning to feel the pressure. Almost every day there were news reports and editorials in the papers which were harshly critical of the police force – the force which he commanded – and which emphasized in great detail exactly how little progress had been made in catching Jack the Ripper. And to make matters worse, Warren, and every other police officer in London, knew that these criticisms were entirely justified. With the single exception of Warren himself, nobody involved in law enforcement in Britain's capital city had the slightest idea of the identity the killer or of his real motive.

And it wasn't just the reference to Catharine Eddowes's missing kidney which was concerning Warren. He knew from the police reports and the few witness statements that each of the murders to date had been performed in a matter of minutes, with both the killer and the victim in exposed positions, with the attendant risk of discovery at any moment. If the murderer could somehow lure a woman into a quiet and secluded location, where he could carry out his work unobserved and at his leisure, Warren knew that the man would be able to produce mutilations which would surpass anything which he had done before, and which would have a devastating effect on Warren's own professional position, and of course on the residents of Whitechapel.

There had to be some way of catching the man before he started work again. And not just catching him. The one thing Warren could not permit to happen was for 'Michael' to appear in court and tell his own side of the story, to explain to a judge and jury what Warren had done in Jerusalem almost twenty years earlier. Although he knew that no proof of what he'd done could be offered, Warren was also aware that mud had a habit of sticking, and even if he managed to avoid being investigated or prosecuted himself, the rumours would spread, and in all probability his army career would at best stall, and at worst might be over.

He realized that he had only two viable courses of action. First, he could simply accede to the man's demands and hand over the Jewish relic. Or, second, he would have to devise some means by which he could get 'Michael' by himself and kill him. It was a desperate solution to a desperate problem, but Warren found he could justify that action, at least to himself, simply because of what 'Michael' had done in London. Not for the first time, he regretted not having pulled the trigger of his Webley revolver during their first and only meeting.

What he had to do was work out some way of engineering another meeting between himself and the other man, in a secluded location with an absence of witnesses, where he could carry out the deed and somehow dispose of the body.

And at that moment, Warren had absolutely no idea how he could achieve that.

A double knock on the door interrupted his thoughts.

'Come.'

The door opened and Inspector Abberline stepped into the office, a large folded sheet of paper held in his left hand.

'What is it?' Warren asked. 'You don't have an appointment.'

'I know, sir,' Abberline began, 'but I thought you would want to see this as soon as possible. I don't know how significant it is, but I've discovered something rather interesting about the locations of the murders.'

The inspector unfolded the sheet of paper he was carrying and placed it on the desk in front of the commissioner.

Warren saw immediately that the map Abberline had prepared

was almost identical to the one which was folded up and tucked away in one of the pockets of his locked briefcase. He had hoped that nobody else would realize the significance of the locations of the killings, but clearly something about this had dawned on the inspector.

'I've marked the location of all of the murders to date on this map of Whitechapel, sir,' Abberline went on, pointing at a series of crosses, each marked by a name and a date, 'and I then drew lines to connect them. As you can see, the first three killings, those of Tabram, Nichols and Chapman, form a clear triangle with a fairly acute angle at the apex. Then, if you use the location of the Chapman killing as a starting point, the murders of Stride and Eddowes also form a triangle, but one with a much larger angle at the apex. In fact, it's almost ninety degrees at the site of the Eddowes killing.'

Warren stared at the map for a few moments before he replied.

'I'm quite sure, Abberline, that if you plotted almost any series of murders you would end up with some interesting geometrical shapes. What, exactly, is your point?'

Abberline glanced up at the commissioner, then down again at the map.

'You might think that this is a bit far-fetched, sir, but when I drew these connecting lines, the thing that struck me immediately was that the shapes were familiar. It took me a while, but then I realized what it was. I'm a Freemason, sir, as I believe you are, and if you don't draw the connecting lines on the map between the locations of the Chapman and Tabram murders, and between Chapman and Stride, you end up with two "V" shapes. To me, they look very like the shapes of the compasses and the square, the Masonic symbol. They don't exactly correspond, but they're very close.'

Warren didn't respond, just looked at the inspector.

'I think, sir, that I was right when I said to you that this man was trying to send somebody a message.'

'What message? And to whom?' Warren demanded.

'I think this man has a grudge against Freemasonry, and he's deliberately carried out these killings to display the shape of the Masonic symbol on the ground in Whitechapel. I think he's trying to suggest that the killer is a Mason, and to discredit the whole Masonic movement.'

Charles Warren relaxed slightly. Abberline's perspicacity had surprised him. He hadn't expected anyone to relate the locations of the murders to the ancient symbol of his Craft, and he was just thankful that the inspector's analysis hadn't led him to the correct conclusion, that the murders were indeed a message, a message to Warren himself. What he now needed to do was throw the inspector off the track as far as he possibly could.

'That's interesting, Abberline,' he said, 'but you're reading far too much into what's been happening in Whitechapel. It's a pure coincidence that you can see these shapes on the ground. It's obvious to me that the killer is simply selecting his victims wherever he can find them, and he's choosing each new location some distance away from his previous murder, to avoid being detected by the increased patrols we have in the area.'

Abberline didn't look entirely convinced by his superior's argument.

'And there's another thing,' Warren continued. 'If by some chance you're right, then now the murders will presumably stop, because he's already created the shape of the two triangles, the Masonic symbol, on the ground. Do you really think that this man has now completed his work, and that we'll have no further killings? Are you so convinced about this that I can order our extra patrols and police officers to leave Whitechapel?'

Abberline shook his head.

'I can't say that, no, sir,' he replied.

'Exactly,' Warren snapped. 'Jack the Ripper is still out there, Abberline. You know it and I know it, and you would be far better employed in trying to find him instead of coming up with a ridiculous fairy story like this.'

Abberline walked out of the commissioner's office, and out of Scotland Yard, with a worried frown on his face, a frown which remained all the way back to the Bethnal Green police station.

He knew that Charles Warren was an exceedingly difficult man to deal with, a man who consistently failed to listen to any advice given to him by any other person, irrespective of their position, background or knowledge, but even knowing that, Abberline still had a strange undercurrent of doubt about the commissioner. A doubt that was beginning to border on suspicion.

It was almost as if the man knew more than he was prepared to say about the killings. He had apparently been unsurprised by the murders, had perhaps even been expecting them, and that simply didn't make sense. He couldn't be involved in them, obviously, because he had been out of the country when the second woman, Mary Ann Nichols, had been slaughtered, and bearing in mind that both the Metropolitan Police and the commissioner himself had been the subject of one of the most angry, focused, intense and aggressive media campaigns the capital city had ever seen, he very clearly had no motive for any kind of involvement.

But if that were the case, why was he always so consistently dismissive of any new information which Abberline – or anyone else, for that matter – placed before him? And the detective inspector still remembered, very clearly, Charles Warren's reaction when Abberline had suggested, almost in passing, that the killings seemed almost to be a message to somebody. The man had gone so white that for a moment Abberline had almost expected him to faint.

Warren clearly knew something about what was going on, something which he was extremely unwilling to impart to his subordinates, to the very people who were trying unsuccessfully to bring Jack the Ripper to justice. But Abberline had not the slightest idea what that knowledge might be, or how the commissioner could possibly be involved.

He shook his head. He would just have to continue the hunt for the mass murderer as best he could, and follow up any leads that he could identify, while at the same time keeping a very close eye on Charles Warren, his ultimate superior, just in case the man let slip anything that could be of value.

Abberline closed his eyes briefly as the cab neared its destination. It was an invidious situation for anybody to be in. He was chasing a murderer who seemed able to evade any and all precautions which were taken to prevent his actions, a man who left no clues to either his identity or his motive for carrying out the killings, and who probably would strike again, perhaps several times. He was a member of a police force that was being reviled on a daily basis by the newspapers, and which had not the slightest idea what to do next to catch this man. And, finally, he now suspected that his superior officer might in some way be involved with either the murderer or the killings themselves.

As well as the grotesque nightmare which had engulfed Whitechapel and Spitalfields, Frederick Abberline now seemed to be held captive in a nightmare all of his own.

Chapter 44

Wednesday, 10 October 1888
Whitechapel, London

Because of the 'Dear Boss' letter received by the Central News Agency on 27 September, the serial killer who had been targeting prostitutes in the East End of London now had a name, and a name that would stick.

The soubriquet the 'Whitechapel fiend' had enjoyed a brief popularity before being supplanted by the specific but misleading 'Leather Apron' and the more prosaic 'Whitechapel murderer', but the name 'Jack the Ripper' spread like wildfire once details of the letter were published. The name was, at one and the same time, both commonplace – 'Jack' was one of the most popular male names of the time – and appropriate in that it described precisely what the unknown killer did. Soon after the 'double event' of the killings of Elizabeth Stride and Catharine Eddowes, the name 'Jack the Ripper' was on everyone's lips. Warnings like 'Watch out for Jack' and 'Careful Jack doesn't get you' were muttered when friends parted, and not in jest. The killer really was still out there – he had just demonstrated that in an utterly unequivocal manner – and everyone knew it.

The first letter received by the Central News Agency was dated 25 September and had carried a London East Central postmark for 27 September and, in the context of what happened on the night of the 30th, some of the sentences seemed particularly pertinent.

'Jack the Ripper', the signatory of the letter, had said specifically that he wanted to start his 'work' again, and that the next time he would 'clip the ladys ears off'.

This letter was sent by the agency to the Metropolitan Police on 29 September, and in the early hours of the very next morning the killer had struck again, twice. He had indeed 'got to work right away', just as he'd threatened. And when he'd mutilated the body of Catharine Eddowes, he'd severed the lobe of her right ear. He hadn't removed it from the scene to send it to the police, but this might simply have been because he couldn't find it. When the body was stripped in the mortuary, Dr Brown noted that 'a piece of deceased's ear dropped from the clothing', so it is conceivable that the murderer cut it off and then dropped it and was unable to locate it in the dark of Mitre Square. And with the regular tramp of a policeman's boots getting steadily closer, he might not have been able to risk taking the time to sever and remove the other one.

The mere fact that the letter had mentioned cutting off the ears of his victim, and that this had then been done, strongly suggested that the writer of the letter – the man who signed himself 'Jack the Ripper' – was indeed the murderer.

And what happened next seemed to confirm this supposition.

In the first post on Monday, 1 October, the Central News Agency received another communication purporting to have been sent by the killer. This time it was a postcard, apparently stained with blood, and again signed by 'Jack the Ripper'. It was undated, but bore a 'London E' postmark stamped that same day. The postcard had clearly been written by the same person who had authored the letter, a fact established both by an examination of the handwriting on the two communications, which had enough points of similarity to establish that a single hand had been responsible for both, and also by the content of the postcard, which referred specifically to the letter.

The postcard read:

> I wasnt codding
> dear old Boss when
> I gave you the tip.
> youll hear about
> saucy Jackys work
> tomorrow double
> event this time
> number one squealed
> a bit couldn't
> finish straight
> off. had not time
> to get ears for
> police thanks for
> keeping last letter
> back till I got
> to work again.
>   Jack the Ripper

Very obviously, the person who wrote this postcard had also sent the letter. It was also obvious that the writer was extremely well informed about the circumstances of both the murders which had taken place on the night of 30 September. It was already popularly believed that the killer might have been disturbed in Dutfield's Yard and would have had to make a rapid escape, and the reference to the ears of the second victim also implied that the writer was the killer.

But in fact this wasn't quite as clear-cut as it at first appeared. News of the murders had spread rapidly through the tenements and public houses of Whitechapel in the hours following the discovery of the two bodies, and details of the circumstances of the two killings quickly became common knowledge. According to some of the Monday newspapers, several Sunday editions had carried details of the double murder and, according to the *Telegraph*, a state of 'almost frantic excitement' had pervaded the East End of London on the Sunday and 'thousands of people visited both Mitre Square and Berner Street, and journals containing details of the crimes were bought up by crowds of men and women in Whitechapel, Stepney, and Spitalfields.'

As far as the timescale was concerned, the fact that the postcard was stamped with the date of the first of October – OC 1 – meant that it could have been written either on the Sunday but posted after the last collection, or very early on the Monday morning. So it was possible that the writer had simply composed a brief message based upon the stories which were already circulating throughout the district. Alternatively, it was possible that the writer knew so much about both murders because he had been at the two crime scenes in person, wielding his knife to deadly effect.

Either scenario was feasible, and there was no obvious way of deciding which was the more likely. The view of most police officers at the time, and certainly that of Charles Warren, who not only knew the identity of the murderer but also his motive, was that both the letter and the postcard were part of a hoax perpetrated by a newspaper reporter, most probably intended to revive public interest in a story which was seen to be dying away. On 10 October, Warren told Godfrey Lushington, the Permanent Under-Secretary at the Home Office: 'At present I think the whole thing a hoax but we are bound to try and ascertain the writer in any case.' The most obvious suspicion was that the communications were the work of a London journalist, but the police never named a suspect, and there were no prosecutions in the matter.

This time, there was no delay in sending the missive to the police, who took it extremely seriously and began a concerted campaign to try to identify the writer. They prepared copies of both the letter and the postcard and on 3 October they published them on a poster which requested that anyone who recognized the handwriting should immediately contact them. A copy of the poster was put up outside every police station in London, and others were sent to the newspapers. On the following day, 4 October, several of the papers published facsimiles of the two messages wholly or in part.

The result of this campaign was almost exactly the opposite of what the Metropolitan Police had hoped. Nobody apparently recognized the handwriting, which had been the purpose of publicizing the two communications, but the fact that the hitherto anonymous killer now had a name seemed to spark a positive flood of letters all, of course, signed by 'Jack the Ripper'. Scotland Yard had already been receiving some twenty letters every day about the series of murders, and the Central News Agency almost double that number. But once the name 'Jack the Ripper' entered the public consciousness, in weeks the combined total of letters being received by both organizations topped one thousand a week.

All of these missives required the allocation of police resources to investigate them. And, perhaps predictably, not one of them yielded any new or useful information, or got the Metropolitan Police any closer to identifying the murderer.

As was his established habit, Alexei Pedachenko purchased copies of all the London papers every day, in order to keep abreast of the latest developments in the hunt for Jack the Ripper by the Metropolitan Police, or at least as up to date as the information in the newspapers allowed him to be. He'd read the first 'Dear Boss' letter with considerable amusement, and was quickly convinced that it was the work of some hack journalist writing for a newspaper, a man who was desperate to keep the story of the murders alive so that the circulation figures would continue to rise.

When he read about the second communication in the papers published on 4 October, he felt a moment's disquiet, especially when he read the information about the postmark. It was almost as if he had been observed at his work, because the writer seemed so very well informed. But then he relaxed again. If anybody had seen him, he would certainly have known about it. And he did know that the Sunday editions of the papers had carried most of the important details about the two killings, and so it would not have been that difficult for the writer – who, after all, was almost certainly a reporter for one of those papers – to put together a convincing message.

And that report about the 'Jack the Ripper' letters, Pedachenko decided, was probably a good enough cue for him to send a communication of his own. But it wouldn't be a letter, and it wouldn't be addressed to Scotland Yard.

Chapter 45

The new chairman of the Mile End Vigilance Committee was a man named George Lusk, a builder who lived at 1 Alderney Road, Mile End. On the evening of Tuesday, 16 October he received an extremely disagreeable object through the post. It was a small parcel wrapped in brown paper and the contents unnerved him, to say the least, and he was unsure what to do about it. In the end, he did nothing, at least not that day.

But late the following evening, he attended the regular meeting of the Vigilance Committee, and immediately attracted attention.

Joseph Aarons, the treasurer, approached Lusk almost as soon as he walked through the door, because the chairman appeared to be in a state of considerable excitement.

'George?' Aarons asked. 'You look as if you've seen a ghost, or the devil. What's happened to you?'

For a moment or two Lusk seemed lost for words. Then he shook his head and tried to explain.

'I suppose you will laugh at what I'm going to tell you,' Lusk said, 'but you must know that I had a little parcel come to me on Tuesday evening, and to my surprise it contains half a kidney and a letter from Jack the Ripper.'

The chairman's statement stunned all the committee members, but then Aarons emitted in a short laugh.

'That must be some kind of a joke, George,' Aarons said, shaking his head. 'It's probably just somebody trying to frighten you.'

But Lusk was clearly perturbed by what had happened, and fiercely rebuffed the treasurer's attempt to laugh the matter off.

'It is no laughing matter to me,' he retorted.

'Well I can see that this episode is concerning you,' Aarons said, 'so I think the best course of action is that I will call on you at your home early tomorrow morning with some other members of the committee so that we can examine the object.'

'That will be satisfactory to me,' Lusk replied. 'I will be glad to see the back of the thing.'

The following morning at about half past nine Aarons, accompanied by the secretary, a man named Harris, and Reeves and Lawton, two other members, arrived at Lusk's house in Alderney Road.

'Good morning to you,' Aarons said cheerfully when Lusk opened the door to them and ushered them inside.

The chairman led the way to his study, and sat down at his desk.

'Here it is,' he said, 'the revolting thing.'

He opened a desk drawer and produced a small cardboard box, about three and a half inches square, and handed it to Aarons.

'Throw it away,' he instructed them. 'I hate the sight of it.'

The treasurer lifted the lid of the box and peered at the object which lay inside it. Almost immediately, he recoiled, as did the other committee members who had crowded round him. Inside the box was half of a kidney which had been cut longitudinally. Completely unsurprisingly, it reeked.

'Oh my God,' Aarons said, his voice subdued. 'I can see exactly why this disturbed you so much, George. It's revolting.'

'And that's not all,' Lusk said, sounding almost pleased at the impact the object had had on Aarons, who he had always thought was too cheerful by half. 'He sent me a letter as well.'

Lusk again reached into the drawer of his desk and extracted a small piece of paper, which he also handed to Aarons.

The treasurer read it silently, then handed the page to Harris to study. The letter was smeared with red marks, very possibly blood, and was written in a spiky and apparently illiterate hand.

Joseph Aarons shuddered involuntarily, and for some minutes he stared at the cardboard box, studying the object it contained.

'I'm not a doctor, but I don't think this is a kidney from an animal,' he said finally, 'so I suggest that we should take it to Dr Frederick Wiles. He has a surgery at 56 Mile End Road and I think he is the nearest doctor to this premises.'

'Yes, take it, take it,' George Lusk said, clearly glad to be rid of the object.

Aarons replaced the lid on the box, tucked the letter into the pocket of his jacket, and the four men took their leave.

They walked briskly to the doctor's surgery, but when they reached the address, Wiles was out.

'I don't know how long the doctor will be,' his assistant, a man named Reed, told them. 'If it is an urgent matter, perhaps I can help.'

'In truth, Mr Reed,' Aarons replied, 'I didn't know if it is urgent or not. It concerns a package our colleague received from somebody purporting to be the notorious killer Jack the Ripper. The package, which I have here, appears to contain part of a human kidney.'

'Good Lord,' Reed said, his interest clearly aroused. 'If I can examine it, I might be able to determine its origin for you.'

Aarons nodded assent, and passed him the cardboard box.

For a few minutes, Reed looked at, and then poked and prodded the object, then sat back and looked up at Aarons.

'I think this is probably human,' he said, 'and it looks to me as if it has being preserved in spirits of wine or some similar medium. But to be certain I think we should take it and show it to Dr Thomas Horrocks Openshaw at the London Hospital. He is the Curator of the Pathological Museum, and he will be able to confirm or refute my suspicions.'

The small party of men, its number now increased by one, walked briskly to the London Hospital and quickly gained entrance to see Dr Openshaw.

Aarons again explained how the organ had come to be in his possession, and the doctor almost immediately began examining it under a microscope. It didn't take him long to come to a decision.

'This is definitely a section of a human kidney,' he said, 'taken from the left side of the body and, despite the smell which I think is partially the result of the preserving liquid in which it must have been placed, I believe it is fairly fresh, probably removed from the body within about the last three weeks.'

That was good enough for Joseph Aarons.

'Thank you, doctor,' he said. 'We will immediately hand this over to the police.'

The closest police station was the one at Leman Street, and shortly after leaving the London Hospital, Aarons handed over the object to a surprised Inspector Abberline, who was at the station.

'It came from where?' Abberline asked.

'It was sent to my colleague Mr George Lusk, who is—'

Abberline nodded and then interrupted.

'I know of Mr Lusk,' he said. 'I believe he's now the chairman of the Mile End Vigilance Committee.'

'Exactly so,' Aarons confirmed. 'There was a letter in the box as well as the kidney,' he added, reached into his pocket and handed over the single sheet of paper to the detective.

As soon as the men had left, Abberline examined the organ for himself, his face crinkling with disgust at the foul smell it was emitting, then called one of the sergeants over to him.

'This might be almost the first useful clue we've found,' he said. 'This could be a part of the kidney that was taken from the woman who was killed in Mitre Square. Instruct a constable to take it at once to the City Police, because that murder was in their jurisdiction. But tell them we'd like a full report on it as soon as they can.'

'Very good, sir.'

At that stage, Abberline had no idea whether or not the section of kidney in the box had been removed from Jack the Ripper's victim, or if it was some kind of an elaborate hoax, possibly being perpetrated by a medical student or some other individual with access to human body parts. But Joseph Aarons had already had the kidney examined by a specialist, and it seemed clear that it was a section of the left kidney, which was a good sign. The autopsy on the Mitre Square victim – a woman he now knew had been named Catharine Eddowes – had shown that it was her left kidney that had been cut out and taken away.

Within the hour, Major Henry Smith, the Acting Commissioner of the City of London Police, had taken possession of the cardboard box and its grisly contents, and had summoned the City Police surgeon, Dr Gordon Brown, to perform an examination on the section of kidney.

It didn't take long for Brown to report his findings to Major Smith, findings which – perhaps to everyone's surprise – provided fairly compelling evidence that the kidney had indeed been cut out of Catharine Eddowes's abdomen by Jack the Ripper.

'The first thing I checked,' Brown began, providing the Acting Commissioner with a verbal report whilst his detailed findings were being typed, 'was the gross appearance of the organ, and I saw immediately that about one inch of the renal artery was still attached to the kidney. When I carried out the post-mortem on the body of the victim, I noted that about two inches of the artery remained inside the corpse. The renal artery is normally about three inches in length, so that was a good match. I also confirmed that the kidney I was given had come from the left side of the body, and again it was that organ which had been removed from Eddowes. Finally, as a part of the post-mortem I also considered the state of the body, and the kidney which remained in the corpse showed signs of chronic nephritis – a condition commonly known as Bright's Disease – and this was also evident on the organ sent to this man Lusk through the post.'

'So are you saying that this kidney *was* removed from the body of Catharine Eddowes?' Major Smith demanded.

Brown shook his head.

'That I cannot say for certain, but it is certainly a very strong possibility, perhaps even a probability. And there is one other piece of evidence, circumstantial evidence, granted, but important for all that, which would seem to confirm it.'

'And what's that?' Smith asked eagerly.

'I took the liberty of asking a colleague of mine, a man named Sutton, who's a very senior surgeon at the London Hospital and one of the most eminent authorities in the country on the kidney and its diseases, to have a look at the organ as well. He agreed with my findings – the diseased condition of the organ and the length of the renal artery that was still attached to it – but he also confirmed my suspicion about one other indicator. And that was the way that it had been treated, presumably by the man who removed it.'

'I don't follow that, doctor.'

'You obviously saw the state of the kidney when it was delivered to you, and the way that it smelt.'

It was a statement, not a question, but the expression of disgust which crossed Major Smith's face was confirmation that he had examined it.

'Bearing in mind how long ago the murder took place, for the kidney to be in that condition meant that an attempt must have been made to preserve it, and both Sutton and I agree that the medium used was probably spirits of wine. We are also quite certain that it must have been removed from the body very soon after death had occurred, and placed in this preserving fluid only a matter of hours after that.'

Major Smith didn't look convinced.

'How do you know that?'

'The moment a person dies, all of the organs in the body begin to decay, some of them a lot faster than others. The section of kidney that you provided showed almost no signs of such decay, which means it had to have been removed from the body soon after death. It couldn't, for example, have been removed from a person who had died a few days earlier, by somebody working for an undertaker. Obtaining access to a fresh corpse is not an easy thing to achieve.'

'But what about a medical student? Couldn't some student have removed a section of kidney from a corpse being used for dissection?'

'Certainly,' Dr Brown agreed, 'but it would have been very different to this organ. All cadavers available for dissection are invariably preserved in formalin, not in spirits of wine, and the conditions of the organs in such bodies are quite unmistakable to any doctor. The one thing which I'm absolutely certain is that this could not be the result of a prank being perpetrated by a medical student. In short, and in my opinion, the most likely, and perhaps even the only, way in which this could have been achieved was for the kidney to be removed from a murder victim by the killer. And that would certainly suggest that the murderer was Jack the Ripper and that his victim was Catharine Eddowes.'

While Inspector Abberline was waiting for the results of the examination ordered by Major Smith, he carefully examined the package in which the kidney had been sent.

'There's only one stamp on it,' he said, 'and that's a two penny stamp. There's a partial and indistinct postmark, but the only letters of that which I can read are "OND".'

'Not difficult to work that out,' Chandler said. 'That must be a part of the word "LONDON", and that might mean that it was posted in the Eastern district, which is the same district as the delivery address. I don't know if you knew that, Fred, but it's normal for items of mail that travel through more than one district to be stamped by the offices in each of those districts. It doesn't prove that that was where it was posted, but it's certainly indicative.'

Abberline nodded.

'I didn't know that, Joseph, so thanks. As you say, it's not proof, but even if we knew for certain that it was posted in that district, and even if we could identify the office from which it was sent, it wouldn't help very much. The chances of any postal clerk remembering who handed over the package are probably non-existent.'

The two detectives turned their attention from the box to the letter which had accompanied the organ.

'I'll tell you one thing, Joseph,' Abberline said. 'Whoever wrote this letter was definitely *not* the author of the "Dear Boss" letter and postcard.'

'I had my suspicions about that letter right from the start,' Chandler growled. 'There were no spelling mistakes in it, and it read to me like the work of an educated man who was trying to appear semi-literate. I still think we were right, and that the author was some journalist with too much time on his hands. The only thing that letter provided was an appropriate name for the killer. And the information on the postcard could have been read by anybody in the first editions of the Sunday papers. I think it was definitely a hoax.'

'You're almost certainly right,' Abberline agreed. 'But this is very different. I know that no matter what Major Smith and the City of London police surgeon discover about the kidney, there's no way we'll ever be able to definitely prove that it came from the body of Catharine Eddowes, but my gut feeling is that it probably did. And I can't think of any way that somebody other than the killer, other than Jack the Ripper, could have got possession of the organ, and could then have sent it to Lusk. That means that this letter in front of us' – he tapped the piece of paper to emphasize what he was saying – 'was almost certainly written by the Ripper himself.'

The two men looked at the blood-smeared piece of paper, and at the clumsy writing on it.

'Now that,' Chandler said, 'really does look as if it was sent by somebody with a very limited command of the English language.'

'Actually, Joseph, I'm not so sure about that. Remember that we are also reasonably certain that the writing found by Constable Long in Goulston Street had to have been written by the murderer, simply because of the bloodstained cloth that was found in the same place. And that writing, at least according to Long, was correctly spelt – apart from the one word "Juwes", and I think we now know why that was – and written by an educated hand. I have a suspicion that this letter was written by the same person, but probably using his left hand to disguise his writing.'

'But this letter is full of mistakes,' Chandler objected, pointing down at the page, at the text which was now so familiar to them:

From hell

Mr Lusk
Sor

I send you half the Kidne I took from one women prasarved it for you tother piece I fried and ate it was very nise I may send you the bloody knif that took it out if you only wate a whil longer
Signed   Catch me when

you can
Mishter Lusk

'Actually,' Abberline responded, 'it isn't. It just looks as if it is. I've studied it. The letter contains fifty-six words and only nine of them are incorrectly spelt, and there's one plural – "women" – that should be the singular "woman". Most of the long words, like "bloody", "longer" and "signed" are correctly spelt, and at least one word – "fried" – which I would have expected to be misspelt if the writer really is illiterate, is actually correctly spelt. And there are two other obvious anomalies which suggest that this is the work of an educated man. Although he has deliberately misspelt "knife" and "while" by missing off the last letter of both words, he has included the silent "k" in the first word and the silent "h" in the second. That is the work of a person who definitely knows how both words should be spelt.'

Chandler looked again at the text of the blood-smeared letter, and shook his head.

'But I still don't understand why he would need to do that. Why would he need to send a letter at all? Or disguise his handwriting? I hear what you say about the Goulston Street writing, and I think it probably was an attempt to throw suspicion on the Jewish community, for whatever reason. But with this kidney, why would he bother? Why didn't he just send the kidney and leave it at that if he didn't want anybody to see his handwriting?'

Abberline shrugged.

'I can't be sure, obviously, but I think he probably wanted to make absolutely sure that George Lusk wouldn't just throw the kidney away as soon as he'd opened the box, which is what most people would probably have done. Jack the Ripper had a very good reason for removing that poor woman's kidney, and then for sending it to Lusk. He wanted to make absolutely certain that both the kidney and the letter would end up in the hands of the police but he still needed to send it to a civilian, because his sole objective in doing this, in my opinion, was to make sure that the newspapers get to hear about it. If he'd just sent it to a police station, there was a chance that it would have remained confidential, but I'm almost prepared to wager money that George Lusk is already giving interviews.'

'I see what you're driving at,' Chandler nodded. 'He's putting on the pressure, isn't he? It's not enough that he's terrifying the women of Whitechapel and Spitalfields. Now he's adding an extra dimension to the horror, because he's also eating them. Or claiming that he is.'

'I remember what you said, Joseph, when you came back from seeing the body of Annie Chapman at Hanbury Street. You said it looked almost as if it had been prepared, the way a butcher prepares an animal's carcass. I had a feeling then that this might be the next step. First he kills them, then he mutilates them, then he takes away trophies, like he did with Chapman, and finally he cuts out organs, as he did with Catharine Eddowes, and eats them. Or at least, as you said, that's what he's claiming he did. We'll never know for sure whether that's the truth or if it's just another way – and a very effective way – of increasing the terror in the East End of London.'

Abberline paused for a moment, glanced down at the text of the letter in front of him, then looked up at Chandler.

'And what really worries me, Joseph,' he said, 'is that we've got no idea what he's going to do next. But the one thing I am certain about is that he hasn't finished yet.'

Charles Warren was of course informed about the kidney, but the information was hardly a surprise to him. Ever since he'd received the last note from 'Michael', he'd been expecting to hear that the missing kidney, or a part of it, would be sent to a newspaper or some other organization. He hadn't expected that one of the vigilance committees would be the recipient, but the effect had been much the same as if it had been sent to a newspaper.

He knew the organ had been sent by 'Michael', and the only real surprise to him was the note which accompanied it. Warren assumed that he had deliberately disguised his handwriting and had taken considerable care with the text to ensure that he appeared to be only semi-literate. The writing was entirely different to that found in the doorway at Goulston Street, and the different hand was presumably another attempt to muddy the waters.

But 'Michael' would be certain that Warren wouldn't be fooled, and that the commissioner would know that the two 'messages' had been the work of the same person, just as Warren was now certain that the 'Dear Boss' letters were a hoax.

Warren knew that and, just like Detective Inspector Abberline, he also knew that Jack the Ripper hadn't yet finished his work.

Chapter 46

Tuesday, 23 October 1888
Whitechapel, London

The inquest into the murder of Catharine Eddowes had been opened on 4 October at the Golden Lane Mortuary under the direction of the City Coroner, Samuel Frederick Langham, but was quickly adjourned to the eleventh of the month. When the jury finally returned their verdict, it was entirely predictable: wilful murder against some person unknown. The fact was that nobody had the slightest idea who the murderer was, except that it was now fairly clear that the police were looking for a single killer, not a gang of two or more people working together.

The report on the inquest published in the *Daily News* summed up the situation quite neatly: 'Practically the world knows nothing more of this crime than it did on the morning when it was first announced. We have some details about the victim, few or none about the murderer. The "person unknown" has every right to his designation.'

The inquest on Elizabeth Stride was conducted by Wynne Baxter and had begun three days earlier than that of Eddowes, on 1 October. Baxter was meticulous in his examination of the witnesses, and reviewed every piece of evidence in great detail, adjourning the inquest four times before finally terminating it on the 23rd of the month. But despite his very different and more exhaustive approach, Baxter fared no better than Langham, and the jury produced precisely the same result.

The fact that Jack the Ripper was still at large, and that the police still appeared to have not the slightest idea who he was, and had no obvious prospect of stopping or catching him, produced renewed calls for a government reward to be paid to anyone who could bring him to justice. Because Catharine Eddowes had died within the City of London, the Lord Mayor was able to offer a reward of £500 to anyone who could provide information which would lead to the capture and conviction of the Ripper.

But attempts to persuade the Home Secretary, Henry Matthews, to do the same were repeatedly rebuffed. The prime mover in this correspondence was the Mile End Vigilance Committee, under the chairmanship of George Lusk. On 30 September, the committee secretary, Mr B. Harris, wrote to Matthews requesting that he reconsider his position. The reply from the Home Office on 2 October was unequivocal: the Home Secretary saw no reason to change his position. On 7 October, some ten days before he received the section of kidney through the post, George Lusk tried again, requesting not only a government reward, but also a free pardon for any accomplice of the Ripper who would provide information that would convict the killer.

Support for the idea of a pardon came from Charles Warren himself, which was a calculated gamble by the commissioner. He had thought long and hard before adding his voice to the proposal, but had reasoned that his relations with the Home Secretary were so poor that he was almost certain any suggestion he made would be rejected out of hand by Matthews. And he was quite right. The Home Office refused to agree and the only response was a bland statement that they would keep the matter under review.

Other citizens and organizations also suggested offering a reward. The editor of the *Financial Times*, Harry Marks, had forwarded a cheque in the sum of £300 to Matthews early in October, but this was returned to him almost immediately. The officer commanding the Tower Hamlets Battalion of the Royal Engineers offered £100 and the services of fifty soldiers. Again, Matthews refused to accept either offer.

But private donors exhibited none of the qualms and doubts which appeared to afflict the Home Secretary, and within days of the 'double event' taking place, the huge sum, for the time, of £1,200 had been committed and would be paid to anyone who could identify or apprehend the murderer.

The Mile End Vigilance Committee was active in other ways as well. It was clear that the police presence in the East End of London was having little or no effect upon the activities of Jack the Ripper, and so the Committee decided upon vigilante action as well as simple vigilance. They selected strong and fit men from their ranks, armed them with stout sticks and whistles, paid them a small wage, and instructed them to patrol the streets of Whitechapel every night, beginning at around midnight and continuing until about four or five o'clock in the morning. In addition, the Committee met every evening at nine in a private room at the Crown public house on Mile End Road to discuss the work of their patrols and to consider other ways in which the safety of the women of Whitechapel could be improved. They also employed a private detective agency, Grand and Batchelor, to provide professional supervision of their patrols.

It's by no means clear what these patrols by the Mile End Vigilance Committee – which were soon supplemented by others from the Working Men's Vigilance Committee, based in Aldgate – actually achieved, if anything.

From the point of view of the Metropolitan Police officers charged with keeping the streets safe, these vigilante efforts were not an immediately obvious help. They simply meant that large numbers of men began walking the streets of Whitechapel in the early hours of the morning, men who had to be watched by the police and their identities confirmed if they appeared to be acting in a suspicious manner. In many cases, it was obvious that there were plain-clothes detectives watching vigilante volunteers, who were in turn watching other detectives, and all of them were being observed by uniformed officers.

But it was also undeniably true that these amateur patrols provided additional observers in the area, and numerous reports on potential suspects were forwarded to the police for investigation. Almost inevitably, these 'suspects' turned out to be entirely innocent men going about their normal trade or business. Several doctors were arrested on suspicion, simply because they were carrying black medical bags, such was the strength of the powerful and enduring belief in Whitechapel that the killer was a medical man. This belief was fuelled further when it was suggested that the murderer was using chloroform to subdue his victims before killing them, though none of the post-mortems carried out on the dead women had shown the slightest evidence of this.

And the police were visibly doing more in their attempts to catch the killer. After the 'double event', additional officers, many of them in plain clothes, were sent into the area to supplement the local force, to increase the number of policemen on the streets, in an attempt to try to deter Jack the Ripper from striking again. These extra officers were also a source of some confusion to the uniformed men, who had to identify them just as they had to check the identities of the unofficial patrols.

And Abberline's decoy officers – the young constables who had been armed with revolvers and dressed in women's clothing – were still walking the darkened streets of Whitechapel but without any results so far, apart from the angry reactions of a handful of clients who had believed them to be precisely what they appeared: available prostitutes. Abberline had inspected half a dozen of these young officers, and was frankly amazed that anybody would mistake them for women, even in poor lighting, but clearly there were men out there who were a lot less discerning and discriminating, or perhaps simply didn't see very well.

And that, really, was about all the police could do. They still had not the slightest idea who Jack the Ripper actually was, apart from the most basic of deductions – that he apparently possessed a certain amount of anatomical knowledge which suggested he might have worked in the medical profession or as a butcher or something similar – and they still had no firm clue regarding his motive, except that he was clearly targeting prostitutes. And even that could simply be circumstantial: they were usually the only women walking the streets in the early hours of the morning. With nothing else to go on, and no apparent way of identifying the killer in the teeming streets of Whitechapel, all the police could do was try to deter him from striking again.

But a suggestion by Sir John Whittaker Ellis, who was a former Lord Mayor of London, that the Metropolitan Police should enter and search every house and premises in the centre of Whitechapel in the search for the killer did spark a new initiative. Ellis's proposal could not be implemented simply because the police had no right to enter and search any premises unless they possessed a warrant issued by a magistrate, and such a warrant would not be provided unless there was sufficient justification for that search.

If, however, the consent of the owner or tenant of the property could be obtained, then the police could legally enter and inspect the premises. The obvious flaw with this scheme was that if by some chance the police did happen to knock on the door of a house occupied by Jack the Ripper, all he had to do was to say 'no' when they asked to be admitted, and the police would have to just walk away. By definition, the only people who would allow their homes to be searched would be those with nothing to hide.

But in mid October they tried the tactic anyway. The Metropolitan Police chose an area that included the most desperate slums in Whitechapel and Spitalfields and for almost a week detectives wearing plain clothes searched every property that they could, checking the interiors of the buildings for hiding places and suspicious persons, examining every knife they could find and questioning everybody there. It was perhaps unsurprising that few owners or tenants refused admission to the police, because the dark shadow that Jack the Ripper had cast over this part of the city meant that everybody, rich or poor, male or female, desperately wanted the man to be caught and for his reign of terror to be finally brought to an end.

Also unsurprising was the fact that the police found absolutely nothing, despite the large number of premises they inspected. In fact, the only positive result of this major effort was that it showed the residents of the East End of London that the forces of law and order were doing *something* about the murderer, even if what they were doing actually made little sense.

The use of bloodhounds in the hunt for the Ripper had been suggested on several occasions by both the press and members of the public, and Charles Warren decided to sanction their use with the support of the Home Office, but this was not a success. For one thing, the Metropolitan Police did not own any bloodhounds, which meant they were forced to approach a private individual for the use of his animals, which raised inevitable questions about funding. Were the dogs to be hired or bought? Where were they to be kept and who would act as their handler? There was no provision in the budget for any such financial outlay, and when Warren requested a comparatively modest allowance to permit bloodhounds to be stationed in London, the Home Secretary only authorized a small proportion of the sum he had suggested.

On a more practical note, bloodhounds are extremely efficient at tracking an individual once they have been given his or her scent to follow, and that was probably the biggest problem the police faced. Jack the Ripper had already proven himself extremely adept at leaving no clues behind at the scenes of his various crimes, and ideally the bloodhounds needed to be offered a piece of clothing or other material which the criminal had worn or at the very least touched. The reality was that most of the scents available at the crime scene were those of the victim herself and of the person or persons who had discovered her body. And even if by some stroke of luck one of the bloodhounds did manage to detect the scent of the murderer, the chances of the animal being able to follow the trail through the crowded and polluted streets of Whitechapel were extremely remote. And, in the event, although the use of bloodhounds was trialled by the police, the dogs were never employed at any of the crime scenes.

Other suggestions and ideas, many of them verging on the ridiculous, were also offered to the police, and in at least one case suggested by a police officer who should have known better. Dr Robert Anderson was the new head of the Metropolitan Police Criminal Investigation Department and, in conference with Charles Warren and the Home Secretary, he suggested that every known 'unfortunate' or prostitute found on the streets after midnight should be arrested. The fact that Anderson was able to make this laughable suggestion shows clearly that he had little or no idea of the conditions that existed in Whitechapel and the East End.

A police report which was prepared in October 1888 estimated that there were at least sixty-two functioning brothels in Whitechapel alone, over 230 common lodging houses together accommodating some 8,500 inmates, over half of them women, many of whom were forced to sell their bodies on the streets from time to time in order to live, and well over 1,000 working full-time prostitutes. Anderson also seemed unaware that many of these 'unfortunates' were forced out onto the streets every night simply to earn enough money to pay for a bed in a doss house.

They were not streetwalkers in the usual sense of the expression, looking for customers they could take back to their lodging. Most of their business was conducted out in the open, on the streets and in the warren of dark back alleys that characterized the Whitechapel area, and if they could find no clients who were willing to pay for their services, they had no option but to keep walking the streets until the following day, or sleep rough.

Despite the lack of any positive information, the police were still active and zealous in their pursuit of the elusive murderer. In October, Chief Inspector Swanson reported that, following the murder of Elizabeth Stride, some eighty men had been interviewed at police stations, and the movements of over 300 other potential suspects had been checked. In all, Swanson reported, in addition to the police reports, nearly one thousand dockets had been created in which details of this vast number of suspects and people of interest had been recorded.

There was plenty of activity on the part of both the Metropolitan and City forces, both of whom were now involved in the hunt for the Ripper, but frustratingly little actual progress had been made. Swanson admitted as much in a report to the Home Office, when he stated that although 'very numerous and searching enquiries' had been instituted, the police had obtained no 'tangible result'.

And the situation was summed up neatly in a note made by Dr Anderson on 23 October, in which he confessed that the police had not discovered 'the slightest clue of any kind' despite now having investigated five separate and brutal murders.

The newspapers were scathing of the efforts by the police to catch the killer, but also caught the mood of the populace of the East End of London, which was approaching a state of hysterical panic and almost supernatural dread.

Abberline and Chandler, who were by now the two most senior officers leading the hunt for Jack the Ripper on the ground, were both frequently appalled by some of the reports and editorials which appeared in the daily press.

'Have you seen this one, Fred?' Chandler asked, holding up a copy of the *East London Advertiser*.

Abberline shook his head.

'No. Give me the bad news.'

'Right, then. Just listen to this: "Men feel that they are face to face with some awful and extraordinary freak of nature. So inexplicable and ghastly are the circumstances surrounding the crimes ... that the mind turns instinctively to some theory of occult force and the myths of the Dark Ages ... ghouls, vampires, bloodsuckers and all the ghastly array of fables which have been accumulated throughout the course of centuries take form, and seize hold of the excited frenzy. Yet the most morbid imagination can conceive nothing worse than this terrible reality; for what can be more appalling than the thought that there is a being in human shape stealthily moving about a great city, burning with the thirst for human blood, and endowed with such diabolical astuteness as to enable him to gratify his fiendish lust with absolute impunity." How do you think how do you think that's going to make the unfortunates of Whitechapel and Spitalfields feel?'

Abberline shook his head. He was, by that time, close to despair, with no idea what else he could do to try to stop the next killing – a killing which he privately thought was virtually inevitable – from taking place. No measures the police had implemented had produced any tangible results, and as far as he could see there was nothing else they could do except wait for Jack the Ripper to unsheathe his knife once again.

'I suppose absolutely the only good thing to come out of the "double event" is that the latest killings seem to have driven a lot of prostitutes away from the streets of Whitechapel,' Chandler added, picking up another paper, the *Daily Chronicle*. 'There's a report here which says that "It is not too much to say that the unfortunate creatures who ply their wretched vocation in the streets are paralysed with fear. How much so this is the case is attested by the deserted condition of the East End thoroughfares after half past twelve, and the unbroken solitude in which the side streets, alleys and backways slumber." I suppose if there aren't any unfortunates on the streets, the Ripper won't find it quite as easy to locate his next victim.'

'There'll always be one,' Abberline said. 'Some poor woman with nowhere else to go, who'll take a chance for the price of a drink or the price of a bed. When he starts again, he'll find someone, you mark my words.'

But the so-called 'unfortunates' of Whitechapel were a hardy breed: they needed to be simply because of their circumstances. In the hours and days which followed each killing on the streets, the women stayed indoors as much as they could, and if they had to venture out after dark they usually did so in groups. But as time passed and the memories of the previous atrocities grew a little fainter, their courage and independence of spirit rose to the fore again, and towards the end of the month they were to be seen patrolling their patches alone or sometimes in the company of one other of their kind, with perhaps just a small and hopelessly inadequate pocket knife for protection.

Many of them even adopted a philosophical attitude to their situation, and some police officers reported that prostitutes would call out to them on the streets late at night, saying that they were 'the next for Jack' or something similar.

Days turned into weeks, and no other murders were committed in the area. Slowly, life in Whitechapel seemed to return almost to its ghastly norm, and some people began speculating that, whoever Jack the Ripper was, his hideous reign of terror was now over.

But in that respect, they were sadly mistaken.

Chapter 47

Wednesday, 7 November 1888
London

Ever since what become known in the press as the 'double event', London as a whole and Whitechapel in particular had been noticeably quiet, and the residents of that depressed and deprived area were finally beginning to feel safe again. Or, at least, safe from the vicious blade wielded by Jack the Ripper, though assaults, robberies and fights were still part of daily life in the district. Even some police officers were expressing the view, at least in private, that the Whitechapel murders had finally ended, the killer having ceased his reign of terror for some reason. Perhaps he had moved away, or died, or had even been taken into custody for some entirely unrelated offence.

Charles Warren, of course, knew better. And he also knew that 'Michael' had told him in his last communication that he had one month before the next murder would take place. Ever since the first of November he had been on tenterhooks, waiting for news of another killing. So far, though, all had been quiet.

But that evening, another handwritten letter was waiting for him at home. And, again, nobody in the household had seen who delivered it, or even knew when it had arrived.

Warren took it up to his study, sat down at his desk and opened the envelope. The note inside was short and very much to the point:

> *You now have two days. Then I start again. First the Masons, then the Jews. Two triangles for the star. Six in six weeks, cut down to the bone. Resign to show agreement, then deliver the relic exactly one week later. This is my last message.*

He held the note in his hand and read it half a dozen times, then laid it down on his desk. It was a stark ultimatum, giving him no leeway, but at least it wasn't unexpected. He had been anticipating something of the sort for the last four weeks, and he hadn't been idle during that time.

Charles Warren had looked at the problem from all sides. And eventually he had come up with a plan that was both daring and dangerous, and with which a number of things could go very badly wrong. But if it worked, he would be able to walk away from the nightmare of the Whitechapel murders, and that was the result he was desperately hoping to achieve.

Central to the plan was one simple assumption, which he hoped was correct. As far as Warren knew, the only person alive right then who had ever seen the menorah was he himself. Every Jew knew what it looked like, but nobody apart from him knew exactly how big it was, and that was the lynchpin of the scheme he had concocted.

The instruction from 'Michael' that he was to show his agreement to hand over the relic by resigning as Commissioner of the Metropolitan Police was unexpected, but the more he thought about it, the less Warren was bothered by this. He hadn't wanted the job in the first place, though he had tried to fulfil his tasking to the best of his ability. The circumstances and events of the last year had meant that he was being publicly reviled in the newspapers almost every day, he had an extremely fraught relationship with his immediate superior, the Home Secretary, Henry Matthews, and he simply didn't get on with the senior officers who were supposed to be his colleagues at Scotland Yard.

Warren himself knew that part of the problem was his personality, and there was little he could do about that, but the biggest obstacle to the smooth running of the Metropolitan Police was the fact that he was a military officer, used to the strict discipline and ordered structure of an army unit, and the London police force was, by comparison, a ramshackle civilian organization. It was no wonder that he hadn't been successful in his post.

If he did resign, he would be able to walk away from all that and return to the military world which he had always regarded as his second home, free from all the problems that he had encountered at Scotland Yard.

But if he was to return to the army without any kind of stigma being attached to his posting as the Commissioner, he couldn't just resign and walk away, because that would imply that he had found the job too difficult to cope with or that he had simply given up in view of the problems which he had faced. What he needed was a reason to resign, some point of principle or other matter to which he could refer in the future and tell people 'I could not work with that man because . . .' or 'that regulation hampered me so much that I was completely unable to continue in the post' or something of the sort.

In short, he needed an excuse, a good reason, to go. And at this point fate, in the person of Henry Matthews, the Home Secretary, played right into his hands.

Chapter 48

Thursday, 8 November 1888
Whitechapel, London

Charles Warren was sitting at his desk in his office at 4 Whitehall Place the following morning when one of the internal messengers knocked on his door.

'Come.'

'I have a letter for you, sir,' the man said and passed an envelope to the commissioner.

As the man turned and walked away, Warren glanced down at the envelope, which bore the unmistakable stamp of the Home Office. He wasn't expecting anything from Henry Matthews, and he assumed that the missive probably contained yet another few suggestions about how he might be better able to catch the Whitechapel murderer, suggestions that in all probability the Metropolitan Police would already have implemented without success. Warren had received a number of such communications, including one which had originated from Queen Victoria herself.

Warren took a paper knife from his desk, slit open the envelope and removed the single sheet of paper which it contained, more curious than anything else.

As he read the closely typed paragraphs, his expression changed from one of casual interest in the contents of the letter to deep anger and irritation.

'How dare that pompous imbecile address me in such a fashion,' he muttered.

Then he read what the Home Secretary had written once more, and at that moment he knew that Matthews had done him the most incredible favour, a favour that would allow him to resign from his post on a matter of principle, and which would also allow him to tender his resignation immediately. That might mean 'Michael' would have no need to carry out any further attacks on the prostitutes of the East End of London. It was a fantastically convenient occurrence, both in terms of what it signified, and in its providential timing.

The crux of the matter was almost triflingly inconsequential. Some weeks previously, Warren had felt strongly enough about the daily criticism being heaped upon the officers and men of the Metropolitan Police that he had spoken out in their defence, largely because criticism of the force was also, obviously, a criticism of him. Specifically, he had written an article discussing the administration and conduct of the Metropolitan Police, and this article had subsequently been published in *Murray's Magazine*. In truth, Warren had virtually forgotten about the article which, though typical of his style in that it was a blustering condemnation of anyone who dared criticize the Metropolitan Police, actually contained nothing particularly contentious, and certainly nothing which most people would have been surprised to hear Warren say.

But what Charles Warren was genuinely unaware of was that a ruling had been approved by the Home Office almost ten years earlier, in 1879, which stated that all serving officers were to

obtain the prior permission and approval of the Home Secretary
before they were permitted to publish anything relating to the
Metropolitan Police force. This meant that anything the commissioner wrote, from the shortest missive to a newspaper to an
entire article, had first to be personally inspected and approved
by Henry Matthews.

The ruling had clearly been designed to prevent police officers
from making intemperate statements to the press which contained information that the Home Office did not wish to be
made public, and was arguably a sensible regulation. Charles
Warren genuinely didn't see it that way. If his relationship with
the Home Secretary had been better, then without a doubt the
two men could probably have come to an amicable agreement
about the ruling, but as far as Warren was concerned on that
morning, Henry Matthews had simply provided him with the
opportunity he needed to get out of a job that he was beginning
to loathe.

The letter which he had just read was a formal reprimand for
Warren over the article which had been published, and also con-
tained an instruction requiring him to comply with this Home
Office regulation at all times in the future.

For a few minutes Warren considered what action he should
take, and what form of words he should use. Then he called in
a secretary and dictated a reply which, he anticipated, would
produce an immediate reaction at the Home Office.

Warren began by categorically refusing to accept either the
reprimand or the instruction to comply with the ruling. He then
went on to question the legal authority of the Home Secretary to
issue any such order to the Commissioner of the Metropolitan
Police, and added that, had he known of the existence of such a
regulation prior to his appointment, under no circumstances

would he have agreed to assume the post. And, finally, Warren tendered his resignation.

The secretary who was preparing this letter looked across the desk at the commissioner with raised eyebrows.

'Are you sure about this, sir?'

'Quite sure,' Warren snapped. 'Get that typed up for my signature immediately and then have it sent to the Home Secretary by special messenger. He is to receive it within the hour.'

The only thing that Warren didn't know at that point was exactly when Matthews would accept his resignation – though he was absolutely certain that the Home Secretary would be delighted to see him go – and his major concern was whether or not it would be in time to prevent 'Michael' from striking again.

He just hoped that it would be.

Chapter 49

Friday, 9 November 1888
Whitechapel, London

Mary Jane Kelly had been born in Limerick in about 1863, but her family had crossed the Irish Sea and settled in Wales when she was still a child. Her father, John Kelly, had found employment in an ironworks, and had risen to the rank of foreman.

When she was about sixteen years of age, Mary had married a collier named Davies, but he had been killed in a mine explosion only a couple of years after their marriage. In 1884, she travelled to London seeking work and, perhaps inevitably given that she was young and good-looking, but destitute, ended up working in a brothel in the West End. Several clients of the establishment enjoyed the company of the young Irish girl, and one reportedly took her on a trip to France.

That relationship ended quickly, but other men supported her financially at different times, and when she found herself temporarily unattached to somebody who would pay her bills, she derived an adequate income from general prostitution, not least because, by all accounts, Mary Kelly was attractive. She stood about five feet seven inches tall with a rather stout build, and had a fair complexion, blue eyes and very long hair which reached nearly to her waist.

Soon after her arrival in London, Kelly also reportedly spent some time working for a French lady who had a property in Knightsbridge, and made a number of trips to Paris in her company. It was probably because of these exotic, for the time, excursions to the continent that Mary Kelly liked to be known as 'Marie Jeanette' rather than 'Mary Jane', and occasionally affected a trace of a foreign accent.

But this phase of her life was soon over and by 1885, with an inevitability that was tragically predictable, she had left the West End and gravitated downwards to the sordid surroundings of the East End of London, her profession remaining the same but her clientele becoming noticeably rougher and more uncouth. She had lodged first in St George's Street and then at Breezer's Hill, Pennington Street, in a house owned by a Mrs Carthy, and which was almost certainly a brothel. She stayed there for two or three years, and then left to move in with a man believed to be in the building trade, who was possibly a mason's plasterer named Joe Flemming. But at more or less the same time, in 1887, she met Joe Barnett in Commercial Street, and began a relationship with him. Barnett was an Irish cockney, a respectable man who was employed as a porter at Billingsgate market. Despite her new paramour, Mary Kelly apparently remained on very good terms with Flemming.

She and Barnett quickly established an intimate relationship, and Mary apparently agreed to move in and live with him at a lodging in George Street during the course of only their second meeting. That was far from being a permanent address, and they soon moved to Little Paternoster Row in Dorset Street and from there to Brick Lane, at least one of these moves being precipitated by their failure to pay the rent. Early in 1888 they moved house again, this time to 13 Miller's Court, at the northern end of Dorset Street.

Kelly could perhaps be considered to be a member of the better class of 'unfortunate' in the area because, thanks to her relationship with Joe Barnett, she was not forced to frequent the common lodging houses like so many other prostitutes in the East End. She had her own accommodation, albeit only a single mean room, located at the northern end of Dorset Street.

This road was dominated by large doss houses, thirteen of them registered but many others not, in all capable of accommodating some 1,500 men and women in the most basic manner imaginable. The largest of these was Crossingham's Lodging House, virtually opposite Miller's Court at 35 Dorset Street, which had a capacity of over 300. There were also a number of courts, narrow passageways surrounded by rooms which had been formed from the subdivision of larger premises, rooms which were let on a weekly basis, principally to prostitutes.

Miller's Court was one of these, a stone-flagged cul-de-sac approached down a narrow passage from Dorset Street itself. Within the court was a T-shaped open space equipped with a single water pump and a gas lamp, and surrounded by tenement houses and individual rooms. Mary Kelly's accommodation at number 13 had previously been the rear parlour of 26 Dorset Street, and lay on the right-hand side of the court at the end of the narrow access way.

Her small room was let furnished and contained a bed, a cupboard, a couple of tables, a chair and a fireplace, and had two windows which looked out onto that section of the court where the water pump and a dustbin were located. It was hardly lavish accommodation, but it did give Mary Kelly a little privacy and also offered her a secure location where she could entertain her clients.

Or, to be entirely accurate, the *room* offered privacy, once the door was closed, but the location itself much less so. Of all the properties located in and around Miller's Court, number 13 was by far the most visible, as its door and windows could be seen from all three of the tenement buildings on the opposite side of the court. The doorway could also be seen from the rear window of the shop on the left-hand side of the passage, and anybody entering or leaving number 13 after dark could be seen clearly in the light from the gas lamp which was positioned on the wall opposite the door.

The rent Mary Kelly paid for her room was four shillings and sixpence a week, significantly more expensive than the four pence a resident of a lodging house would pay for a single bed every night, and she had considerable trouble in keeping up the payments. In fact, she was over six weeks in arrears, and her only means of raising funds was to sell herself on the streets. To clear the backlog of her rent, she needed to find a lot of clients willing to pay her a minimum of four pence for her services. Just to maintain the status quo, she would have needed to have sexual relations with over a dozen men every week, almost two each night, and far more than that if she wished to earn enough to buy food and drink as well.

One reason for the arrears was that earlier in the year Joe Barnett, who could perhaps be considered to have been her common-law husband, had lost his job as a fish porter at the Billingsgate Market for some infraction of the rules. Since then, he had been out of regular employment and was no longer able to provide her with funds. Another reason was that Mary Kelly, like most of the other 'unfortunates' in Whitechapel, frequently sought solace in the oblivion provided by alcohol, and was often to be found drunk, either out on the streets or singing Irish songs in her room. Drink cost money, and buying alcohol was probably a higher priority for Kelly than paying her rent. When sober, acquaintances reported that she was a generally quiet woman, with only a few close friends.

By the end of October, Kelly was occupying the room by herself, Joe Barnett having walked out of the place after an argument. Barnett didn't like Mary Kelly walking the streets, though in the absence of any other income, now that he was unemployed, it is difficult to see what other option she had, and he had frequently stated that he couldn't live with her while she was pursuing that precarious lifestyle.

But in fact, it wasn't Mary Kelly's means of employment which had caused their separation. Mary had befriended a fellow prostitute, a woman named Julia Venturney, and had invited her to stay with her in the room in Miller's Court. Barnett had endured the presence of this unwelcome visitor for a couple of nights, but had then left to find accommodation in Buller's Lodging House in New Street in Bishopsgate. Despite their parting of the ways, the two remained good friends and Barnett was a frequent visitor to Miller's Court, and continued to provide Kelly with funds when he could.

But it wasn't just fellow 'unfortunates' and clients who shared Mary Kelly's hospitality and her bed. She was very friendly with a laundress named Maria Harvey, and had allowed her to stay in the room at Miller's Court on the nights of 5 and 6 November, though Harvey had subsequently found lodgings of her own at New Court in Dorset Street. On the afternoon of 8 November, Harvey called on Mary Kelly and the two friends spent the rest of the afternoon together. In fact, she was still there when Joe Barnett knocked on the door at about 7.30, though she left soon afterwards, leaving a few items of clothing in Kelly's room. Another friend of Kelly's, Lizzie Albrook, called round at Miller's Court at just before eight, and spoke to both Barnett and Kelly.

The two of them had recently quarrelled, but they were then on good terms again. Barnett apologized that he still had no work and so was unable to give her any money. He didn't stay at Miller's Court very long, and left at around eight in the evening, the two of them having discussed the Whitechapel killings. Like all the prostitutes operating in the East End, Mary Kelly had taken a keen interest in the Ripper murders, for obvious reasons, and Barnett had frequently read the newspaper accounts of the killings aloud to her, as she herself couldn't read.

That evening, Kelly was in a particularly good mood, as the next day was the Lord Mayor's Show, when the new holder of that ancient office, the Right Honourable James Whitehead, would be driven along the Strand to the Royal Courts of Justice. It would be a splendid procession, and Mary was keenly anticipating the celebration. At about nine that evening, she called on one of her neighbours, Elizabeth Prater, who lived in one of the rooms above her in Miller's Court and was another part-time prostitute, and told her that she was hoping it would be fine the next day 'as I want to go to the Lord Mayor's Show.'

Chapter 50

Joe Barnett's lack of funds to support Mary Kelly meant that the young woman had no option but to try to earn some money walking the streets of Whitechapel yet again, and shortly before nine o'clock, after Barnett had left Miller's Court, she got dressed and, after chatting for a few minutes with Elizabeth Prater, walked out into Dorset Street to search for clients and, predictably, enjoy a drink or two.

Between about ten and eleven, she was in the Horn of Plenty pub with a group of companions, including Julia Venturney. At about fifteen minutes before midnight, a woman named Mary Ann Cox met Kelly in Dorset Street, in the company of a man, who was presumably a client. Cox, a widow of 31 whose only source of income was prostitution, and who would later be described by the *Star* as 'a wretched-looking specimen of East End womanhood', had known Kelly for about eight months, and also lived in Miller's Court, at number 5.

Cox had been looking for customers along the pavements of Commercial Street, but because the night was so cold she decided to return to her room and get warm before venturing out once again. She saw Kelly walking along with a man beside her when she entered Dorset Street, and saw that her neighbour was clearly intoxicated. The couple continued along the pavement and then entered Miller's Court a short distance in front of Mary Cox. By that time, Cox was close enough to call out a greeting to Mary Kelly, but the young Irish prostitute was so drunk she could barely even manage a reply.

Cox described Kelly's client as a short and stout man in his mid thirties, with a thick reddish moustache and a blotchy face, who was shabbily dressed and carrying a quart can of beer. Kelly was evidently enjoying the man's company, as Mrs Cox reported that she was singing, and the sound could be heard in Cox's own lodging, a short distance away.

Mary Cox remained in her room for a brief period, then returned to the streets shortly after midnight, staying out looking for clients until about one o'clock. She then again returned to her room to get warm before trying her hand once more at soliciting. She left her room shortly after one, at which time she saw a light burning in Mary Kelly's room, and the Irish girl was still singing. When she returned to Miller's Court shortly after three in the morning, the light in number 13 had been extinguished and the room was quiet, which could have suggested that Kelly was in bed with a client with her candle extinguished, or asleep alone, or back out on the streets.

Although she was tired, Mary Cox found it impossible to get to sleep that night, possibly because it was then raining hard. Throughout the rest of the early morning hours, she heard the sound of loud footsteps as visitors – presumably men visiting one or other of the prostitutes who lodged in the court – came and left. She heard the last man leaving at about 5.45.

Mary Cox might have assumed that her neighbour had remained in her room, but by about two in the morning, while Cox herself was out soliciting, Mary Kelly was also back on the streets of Whitechapel.

A labourer named George Hutchinson, who had a lodging at the Victoria Working Men's Home in Commercial Street, met her near the end of Flower and Dean Street shortly after two. He had known the young Irish girl for about three years, and had occasionally provided her with money.

'Mr Hutchinson,' Mary Kelly asked him, 'can you lend me sixpence?'

'I cannot,' Hutchinson explained, 'as I am spent out going down to Romford.'

'I must go and look for some money,' Kelly said, and headed off towards Thrawl Street.

Almost immediately Hutchinson saw a man who had been standing on the corner approach Kelly and tap her on the shoulder. He said something to her and they both began laughing, and then the two of them walked down Dorset Street and entered Miller's Court, where Hutchinson lost sight of them. Something about the man interested or bothered the labourer, and for some three-quarters of an hour he loitered outside the court, waiting for either the man or Mary Kelly to reappear. But eventually, at about three in the morning, he gave up and continued on to his lodging.

If Hutchinson had waited perhaps fifteen minutes longer, he would have seen the man open the door to number 13 and bid farewell to Mary Kelly. And if he had stayed for a further half hour after that, he would have seen the young Irish girl emerge from her room and head back towards Dorset Street. She hadn't had a bad evening, managing to attract two clients who had each paid her the usual fee, and perhaps she thought she might find a third man out on the streets.

Perhaps she thought it was her lucky night. If she did, she was sadly mistaken.

The killing spree that Alexei Pedachenko had embarked on had had one predictable and extremely unwelcome – to him – effect on the traffic on the streets of Whitechapel. Groups of men wandered along the pavements during the early hours of the morning clearly looking out for any individual who aroused their suspicions by either his appearance or his conduct, and Pedachenko was no longer able to appear in his own persona in the area for fear of attracting such unwelcome attention. His adoption of a female disguise had proved to be very effective, as he became yet one more 'unfortunate' roaming the streets in the hope of earning a few coppers, and in consequence was essentially invisible and ignored by almost everyone.

But the other consequence of the murders was that he no longer felt safe in attacking a woman actually on the streets. There was just too much activity, too many people walking the pavements, and too many eyes that might see him performing his task. That was one reason why the Russian had refrained from carrying out a further attack after the so-called 'double event'. He had been waiting for the vigilante action and increased police patrols to be scaled down to a level where he felt he would be able to find his next victim without being observed.

That hadn't happened, and there were still too many people wandering the streets for Pedachenko to be able to risk carrying out another attack in the open air, and with the next one he also wanted to take his time. So he had decided to find a prostitute who had her own accommodation, a private room somewhere, a place to which he could accompany her and where he could carry out the murder and then mutilate the body at his leisure without any fear of being interrupted. And he was determined that this killing should be so shocking, and the mutilations so massive and so brutal, that Charles Warren would then have absolutely no option but to accede to his demand.

He had hoped that the man would already have resigned his post as Commissioner of the Metropolitan Police following the last note he had sent him, but this hadn't happened. Or, at least, that event had not yet been published in newspapers. But it didn't matter. After what he intended to visit upon the first suitable woman he found, he had not the slightest doubt that Warren would be forced to do his bidding.

For the past week he had been patrolling the Whitechapel area in his female disguise, and especially Dorset Street and Flower and Dean Street, taking mental note of which prostitutes took their clients into the nearest convenient alleyway or open doorway to perform their services, and which of them linked arms with their customers and walked them to their lodgings.

Pedachenko had several times seen a young Irish girl who was addressed by her acquaintances as either 'Mary' or 'Marie', and he had even established that she lived in one of the rooms off Miller's Court, though he hadn't so far discovered which one. But that didn't matter. She was a working prostitute, young and attractive by the standards of her class, and with her own room. That was all that concerned him.

The other difficulty he faced was that although in his female disguise he was able to walk the streets of Whitechapel without interference, he doubted very much if the Irish girl would be prepared to take a fellow 'unfortunate' back to her room during her working hours: in other words, from about midnight until four in the morning. But if he presented himself to her as a man, he had little doubt that he would be able to persuade her that he was a genuine client.

And once he was inside her room, there would be nothing to stop him.

At two o'clock that morning, the Russian was still wearing skirts and a bonnet, though with his male apparel underneath. He could change his identity – and effectively his sex – in a matter of minutes. He was strolling down Flower and Dean Street, looking for Mary or one of the two other possible victims he had already identified, when he saw her at the end of the road.

For a couple of seconds, Pedachenko considered removing his disguise immediately and approaching her straight away, but then he paused, because he'd just seen Mary walk up to a man on Dorset Street and greet him in a friendly fashion. He wondered if the man was a regular client of hers, or just an acquaintance, and in moments he saw that it was the latter, because the two spoke together briefly and then separated.

But almost immediately the woman was accosted by another man, in such a friendly fashion that she burst out laughing, and together they walked away along Dorset Street, clearly heading in the direction of Miller's Court. As they strode along together, the girl said something and the man pulled a dark-coloured handkerchief, possibly a red one, out of his pocket and gave it to her. Oddly enough, the first man Mary had spoken to walked in the same direction, and it almost looked as if he was following them.

Pedachenko brought up the rear of the procession, and watched as Mary turned into the narrow passage which gave access to her lodging, holding the man firmly by the arm. The other man took up a position from which he could see into the court, and appeared to be waiting for either the man or the prostitute to come out again.

For a few moments, the Russian halted in indecision, but then he realized that fate had probably delivered the Irish girl into his hands. He knew exactly where she was, and precisely what she was doing. He anticipated that within about half an hour to an hour her client would leave her room, and then she would either remain inside for the rest of the night or step back out onto the streets. And there were now far fewer people walking the pavements in Whitechapel, so he felt safer in removing his disguise.

The only problem was the second man, the man who was still standing at the entrance to the passageway, leaning against the wall, and clearly waiting for one of the two to emerge. He could, Pedachenko supposed, perhaps be a friend of Mary's client, and simply be waiting for the other man to complete his recreational activity and rejoin him. Or perhaps he wanted to take his turn with Mary when the first man had finished. Whatever the truth of the relationship between the three of them, for the moment Pedachenko felt content to just watch and wait.

And within about forty-five minutes, at just after three in the morning, his patience was rewarded. The 'watcher', whoever he was, apparently got bored or tired of waiting, and continued on his way along Dorset Street. There was no sign of either Mary or her client, and the street was almost empty of pedestrians. The Russian realized that this would be the ideal time to strike.

He headed away from Dorset Street and made his way down one of the innumerable alleys, then slipped into the doorway of a building only a few tens of yards down Dorset Street from the passageway entrance to the court, and swiftly removed both his bonnet and the skirts, and tucked them into a corner where he could retrieve them later: he intended to walk away from the scene dressed as a woman, for his own safety.

He straightened his clothes, checked up and down Dorset Street to confirm that he was still unobserved, and then began walking casually towards the entrance to Miller's Court. As he did so, a male figure stepped out of the passageway, turned to his left and began striding away.

Pedachenko recognized him immediately as the client Mary had taken to her room, and muttered under his breath. He had hoped to be in position, either in the passageway or in the court itself, before the man emerged, so that he could identify the room from which he had come, just in case Mary decided to remain in her bed rather than seek out another customer.

He would just have to hope that she needed more money than she had so far earned that night.

The Russian turned down the passageway leading into Miller's Court and paused at the end to look around him. There was a single gas lamp on the wall to his left, and the backs of tenement houses, each with windows and a door, in front of him and lying along the left-hand side of the court. To his right was a short and wider blind alley, at the end of which was a water pump.

All of these details Pedachenko registered, but his attention was drawn to the faint illumination he could see near the pump, illumination which was obviously coming from two small windows of the room on his right, probably from the flame of a candle. No other lights were visible anywhere in the court, and it was a reasonable assumption that he was looking at the room occupied by the Irish girl, and that she was still inside.

Pedachenko walked across to the door of the room. If he could open it, and take her by surprise, it would all be over in seconds. But in the faint yellowish light cast by the gas lamp on the opposite wall, the Russian could see that that wasn't going to work, because the door was clearly secured by a latch operated by a key, and when he tried turning the handle and applied gentle pressure on the wood on the left-hand side of the door, near the keyhole, it didn't move at all. The door was locked and could only be opened from the inside, or with the key, and that meant he would have to wait.

He didn't want to knock on the door, in case the noise alerted any other residents of the court who might still be awake, and who might then look out of their doors or windows and see him, so he retreated along the passage almost to the end, and then stopped in a position from which he could see the door of the room on the right-hand side.

For what seemed a very long time nothing happened. And then, about thirty minutes after he'd taken up his position, he was rewarded by the sight he had hoped to see. He heard a click, and then saw the door swing open inwards. Obviously the girl had decided that she needed to try to find some more trade before she retired for the night.

Pedachenko stepped out of the passageway and out into Dorset Street. He looked round, but the handful of pedestrians who were visible were all some distance away, and would certainly not be able to see him clearly enough to identify him, or hear anything that he said or did to the young prostitute.

And at that moment, the Irish girl strode out of the end of the passageway and turned directly towards him. It was 3.45 in the morning.

Chapter 51

Friday, 9 November 1888
Whitechapel, London

Alexei Pedachenko turned to look at his latest victim.

Mary was again dressed as he'd seen her earlier, wearing a linsey frock and a red knitted crossover – a kind of shawl worn over the shoulders and tied at the front – and was bareheaded. She was staggering slightly, clearly the worse for drink.

'Hello, love,' she murmured, her soft Irish lilt smoothing the words, 'looking for a bit of company, are you?'

'I might be,' Pedachenko replied.

'It'll be sixpence to you, my dear, for as long as you like. Nice comfy room and a decent bed. You interested?'

Pedachenko took a quick look up and down the street before he responded. He needed to be certain that they were still unobserved.

'You won't find nobody better than me,' the girl said, misinterpreting his glance, 'not at this time of night. And probably not anyway. I'm real good.'

Pedachenko nodded.

'I'm sure you are,' he replied, satisfied that nobody could

either see or hear them. 'And it looks like I'm going to find out just how good you are. Lead the way.'

Mary turned back the way she'd come, escorting the Russian down the narrow passageway and into the court. At the door she paused and glanced at him, but made no move to insert a key in the lock.

'Got a bit of a problem with this door,' she said, giggling. 'Can't find the key nowhere.'

She grinned at him, then stepped around the side of the room to the first of the two small windows set into the wall. Pedachenko took a couple of paces after her, so that he could see what she was doing. Mary extended her left hand through the window, in which the pane of glass was broken, pushing aside a coat that obscured the view into the room. A moment later, the Russian heard a click as she released the latch on the door from the inside.

'Here we are, love,' Mary murmured, stepping back to the door and pushing it open wide.

She took a match and lit a candle which provided a dim and flickering light, barely enough to chase away the shadows, then undid her crossover and placed it clumsily on a chair.

Pedachenko pushed the door closed behind him, listening for the click as the latch made contact and secured it. Then he glanced around the room, which was tiny, dirty and very scruffy. But it was warm, the remains of a fire still burning in the grate, which was welcome after the chill of the night outside. The bed was small and cramped, and the sheets looked extremely insanitary, showing the unmistakable signs of recent sexual activity, and he knew that if he had been a genuine client of this particular prostitute, he would've thought sixpence to be quite an expensive price for what he expected to receive.

But he had an entirely different outcome to the evening in mind.

'You can put your clothes on that, if you'd like,' the Irish girl said, gesturing to the chair she was using, 'or keep them on, just as you prefer.'

'I'll let you make yourself comfortable first,' Pedachenko replied, taking a small step backwards and looking at Mary with an expression that he hoped conveyed eager anticipation. There was no harm in letting the woman enjoy her last few minutes of life, and the belief that the man standing in front of her found her sexually attractive. The reality was that Pedachenko would rather have forgotten all about the prize he sought than engage in any kind of sexual activity with such a creature.

'You'll have to take off them trousers to take me proper, love,' the woman said with a suggestive smile, 'but just as you like.'

Mary hummed contentedly to herself as she removed her frock and woollen stockings, shedding her clothes with practised speed and economy of effort. As she did so, she made sure that she showed off her figure to the best advantage, affording her client glimpses of her breasts and buttocks while she disrobed.

Finally, she stood before him wearing only a thin linen undergarment that barely covered her torso.

'You like what you see?' she asked playfully, lifting the base of the garment to reveal her groin.

'Oh, yes,' Pedachenko replied. 'Go and lie on the bed.'

Mary smiled at him again, turned away and walked the three or four steps to the old bed with its stained and discoloured sheets, wiggling her buttocks as she did so. At the edge of the bed she turned back to face her client and gestured for him to join her. Then she sat down on the edge of the bed, swung her legs up so she could lie flat, wriggled over to the other side to allow him room to get on it as well, and spread her thighs wide.

'I'm ready,' she said, giving another smile.

'And so am I,' the Russian said, and strode quickly across the bed to stand beside her, looking down.

And then, with the speed of a striking snake, he ripped the pillow from underneath the woman's head, lunged forward and immediately forced the fabric down over her face.

But though Pedachenko was quick, and despite her drunken and befuddled state, Mary still had the presence of mind to call for help in those last few seconds of her life.

'Murder!' she yelled.

But then the killer forced the pillow down hard, muffling any further sound that she might make.

She writhed and struggled desperately, fighting for her life, kicking out with her legs and flailing at Pedachenko with her fists. But it was to no avail. He was a man, strong and sober, and she was a slightly built woman who was much the worse for drink. In less than a minute, she began to weaken, and within three minutes she ceased moving altogether.

The Russian lifted the dirty pillow off her head and stared down at her for a moment. Then he reached into his pocket, pulled out his knife and bent forward over her. It was time to complete the task he had set himself.

He wasn't sure whether or not the woman was dead, but he would take care of that straight away. He just needed to make sure he didn't get covered in her blood.

Pedachenko pulled the sheet out from under the still and silent figure in front of him and covered her body with it. Then he pressed the sheet down on her head to hold it in place, slid the point of the knife through the fabric and with a single swift stroke drove the blade of the weapon into, and then pulled it through, her throat.

Blood spurted from the severed arteries and veins, turning the sheet crimson in an instant, but within a matter of seconds the flow stopped as her heart ceased pumping.

Then the Russian stepped back from the bed and looked around the room, listening intently. The woman's cry had sounded alarmingly loud to his ears, and it was always possible that somebody outside had heard her call out. If so, he would need to get out of the room as quickly as he could, before a policeman could be summoned.

He walked across to the window by the door, pulled aside the material covering it and peered out, but the court outside was still and silent, nobody visible, and he could hear no sound of footsteps. It looked as if he'd been lucky. Or perhaps a cry of 'murder' was not that unusual in that district of London in the early hours of the morning. Satisfied that the alarm had not been raised, Pedachenko stepped back and glanced around the room again.

The only illumination came from the single candle the woman had lit when the two of them had entered, and the dim red glow of the embers of the dying fire in the wall opposite the door. He wanted to see what he was doing with this victim, and that meant somehow getting better light into the room.

But before he did anything about that, Pedachenko stepped over to the door and tugged on the handle to make sure that it was still locked, and then turned his attention back to the windows. Obviously he needed to be certain that nobody could see into the room. The window beside the door was already covered by a coat hanging from a hook above it, the material hanging down and completely covering the panes of glass. The other window had a pair of thin and grubby muslin curtains pulled partially across it, and they would probably be enough to prevent anyone witnessing anything. He pulled those curtains completely closed, and then stepped over to the fire.

There were a few small bits of wood and kindling on the floor beside the grate, and he put those onto the embers. The kindling immediately caught light and within a couple of minutes flames were licking at the wood, but it was obvious that within a very short time the fire would be extinguished. He needed more fuel for it.

Pedachenko looked around the room. The chair and tables were of course made of wood, but he would need to break them up in order to put them on the fire, and that would create enough noise to wake up some of the neighbours. He had already ascertained that the partition between the room he was standing in and the adjacent accommodation was made of wood, and sound would travel through that medium very easily.

He would have to use something else. His eyes fell on the clothes that the dead prostitute had discarded just minutes earlier. They would burn, he was certain, as long as he could cut them into reasonably small pieces. If he tried putting her entire frock on the fire, it would probably extinguish it immediately, or at best simply smoulder, producing smoke but no flames or illumination.

He picked up the garment in his left hand, trod on the base of it with his foot, and slid the sharpened blade of his knife downwards, through the material, separating it into two halves. Then he cut each of those into about half a dozen smaller pieces, and placed the first of them on the fire. In moments, the flames had already started licking around the material, and shortly after that the cloth began burning fiercely.

Now he had enough light to see exactly what he was doing. Pedachenko walked back to the bed and pulled the blood-sodden sheet off the body. The woman's eyes were open, staring sightlessly at the discoloured ceiling above the bed, her limbs limp and flaccid in death. She looked almost peaceful, apart from the gaping wound in her throat, a slash which had virtually severed her head from her body, and the almost circular pool of blood on which her shoulders rested.

The Russian stared at her for several seconds, then shook his head. He seized her left arm and left leg and dragged the body a couple of feet closer to him, towards the left-hand side of the bed, so that he could more easily perform the rest of his tasks.

Before he used the knife again, he first positioned the dead woman's limbs to his satisfaction. In life she had been a prostitute, arguably even an attractive prostitute, and in death he thought it was only fitting that her body should assume the same stance that it must have occupied so many times while she was working. He bent forward and opened both her thighs wide, so that they were almost at right angles to each other, completely exposing her genitals.

He would do some work in that region later on, he decided, but first he would attend to the upper part of the torso and then her face. He changed his grip on the knife, placed the blade inside the neckline of her linen undergarment, and drew the blade swiftly down her body, easily cutting through the thin material, which he pulled to the sides to expose her breasts and stomach.

The light from the fire was dying as the last of the material was consumed, so Pedachenko placed a couple more pieces on it to provide more light before he carried on.

Then he stabbed the point of the knife into her chest below and between her breasts and began cutting his way down towards her groin. There was a lot that he wanted to do to this woman and, fortunately, he had all of the rest of the night to do it.

Chapter 52

The landlord of Mary Kelly's pitiful room was a man named John McCarthy, who operated from a shop located at 27 Dorset Street, and by the end of that week he was getting seriously concerned about the amount of rent Kelly owed. She was supposed to be paying him four shillings and sixpence every week, but she had failed to make payments for over six weeks and now owed him some twenty-nine shillings. Obviously the situation could not be allowed to continue, and that morning McCarthy summoned his shop assistant, a young man named Thomas Bowyer, and told him to call at 13 Miller's Court to try to recover some of the arrears.

Bowyer walked around to the premises and knocked twice on the door of the room but received no response. On the adjacent wall and close to the corner of the building, near the door, was a small window, inside which a piece of material was drawn across. Bowyer noticed that one of the panes of glass in the window was broken, and he reached in through the window to tug the curtain aside and see if Kelly was there.

The first things Bowyer saw were two lumps of bloody flesh

sitting on the table beside the bed and, beyond that, a mutilated corpse on the bed itself.

Bowyer recoiled in horror at the sight and ran back to the shop in Dorset Street in a state of panic. When he got there, he stumbled out a halting and incomplete explanation of what he'd seen: 'Guvnor, I knocked at the door and could not make anyone answer. I looked through the window and saw a lot of blood.'

John McCarthy immediately returned to Miller's Court with Bowyer to investigate for himself. When he looked in through the window, as his assistant had done, the scene was even more dreadful than he had expected. The lumps of flesh lying on the table were bad enough, but it was the body itself which shocked him the most. Bone glistened white in the dim illumination, and the corpse looked like a butchered animal.

McCarthy stepped back from a window and ordered Bowyer to go at once to the nearest police station to summon help.

Bowyer did as he was told. He ran to the Commercial Street police station and burst in through the doors, panting from his exertions and clearly in a state of abject terror. Two detectives – Inspectors Walter Beck and Walter Dew – were talking together when he arrived, but it was several seconds before Bowyer was capable of uttering a coherent sentence to explain what he had seen. Finally, he blurted out: 'Another one. Jack the Ripper. Awful. Jack McCarthy sent me.'

Very shortly afterwards, John – also known as 'Jack' – McCarthy himself arrived at the station, having decided to follow his assistant, and was able to explain the situation in more detail.

Beck and Dew pulled on their coats and hurried out of the police station along with McCarthy and Bowyer, and reached Miller's Court at about eleven o'clock. McCarthy indicated the door to number 13, and Dew tried to open it without success. Inspector Beck moved to the window on the other wall of the building, stretched his arm through the hole in the glass to move aside the fabric – the old coat – hanging there so that he could see inside the room.

Almost immediately he stepped back, white with shock, and told Dew not to look. But the other detective disregarded his superior officer and peered through the window himself. He later stated that: 'When my eyes had become accustomed to the dim light I saw a sight which I shall never forget to my dying day.'

Within a very short time, the area around the room and Miller's Court itself had become the principal focus of attention of the investigative machinery of the Metropolitan Police. At about 11.15, the divisional police surgeon, Dr George Bagster Phillips, arrived to inspect the body. Phillips took one look through the window and came to the immediate and reasonable conclusion that Mary Kelly was far beyond any medical help that he or anyone else could administer.

Detective Inspector Abberline reached the scene about a quarter of an hour after that and took charge. At least, this time, there was no doubt about the identity of the victim because of where the body lay. But for some considerable time, none of the assembled officials entered the room, though it wasn't the locked door that stopped them. The reason for their decision not to enter the crime scene was because of some confusion over the use of bloodhounds.

'You are sure that dogs have been sent for?' Abberline asked Inspector Beck for at least the third time.

Beck nodded.

'That's what a constable told me. He was sent here with a message from the station.'

'Very well,' Abberline said. 'So I suppose we'd better carry on waiting. The dogs will only be able to do anything useful if the body and the crime scene aren't touched.'

In the absence of anything better to do, Abberline had ordered that the area around Millers Court should be secured and cordoned off to keep out any spectators or reporters, and once that was done he sent uniformed constables to every building in the near vicinity to take statements from neighbours and any potential witnesses. Remembering what had happened at Goulston Street, he also summoned a photographer to record details of the scene. Not that there was any chance of this evidence being wiped away.

At 1.30 in the afternoon, Superintendent Arnold arrived at the crime scene, with the unwelcome news that no bloodhounds would be coming.

'I wish I'd known this earlier, sir,' Abberline complained. 'We could have been in this room almost three hours ago.'

'There was a misunderstanding,' Arnold said, 'and I only had the information confirmed a short while ago. Now let's get inside here and see what we've got.'

'The door is locked on the inside,' Abberline pointed out, 'and we've no idea where the key is, so we're going to have to break it down.'

None of the officers present had noticed that the broken window was close enough to the door to allow somebody to reach inside and just release the catch.

John McCarthy, the landlord who actually owned the premises, was the obvious person to effect an entrance, and he used a pickaxe to force the door. The first person to enter the dwelling was Dr Phillips.

When he stepped inside, he saw a very small room, perhaps

about twelve feet square, and cluttered with furniture. The bed-side table was so close to the entrance that the door had banged into it when it was opened, and there was little space for the investigators who had followed him to move around. The right side of the bed was pushed tight up against the wooden partition which divided the old back parlour of the house and formed one wall of Mary Kelly's room. There was a second table in the room, a wooden chair, a wash stand, a cupboard and an open fireplace, over which was hanging a cheap mass-produced print entitled 'The Fisherman's Widow'. The floor was bare and dirty, with a single small ragged rug on it, and the walls were papered, but so encrusted with the dirt deposited by years of neglect that the pattern – if any – was impossible to make out.

The sight which greeted Phillips and the police officers who entered the room hot on his heels was undeniably the stuff of nightmares.

John McCarthy was one of the first to go inside the premises and he, of course, knew Mary Kelly personally. Later that day he made a statement in which he described what had greeted them in the room:

The sight we saw I cannot drive away from my mind. It looked more like the work of a devil than of a man. The poor woman's body was lying on the bed, undressed. She had been completely disembowelled, and her entrails had been taken out and placed on the table. It was those that I had seen when I looked through the window and took to be lumps of flesh. The woman's nose had been cut off, and her face gashed and mutilated so that she was quite beyond recognition. Both her breasts too had been cut clean away and placed by the side of her liver and other entrails on the table. I had heard a great deal about the Whitechapel murders, but I declare to God I had never expected to see such a sight as this. The body was, of course, covered with blood, and so was the bed. The whole scene is more than I can describe. I hope I may never see such a sight again.

Even before the police had entered the room in Miller's Court, it was perfectly clear to them that they were dealing with another atrocity perpetrated by the man known as Jack the Ripper, and it was also obvious that the most senior officers of the Metropolitan Police force needed to be informed as quickly as possible.

Inspector Beck had dispatched constables to carry the news of the killing to the police station at Commercial Street shortly after he had arrived at Miller's Court, and an initial report was then sent to Scotland Yard by telegraph.

Charles Warren was at his desk in his office at Scotland Yard when this report arrived, and read it with a growing sense of dismay. News of his resignation had yet to be published – indeed, he hadn't heard from Matthews since he'd sent his letter, though he had no doubt that it would be accepted imminently – but clearly 'Michael' had decided not to wait any longer, and had got started on the next phase of his campaign immediately.

Warren had no option, and did his duty. As soon as he had acquainted himself with the details of the murder, he passed on the information to Godfrey Lushington, the Permanent Under-Secretary at the Home Office. His note read: 'I have to acquaint you, for the information of the Secretary of State, that information has just been received that a mutilated dead body of a woman is reported to have been found this morning inside a room in a house in Dorset Street, Spitalfields.'

The information produced an instant reaction from the Home Office, where a member of staff immediately telephoned Charles Warren and instructed him to advise them of any further developments. In response to this, Robert Anderson, the Assistant Commissioner and the head of the Metropolitan Police CID, went to Miller's Court in person to inspect the scene of the crime and the victim and then telephoned the Home Office. The person to whom he spoke made a brief note of the substance of his message. It read: 'Body is believed to be that of a prostitute much mutilated. Doctor Bond is at present engaged in making his examination but his report has not yet been received. Full report cannot be furnished until medical officers have completed enquiry.'

But it wasn't just the Home Office which was concerned about the brutal murder. News of this latest atrocity spread quickly throughout Whitechapel and the East End and, like all of the earlier murder scenes, Dorset Street and especially the area around Miller's Court quickly became the focus of crowds of people, their mood both angry and frightened. The court itself had already been placed off-limits to spectators on Inspector Abberline's orders, and the police also set up cordons at both ends of Dorset Street. News of the latest atrocity even spread into the crowds which had assembled in and around Fleet Street, and thousands of people deserted the route of the Lord Mayor's procession to head to the scene of this new killing by the fiend of Whitechapel, Jack the Ripper.

At around four o'clock that afternoon, a cart pulled by a

single horse, and with a tarpaulin covering the cargo area at the rear of the vehicle, drove down Dorset Street and stopped close to the narrow passageway which gave access to Miller's Court. The tarpaulin was removed and a battered old lightweight coffin was lifted from the cart and carried down to number 13. It was obvious that the police and doctors were about to remove the body and take it to the mortuary, and this generated a huge wave of excitement through the crowd, and people made a determined effort to push through the police cordon at the Commercial Street end of Dorset Street itself.

The Times report was typical of those describing the scene: 'The crowd, which pressed round the van, was of the humblest class, but the demeanour of the poor people was all that could be desired. Ragged caps were doffed and slatternly-looking women shed tears as the shell, covered with a ragged looking cloth, was placed in the van.'

The coffin containing the pitiful remains of Mary Kelly was carried out of Miller's Court and placed in the cart, after which it was driven to Shoreditch Mortuary where the post-mortem examination would be conducted. As soon as the cart had driven away, the police boarded up the windows of number 13 and placed a padlock on the door of the room to secure the crime scene. Shortly afterwards, the police cordons at the ends of Dorset Street were removed, but access to Miller's Court itself was restricted to only the occupants of that grim residential area, and the passage from Dorset Street was guarded by two constables for the rest of the day and all that night.

The quantity of blood found in the room at Miller's Court confirmed that Mary Kelly had died there, on her bed, before the mutilations to her body were carried out and that, together with the fact that she was lying on her back and was virtually naked when she died, obviously suggested that her killer was one of her clients, or had at least been pretending to be a client.

But beyond that, and as with all the previous killings, Jack the Ripper appeared to have left no clues in his wake.

Chapter 53

Saturday, 10 November 1888
London

On the Saturday morning, the day after the mutilated remains of Mary Kelly had been discovered, Warren received a terse note from Henry Matthews telling him that his resignation had been accepted and that the London press would be informed accordingly. The note also reminded him that until a replacement was appointed to the post of Commissioner Warren was to continue discharging his duties.

When Warren's resignation was later announced in the House of Commons it would be greeted with cheers and catcalls, and the London newspapers, especially the more radical elements of the press, would go to town on him.

At that stage, Warren was unaware just how long he would have to continue acting as Commissioner, and it would be over another two weeks until his successor – James Monro, the former head of the CID, and a man with whom Warren had argued vehemently earlier that year – would be appointed, in fact on 27 November.

At the same time as Warren was mulling over the entirely anticipated response from Henry Matthews in his Scotland Yard office, over in Spitalfields the police had returned in force to Miller's Court.

They were led by Detective Inspector Abberline who, despite the commissioner's entirely negative response to his suggestion about the geographical positions of the previous murders, had also plotted this killing on his map. Unfortunately for his theory, the location of the latest murder seemed to be entirely random, and nothing whatsoever to do with the neat triangles he had discovered that the locations of the previous five killings had formed. He hadn't dismissed his earlier conclusion, but even he had to admit that his logic was now looking somewhat suspect.

The police officers had returned to the scene of the crime to carefully inspect the premises in daylight. Unfortunately, despite studying the contents of the tiny room with considerable care, they discovered little more than had been apparent the previous day, and what they did find added nothing useful in their hunt for the killer.

The only significant evidence was found in the cold ashes of the fireplace. It was obvious that the fire had been burning while Mary Kelly was being slaughtered and then butchered, and it had clearly been a very significant blaze, so hot that the spout of the kettle had actually melted.

Abberline instructed one of the officers to sift through the ashes left in the grate, just in case the killer had by some chance been trying to burn a crucial piece of evidence. The detective spent the better part of half an hour looking closely at every single piece of ash that was big enough to appear useful, and at the end of it he called Abberline over to show him what he'd found.

'It's not much, I'm afraid, sir,' the detective said, 'and I don't think it's going to be very much help to us. All I found were these few pieces of burnt material. They look to me as if they might have come from a woman's clothing, and my guess is that they're probably the remains of a skirt, and possibly also some bits of a hat.'

Abberline prodded the charred fragments with the end of his finger in a thoughtful manner. There seemed no obvious reason why the killer should have wished to destroy the clothes which, he presumed, Mary Kelly had been wearing before her death, or even when she was killed, but it looked as if that was what he had done. It was difficult to imagine how any clue could have been a part of those clothes, and Abberline was keenly aware that trying to recover any evidence from the handful of burnt fragments would be simply impossible. So whatever the killer had done to the garments didn't matter, and would under no circumstances help to identify him.

Then a thought struck him, and he suddenly realized that he might have identified the clear and logical solution to the mystery.

'I know why he did it,' Abberline said. 'It's obvious. Just take a look around this place.'

The other officers glanced around the tiny room, their complete lack of understanding manifest in their facial expressions.

'Think about it,' Abberline continued. 'This room is really small and very dark. It's only got two tiny windows. We're standing here with the door open, both windows uncovered and in full daylight. At night, with only that single gas lamp outside in the courtyard, even if there was nothing over the windows, it would still be dark in here. With the windows covered, it'd be pitch black, and the killer would definitely have covered the windows so that nobody could look inside and see what he was doing. The only source of illumination we found in here was one small candle. I think the reason he built up the fire was to provide enough light for him to see what he was doing. There's no fuel – no wood or coal, I mean – so he had to burn whatever he found in here, which was the clothes Mary Kelly had been wearing.'

Whilst the police officers were picking over the contents of Mary Kelly's room, three doctors – George Bagster Phillips, Thomas Bond and Frederick Gordon Brown – were together performing the post-mortem on the body at the Shoreditch Mortuary, a procedure that would last for some six and a half hours due to the severity of the mutilations.

Dr Thomas Bond, who had also worked with Phillips at Miller's Court, provided a detailed, if gruesome, and extremely accurate description of the injuries he had seen on her body when he'd inspected it at the crime scene. Bond was highly qualified, having had over twenty years' experience as a police surgeon, and had been asked to help with the Ripper investigation by Assistant Commissioner Anderson, who was trying to determine what degree of anatomical knowledge the murderer actually possessed, in view of the comments made by various doctors at the previous inquests. Anderson hoped that a definitive statement by Thomas Bond would help him to identify the likely trade or profession followed by the murderer, which in turn might narrow the list of potential suspects.

With regard to the killing of Mary Kelly, Bond stated the following:

The body was lying naked in the middle of the bed, the shoulders flat, but the axis of the body inclined to the left side of the bed. The head was turned on the left cheek. The left arm was close to the body with the forearm flexed at a right angle & lying across the abdomen, the right arm was slightly abducted from the body & rested on the mattress, the elbow bent & the forearm supine with the fingers clenched. The legs wide apart, the left thigh at right angles to the trunk & the right forming an obtuse angle with the pubes.

The whole of the surface of the abdomen & thighs was removed & the abdominal cavity emptied of its viscera. The breasts were cut off, the arms mutilated by several jagged wounds & the face hacked beyond recognition of the features & the tissues of the neck were severed all round down to the bone. The viscera were found in various parts viz: the uterus & kidneys with one breast under the head, the other breast by the right foot, the liver between the feet, the intestines by the right side & the spleen by the left side of the body.

The flaps removed from the abdomen & thighs were on a table.

The bed clothing at the right corner was saturated with blood, & on the floor beneath was a pool of blood covering about 2 feet square. The wall by the right side of the bed & in a line with the neck was marked by blood which had struck it in a number of separate splashes.

Detailed though Dr Bond's statement was, it was incorrect in one particular: Kelly's body was not naked because when she was killed she was wearing a linen undergarment. However, the ferocity and extent of the mutilations performed on her meant that the killer's knife had sliced through the material of her underclothes, which had then been pulled aside to reach the flesh underneath, and so she had appeared to be naked upon initial inspection of the crime scene.

The appalling state of the corpse, the mutilations so extensive and terrible that the body was only barely recognizable as a human being, had meant that the three doctors needed to work slowly and carefully to ensure that they didn't miss anything. But, actually, that was exactly what they did: they missed something. One of her organs.

'He took her heart,' Dr Bond said flatly as he took a step back from the expanse of raw meat that twenty-four hours earlier had been the torso of a young woman.

'Are you sure?' Phillips replied, gesturing wordlessly not just at the corpse but at the piles of flesh which had also been removed from the room at Miller's Court. 'It's not somewhere in amongst all this lot?'

'No. I've checked twice. The organ is definitely not here and I can see where the major blood vessels have been severed. He must've taken it with him.'

Dr Phillips made a note, but then another thought struck him.

'Actually, there's another possibility,' he said. 'At the scene, we all noted that there had been a very intense fire burning in the grate, presumably at the time that the mutilations were being committed. Perhaps the killer didn't take the heart with him, but burnt it instead. As soon as we've finished here I'll go back to Miller's Court and check the ash.'

When the examination was complete, and the three doctors had written up their notes, Phillips voiced his concern to the district coroner, Dr Roderick Macdonald, and later that day the two men returned to Miller's Court to inspect the ashes in the fireplace which Inspector Abberline and his men had already picked through. The police had been looking for clues; Phillips had a different objective in mind. But no trace of the woman's heart, or in fact any evidence of burnt human tissue, was found in the ashes discovered in the fireplace.

The conclusion was as obvious as it was inescapable: just as he'd done with Catharine Eddowes's kidney, the killer must have taken the organ away with him.

Following the post-mortem, Dr Bond was able to turn his attention to the request from Assistant Commissioner Anderson concerning the degree of medical expertise displayed by Jack the Ripper. He had studied the police notes and files relating to four of the previous murders, those of Nichols, Chapman, Stride and Eddowes, and of course he had examined the body of Mary Kelly both at the scene of the crime and during the post-mortem examination.

He was of the opinion, he said, that all five of these women had been murdered by the same man. The cuts which had severed the throats of the previous four victims had been made from left to right, and had presumably been inflicted by the killer standing or crouching on the right-hand side of the victim. In the case of Mary Kelly, a different technique must have been used, simply because of the position of the bed in the tiny room, and so that attack must have been launched either from in front of the woman, or from her left hand side.

In Dr Bond's opinion, the mutilations performed on Nichols, Chapman, Eddowes and Kelly were 'all of the same character' and had most probably been inflicted with the same knife or at least the same type of knife. This, he said, was a strong and very sharp knife, the end of the blade pointed, and the blade itself at least six inches in length and an inch in width, and probably straight.

But on the question of the anatomical knowledge displayed by Jack the Ripper, Bond was in complete disagreement with the other doctors who had examined the victims. Alone among these medical experts, he stated that the killer had neither anatomical nor scientific knowledge: most probably, he said, not even the understanding of anatomy that would be possessed by 'a butcher or horse slaughterer or any person accustomed to cut up dead animals.'

But notably, after making this definitive statement, he failed to offer any explanation as to how an entirely unskilled person – as he was suggesting – could have successfully removed the left kidney from the body of Catharine Eddowes without damaging any of the surrounding tissues. Her kidney had been extracted through the vascular pedicle from the front, and the organ lay behind the peritoneum, the stomach, spleen, colon and jejunum, and was itself embedded in fat. Even a fully qualified surgeon would have found that a lengthy and taxing procedure to perform in a properly lit operating theatre with the correct surgical instruments to hand, and Bond seemed either unaware, or at least unwilling to acknowledge, the fact that the murderer had achieved this in a time of under ten minutes in the middle of the night on a stone pavement in a poorly lit square, working under the pressure of the danger of imminent discovery. Even at the time, the other doctors dismissed his opinion as both ill-informed and quite simply wrong.

The other question on which Dr Bond had been asked to give his opinion – this time by Inspector Abberline – was exactly when Mary Kelly had met her death, but the doctor was unable to provide a definitive answer. Bond had arrived at the crime scene at about two o'clock in the afternoon, and making an accurate determination of the time that had elapsed since the killing was difficult because of a number of factors.

When he'd seen the corpse, rigor mortis had already set in, and he noticed that it increased during his examination. The body had been found virtually naked and suffering from grotesque and severe mutilation. It was clear that a fierce fire had burned in the grate for some time following her death, which would have warmed both the room and the body. Another indicator was the partially digested food which had been found in her stomach. This suggested that death would have probably occurred about three or four hours after the meal had been eaten. All in all, Bond was unable to do more than suggest that the killing had most likely taken place roughly twelve hours before he saw the body, which probably meant between about one and three o'clock in the morning.

The latest killing appalled and terrified the residents of Whitechapel and even provoked a response from the government. Although the official position was that the Home Secretary's decision not to offer a reward was still correct, it was agreed that a free pardon would be offered to any accomplice of the man who had killed Mary Kelly, and who would deliver that man to the police. Accordingly, later that day, Charles Warren was authorized by Godfrey Lushington, the Permanent Under-Secretary at the Home Office, to issue a notice to be prominently displayed outside every police station in London, and also printed in the newspapers:

MURDER. – PARDON. – Whereas on November 8 or 9, in Miller Court, Dorset Street, Spitalfields, Mary Janet Kelly was murdered by some person or persons unknown: the Secretary of State will advise the grant of Her Majesty's gracious pardon to any accomplice, not being a person who contrived or actually committed the murder, who shall give such information and evidence as shall lead to the discovery and conviction of the person or persons who committed the murder.

CHARLES WARREN,
the Commissioner of Police of the Metropolis.
Metropolitan Police Office,
4 Whitehall Place, S.W., Nov. 10, 1888

Whoever compiled the notice got Mary Kelly's real name wrong, but that didn't make any difference. It is doubtful whether anybody in authority seriously expected this somewhat optimistic offer to be taken up by anyone close to Jack the Ripper. Certainly Charles Warren knew for certain that there would be no response.

The fact was that most of the indications were still that the killer was a man who worked alone, without an accomplice or even a lookout. It was true that in the case of Elizabeth Stride, one of the possible witnesses, Israel Schwartz, had claimed to have seen two men near the scene, though there was no definitive proof that either of these men had perpetrated the crime, were acquainted with each other, or had been involved in the murder in any way.

And there would be challenges to this decision within days, the matter being raised in the House of Commons, when the Member for Aberdeen North asked if this pardon was retrospective and could be applied to the group of men who had been participated in the murder of Emma Smith the previous year. And certainly, in the case of Mary Kelly, there was no indication whatsoever that more than one man had been involved.

But they made the offer anyway.

Chapter 54

Monday, 12 November 1888
London

The inquest into the latest killing was held on Monday, 12 November. Because Mary Kelly had been murdered in Spital-fields, her body had been taken to the Shoreditch Mortuary, and the proceedings were held in Shoreditch Town Hall under the auspices of the Coroner for the North Eastern District of Middlesex, Dr Roderick Macdonald.

Even two days after the murder, there was still huge public excitement and concern about the events which had taken place in Miller's Court. Crowds of people meandered up and down Dorset Street throughout Monday, although they were pre-vented from entering the court itself, which was still protected by two constables. The second focus of public interest was Shoreditch Town Hall. When the inquest began at eleven o'clock in the morning, dozens of people tried to get inside to witness the proceedings, and had to be forcibly restrained from doing so. Eventually, the door to the building had to be locked and a police officer positioned outside to quell any further unrest. The room in which the inquest was to be held was already filled to bursting.

As was the practice in those days, once the men chosen for the jury had been sworn in, they were escorted by Inspector Abberline to the Shoreditch Mortuary to view the body of the deceased. She was a pitiable sight. The worst of her jagged wounds had been roughly stitched together and her body placed inside a coffin shell, with only her face left visible, a grubby grey cloth covering her torso and legs. The mutilations to her face were so brutal and extensive that, as the *Pall Mall Gazette* reported: 'The eyes were the only vestiges of humanity. The rest was so scored and slashed that it was impossible to say where the flesh began and the cuts ended.'

Having viewed the remains of Mary Kelly, the twelve members of the jury were then taken to Miller's Court, where they were led in single file down the narrow passageway and into the room the dead woman had called home. The room was so small that not all the members of the jury could be inside it at the same time, and so they viewed it in batches. The viewing was supervised by Inspector Abberline, who held a single candle aloft to provide enough illumination for the jury members to see by, while pointing out to them the important evidence – such as it was – at the murder scene. The wall was still splattered with bloodstains, and there had clearly been a large pool of blood under the bed, on the side nearest the partition.

Back in the jury room, the first witness, Joseph Barnett, told the jurors something of Mary Kelly's life, and Thomas Bowyer and John McCarthy explained how they had discovered her body. Various neighbours, nine of them in all, from Miller's Court and Dorset Street, provided a little more information about her final hours. Their verbal testimony confirmed and supported the written statements they had already made to Inspector Abberline and other officers three days earlier.

Two of the neighbours told the inquest that they had heard a muffled cry of 'Murder!' in the early hours of the morning, but neither of them had reacted in any way. One of these putative witnesses to the time of the crime was Elizabeth Prater, a woman who had a lodging at 26 Dorset Street, the same building as Mary Kelly, albeit approached from Dorset Street itself rather than from Miller's Court. She lived in room 20, located above Kelly's lodging, and had known the victim quite well.

Her evidence was, by any standards, somewhat confused. In her initial statement to the police she had claimed that she heard a woman scream 'Murder!' two or three times between 3.30 and four in the morning, but at the inquest she modified her evidence.

'And then you heard what, Mrs Prater?' the coroner asked.

'A woman crying "Murder!",' she replied.

'Was that one cry, or was it repeated?'

'I just heard it the once. I'm sure a woman shouted "Oh! Murder!" somewhere nearby.'

'And what time was this?'

'I don't know exactly, but probably some time after four in the morning,' Prater replied.

The other witness was a laundress named Sarah Lewis. She actually lived at 24 Great Pearl Street in Spitalfields, but was staying at a lodging in Miller's Court which had been taken by her friends, a couple named Keyler. She had arrived there early on that Friday morning following a quarrel with her husband. The Keylers lived at number 2 Miller's Court, and Lewis didn't have a very good night there. There was no bed available for her to use, so she sat in a chair to try to get what sleep she could, but was awake by 3.30 and remained so until almost five in the morning. Just before four, she heard a cry of 'Murder!' from somewhere fairly nearby.

'What did you do when you heard this?'

'Nothing, sir.'

'You didn't, for example, get up from your chair and look out of the window?'

'No, sir. I stayed right where I was. I've heard shouts like that at all hours of the night in Whitechapel and Spitalfields.'

Although Dr Phillips had been the first medical man – and indeed the first person – to enter the room, his description of the condition of Mary Kelly's body at the inquest was hardly comprehensive. He contented himself merely by stating that the immediate cause of death was the severance of her right carotid artery, which was undeniably true, but which certainly shaded the truth, and again he deliberately suppressed any details of the mutilations which had also been visited upon her.

Calculation of the time of death was difficult because of a number of different factors. Dr Bond had suggested one or two in the morning at the earliest, while Dr Phillips, who had examined the body at just after eleven, believed that the woman had been dead for only about five or six hours, so possibly was killed as late as six.

The unspoken probability was that Elizabeth Prater and Sarah Lewis had both heard the victim's desperate cry for help at four o'clock, and both of them, for reasons of their own, had ignored it.

Inspectors Beck and Abberline, in their turn, provided what little information was available about the police investigation. At the end of the proceedings, Dr Macdonald gave the jury members a simple instruction: all they had to do was to decide on the cause of Mary Kelly's death, and leave the investigation of the crime in the hands of the Metropolitan Police.

The foreman duly returned a verdict of 'wilful murder against some person or persons unknown.'

One witness whose evidence was not heard at the inquest was George Hutchinson, and this was simply because he did not come forward until six o'clock that evening, when he walked into the Commercial Street police station to make a statement. That same evening, Detective Inspector Abberline, who had been informed that the man had possibly seen the murderer with his victim, interrogated the labourer.

'We've established that you had this man in clear sight for some time, Mr Hutchinson,' Abberline said. 'So can you please give us the most accurate description that you are able.'

Hutchinson nodded.

'I'll do my best, sir. The man was about five feet six inches in height and I think about thirty-four or thirty-five years of age,' he began, 'with a dark complexion and a dark moustache that was turned up at the ends. He was wearing a long dark coat, trimmed with astrakhan, and a white collar with a black neck-tie affixed with a horseshoe pin. He wore a pair of dark spats with light buttons over button boots, and displayed from his waistcoat a massive gold chain. His watch chain had a big seal, with a red stone, hanging from it. He had a heavy moustache curled up and dark eyes and bushy eyebrows. He had no side whiskers, and his chin was clean-shaven. He looked like a foreigner.'

It was, by any standards, an extremely comprehensive description, but if the events had taken place as Hutchinson had described, then he had must have had the man in view for some considerable time, and if he was possessed of keen observational skills, and if – of course – this man *was* the person who killed Mary Kelly, it was vital information for the police.

Certainly, Inspector Abberline believed him. Following his interview with Hutchinson, the Detective Inspector forwarded the statement to Scotland Yard that same evening, together with a note in which he stated: 'An important statement has been made by a man named George Hutchinson which I forward herewith. I have interrogated him this evening, and I am of the opinion his statement is true.'

And for Abberline, it wasn't just a case of circulating the detailed description which the labourer had provided to the police. For that same night, Abberline sent Hutchinson out onto the streets of the East End in the company of two detectives in a search for the man who'd been seen entering her room. The three trudged around the streets until about three in the morning, but without success, and they would repeat the exercise, with the same lack of a positive result, on the following night as well.

George Hutchinson's evidence was later discovered by the London press and the description he had provided of the man he'd seen was widely published and circulated as a result of the various interviews which he gave to the newspapers.

But no trace of the foreign-looking man with the moustache with the turned-up ends and wearing an astrakhan coat was ever found.

Chapter 55

Alexei Pedachenko read the reports in the newspapers with a good deal of satisfaction. The news that Charles Warren had resigned from his post as the Commissioner of the Metropolitan Police had been announced the previous day, and was vying for space with further details about the murder of the woman he now knew had been named Mary Kelly.

That was the result he had been hoping to achieve from the very first, signifying the Englishman's agreement to hand over the relic he had stolen in Jerusalem so many years earlier. The fact that the man's resignation had ostensibly been due to a difference of opinion with the Home Secretary was of no interest to Pedachenko, because he had expected Warren to produce some kind of a believable excuse for leaving his post. The important thing, as far as Pedachenko was concerned, was the simple fact that he had resigned.

He wasn't sure how long it would take for Warren to recover the menorah from wherever he had placed it for safekeeping, but his ultimatum had given the man ample time to place the relic in a box and have it delivered to the warehouse in Bermondsey within the week he had specified.

Although news of Warren's resignation hadn't appeared in the newspapers until 10 November, all the reports stated clearly that he had actually resigned two days earlier, on the 8th. That meant that he should be delivering the menorah to the warehouse on the south bank of the Thames seven days later, on the 15th. Pedachenko decided he would make absolutely sure they were both working to the same timetable, and penned another short note to Warren, which he would arrange to have delivered by one of the street urchins who were always hanging about in the area. The note read:

Bermondsey. 15th, by three after the noon.

By that time, he was certain, the box would have been delivered, and he would be able to complete the task he had set himself. And if for some reason the box wasn't there, both he and Warren knew he still had his knife, which was still sharp, and if it was necessary he could resume his work among the 'unfortunates' of Whitechapel, and as an additional refinement apply further pressure on Warren by threatening to reveal his secret to the newspapers. But he didn't think that would be necessary. That final killing, of Mary Kelly, would have clearly shown Warren exactly what Pedachenko was capable of, and the last thing the – now former – commissioner would want would be a series of similar murders across London.

The Russian nodded to himself. It was all, he was sure, going to end in an entirely satisfactory manner.

When Charles Warren returned to his home that evening after another frustrating day at Scotland Yard, he found the note from his nemesis waiting for him. As was his habit, he took the letter upstairs and read it in his study. Then, again as usual, he copied down the contents and burnt the original in the fireplace.

In fact, the instruction from 'Michael' pleased him, because it eliminated the one uncertain element in his plan. And now it was time to put that plan into operation.

Warren rang the bell and about a minute later Ryan knocked on the study door and entered the room.

'I have a job for you,' Warren began. 'It will probably take you most of tomorrow to complete it, and it must be done no later than midday on Thursday. What I want you to do will also probably seem most peculiar to you, but all you need to know is that the task is essential, so please do not ask me any questions about it.'

'If I may say so, sir,' Ryan replied, 'I have been in your service for some time, and I do not recall ever questioning one of your decisions or instructions during that period.'

'Good,' Warren said, and gestured for Ryan to approach his desk.

For just under five minutes Warren explained precisely what he wanted his manservant to do, and exactly how he wanted it done.

'Do you understand all that?' he finished.

Ryan nodded.

'Yes, of course, sir. None of it seems particularly difficult, and I would expect that I would have the first part of the job finished by early afternoon tomorrow. Obtaining a cart should not prove too difficult, and there would be no problems in arriving at the location at the time you have specified.'

'Excellent. And you are happy to carry out my other instructions?'

Ryan nodded and smiled.

'It will be a pleasure, sir.'

When Ryan had left the study, a piece of paper in his hand on which Warren had sketched the object he wanted building, the former commissioner began making his own preparations. The first thing he did was precisely as 'Michael' had instructed: he created two copies of a postage label which read:

Consignor Charles Warren
c/o 4 Whitehall Place
London
Consignee Miss S Winberg
To be collected.

Then he sat in thought for a few minutes, trying to decide exactly what else he needed to do. Finally, he wrote a third postage label with an entirely different address on it.

He again sat back in thought for a short while, then stood up, walked over to the study door and turned the key to lock it. He fished in his trouser pocket and pulled out a small but complicated key, and crossed to the corner of the room where one of the bookcases ended. Warren reached up, released a hidden catch and pulled on the end of the bookcase. A section of it swung back on concealed hinges to reveal a large steel safe set into the wall.

Warren used his key to open the safe door wide. In the middle of the steel container was a large object draped in a woollen blanket. He reached inside and with some difficulty, because it was heavy, lifted out the object and carried it over to his desk. He placed it on its base in the centre, and then removed the blanket. Years earlier, he had carefully and painstakingly cleaned off all the black paint which had covered the menorah, and now the ancient relic gleamed golden in the light from the evening sun spearing through the window.

Almost tentatively, Warren stretched out his hand and ran his fingers down the battered old gold shaft and then traced the seven curved branches, each of which led to a lamp holder shaped like an almond flower. Every time he looked at the relic, he was struck anew both by its stark beauty and the enormous sense of age that it seemed almost to radiate. The object in front of him was ancient even before the time of Christ; it had been created an almost immeasurably long time ago. Stolen by invading armies, paraded in triumph through Rome and Constantinople, and then lost for centuries until he himself had peeled away the fabric that had shrouded it in that dark and hidden chamber under the Temple Mount in Jerusalem. It was an object of awe-inspiring beauty and enormous, almost unbelievable, power and religious significance.

He hated to think that it would no longer be in his possession, but the events in Whitechapel and Spitalfields over the last few weeks had shown him clearly that he needed to let it go. It was probably not the killing and mutilation of Catharine Eddowes, or even the savage butchery inflicted on Mary Jane Kelly which had brought this home to him, but the casual and cold-blooded execution of Elizabeth Stride. He'd travelled to Dutfield's Yard, the site of that murder, and had seen the pool of blood on the ground, and then the sight of the woman herself, laid out on a rough table in St George's Mortuary. He'd looked down at the body of a woman whose only asset, whose only possession, had been her life, and that had hit home more forcefully than Warren could possibly have anticipated.

Her death had sent a message to him, and it was a message

that he had finally fully understood. No relic, no matter how ancient or how important, was worth the sacrifice that the 'unfortunates' of Whitechapel had been having to make on his behalf. Warren still had the most profound dislike and contempt for women of that class, but the sight of Stride's body, the head almost severed from the neck by the brutal stroke of a knife, had touched him deeply. For the briefest of instants, he had visualized his beloved wife Fanny lying on just such a table, the victim of a murderous attack, and had stood in silence before the body, shock and rage coursing through him.

At that moment, he had known it was time to end it.

Warren stared at the menorah for a few moments longer, then nodded. In his heart, he knew it was the right decision to make. The object had come into his possession purely by accident, and there really was neither reason nor justification for him to keep it any longer. It was time to let it go, to pass it on to a new keeper, to someone who would surely appreciate its value and enduring power.

He picked it up and replaced it in his safe, where it would remain for only a couple of days longer.

Chapter 56

Thursday, 15 November 1888
Bermondsey

Just after 2.50 that afternoon, Ryan pulled back on the reins and eased the pony to a stop outside the warehouse where Charles Warren had told him to deliver the box, then climbed down from the cart and knocked on the door.

A heavyset man wearing dark trousers and a pea jacket opened it after a few seconds and stepped out.

'Got a delivery, guvnor?' he asked.

Ryan nodded.

'It's the box in the back of the cart,' he confirmed, and walked back to the vehicle behind him. 'It's quite heavy, so could you get a couple of your men to lift it down?'

'No problem.'

The man – Ryan assumed he was the foreman, or perhaps even the owner of the establishment – strode back to the door, opened it and called out to some unseen person inside the building.

A few seconds later two more heavily built men stepped out and walked over to the cart.

The wooden crate was lying on its side in the centre of the

cart, and the two men climbed up into the vehicle and manoeu-vred it towards the tailgate. Grunting with the strain of its weight, they carefully lifted it down and took it back into the warehouse through the same door they had emerged from minutes earlier.

'It's to be collected by a lady,' Ryan said as he stepped over to the front of the cart. 'She'll be paying your fee.'

'I saw the label,' the man said, 'and that won't be a problem. If she doesn't pay, we've still got the goods,' he chuckled.

'I'm quite sure she'll be along soon,' Ryan said.

Then he climbed up and sat down in the driving seat, picked up the reins and flicked them lightly over the horse's back. The animal stepped forward, and Ryan eased back on the right-hand rein to turn the horse around to the right, to head back the way he'd come.

At 3.15 precisely, another very similar cart drew up outside the warehouse, but this one had a person wearing female attire, complete with a veil, sitting in the driving seat, the harness in one hand and a whip in the other. For a few moments after the vehicle came to a stop, the driver looked around, checking the surroundings.

Alexei Pedachenko wasn't expecting any problems, but he certainly wasn't going to step down out of the cart until he was certain that there was nobody lurking in the vicinity. Charles Warren still controlled the Metropolitan Police, and it was always possible that he had some plan afoot to follow Pedachenko when he left the Bermondsey warehouse.

But as far as he could see, the street was completely deserted.

Satisfied, he climbed down and, taking small steps which he hoped would make him look like the woman he was trying to impersonate, he walked over to the warehouse door. The Russian had been born with very fine and delicate features, and had on several occasions been able to pass for a female during his career with the Okhrana. And if anybody challenged him, or recognized him as a man, he had two compelling arguments which he could use. In one pocket of his voluminous skirt he had a fully loaded revolver, and in another what had recently become the tool of his trade, his six-inch bladed knife nestling snugly in its leather sheath.

He rapped on the door with the handle of his whip and waited for an answer.

In less than a minute, the same heavyset man who had taken delivery of the crate only about half an hour earlier opened it and peered out.

'Yes, miss?' he said. 'How can I help you?'

Pedachenko smiled in what he hoped was a winning fashion.

'My name is Winberg, Miss Stephanie Winberg,' he said, his voice both softer and much more high-pitched than his normal speaking voice, 'and I believe you may have a package ready for me to collect.'

The foreman returned the smile and nodded.

'Blimey,' he said. 'You didn't waste any time, did you? It only arrived about half an hour ago.'

He turned away from the Russian and issued instructions to two of the workers.

'Sam, Edward. That crate we just received, bring it out, will you? Customer's here to collect it already. Now,' he said, turning back to Pedachenko, 'there's a fee to pay for storage and handling. So that'll be two shillings and eight pence, please.'

'For half an hour's storage?' Pedachenko queried. 'That seems very expensive.'

The foreman shrugged.

'Take it or leave it, miss, but that's the rate.'

'Oh, very well,' the Russian replied, and delved into another pocket of his skirt and pulled out a handful of coins. He counted out precisely two shillings and eight pence and handed the money over to the foreman.

'I don't think I will be using your facilities again, not at that rate,' Pedachenko said.

Then he stepped back and watched as two labourers carried out a large wooden crate marked with two address labels. It was bigger than he had expected, and clearly heavy, and he guessed that Warren had probably secured the menorah in a steel box inside the crate for safety.

'In the back of the cart, please,' he instructed.

A few seconds later, he climbed back up into the driving seat and cracked the whip over the back of the horse, which immediately moved off at a trot.

Pedachenko had studied maps of the area, and he had decided to get clear of Bermondsey before he stopped to examine his prize. He didn't think that Warren would have dared not supply the menorah, but he was certainly going to check it as soon as he possibly could.

The road was cobbled in places, beaten earth studded with rocks and stones in others, but reasonably straight, and within a matter of minutes the Russian could see that he was leaving most of the buildings behind him. He was also encountering some other traffic, some riders on horses, but mainly carts pulled by one or two animals. There were a couple of carts following behind him, but they were both well back.

He reached a large open area and eased back on the harness, directing the horse over to the left hand side and moving a few yards off the road. He waited, sitting in the driving seat, until one of the carts which had been behind him passed and continued heading east along the road. He looked back to see where the second vehicle was, but it was nowhere in sight, so he assumed that it had turned off onto one of the side roads or stopped beside a building somewhere.

The road was clear in both directions, which gave Pedachenko the opportunity he needed to lift the lid on the crate. He stepped around the seat and into the load section of the cart, picked up a heavy screwdriver which he had earlier placed there, and jammed the point into the gap between the lid and the body of the wooden box. He glanced around once more, ensuring that he was still unobserved, and then levered the lid upwards.

It was secured with nails all around it, and the Russian had to move around the box, freeing the lid in stages. One of the nails squealed in protest as it was dragged out of the wood. Then he dropped the screwdriver, grabbed one side of the lid with both hands and lifted it up. Underneath the lid was another flat section of very thin wood, and Pedachenko grasped this eagerly and pulled it away, desperate to get at the prize which lay underneath it.

And then he recoiled, an expression of disbelief clouding his features.

Chapter 57

'I almost didn't recognize you, Michael,' Charles Warren said, looking up at the hard, cold eyes of the man who had brought so much fear, misery and suffering to the East End of London for the last four months.

Pedachenko stared down in shock at the figure of the man lying in front of him. Warren was holding a heavy-calibre revolver, the muzzle of the pistol pointing directly at him. The inside of the box was padded with cushions, so that even if it was tilted on one side the action would not harm the occupant, and for the first time the Russian noticed the line of small air holes which had been drilled around the perimeter to allow Warren to breathe.

For what seemed like a very long time, the two men stared at each other, neither of them moving.

Then, before Warren could react, the Russian leapt sideways, over the edge of the cart, grabbing for his own pistol as he did so. He landed lightly on his feet and raced away.

In the back of the cart, Charles Warren was struggling to sit up. He'd been confined in the box for well over an hour, hardly able to move, his joints were stiff and aching, and his movements clumsy. He clambered to his knees and turned round, his pistol held in his outstretched arm as he looked for his target.

He'd seen the man – clad incongruously in a skirt – jump over the side of the cart, but he didn't know which way he'd gone after that.

Warren knew, without the slightest shadow of a doubt, that despite the disguise 'Michael' was wearing, it was the same man who had called at his house and who was the author of the nightmare murder spree that had engulfed London. His cold dark eyes were unmistakable. And whatever happened now, Warren was determined to kill him.

He saw the faintest of movements over to his left, beyond where the horse was standing. Warren turned clumsily, his limbs still refusing to obey him properly.

A shot rang out, and the bullet slammed into the back of the driving seat of the cart, sending wood splinters flying in all directions.

Warren ducked down again, relying on the heavy wood construction of the vehicle to shield him. He had guessed that his opponent would be armed, but he simply hadn't expected him to move so fast.

The cart lurched suddenly. The horse had obviously been spooked by the other man firing his pistol so close to its head. Warren tumbled backwards, his revolver falling from his hand. The weapon slid along the wooden floor of the cart and then disappeared over the end.

At the same moment, he heard a sharp cry of pain from nearby, and guessed that the horse had bashed into his opponent, or maybe trodden on his foot.

The cart was gathering speed as the horse panicked. Warren jumped forward, sat down in the driving seat, grabbed hold of the harness and pulled back on it as hard as he could. The vehicle lurched and bucked as it rolled over the uneven ground, but within about thirty yards Warren had hauled it to a stop.

Then he glanced back over his shoulder, and realized his instinctive action had possibly cost him his life.

The man in the skirt clearly hadn't been injured by his contact with the animal, and had run after the cart. He was now perhaps only ten yards behind it, a pistol in each hand, both pointing straight at Warren. He had obviously picked up the fallen revolver as a backup to his own weapon.

Warren realized it was too late for him to coax the cart into motion again. He was certain that at the first sign of such an action, the man would shoot him.

He only had two possible cards left to play.

'If you kill me,' he called out, 'you'll never get the menorah.'

The other man didn't respond, just continued walking steadily towards the back of the cart. When he got to it, he placed one pistol on the ground, then reached down, fiddled with the skirt for a moment and stepped out of the garment, tossing it to one side. The bonnet on his head followed, and then the blouse he was wearing. Underneath, he was clad in normal male attire.

He picked up the second pistol, walked around to the front of the cart and stood there for a few seconds, both weapons aimed at Warren.

'That's better,' Pedachenko said. 'A useful disguise, but one I never feel entirely comfortable wearing.'

'Who are you?' Warren demanded. 'I know your name isn't "Michael", and you sound Russian to me.'

'That's a good guess. I am Russian, but my real name doesn't concern you. You reneged on our agreement. Where is the menorah? If I don't get it, you know what will happen.'

'I changed my mind,' Warren said.

'Then you'd better change it back,' Pedachenko snapped. 'If you don't, I can guarantee that you'll never leave this place alive.'

'As I said before, if you kill me that will simply ensure that you'll never get it.'

Pedachenko shrugged.

'Maybe not, but you'll be dead and at this moment that seems to me to be about the best outcome I can expect. But it won't be quick. I've got two pistols now, and eleven bullets. I can do a lot of damage to you with eleven bullets. And once you're dead, I might be able to persuade your wife to hand over the relic to me.'

'She has no idea I even have the menorah,' Warren said hastily. 'She would have no idea where I've hidden it.'

'Then I'm sure I can persuade you to tell me the hiding place before you die, just to relieve the pain of your wounds. And if I know where the relic is hidden, that means I will be able to spare your wife, Fanny Margaretta. That would be a last small service you could perform for her. After all, I would hate to have to use my knife on her while she was still breathing. At least I gave the whores that small mercy. They were all dead before I started the cutting.'

Warren knew that he was facing a protracted and incredibly painful death, and his beloved wife an even more hideous fate, but there was one question he needed answering before the man in front of him started shooting.

'One favour,' he said. 'I just need to know for sure. You

were responsible for all those killings in the East End? The six murders?'

'You know I was. The other one, the very first killing of the woman called Smith, that was nothing to do with me, but it gave me the idea.'

'Thank you,' Warren said. 'I just needed to hear that from your own lips.'

'Why?' Pedachenko asked, clearly puzzled.

'For justice,' Warren replied, and lifted his right arm high above his head.

Instantly, a shot rang out, the flat crack of a heavy-calibre rifle rather than the more distinctive noise of a pistol.

Pedachenko screamed and fell backwards to the ground, dropping both weapons and clutching at his stomach, a crimson stain instantly blooming across his clothes.

Warren jumped down from the cart and picked up the two pistols, then stepped over and looked down at the badly wounded man.

'Who?' Pedachenko gasped.

'My manservant,' Warren replied. 'Ryan is a very accomplished shot, and I provided him with one of my favourite rifles, my Martini-Henry. He delivered the box to the warehouse, then drove away and waited for you to turn up. I was glad that you were prompt. I could breathe without too much difficulty inside that box but it got very hot and extremely uncomfortable quite quickly. And when you did appear, he simply followed you in his cart at a distance until you turned off the road, when he stopped and continued on foot.'

Warren paused and glanced back the way the cart had come, and then pointed.

'He's obviously been watching us from that small copse of

trees just over there, waiting for my signal. It was an incredibly easy shot for him, but I told him to aim for your stomach, because I wanted you conscious, at least for a while.'

Pedachenko moaned in pain.

'You mean you dropped your pistol deliberately?' he murmured, his voice racked with agony.

'No. I had hoped to take care of you myself. Ryan was my insurance policy.'

'Unfair,' the Russian whispered. 'I thought you English were supposed to be sporting?'

Warren shook his head.

'I gave you more of a chance than you ever gave any of the women that you butchered on the streets of Whitechapel. And I will extend you one small mercy now.'

'What?'

'This,' Warren replied.

He raised Pedachenko's own revolver, aimed the weapon at the Russian's chest and pulled the trigger. The Russian's body jerked once and then lay still.

'Was that the way you wanted it, sir?' Ryan asked, walking up to where Warren stood, looking down at the dead body of the man who had become known as Jack the Ripper.

'Thank you, Thomas,' he said. 'That was exactly the way I wanted it.'

'And it was definitely him?'

'Definitely. He admitted it to me himself, though of course we'd never have managed to prove it. But this way, we don't have to. Now give me a hand with him.'

The two men dragged the corpse of the Russian around to the rear of the cart, hoisted it up with little difficulty – he wasn't a big man – and dropped it unceremoniously into the box. They replaced the inner wooden panel, then nailed the lid firmly shut. Warren took an address label from his pocket, ripped off the ones which he had been told to attach to the box and applied the new one.

'Right, Thomas,' he said, as the two men climbed up into the driving seat of the cart. 'There's another warehouse not too far away where we can get rid of this. Then we'll collect the other cart and head home.'

Ryan turned the vehicle round, and they drove a short distance back the way they'd come, towards Bermondsey. Twenty minutes later, Warren and Ryan lifted down the box from the back of the cart and handed it over to a company which specialized in shipping goods abroad. Warren paid the charge the foreman demanded, and then the two men drove away.

Chapter 58

Monday, 19 November 1888
London

Mary Kelly's funeral was characterized by a wave of emotional distress on the part of the public. None of her relatives made themselves known, and so the cost of her funeral was borne in its entirety by the verger of St Leonard's Church in Shoreditch, Henry Wilton. Mary's body had been lying in the mortuary attached to this place of worship since it had been discovered.

The funeral began at noon, the time signalled by the tolling of the church bell, and a crowd of spectators which numbered several thousand quickly assembled outside the building. At about half past twelve the funeral cortège left the church. Mary Kelly's coffin – a clearly expensive piece of work made from oak and elm, and with polished metal mounts – was carried in the leading cart, which was drawn by two horses. On the coffin was a metal plate which bore the tersest of inscriptions and the name by which she liked to be known: 'Marie Jeannette Kelly, died 9th Nov. 1888, aged 25 years.'

Following this cart were two mourning coaches, but with only eight occupants in total. The crowd which had gathered outside the church accompanied and surrounded the procession as it started moving down the road, immediately blocking the thoroughfare and preventing other traffic from moving, and the police had to force their way through the mass of humanity to clear a path for the three funeral vehicles. The procession took some time to traverse the length of the Hackney Road before arriving at Leytonstone and the Roman Catholic Cemetery of St Patrick, where the coffin and the mutilated remains of its young occupant were laid to rest.

Because of the ferocity of the attack on this latest victim of Jack the Ripper, the mood of the crowd ran the gamut of emotions. Anger, fear and sorrow vied for supremacy. Men removed their hats and bowed their heads as Mary Kelly began her sad final journey. Women – and there were far more women than men there – cried openly, and many tried to touch the coffin as it passed. According to the report in the *Advertiser*, 'the sight was quite remarkable, and the emotion natural and unconstrained.'

Unfortunately, the police were no further forward in their hunt for the killer after the brutal murder of Mary Kelly than they had been before, and the newspapers were quick to point this out. *The Times* summed up the situation thus:

The murders, so cunningly continued, are carried out with a completeness which altogether baffles investigators. Not a trace is left of the murderer, and there is no purpose in the crime to afford the slightest clue, such as would be afforded in other crimes almost without exception. All that the police can hope is that some accidental circumstance will lead to a trace which may be followed to a successful conclusion.

But no such 'accidental circumstance' appeared in the least bit likely to occur, at least in the considered opinion of Inspector Frederick George Abberline, still based at the Bethnal Green police station and hoping for either a clue or inspiration, unless the man known as Jack the Ripper suddenly became very careless indeed.

The Metropolitan and City Police Forces would just have to continue their investigations and their interviews, and their plodding and routine police work, but nobody in either force seriously expected that they would ever manage to identify the killer and bring him to justice.

'Have you got any more good ideas, Fred?' Inspector Chandler asked, as the two men sat on opposite sides of the conference table at Bethnal Green looking at the latest crop of interview reports and statements from neighbours and residents of the properties surrounding Miller's Court, all of which – just as the two officers had expected – contained no useful information whatsoever.

Abberline shook his head.

'No,' he said shortly. 'I think we've tried pretty much everything we can. I hate to say this, but I think the newspapers are right. I don't believe that detection, that police work, is ever going to bring this man to justice. The only way he's ever going to be caught is if somebody stumbles upon him when he's carrying out a murder, and if you want my opinion, I think he's too clever and cautious to ever allow that to happen. After all, he's now done six murders in Whitechapel and Spitalfields, and the only solid leads we've had are from a tiny handful of people who've seen a man either with the victim or in the vicinity at about the time the murder was committed. We don't even know if any of those people actually saw the killer. As far as I can see, there's nothing we can do to stop him carrying on murdering prostitutes in the East End of London. As many as he likes, and as often as he likes.'

'It might be better now that Warren has gone,' Chandler suggested. 'The new bloke, whoever it is, might be more amenable to some of our ideas.'

'Maybe.'

'I meant to ask you,' Chandler went on, 'I know you had that idea about the locations of the killings perhaps being important for some reason, because of the shape they made on the ground. Did you ever get anywhere with that?'

Abberline shook his head.

'No. I thought there was something there when I plotted the position of the first five, but the last killing, Mary Kelly, that doesn't fit at all, as far as I can see. So I suppose that Warren was right about that, at least. It was just a coincidence that the murders formed those two triangles.'

'Unless the killer was starting a completely new pattern with Kelly.'

'I never thought of that. Maybe you're right. We'll only know when he's done a couple more, I suppose.'

'So you do think that there'll be more killings?' Chandler asked.

'I think it's almost certain,' Abberline replied. 'After all, what is there to stop him?'

Chapter 59

Thursday, 22 November 1888
London

In the early evening, two men sitting in a cart drawn by a single horse proceeded along the Strand at a leisurely pace. In the back of the vehicle was a sturdy wooden box measuring perhaps three feet by four feet and around a foot deep, to which was attached a single address label.

'I think that's it over there,' one of the men said, and pointed across to the other side of the road, where he had seen a street sign indicating Denmark Court.

The other man steered the cart through the traffic that was proceeding up and down the main road and pulled up outside one of the buildings in the court. They both climbed down from the vehicle and one walked back to the rear of the cart to release the tailgate while the other knocked on the door of the adjacent building.

After a few moments, the door opened and an elderly grey-haired man peered out curiously.

'Got a delivery for you.'

'We're not expecting anything,' the old man replied.

'Dunno about that, but we've been told to bring this here. This is the Westminster Synagogue, in't it?'

'Yes, but – oh, very well. You'd better bring it inside.'

Three minutes later, the two deliverymen turned the cart around and retraced their steps. It had been the last delivery of the day for them, and they were now able to return to their homes.

Inside the synagogue, the elderly rabbi searched for a few minutes until he found a screwdriver, then he began raising the lid of the wooden box. When it came free, he put it to one side. On top of the mass of packing material which concealed the contents was a small piece of white card on which a few words had been printed in block capitals. He picked it up and read the text: 'FOUND UNDER THE TEMPLE MOUNT, JERUSALEM'.

The rabbi read the words twice with a puzzled expression, then put the card aside and lifted out the packing material. For a few moments, he simply crouched beside the wooden box and stared in incomprehension and disbelief at what it contained. He wondered if it was some kind of an elaborate joke, but that made no sense at all.

Finally, his mind managed to process what his eyes were showing him, and he fell slowly to his knees, heedless of the tears streaming down his face. Tentatively, hardly daring to breathe, he reached out and reverently ran his fingers down the stem of the golden menorah. The metal was cold to the touch, but his body felt as if it was flushing with heat, almost ready to burst into flames, with the strength of the emotions coursing through it.

His lips began to almost silently recite the preamble to every Jewish prayer, a preamble which every Jew knows as well as his own name:

'*Barukh atah Adonai Eloheinu, melekh ha'olam.*'
Blessed are You, Lord, our God, King of the universe.
The sacred relic, the single most precious possession of the entire Jewish nation, lost for almost two millennia, had finally, and completely inexplicably, come home.

Chapter 60

Wednesday, 12 December 1888
Paris

The smell in the warehouse had been getting progressively worse for the last two weeks, and finally the foreman of the shipping company had had enough. He called up two of his men and between them they worked their way from one end of the warehouse to the other, using their noses as they tried to track down the source.

Eventually, one of them pointed to a wooden crate placed against the wall on one side of the warehouse. It was marked only with the Paris address of the shipping company, and the annotation that it would be picked up by a Monsieur Duvall.

One by one, the three men leant closer to the crate to take a sniff, and each quickly recoiled. The foreman told the two men to wait there, collected a crowbar, stuck the point into the gap between the base and the lid and levered it off.

The moment he did so, the smell redoubled in strength, and a rotting corpse tumbled free onto the floor.

The gendarmes were called immediately, and quickly ascertained that the dead man had been shot twice, once in the stomach and once through the heart. But they found no identification on the body, and all their enquiries were inconclusive.

All they did discover was that the crate had been sent from London, but nobody at the shipping company there recalled who had delivered it, or anything about them. Enquiries for a Monsieur Duvall produced hundreds of possible suspects, because 'Duvall' was an extremely common name in France. None of the people interviewed by the gendarmes appeared to have any connection whatsoever with the body.

The corpse was quickly buried in an unmarked grave in a local cemetery, and after a month or so, during which they made no progress whatsoever with their investigation of the murder, the French police closed the case.

Epilogue

1889
London

Within a month of his resignation, Sir Charles Warren returned to military duties, and in 1889 he was sent out to command the garrison at Singapore, taking his household with him, and doing his best to forget entirely the events of the autumn and winter of 1888.

One entirely unexpected benefit of the Whitechapel murders was that the killings focused the attention of the world on that small area of the city of London, which resulted in calls for the appalling conditions there to be improved. Numerous public benefactors and other prominent individuals whose names are well-known even today – people like Dr Thomas Barnado, George Bernard Shaw, the social reformer Beatrice Potter and Sir Arthur Conan Doyle – looked at the conditions in the East End of London and found them severely wanting.

The evangelist General William Booth established a Christian mission in Whitechapel to provide food and shelter to the destitute, albeit with a fair dose of compulsory religious indoctrination making the pill rather more bitter to swallow, and this organization later metamorphosed into the Salvation Army.

Members of Parliament and the newspapers took up the banner as well, and the desperate conditions in Whitechapel and the surrounding areas would, over the coming years, slowly – very slowly, in fact – begin to improve.

In the weeks following the murder of Mary Kelly, the police presence in the Whitechapel area, both of uniformed officers and plainclothes detectives, and that of the volunteer patrols and vigilante groups, was maintained at a very high level.

As had occurred with the previous murders, the police were deluged with letters offering advice and possible leads to the identity of the killer. The total ran into the thousands, and every one of them had to be investigated, at least to some extent. But by the following spring, with no further murders to investigate, Inspector Abberline issued orders for the various patrols to be scaled back and the amateurs began to give up their voluntary duties. The extra police who had been appointed to the East End of London were recalled and redeployed.

But for months afterwards Abberline puzzled over the killings, wondering if it was purely coincidental that they had ceased on almost the very day that Sir Charles Warren had resigned from his post as the Commissioner of the Metropolitan Police. But he still had no leads, and nothing to go on, and finally turned his attention to other matters.

In the course of the investigation, hundreds of people had been questioned and numerous arrests made, but all without a single positive result. Nobody – not one person – would ever be charged in connection with any aspect of the Whitechapel murders.

Like the snow in the spring, and as silently and as inexplicably as he had arrived, Jack the Ripper seemed to have simply vanished into thin air.

Author's Note

Jack the Ripper

In reality, the true identity of the mass murderer or serial killer known as Jack the Ripper will almost certainly never be discovered. Much of the original evidence about the case has been mislaid, lost or destroyed, and the written recollections of many of the people involved in the investigation can be shown to contain serious errors of fact and/or timing. At this remove, it is very difficult to confirm any fact or theory, but despite that almost every year some new suspect appears briefly in the limelight, only to fade away again in the face of critical analysis.

Literally dozens of books have been written on the subject, and in almost every case the author has started out with the name of the killer already firmly established in his or her own mind, and has then cherry-picked the evidence to support that conclusion, in some cases to the extent of ignoring established facts, bending or at least shading the truth, or even inventing new 'facts' to help make the case.

If the same type of killings took place today, it is almost

certain that the murderer would quickly be apprehended because of the enormous advances in investigative technique, and especially in scientific detection methods such as DNA analysis, which have been developed. But at the end of the nineteenth century, the apprehension of criminals primarily depended upon them being caught in the act, and Jack the Ripper seems to have been particularly adept at avoiding detection.

My personal opinion, for what it's worth, is that Jack the Ripper was an intelligent criminal, not some common thug who just got a thrill from murdering women. I also believe that, because of the circumstances of the killings and the speed with which he is known to have carried out some of the mutilations, he almost certainly had had considerable medical training and experience. The removal of Catharine Eddowes's left kidney, which had to have been accomplished in the dark on an open street in no more than about ten minutes using a single heavy knife, is sufficient proof of this. What he did to her body showed unarguable and impressive medical skill.

As described in this novel, an impartial analysis of the descriptions of the murders does show a steady progression from simple stab wounds – if Martha Tabram was the first victim of the Ripper, which has never been established for certain – through increasing mutilation which culminated in the horrific butchery visited upon Mary Kelly. That could suggest, as in this book, that the killer was trying to send somebody a message, and the escalating brutality in each case simply served to reinforce that message.

It could also, equally, mean that the Ripper was a lunatic and that his madness was getting progressively worse and that after the final killing he, for example, committed suicide, or was apprehended for some other offence, was incarcerated in an asylum, or simply left London. Or there could be a dozen other reasons for the way that the mutilations increased in ferocity, and why the killing stopped. The short version, in fact, is that nobody knows who Jack the Ripper was or why he was doing it.

Alexei Pedachenko

Although this man lies well outside the group of the more usual suspects, he was named categorically as Jack the Ripper by the equally notorious Russian monk Rasputin. Or, at least, that's according to a man named William Le Queux, who in a book published in 1923 claimed that some six years earlier he had been given a number of manuscripts found in the cellar of Rasputin's house by the Russian provincial government. Among these documents was a manuscript written in French entitled *Great Russian Criminals*, and this identified Pedachenko as Jack the Ripper. However, it also fair to say that as far as we know, Rasputin neither spoke nor wrote French and lived in a fourth floor flat, so it's arguable that Mr Le Queux's source is at best somewhat suspect, and at worst entirely fictitious.

There is evidence that Pedachenko was a real person, apparently born in 1857 and who died in 1908, and he may well have been an agent of the *Okhrana*. According to some sources, he had trained and worked as a doctor in Russia, principally in the maternity wards of hospitals in Tver. He was also believed to have been living in Paris in 1886, and may have killed a woman in Montmartre while he was there, as a result of which he fled to Britain, and in 1888, when the Ripper murders took place, he was supposedly living in Walworth in south London with his sister.

Another somewhat questionable source suggests that Pedachenko did carry out the Ripper killings, but that he had been ordered to do so by his Russian masters either to embarrass the British police or to try to have expatriate Russian anarchists blamed for the murders, but there is no documentary evidence for either of these suggestions. A further source claims that following the Ripper murders Pedachenko was recalled to Russia and returned to St Petersburg, but he murdered another woman there in 1902, after which he was confined in a lunatic asylum where he died six years later.

Pedachenko was known to cross-dress, as I've described in this novel, and was able to successfully pass himself off as a woman when he needed to do so.

There is no evidence that he was ever stationed, in any capacity, in Jerusalem.

The young woman in the night

One chapter of this novel shows 'my' Jack the Ripper, Alexei Pedachenko, stopping a young woman on the street late at night and engaging in conversation with her. This is actually a fictionalized account of a real event. The great-grandmother of one of my good friends was actually walking back through the streets of Whitechapel after visiting her husband in hospital, when she was stopped by a well-dressed gentleman and engaged in a conversation very similar to the one that I have described. And immediately before the man continued on his way, he gave her a few words of warning about being out so late, and then handed her the enormous sum of £5.

She told and retold this story throughout her life and, although she obviously had no definite proof as to the identity of the man, she always believed that he could have been Jack the Ripper, and that he had only let her pass because she was so clearly terrified of him. The truth of this story, too, will never be known.

The Jewish Menorah

The fate of this most sacred of all Jewish religious artefacts has never been clarified. Beyond any doubt, at some point during the suppression of the Great Jewish Revolt it was seized by the Roman legions under the command of Vespasian and then his son Titus, and was carried back in triumph to Rome. The frieze on the triumphal Arch of Titus in Rome shows the relic quite unambiguously. Just as an aside, until comparatively recently tourists were able to walk through the arch unsupervised, and Jewish visitors in particular were known to spit on the sides of the arch as a somewhat messy protest against the events which had taken place almost two millennia earlier and which the arch commemorated.

It is also known that the menorah was placed on display in Rome and remained there for many years, but when the Western Roman Empire crumbled because of internal strife and attacks on the Eternal City by, particularly, the Vandal armies, the relic vanished from the pages of history, and has never been seen since. The Byzantine general Belisarius did conquer Carthage and managed to recover many of the Roman Empire's lost treasures, but it has never been established whether or not the menorah was among these items.

However, if it was, and if the emperor Justinian decided to return the treasure to Jerusalem, then concealing the object in the maze of tunnels and chambers under the Temple Mount would have been a logical thing to do, in view of the situation in Jerusalem at the time. With Muslim forces governing the city, it would have been far too dangerous for the menorah to have been returned to Jerusalem openly. It would have had to be smuggled in and then hidden somewhere, and because of the enormous cultural and religious significance of the Temple Mount itself, the most obvious, and in fact probably the only sensible, place to conceal the relic would have been in the labyrinth underneath it.

It might even still be there today.

Acknowledgements

No book is a solo effort. It's the product of a team of professionals, and I consider myself lucky to be working with one of the best teams in the business. My agent, Luigi Bonomi, is a good friend as well as a wonderful agent, a font of ideas and suggestions which always seem to work. At Simon & Schuster, Maxine Hitchcock and Emma Lowth have shaped the manuscript with care and skill, and vastly improved the book, and my thanks go to them and everybody else at the publishing house. And I suppose I also need to thank two men, both long dead, who were intimately involved in this story, one well-known for a number of reasons, and the other whose identity remains as much a mystery today as it was at the end of the nineteenth century

**SIMON &
SCHUSTER**

Jack Steel

TITANIC SECRET

**Discover the *true* story behind the sinking of the
Titanic . . .**

10 April, 1912 As the RMS *Titanic* leaves from
Southampton Docks for her maiden voyage to New York,
little do her 2,223 passengers dream of the powers at play
on board the ship and the terrifying fate that awaits them
far out in the icy wastes of the Atlantic.

For on board the *Titanic* are three men – among the richest
in America – who, with the President of the United States
an unwitting pawn in their scheme, are about to make an
announcement that will change the course of history.

Aware of the gravity of the situation, the head of British
Intelligence dispatches his best and most trusted agent,
Alex Tremayne, onto the *Titanic* with one objective in
mind – he has to stop the men from reaching New York, by
whatever means are necessary.

Aided by the cooly beautiful American agent Maria
Weston, is Alex prepared for the lengths he will have to go
to to fulfil his mission?

**Paperback ISBN 978-0-85720-862-0
Ebook ISBN 978-0-85720-861-3**